PRAISE FOR (AND PRAISEWORTHY REJECTION OF) VINCENT CZYZ

"There is something of Virginia Woolf's toxic perfume, the tincture of bemused sadness, the glorying in the jewel-tones of the half-healed bruise, the thing that–in being left one-quarter undone–is therefore promising forever."

–Allan Gurganus,
author of *Plays Well With Others*

"[*Zee Gee and the Blue Jean Baby Queen*] has poise, subtlety and charm."
–Paul West,
author of *Rat Man of Paris*

"It's frustrating to read stories that are as well written as yours are and to still feel unable to take them on for publication."
–a New York publishing house

"[*Bring On the Night*] is an erudite and evocative narrative, reminiscent at times of the tricky, allusive progresses of Nabokov."
– Ben Nyberg,
former editor, *Kansas Quarterly*

"...eloquent and sensual..."
–another New York publishing house

"...lively, vivid, original..."

–Marilyn Hacker,
author of *Winter Numbers*

ADRIFT
IN A
VANISHING
CITY

BY

VINCENT CZYZ

VOYANT PUBLISHING
RUTHERFORD

Grateful acknowledgement is made for permission to reprint
lines from the following selections:

From "Rock On" by David Essex, copyright © 1973, Rock On
Music.

From *The City in History: Its Origin, Its Transformation and Its Prospects*,
copyright © 1961 and renewed 1989 by Lewis Mumford, reprinted
by permission of Harcourt Brace & Company.

From *Ozark Magic and Folklore*, copyright © 1947, originally published by Vance Randolph, Columbia University Press. Reprinted
by permission from Dover Publications Inc.

Zee Gee and the Blue Jean Baby Queen previously appeared in The
Double Dealer Redux.

Author photograph by Kimberly Ross.

Library of Congress Cataloging-in-Publication Data
Czyz, Vincent, 1963-
Adrift in a Vanishing City/Vincent Czyz–1st Voyant ed.
p. cm.
ISBN 0-9665998-0-2
98-061077

ACKNOWLEDGEMENTS

The writer would like to acknowledge a creative debt to Paul West and to Millo Farneti–a debt he has attempted to repay in the form of the pages herein. He would also like to thank Rocco Gratale, Carole Maso and Peter Blauner for their encouragement and wisdom; Michael Trotman, Suzanne Riss, and Stephen R. Pallucca for going the distance with him; his agent, Mary Jo Phelps, for her infinite patience and faith; and his brothers, Robert and Anthony, who have been Theos to this Vincent. Special thanks to the New Jersey Council on the Arts, without whose support this collection would not have been possible, and to Joseph J. De Salvo, Jr., Rosemary James and the rest of the Pirate's Alley Faulkner Society. Special thanks also to Michael P. Dyer of the Kendall Whaling Museum, the only scholar able to help me track down the documented fate of the Octavius. Finally, thanks to Samuel R. Delany for offering his time, his literary expertise and his inimitable touch both to me and this collection.

CONTENTS

Prefatory Note to Vince Czyz's
Adrift in a Vanishing City

by Samuel R. Delany

L IKE *EVERY* ONE OF THE LAST THREE DOZEN MFA THESES
I've read, the following text is neither a novel nor, really,
a collection of stand-alone stories. Familiar characters—
Zirque (rhymes with Jerk), Blue Jean, the Duke of Pallucca–
disappear or are abandoned, reappear or are revisited tale to tale. But
equally clearly these are not novel chapters. Our young writers seem
unhappy with the strictures of both genres and are struggling to
slough them.

If you are a reader convinced of the irrevocable sociality of fiction,
I warn you: By and large, the text won't linger on how characters
manage to pay for their various flights from Pittsburg to Paris, from
Kansas to Amsterdam, how most of them make their living, or even
scrounge up change for that next pint of booze, not to mention
make the rent on an apartment in Budapest–another trait Vincent
Czyz shares with many of his contemporaries; although, in their con-
viction that the world's socio-economic specificities are every self's
necessarily distinctive background, neither Austen nor Flaubert,
Knut Hamsun nor James Joyce, Virginia Woolf nor Henry Miller
could have let such an omission by in their successive attempts to
delve more and more deeply into some more and more highly fore-
grounded presentation of the subject. But the clash of micro-class
and micro-class, macro-class and macro-class, that make fiction
interesting, or even useful, to the average Joe or Sue (not to mention
to the commercial editors riding shotgun on the stopcock of the

smoky trickle of confused tales—overplotted, understructured, and as incoherent and mixed in metaphor as the images within these parentheses, outside these dashes—throughout our Barnes & Nobles, onto our Big Name bookstores shelves) are simply not in focus on Czyz's screen. They are bracketed along with all notion of labor.

If you feel art is an enterprise in which, when you have found an artist doing what every other artist is doing, you have necessarily found an artist doing something wrong (yet *another* story or poem voicing its appeal to aesthetic distance in that artificial and so-easy sign of the literary, the present tense: *Yawn....*), some of the elements—or absences—I've highlighted here, in a book such as this, might give you pause.

What's extraordinary here, however, what recommends and finally makes such work more than commendable, what renders it a small landmark in the sedimentation of new form in fiction, is a quality of language, a surface that signals that the structure of anything and everything that surface evokes beyond it is simply other than what we have grown used to. Finally such a surface signs to the astute that the reductions our first three paragraphs suggest are, in this case, wildly off the mark. (Czyz is *not* an MFA product.) Such language as we find here projects an esthetic consciousness, rather, it might be more profitable to read as interested in other things, and not as one merely slovenly, unthinking, or ignorant of the tradition.

Nothing is careless about this writing at all.

Poetry is about the self, as it is defined in the response to love, death, the changing of the seasons... However indirectly, however mutedly, traditional fiction has always been about money. I could speak easily, and easily speak honestly—and at length—about how much I admire Czyz's considerable talent, his fictive range, his willingness to plunge naked into the gutter, to leap after stellar contrails, his grasp of how ravenously one body grasps another, or of how his impossible apostrophes out of the night are the necessary utterances that make life possible, confronted with the silence of the day, with the deafness of those who never hear. But this is still a more or less rarefied, a more or less dramatic bit of lit. crit. It only becomes a recognizable "story" when I write that Vincent Czyz is a long-haired, newly-married taxi driver living in New Jersey, who wants to self-publish his first book and, as such, has sought my help-a gay, gray, pudgy professor with income tax problems, who commutes to work in Massachusetts by Peter Pan (cheaper than Amtrak), and who has published thirty over as many years with various presses, commercial and university... But Czyz's are *not* traditional stories. Indeed, they are part of a counter-fictive tradition that attempts to appropriate precisely the substance of poetry for prose: Novalis's *Heinrich von Ofterdingen*, Rilke's *Die Aufzeichnungen des Malte Laurids Brigge*, Toomer's *Cane*, Keene's *Annotations*... Average Joes and Sues are just not Czyz's concern. He's fixed his finger, rather, on yearningly romantic figures who combine rough American- or foreign-tinted-dialect with pristine insight; men and women who, clawing at the evanescent tapestry of perception as it unravels madly from the loom of day, are as concerned with myth and cosmology as they are with moment and the night, and who now and again have more consonants in their names than vowels, many of those names not commencing till the terminal handful of letters flung from the alphabet... Though they fixate on indirectly answering just such questions as Czyz here sets aside, not Proust, not Musil, not Ford of *Parades End* or *The Fifth Queen* is "easy reading" either; and finally for much the same surface reasons. Though the sexuality is more or less normal, the poetic method is closer to Genet's-another writer whose novels tends to ignore those grounding questions, unless the characters are pimps (i.e., living off prostitutes of one sex or another) or in jail (i.e., living off the state).

As an appendix to his 1934 collection of essays, *Men Without Art*, Wyndham Lewis proposed "The Taxi-cab Driver Test" for good fiction. Suggested Lewis: Open the text to any random page and give it to any average cab driver. (Fascist Lewis assumed the driver's first language would, of course, be English; Czyz converses in several–besides working as a cab driver, he's also been an English teacher. He has lived in Poland, Turkey, Lyndhurst...) Tell him to read it. Then ask: "Is there *anything* here that seems strange or unusual or out of the ordinary for a work of fiction?" If he answers, "Yes," then you *may* have some extraordinary fiction. If he answers, "No," then you don't. Lewis went on to apply his test to, respectively, a Henry James short story and a banal society novel by Aldous Huxley (*Point Counter Point*, that was thought much of back then because it was a *roman à clef* about the Lawrences and the Murrys–I remember reading it when I was around seventeen. I said, "Huh...?"). James certainly wins; Huxley doesn't. (Today, does anyone read *anything* else he's written other than *Brave New World*, possibly *Island*?) I don't think the Taxi-cab Driver Test is a hundred-percent reliable. Still, it's a good one to keep in mind; and it's a salutary corrective to today's mania for "transparent prose," even (or especially) among our most radical experimenters. I mention it, because Czyz's work (as does Melville's, Joyce's, Hemingway's, Woolf's, Faulkner's, Patrick White's, William Gass's...) passes the Taxi-cab Driver test admirably. The work of the vast majority of Czyz's contemporaries does not.

That is to say: Czyz is telling stories many of his contemporaries are trying to tell–and telling them much better!

If you are a reader who can revel in language–in the intricate and intensely interesting "how" language imposes on its "what"–then, however skew his interests are across the fictive field (and how refreshing that skewness!), Czyz is a writer rich in pleasures; it's a pleasure to recommend him.

–New York City,
May 1998

Are You a "Finely Tuned Reader"?
author's introduction

WHILE IN MANUSCRIPT FORM, *ADRIFT IN A VANISHING CITY* circulated among some 14 editors at various publishing houses. The responses were strikingly similar: praise for the writing, but dismay over the possibility of finding a market for the collection.

My favorite such rejection slip, addressed to my agent, reads like this: "Thanks for letting us see Vince Czyz's collection. He had two readings up here, both good, but we both scratched our heads as to how we could reach 5,000 people ready for this kind of hot-house writing, very lyrical, experimental, Joycean. I don't think we could do it, find that many finely tuned readers. Too bad. He's very good."

While the commentary was flattering, the work remained unpublished. I sent a letter to the editor in question, minutely detailing why I felt this collection would sell 5,000 copies.

I received no reply.

One of my contentions in that letter was that there are more finely tuned readers out there than one might suspect, and that they are more open to novelty than one might suspect. Some editors have turned down the collection on the basis that what I've written are not actually "short stories" and so, like foreigners in odd garb speaking a strange tongue, should be left outside the city walls.

It's true, most of the narratives do not move from point A to B or end neatly with a final sentence that wraps everything up like a Christmas bow. Instead, they *tend*, they point into the distance, offering direction but not destination; they overlap, they are fragmented, with characters chasing each other from one story to another as well as through time (the final piece takes place centuries before Christ was born). Taken together, they form a kind of constellation, implying a shape edged in light rather than delineating a clear form, drifting aimlessly overhead rather than fixed in a particular corner of the sky.

The primary setting for these stories is a "small-time city" in the southeast corner of Kansas. From time to time, however, the subterranean current moving things along carries characters as far afield as Amsterdam and Paris (not to mention ancient Palestine). The ascendant point in the collection around which the others have gathered is the romance between Zirque Granges and Rae Ann Kelly (a.k.a., Blue Jean). In the words of Allan Gurganus, it is a story about what happens when "one woman loves the wrong man–perfectly."

Now while many a short story is composed of sentences that are disposable–there to move along a bit of plot and nothing more-I was interested in how the language in which these narratives have been written seemed to be part of the tale: to tell them any other way would be to lose something vital. I think this is what prompted one of the editors who declined the collection to tell my agent, "American readers aren't ready for him yet."

All I have to say to that is, *Sure you are.*

–VC

P.S.: Although some of these stories would hold up outside the collection, some would not. To bring them into sharpest focus, it's best to read them in the order in which they appear.

Fiction is a true story that never happened.
—Robert E. Bostwick

Memory is like a vanishing city on the horizon,
now there, then not.
—*Vanishing Cities*

ADRIFT
IN A
VANISHING
CITY

ZEE GEE AND THE
BLUE JEAN BABY QUEEN

"THE HEART HAS ITS REASONS THAT REASON DOESN'T KNOW."
—BLAISE PASCAL

HALLEY'S, SHE SAID TO HIM ONCE, FLAT ON HER BACK, looking up at the bedroom ceiling, distant as one of those alternate higher planes fortune tellers talk about, you're like that.

He didn't understand.

You're far away, some place I can hardly imagine (she was still talking to the hazy ceiling mostly lost in the half dark), but I know you're coming back. You always do.

She thinks of him during long winter nights silent and clear as a sky full of constellations (he has shown her the place where her sign rises, how his is framed at certain times of the year by her bedroom window). The ice jackets on tree branches, on overgrown grass, shiver and crinkle with the slightest breeze, tinkle like chimes. During the season of changing colors with its misty-breathed mornings, she wonders who is waking up next to him. One of those free-love girls with big tits and too much mascara he likes so much most likely, shaking her can all over the bar he met her in. And on those sweaty evenings her hair just won't stay, a hot orange moon big over the fields, crickets rub against each other's solitude and she misses him most.

Memory is like a weird city, he said, when you're in it, the street names keep changin, or the signs disappear. You try to find your way back but you're never sure which direction you're goin in.

He did some sleight of hand: Now you see it, now you don't.

In the dream that comes to her most often, she's in an abandoned mine sunk into this coal-shaft region of Kansas bucked up by railroad-ties, tracks for the coal carts careening off into darkness. No windows down there but she knows it is always winter of nothing growing, no wind, no resin smell of rising sap or cut grass, no whiff of the old barn soaked to the wood's grain in the earthiness of hay, manure, horse sweat reaches her in the cold of uncut diamonds and dull gold. Feeling her way with blue hands (bluer veins hard as marble), mostly numb, trapped beneath the fields in a footsteps-echo-on-the-stone vault of glassy black, the glittering hard eyes studding the rough walls are no light but cold light.

A place memories are put away for safekeeping (with no beam of a miner's helmet to set them off), a home for the restless shades of people badly missed–Old Man Varanelli who was always smoking Toscana cigars even the day he never made it up from the mine when the timbers cracked and gave in they say it was like God granted him a last request he had a Toscana in his mouth; the Thomas boy who was only 18, taller than Zirque and handsome as all get-out, a wonder to see on the baseball field, electrocuted that rainy night on farm machinery (that's what brought on the early frost that year); poor Pap, only five feet two inches of him, he said the funniest things before he turned up face down, naked as you please, in a flooded drainage ditch.

She hears the sound of their picks clanging clinking digging for something generations of miners failed to turn up, but never catches sight of one, is never anything but alone with the shadows of things that sank–slow as the fall of evening–out of sight, a fancy spinning lure flashing, then gone in deep waters. Nothing but blue-black dark down there, only a vague remembrance of what orange might be like, of a moon that will rise in the hot sky to watch over her, summertime, when he is not there.

Her voice echoes in the shaft, boomerangs eerily back as if

someone else has called him. The picks of the invisible miners fall into silence, but he doesn't hear and the next scream turns into a fist in her throat. She wakes in a fit of shivering.

Sometimes her nose right up against the back of his neck, the smoothness of his body warm with sleep, mixed in with his smell, an odd whiff of the last place he'd been. Other times there were only the sounds the wind makes. She's gotten used to reaching in among put-away clothes, pulling a bottle of Cold Duck out of the cedar chest Mamma left her, sinking into the edge of the bed, drinking herself back to sleep.

My Grandma was Creek, he says by way of explanation, I can't help the way I am.

Creek nothin, Willie liked to cut in, anybody takes a good look can see he's quarter-blood ky-yoat.

All comes out t'the same thing if y'ask me—wouldn't you know Earl wasn't above shouting it across the bar?

Doesn't matter who's right, the upshot bein Zirque chases what he fancies on a mean horse that bucks him every time, he just gets up and slaps the dust off his jeans.

Could have been a pool hustler, but that was nothing next to being the first country singer out of Pittsburg, Kansas to make a name for himself. Switched saddles and decided to be a rodeo rider, hardly ever winning a thing but having a grand time being tossed into the chewed-up dirt, the crowd holding its breath while he high-tailed it out of there, clowns trying to keep the bull from gutting him, stomping him, marking him permanent. He sang jazz in cramped St. Louie dives (Louie of old was king of France he always says) where some of the drinkers eyed him the way rodeo bulls stared him down. Moaning blues to anybody within earshot, he wrote songs on candy wrappers and inside matchbook covers even though he can't play a note. When nothing else was going for him, he washed dishes in Chicago. From the front seat of the cab he drove in Kansas City he talked Golden Gloves, that time he got dropped for a five-count, the crowd's roar not as loud as the ocean breaking in his skull, took a standing eight a round later, remembering the hot white lights hazy in the smoke and that stumpy Italian kid with a head like a cinderblock coming out, thick arms up, to get it over with.

He beat me for first, but I finished on my feet.

Quiet times he sold magazines door to door, Mornin ma'am now hold on just a minute this won't take but a minute and it's painless I promise because he was always making promises, hardly ever making good but not a person can listen to him and still say no–he'll take in anyone not chained to her better judgment. Somehow or other he always manages to make off with whatever he's set his sights on, getting by on roughed-up good looks, neighborly smiles, words as smooth and pretty as glass. Only Helen Keller is safe.

If life were a pinball game, my name'd be right up next to the tilt for having hit the highest score. He winked.

Oh there are six feet of you Zirque, too much to be a kid anymore. When are you going to stop acting like one? You've about run out of quarters.

He smiled because he could always borrow another, steal it, lease his soul if he had to (fine printed so ownership would revert to him at year's end). But that year costs him. Last time he was missing a tooth. Coke deal gone bad, is all he would say. He used that smile (slow as cigarette smoke making itself into a graceful coil) to show off his new space, like he was proud of it. God only knows how he could be glad to be missing a front tooth.

I only do drugs to keep em out of the hands of little kids, you know that.

She slapped him in the chest for that, knowing she couldn't be the one who hurt him the way he comes home sometimes. So bad once the hospital had to wire his jaw shut, one of his eyes purpled up, swollen shut, just lashes sticking out, and his nose–he has such a nice one it could have been on a Greek statue–his nose was twice as wide as it should have been. If something had to get broken though, thank heaven it was his jaw, shut him up for a while. He was an honest-to-God saint the way he took his daily punishment, drinking meals through a straw, hardly moving from the house, reading all day practically, so quiet she kept checking up to make sure he hadn't slipped out.

Five uv em Blue Jean. I took out two clean, but one uv em got me from behind and they were still in a world a trouble, I wuzh gonna put a good hurtin on all five only I got cracked with a bottle an it wuzh downhill from there. Got t'admit, my head, hard azh it izh, ain't no match for a bottle a old Number Seven. Glass ain't quite azh fragile azh it'sh cracked up to be.

There were probably two, three just maybe, but he liked to blow things up balloon size, carry you off to Oz or some such place where there were emerald cities and talking scarecrows and Zirque could whip five guys as long as none of them had an empty bottle of Jack Daniels handy.

In the beginning when it was too painful to talk, he wrote little notes. Most she saved and most ended with You know I love you. He stayed for a whole year that time. Things were so beautiful she wouldn't mind if he got his jaw busted again.

Most often he comes back just bucked, still slapping at the dust, with nothing but the clothes he's wearing, that jean jacket he'll never let go of with a hundred pockets, she's patched it up at least that many times. Now and again he comes cruising down Broadway (all the buildings lined up to watch) as if he's an astronaut back from the moon, a car twice as fancy as the mayor's, a cream-colored Continental with spoked tires, a convertible of course, the roof immaculate white when it stretched itself out, rode her all over town, the front end so long she didn't know how he steered it right into a parking space in front of Toni's Place thinking he could get a kiss outta her just because he bought her those dresses and that handbag, those fancy two-tone Texas riding boots besides, just because the money he was carrying around in his pockets was enough to pay his debts ten times over.

You could've done anything you wanted to...

They were swaying on the swing seat out back, the acreage flat except for a clump of trees in the west, silhouetted in the evening.

Chiaroscuro, he said, talking about light falling a certain way, Italy has its own light its own word for it, a thousand painters died never getting it right but they tried.

The copse of trees blacked out, a break in the west from everything flat else, while the swing he always promised to oil but nearly always forgot went on creaking, forward and back, between now and then, between what was and what could still be...

You could've done anything, she said, anything at all.

This way is better: I don't know exactly what it is I want, might as well see the hand I been dealt before I throw away.

But you'll never catch up with yourself, there's always something ahead of you that goes faster whenever you do, like chasing your own tail.

She knew she was right, but he had this way of putting his arm around her, making the floor tilt and from that off angle, that skewed way of looking at the world, nothing looked impossible, nothing was worth complaining about with her head on his chest and his particular smell coming through an old flannel shirt worn smooth by a thousand washings. She doubted herself, lost the resolve that had hardened while she looked out a kitchen window, meticulously cutting onions for dinner as if he were going to be home for it. Setting a perfect table for one, but always making a little extra just in case. Everything fresh from Pallucca's Market, the green peppers, the red ones, the tomatoes for making sauce (nothing he likes eating better than Italian or Mexican), the garlic, the red onions for salad, white for the too-sweet tomato pureed by hand, an all-day event making sauce the right way, especially getting caught up cutting green peppers, sometimes taking an hour just to do one because it's good to concentrate on the shapes of the strips. This one looks like a Z, maybe I can spell his name before I throw it into the pot and that'd get him over here, how could he resist? Never powdered seasoning, always the hard teardrop clusters of garlic, though the smell sinks into her skin, whoof the smell, but all the Italian women say it's good for you, and olive oil too—only cook with olive oil—and for a cold, a little red wine is best and to settle your stomach after a big meal, red wine and red wine if you're having trouble sleeping. And what is he up to just now when this sauce is just getting to the thickness it's supposed to be, smelling up the whole house, and the bread is about done, too. How far is he from here she wanted to know, could she measure in teaspoons laid end to end? A bell should ring when he comes within a thousand, when he's anywhere in the state, the whole damn country. God knows he doesn't have the courtesy to call, or even to barge in and give her a big kiss and hug hello. He likes to be found, like a dug-up bone, let you show him how much you missed him, probably got his sense of dramatics from his Creek grandma, too. A bell to keep her from getting up all the time, she wouldn't mind at all, just look the floor tiles are worn smooth practically, a direct line from the back door to the stove, her feet did that she knows, but how? She never saw it till one day she noticed the grooves were going out of the linoleum in a whitening trail, a tiny Milky Way on the white floor of her kitchen, hazy undefinable inexplicable, an object of ceaseless wonder but there it is, questions about its origin a source of constant curiosity, she doesn't remember so much back and forth, back and forth looking out the back door again and again, odds against finding him, but once or twice she found him there sitting on the edge of the porch, beat him silly with a rolled-up newspaper for making her wait like that.

In the old days, Pap would come by, too shy to knock for a whole ten minutes sometimes, of course she'd invite him to stay for dinner. He'd limp inside, usually a bottle of red wine in his hands, kee-auntie, a basket covering the bottom, she always saved the bottles for the basket. It was kind of nice, listening to him talk nonstop, lisping kind of because what a shame he's got a harelip besides one leg being shorter than the other. Always a gentleman, never a cuss word, he'd make her laugh gossiping about Earl or Red, their latest bet, Earl was putting up his car against Red's pickup that he'd get that new woman who'd just moved to Pittsburg to marry him by Christmas. Sure you will, Pap said and wanted in on that bet.

Somehow he always seemed to know when she was starting to miss Zirque in a way that company made her feel even more alone, he'd know, say he had to get going, and off he limped. And she'd look at that worn part of the floor and say to herself next time I'll avoid it, take a different way, walk anywhere but there, even out the rest of this damn floor, but what was the use with a whole kitchen full of reminders of him? Tiny slant-roofed houses he'd brought from a ceramic shop in Paris, an elegant blue-glass candle holder he'd bought from a wrinkled little man with a gray goatee in Miami (Arizona, not Florida), a Dutch plate he came by in Amsterdam (It's legal for the girls to be right up against the glass, mannequins in lingerie except they wink atchya, wave atchya, tempt you sore), a '40s-style beer glass stolen from the Grand Emporium in Kansas City where there's a neon outline of John Lee Hooker.

She never did make good on that promise to put away his picture, the one she took of him on Locust Street, leaning against the red brick of a building boarded up since Prohibition, standing there in a long, blue-black Navy coat with the collar turned up against the wind. Like a postcard sent to her from one of his trips. Greetings from Locust Street. Wish you were here. His dark eyes holding the spark of train wheel on rail, his mouth set like a promise still unkept. A feeling comes and goes too quickly to warm her or even to catch its name.

He's told her what the canals in Venice look like at night,

in winter, when there are no tourists, just the lights on the boats and the sound of water slapping against the mossy stone buildings.

Wish you were here.

He's spent his money in sight of the Mediterranean, on islands she's never heard of, probably making the same bad name for himself, taking on the same shady debts on that side of the world. Comes back with fancy words he learned right after *bonjour, comment t'allez vous,* hi how are you? *Estoy bien, dankeschön,* fine, thanks a wagonload for askin.

Picked up a whole bunch in Germany, along with a fancy beer mug with a silver lid on it. *Weltanshauung.* That one sounds like a big brass bell ringin, don't it?

It's sitting on a shelf in the kitchen losing its shine because beer doesn't suit her. Except for now and then a shot of Kentucky bourbon, it's about all he drinks. Zirque in Germany must have been like a bookworm locked in the library. But he hardly talked about small-town breweries and yeast-bottomed beers when he got back. Instead he said things like German Expressionism isn't just music made with metal-on-metal percussion or distorted faces painted in warring colors, in black and red, it's all over Berlin, in the streets, at the dinner table, in museums.

They're so unhappy they name their kids after it, imagine callin a little fella Max Angst. Cities, he said, are built around it, neon clubs and all.

He doesn't have the slightest idea what cities are built around, he doesn't know what it's like waiting out the turn of the seasons, thinking you recognize the back of his head, only to find the face unfamiliar. What she's really looking at in town are her display-window memories arranged just so, behind glass where dust won't settle, where you can have a look but you can't put a finger on a familiar feel for reassurance. He's not there when she doesn't have the energy to get out of bed and face the day. When she turns on the television for the sound of voices, even a commercial. Anything but the wind chimes. The clock. The summer insects. There are times when swallowing a whole bottle of aspirin with a pint of whiskey doesn't seem a bad idea.

Just once she wants to be dead when he gets home. If she could just time it so he'd be the one to find her. Before the flies really got to work. If not dead, at least gone. It'd be worth the look on his face if she could see it, him climbing in a window and some people living there he doesn't know. Just to know what he looked like when that happened, when he realized she'd sold the place and moved on. And there's no way he can find her. Wouldn't that be something? It doesn't matter the look would only last for a moment, that he'd shake his head and drive off.

She can call the real estate office this afternoon and make the arrangements. She just might do that.

Summer always worse because she doesn't teach aside from riding lessons here and there, her kindergartners aren't around to take her mind off anything, she winds up clip-clopping into town on Baldy, that horse the only thing that keeps her sane sometimes, a quiet ride better than a bottle of Cold Duck any day. Baldy (his head is white as an eagle's) tied up outside, she sits at Carol's Corner Cafe for all-morning breakfasts (Carol's old clock with its fancy Victorian hands is always wrong any-way), talking to Carol's sister Connie who never slept through a night in her life and looks it, wrinkled as an old dollar bill, a cigarette always burning in her hand, green with snaking veins, speckled brown.

Oh the things I seen in this town, honey.

Connie can tell you them all, pink hair rollers in the whole time, cheeks drawn hollow as she smokes, she was there for the 1888 mine disaster, the worst in Crawford County history, the men trapped and their dark-skinned, black-dressed women waiting in the steadily falling snow, hardly a one of them who spoke English, they'd come from Italy for the better life.

If you could have heard what was coming from the mine you'd've thought the center of the earth haunted. Sixty-eight men died that day.

Looking out the window of the Hotel Stilwell where she slept last night, thinking of youth gone beneath the hard autumn frost brings back that college summer, Zirque and Earl pulled up alongside her in Earl's '56 pick-up, doing three miles an hour while Zirque tried to talk her into a ride, what little patience he had snapping like an old rubber band, he hauled her into the back like some kind of oversized bird. Earl gunning the engine the two of them fell, Zirque cracking his knee good, he laughed the whole way to the 1106 Burger Drive-In anyway. She wouldn't eat anything though, not for all their come-on politeness thick as cooking lard.

Ain't you heard poutin is hazardous to my social life?

Seven french fries was all she would go for–and about as many words, Earl winning a coin toss for her burger, Zirque finishing off the fries.

Who can say how she wound up sneaking out of the house in the middle of the night, easing the screen door so it didn't suck itself closed with a slam, the spring softly squealing anyway, the crickets so loud a wonder her parents could sleep with them chirping away. He'd be there in the dark, the warm air sticky with something honey-suckle sweet, what the wind picked up on its travels through southeastern Kansas. She'd reach for his hand without much looking, without much thinking about it, because once he had it he never let go, she never worried, he could have walked her over water she trusted him so much, but he only took her up the block to his car, past the row of silent front porches, the flickering blue glow of a TV set left on in Mrs. Breddafeld's house coming through the window. She was always there, fast asleep in her pink nightie, her hair a Medusa's nest of curlers, sunk into a huge brown easy chair that seemed ready to swallow her.

A hundred times at least Zirque took her down Cayuga

Street to his Chevy Impala as loud and heavy as a locomotive coming at you and they drove along the train tracks, the poles lining the rails planted in the darkness, a row of crosses against the sky tapering into the distance, drove until they came to their place, where he'd taken her a hundred times, but this time was different, this time she let him unbutton her favorite white blouse, the August breeze cooling against the dampness underneath (it was hot, she couldn't help she'd begun to sweat), let him take her panties down past her knees, over her bare feet, but he wouldn't go any further, wouldn't do one more thing besides kiss with his shirt off, skin pressed against skin, the moon up there over his shoulder and all the stars in the leather back seat of that old Chevy convertible (tinny blue with rust eating away the back fenders), the leather making her sweat more than she wanted to, more than women ought to, but it didn't bother him slipping over her, his denims rough across the soft white where her panties had been, pulling the hair just a little while she undid his belt buckle which scratched her once, made her jerk underneath him, he smiled as she tugged at his pants, down to his ankles—whose idea was it that she couldn't stay just like that, her legs wrapped around him couldn't he see how perfectly they fit together, moved together, could live together? She wanted it to be like that always, their first time, why couldn't it always be that way when they were so in love? The moon a halo behind his head, and her hands pushing against his chest, her head thrown back into the leather of that musty old Impala too noisy to start unless it was a whole block away from her house, her fingers passed right through his skin, tightened on bone and muscle and lodged in both, and somehow she was breathing through him, her lungs feeling grand and cavernous enough for an echo but breathing through his mouth, a tunnel of wind where his mouth met hers, who needed to breathe anyway in the last moment when for the last time she shuddered against him, her fingers digging into his back, her body filled with the beating of tiny wings, softly dusting mothwings everywhere from her feet to inside her skull tingling just under her scalp so lightly feathery barely touching that maybe they never did touch just stirred up the baby's breath she felt, had already carried her to the stillest most unimaginably still place, everything around her absolutely at rest, it had all stopped forever, or maybe was just gone, burned up in a long beautiful fall and drifted away as ash, dust, nothingness, but she knew it hadn't, it was just that the thrumming wings had taken the place of her body, their gentle swarming intimating the shape she'd once filled out with something a lot more clumsy, a human-sized constellation made of the invisible trails moths trace out in their fluttering erratic patterns, the gorgeous easy warm breeze going right through her there's no sensation in the world like the air moving through skin you don't have anymore but you're still solid enough, sweaty enough, pressed tightly enough against him to feel it until at last when her eyes opened again, she realized she couldn't breathe he was so heavy, Oh please Zirque I love you but please get off me. His head hanging over her shoulder as if he'd died came up and even in the moonlight she saw the hard lines of his stomach, ran her hands along his flanks, down his narrow hips.

It was years later he called her Blue Jean, smiling down on her in the backseat of a new Cadillac even though she had her own place by then, they went ahead for old times' sake, my Blue Jean Baby Queen he called her from his favorite song.

I wrote it you know, they stole my lyrics.

He was joking when he said it, but only half. There's a song they play on the radio which haunts him because he hadn't known who to show it to and when he did, they put a different name on it, he never got any money or credit. Okay, a teaspoon of angst for that one. She still remembers picking up the matchbook-cover song while dusting, years before it made it to radio, his jaw still healing. She found them all the time—on envelopes the electric bill came in, torn movie tickets

[13]

(the words so tiny she could hardly read them), the insides of book covers, the corners of newspapers, she saved every word of every song in the making.

Rock on.

Some of the best times were in the Pan Club where you have to buzz just be let in they want a look at you first, Willie bartending and Red talking. Red (his hair is about orange) had done time with Zirque in Jeff City and has the shiny white thread of a scar splitting his left eyebrow to prove he was watching out for him.

Red who told her of destiny altered by a drunken sign maker who mistook the sound of the F in Fan for the P in Pan. Rather than rework what had already been cast in neon, he offered to knock a hundred off the price to keep it that way.

Pan's a mischievous, half-pint forest god with the horns and legs of a goat, Zee Gee told Willie, most often sighted chasing beautiful women if Greek fairy tales are to be believed.

Accidents that pan out are signs of God at work, Willie announced, pocketing his good fortune. Willie used up some of it at a county-sized flea market in Texas where he picked up an alabaster likeness, woodsy setting and all, which he kept behind the bar in a forest of gleaming long-necked bottles.

While Pan grinned from the other side of the bar and Red scratched his stubbly chin and smiled, Zee Gee hustled some 19-year-old biker in a pool game, then beat out Willie for 10 bucks.

I been practicin up for ya Granges, Willie says with a smile clamped on a cigar stub, his cue twisting in blue chalk, a wink at Blue Jean because it's a game they play so Zirque won't feel he has to pay it back.

He plays pool by instinct, he says, which makes her roll her eyes and look away. Maybe Pittsburg U doesn't give out degrees on the topic, but he had to put in his time at Bartelli's Blue Goose Bar before he got any good. Leaning on the table's edge (white Tee sleeve pulling back to show his dark-

Thank you for choosing the

BURLINGTON Marriott®

Routes 128 and 3A, Burlington, Massachusetts 01803
(781) 229-6565   FAX: (781) 229-7973

complected skin), he'd line up a shot with a style distilled from the best he'd seen in pool halls up and down the Midwest, watching him play kind of like the fair being in town, listening to him talk himself up, a sideshow act–keep yer eye on the ball–sinking a shot in his careless way, smile like it was nothing, counting on luck like it's something to lean against, the brick side of a building that won't let him down short of a California quake.

Then he'd sit down, a good sweat going, put his arm around her and the floor'd begin to tip to one side, his eyes black volcanic glass while he talked about where he'd been (careful to skip the pages where the names of women are written). Red, Willie, Earl (his over-white dentures the only thing smooth in his craggy face) would be at their table, full beers showed up while the stories flowed and only the question of why it couldn't always be that way went unasked.

One story about a Navajo dance he called Yay Bi Chay (spelling it a mystery right up there with the Trinity) down there in New Mexico, winter, the dusty earth gone cold, smoke from the fires headed for the ancient light of stars. The men wore masks, he said, opted for paint rather than shirts, and danced all night with a strange little hoo-hoo sound like no animal he ever heard, around and around with the gravity of a planet and only firelight to see them by. The faces watching dark and rigid, one with glasses on like a bright-eyed demon, the dancers kept up until the stars faded (the fires still burned) and the sky grew gray-blue light. He stayed and watched and drank, passing his bottle around, later picking up a toothless Navajo hitcher who smelled like smoke and beer, both of them with eyes itching and red, running on something the dancers passed on. Zirque rode him near 200 miles home for which he received a blessing in a language he didn't understand.

Jack Hanes interrupted, complaining loudly the painting business was damn well bad enough to make another beer about as hazy a possibility as the Second Coming.

Hope the beer makes it first, Zirque said, taking a swallow of his own before going back to the dance.

It was hypnotic, he said, staring down something at his feet, like watching the waves roll in over the shore. No matter how many you watch, you can still sit for one more. Felt it about the same place, too, gut-center, a deep, deliberate pull, like a peek at infinity and the big surprise is you're part of it.

The dancing painted men in their masks, antlers branching from their heads (he mentioned antlers, didn't he?) got her thinking maybe he's not ... well maybe he's just wearing a mask himself, he'll never die, just change the mask. Right about the time something like that came to mind, he'd put a quarter in the jukebox and play his favorite song and sing to her.

See her shake on the movie screen.

Hollywood doesn't know what it's missing. Tall, shapely, green-eyed as cut glass, hair the color of a two-year-old penny, the shine of a fish cutting away, a flash and gone, still a few shades darker than Red.

Prettiest girl I ever seen.

Red always reminded them, before the night burned softly down to gray ashes they threw to the stars, what a right handsome couple they made. The three of them driving off in a convertible if Zee Gee could manage one, up route 69, on to the place where dawn meets the road.

Zirque the Jerk, Red would say shaking his head when he got stood up for drinks. Red—he has about the most angelic smile you've ever seen and hands wide enough to palm a truck tire—wouldn't know what to say or do to make her feel there was anything between Kansas and the moon worth living for.

He'll be back, was the best he could manage.

He's a refrain from a song, she wanted to tell Red, you never know when you'll hear it again, but when you do, you keep hoping the words will be different. They never are. Maybe because everyone's willing to grant forgiveness, she the abused saint of them all.

It makes her wonder if he feels any difference between pain and pleasure, he seems to give it out in equal amounts.

Life is like that theater mask, it's two-faced, you know, one face with a big Cheshire Cat grin, the other with that same grin upside down, in reverse.

In college they told her comedy is when everyone at the end of the play marries everybody else. Tragedy is when everybody dies in the last act.

What about utopia, you ever heard a that one? he asked, probably to get at some obscure fact, offer it like a pretty shell for her collection.

Sure, I know what it is. It's when your man stays with you all year round and it ends with they lived happily ever after. It's comedy.

C'mon now Blue Jean, have you ever known me not to come home?

No, but I've never known you to take me with you either.

Except that once they went to Mexico. There were pyramids down there that stacked up to the ones in Egypt, he told her, and could have shown her pictures in a library book but he told her to pack a trunk and throw it in the car.

We're going to Meh-Heeco.

She'd never seen so many poor people in all her life, outside of town in shacks with plywood walls, sadly faded colors much too bright in the first place but maybe it took their minds off walking on dirt floors, off the fact water had to be carried in pails. There were plenty of penniless families in Kansas she knew, but not all in one place.

In town, crowded as church on Sunday morning with no end to the shops and souvenir sellers, he bought her silver jewelry, carna-vollay-colored dresses and blankets from men who stopped them in the streets. He never paid asking price because when he spoke, pesos evaporated.

A thief would offer 2,000 pesos. Un ladron.

One thousand.

Madre de Dios! Giving it away would be better.

Be my guest.

He started to walk away, but they wouldn't let him, first giving chase, then giving in.

The first night he sang in Spanish with three little men, in colorful ponchos, darker than him, playing tiny guitars and shaking maracas. La Rubia they called her, so air-mosa.

They think you're about as pretty as a sunrise, Zirque said. They'll be wanting to name a drink after you before we leave.

She drank salty margaritas, Zirque playing the big spender, taking shots of tequila, buying for the men who joined in. That night, with mostly table candles for light, she could see he was kin to those people, pure cannibal if he did up his face right. His eyes more squinty than ever but his smile innocent and generous, her father's smile. They danced till sun-up, those men making music out of clapping, calling La Rubia! La Rubia!

Morning was a beach near Ensenada with sad, half-starved horses. He took her riding anyway and paid the straight-haired boy with big brown eyes twice what he should have, making him promise to get the animals more feed. She'd never ridden on a beach and fell in love with the smell of the sea and the spray kicked up by the hooves, all with bluish mountains dissolving in the gray distance.

They kept driving south, climbing winding badly paved roads through tiny towns where the goats crossed the street in bunches and short men in ponchos and sandals (cut from old tires Zirque told her) looked up inquisitively at the red, finned Cadillac convertible. They passed the religion of the land housed in stained, once-white walls and roofed in cracking Spanish tiles as orange as sunbaked clay brought a long time ago (rusting crucifix askew now) on the armored backs of bearded foreigners, the road empty except for them and the goats, out of place in the moss-green mountain stillness. Zirque drove with one hand on the wheel, the other holding hers, the air getting thinner all the while, the mornings cool enough to make their breath mist.

It's not like those westerns that make you think Mexico is one big desert, he said, is it? He put his arm around her. We're half way to god up here.

Finally they made it to a city so old it was already abandoned (weeds growing through cracks in stone streets) by the time the Aztecs got to it. The Indians who'd built it, he said, had become extinct. Sure enough, the wide perfectly straight Calle de los Muertos was empty except for the tourists and souvenir sellers. And there—she could hardly believe her eyes—were pyramids, two of them.

Piramide del Sol, he said pointing at the one closest to them, Pyramid of the Sun. And over there's the Moon.

Flatter and wider than the ones in Egypt, settled not in sand, in the desert, but in the green mountains, with steps going to the tops. The Moon Pyramid was smaller but prettier, terraced, not so much the pile of stone the Sun turned out to be, cement holding in place the old broken stones. She tried to imagine what it was like when it was a city—did they really have sacrifices up here? Thought of herself on her back, stony cold altar underneath her, at the flat peak of the Pyramid of the Sun, a man whose head was wild with feathers—great long ones like a fanning peacock tail—standing over her bared chest with a knife—

A flint knife, he told her, no metal back then, not here.

—a strange cry going up from the bird-priest before plunging the jagged blade in the name of the sun, in the name of a great serpent whose image she'd seen in stone, a dragon more like, with a few feathers around its head, Ketzal-whatever.

Gives me the creeps thinking about it.

They're all gone, long time ago. Come on, let's go to the top.

There must have been a hundred steps to the Sun and when they got there, a little out of breath, it seemed she could see enough land to cover the whole state of Kansas, except there were mountains grander than anything in Kansas. She'd never seen so far in her whole life—had anyone back in Pittsburg? She knew then where eagles got off looking so arrogant, a view like that an everyday thing for them, up there where gravity lost its grip, the earth a more majestic place than you want to give it credit for when you can only see a little piece at a time.

Beautiful ain't it?

Oh yes, this must be half way to heaven.

But he's left her somewhere on that stairway one too many times. She's not going to take him back again. Not when she's got the card of that real estate woman in her pocket and the one parent God left her on this earth in Joplin, her mamma, who would take in her only daughter, Joplin hardly any distance to speak of. A new place, a new man, a new life. Lord only knows when he'll be back again. Years could be. He can make someone else Mrs. Granges.

She pulls aside the thick brown drape—heavy enough to have covered a settler's wagon—to look out the third-floor window of the Stilwell Hotel, the oldest building in Pittsburg (Arthur Stilwell put it up around 1889 if she remembers right), where she's spent the night with a man who is asleep still. If she can get out of the room without waking him—if she never sees him again—her faith in a guardian angel will be renewed. Younger than her, he was sweet, it's true, but stupidity showed on his face like a price tag someone forgot to take off. If it weren't for Zirque, she wouldn't have to go out and do this out of spite. To get coke or sleeping pills. Just for company.

Outside, big slow flakes drift in a slant past the glass storefronts—the old Gutteridge Pharmacy with its baseball black-and-whites, Pittsburg's Hardware Company, Carol's Corner Cafe where everyone goes for the breakfast special. And she can hardly believe it, but there he is at a stop light. Sitting in a red Cadillac convertible, the kind with fins. Top down, flakes of snow gathered against his dark hair like lost stars, that Steely Dan in-a-room-with-your-two-timer song on the radio fading as he pulls away.

She really doesn't mean to bother God about all this but, her eyes fixed on his glowing tail lights, she can't help it. Lord in Heaven I couldn't stand to go to the bottom of any mineshaft again even if it is a dream. I don't want to be like that Greek girl he told me about, who was stolen away, who let herself die a little, turn brown like autumn grass—just for a while—saving herself for better days, waiting for spring. I know he'll be back, he'll bring spring with im—never mind this light snow—Zirque you always do, please Zirque, I want it to be spring, not any mineshaft winter, please can't you be on your way to my house?

OVERHEAD, LIKE ORION

"MID THE UNEASY WANDERINGS OF PALEOLITHIC MAN,
THE DEAD WERE THE FIRST TO HAVE A PERMANENT
DWELLING: A CAVERN, A MOUND MARKED BY A CAIRN,
A COLLECTIVE BARROW."
—THE CITY IN HISTORY, LEWIS MUMFORD

THE DOWNTOWN IS BRICK; A SENSE OF PERMANENCE IN THAT, somethin you can lean against after last call. The pitted surface a local history, a mason's hand in all in those neat layers and straight corners showin in the scanty light. Scanty all right, mostly from poles overhead, lettered neon thrown in, free floatin in shop windows. North-South Broadway, wide an two-way, goes off to meet a dark sky. Broadway or Main Street, every town big enough to have a name has one.

A light turns red (in quiet enough to hear the metallic click).

From a few hotel stories up this town don't look like much, a little cross-hatchin a tar an sidewalks on the plains, could be swept away by one a those summer thunderstorms, angry clouds comin in like a dark billowin herd driven by wind riders, winds up takin up the whole sky, lightnin spiderin across a stretch a black big as the entire state but town's still here, dust a worn-out years blowin down Broadway, the centerpiece I guess bein the Hotel Stilwell, a fancy one in its time, run down now, what's left around here a the grandness of Old World Europe, quite a sight in its day, sometimes Pittsburg seems to me a Hollywood town almost, all façade, mostly sky an field behind, alleys, streets an backsides a buildins don't make much of a maze—no New York or Kansas City—but it ain't the way home gets people lost around here.

Take a left down 5th Street, Farley's Tavern stands an aged landmark, an anchor for things lost'n uprooted. Slow fans hangin from one a those high fancy tin ceilings. The higher the better. A place bygone travelers would haunt given the chance. Weightless, transparent moths flutterin in the mellow light, brushin up against the front window, see-through but impassable.

Here on Broadway the neon Gutteridge Pharmacy sign burnin silently red lets you peek at what's behind the window: antique drug bottles, boxes of imported cigars, black-&-whites a baseball greats like Ted Williams, Ty Cobb, a tall freckled boy from these parts whose name I don't recall, on his way to bein a major leaguer when he got electrocuted on farm machinery one rainy night. Two greats, one woulda-been, all three gone—the Thomas boy, that's him, a black-cat-crossed path, eyes closed peaceful now, celluloid mask all that's left a him an the rest. The ghost of an entire world that lived an died a billion years before this one moves through me—I can't explain it—leavin somewhere insida my ribs the kinda space could fit a mountain range.

After miles an months, Pittsburg (we got one here in Kansas) was a promise kept. I'd had my share a dead ends an one ways, of unmarked dirt drives without a single lamp to let you know what you were gettin yourself into.

A man gets tired a trackin down the source a the forces that shape his life. There are lines of energy in this world that show themselves on rare occasions in unexpected ways. Cagey as the secret shapes of woman in curves a flame. You grab holda the main circuit an hang on for all yer worth. Makes you feel like a nine ball sent reeling by the cue, makes you glad to have land-ed in a pocket.

Other times—right now is one of them—I need to be movin. Preferably through open spaces. (Conveniently forgettin those empty ones only a woman knows how to fill.)

You make do.

Wherever they finally plant my body, I'll always live in Pittsburg, alongside Gutteridge's baseball heroes, the invisible mothswarm outside Farley's, Blue Jean (prettiest girl I ever seen), and the rest of em.

Red, with that scar like a lightnin bolt through an eyebrow, likely to be drinkin at the Pan Club right about now (Hey, where's your green card? Willie said first time I walked inta the Pan Club, can't serve an illegal, Earl threw a beer cap at me, both of em laughin. Wouldn't it be somethin if one a them drove by right now and gave me a lift outta town?)

Somewhere up in KC, Skunk is cleanin those glass circles he wears on his nose an complainin the price The Cordoba charges for its girls has gone up. Who knows maybe Pap's with im.

Blue Jean at home earlier this evening, pannin the sky like a prospector for her sign risin, sleepin now, the pillow held tight.

The Earl, silver-haired though he is, married again, cheatin on his wife. Again.

Watch y'up to Earl?

Pickin m'nose an rubbin m'ass. Earl'd lift his KC Royals cap (always there to hide where he's going bald), settle it back on his head.

The Duke a Pallucca, his short legs carryin his thick body, Branson-bought walkin stick in hand, logs endless miles in Frontenac an Pittsburg, talkin to Indian ghosts who greet him in dawndusk mists an call im Troubled Heart because a virus about shut down his primary pump.

How are ya Duke?

Fair t'middlin.

Me—No Trail, False Trail, Lost His Way—the least likely of all to be tracked down. One a these shoulda been my God-given name.

As a boy it started (called me by my initials, Z.G., even then), never got my filla empty places, abandoned buildins, mine shafts. Exhaustin things hereabouts I discovered the railroad tracks one winter, desolate but promisin, most a them rustin destinies since the coal mines died out an the miners had mostly gone to the earth they worked. Ran alongside a train, jumped it, cold wind squintin my eyes, yankin back my hair, occurred to me borrowin a ride beat payin. Came to the conclusion there're things enough in the world, why add t'the pile? Course, you can do time for borrowin without permission.

Once used a waiter's uniform, posed as a valet parker at a fancy restaurant in Chicago. By the time the maitre d' came out to see what was goin on, all he got was a good look at the tail lights. Mercedes Benz that time. Shopliftin, bad checks, dope deals, too. New York, Chicago, California, Oklahoma, Mexico. Places somehow tied to what's been done in them—not necessarily by me.

There are ways to tell.

First night I sleep in a place somethin that happened there happens again in my dreams. Leaves owners with astonished faces hoverin over steamin breakfast eggs often enough. Well I'll be... Somethin sticks to the wooden ribs of a house, stains the earth like blood from a biblical killin never dried up.

Blamin my restlessness on anythin that can't get up and argue the point, I take the way of greatest desire, whatever the moment dangles before me. A blueprint drawn up by expectation, most often endin in disappointment. Tempered by the Nowherevilles that no one's ever heard of but you spend a good part of a lifetime there, not measured by a clock but by what happens to you, how deep it presses into memory.

Half my years it seems rose an fell in the Duke's half-lit basement. College educated, sternly Catholic, his face somethin saintly an weathered, a stone likeness that's been standin an watchin in the archway of a gate since Roman times, ain't much gets past without his noticin. He's like that card in a fortune teller's deck, wavin around a lantern, leanin on a walkin stick, always on his way somewhere, mostly alone, whether readin from the books stacked ceiling high in his basement or strollin the hazy beginnins of day on Cayuga Street. He can go off on a one-sided conversation like no one I know, every sentence a keeper till you have so many you don't know what to do with em. Talks insteada sleeps, right through the night, pullin down a book every now and then for cross-referencin, losing me in funhouse turns till just when I think there's no way back I find familiar ground.

Memories, he says, are handles connected to time.

What he learned from his illness, he said, is the heart ain't a muscle but a place, where you either live, or you don't.

Blue Jean says I broke hers a hundred and fifty times at least. But I always come back. I've got a chronic case of claustrophobia that'll turn terminal if I don't get away from time to time. You can't call it id or superego, it's an illness a the spirit around since the time a the ziggurat-builders in Sumer.

Man's always been hollow, since the day a goddess breathed him alive. Just solid enough to build cities. Me, just empty enough for dust storms to kick up. Not somethin to wait out, but somethin that wants out. Aren't too many ways either. To pass the time, I useta rope steer, sell door to door (I still do), steal cars (I always will). When I get the chance, I don't mind singin in my half-assed voice, watchin twists a cigarette smoke drift up toward the hot light. The music sounds out the deepest places in you, leaves you alone in them, a disappearing act kinda, turns you for a little while into the answer to the prayer you been prayin all your life. Till the house lights come on, the song ends, the spell's broken.

I do the same things over and over it seems, the place what changes. For some reason, a beer can take on a different taste in a bar you never been to, Mexico maybe. Or Nebraska. Greece if yer the kind who gets around.

There's quite a feelin to be had sittin on a white-stoned veranda overlookin the darkened cone of a volcano—set in the waverin blue shimmer a the Mediterranean—that downed a civilization around 400 BC. I watched the sun settle behind that blackened rim a disaster, the meltin bronze while ships dwarfed by distance set out for wherever. And even though I was in a place where ships arrived everyday, a twinge a me wanted to be on one.

It's always that way. In a pocket fulla crumpled, unanswered (or once-answered) desires, we keep a photo of what it is we want (again maybe) an hold it up to everythin we get. Time after time there's a shakin a the head, a return a the photo.

There's a still of me in Blue Jean's kitchen, standin alongside the reddish pillars at Knossos, the labyrinth island a Crete. Inventors a the flush toilet, keepers a sacred bull rites, a the bull-beast with a man's body. Lost at night in the dark cobblestone alleys a cities, adrift in streets, in half-lit stone-walled bars fulla men with heavy heads an thick black mustaches, there's an invisibly thin thread ties me to her I never lose sight of.

A detour takes me to Delphi under sea winds, not a streamlined Minoan boat with sails (black or white, dependin on the occasion), but a ferry stinkin a diesel with no sleep for the worn-out on an oil-slick deck, the vibrations a the engine like a star about to explode. Delphi, center of the world the old Greek told me, bald as Telly Savalas, Ev'reeteeng at Delphee.

No, just some ruins an beautiful mountains. Remnants of an oracle.

Used to be, Apollo's priestess was go-between for the god an questioners. Sometimes great men, sometimes small-timers with great questions. The oracle answered true, but had a likin for curve balls. Some king went there with startin a war on his mind, asked the oracle what would happen if he did. Oracle said a great empire'd fall. The king got excited and headed off, sword in hand. Was his own empire that went to dust.

The whole point bein, like anythin else, even a statement that would hold up in court can lead you astray.

Keen as we are to pick up the hint as to which way things in this world are goin, don't take more than an onion to send us headin off in the wrong direction. Take what Blue Jean said to me while makin dinner one evening. Looked at the onion she was cuttin an wondered how it got that way, with its layered arrangement—peeled neatly away, or made rings if you sliced it right—and couldn't bring herself to believe the complicated nature a the onion was a chance act. Based on this evidence, she cast her vote for God. Like late-night neon, an onion can say something without meanin to—specially when Blue Jean's the one listenin. Mainly what an onion says to me is come and get it.

I can smell her kitchen a thousand miles away.

Watchin her cook, one a those scratched-up Chet Baker records she borrowed from Pap wearin out the needle a that antique phonograph player used to be her daddy's, the back door open to let in the August breeze and the evenin sun fadin amber while behind the salt an pepper shakers, winged Eros—painted black on burnt orange—forever offers white-skinned Athena a plate a fruit (a bit a pottery I managed t'bring back for her by stickin it dead center a the clothes stuffed in my duffel bag). Postcards an photos on the walls, wine bottles an porcelain vases arranged with dry flowers on countertops, glass do-dads an antique what-nots found at second-hand shops in Joplin or front-lawn junkyards, she's got quite a collection goin.

She cooks meticulously, favorin oregano, onions, garden-grown green pepper, garlic fresh from Pallucca's Market, parsley an black pepper. Never measures a thing and never mis-seasons down to a grain of salt. Home never smelled so good.

Get your feet off my table, Zirque.

Summer in Kansas brings out the mature lines in her face, reminds me what she'd look like if she lived in a place like New Mexico or Arizona. Her body with the smooth hardness of a reclinin rock.

Sometimes, she says, it's so flat and plain around here I can't stand it.

Sometimes I think exactly that: I can't change it, I can't stand it, I might as well get as far away from it. (Each bootfall takes me further.)

From time to time I take her with me. Monument Valley, rock formations like gigantic sailin ships stranded in an ocean expanse a desert, oddly masted, too heavy to be carried on a light dry breeze headed for livelier seas. The crown a creation, the sun wrote its epitaph in afterglow on the dark sandstone, Venus rose in the last a the blue an the towerin stone became stoic silhouettes, like time still standin. I bet you could catch sight a the next day from the top a one a those, she said.

First light in Kansas (summertime when school's out an she doesn't have t'teach) most often finds her in the barn, brushin down Baldy, her favorite horse. On cool mornins toward September Baldy's flared nostrils steam, the wind streaked with the color of her hair when she rides, she's probably better'n I am but defers to me because a rodeo rings.

This mornin we came to the fence around her land, I wanted to jump it an keep goin. I looked at her, she looked away, she knew what I was thinkin.

This mornin leavin was right there in the room with me, holdin the door open, pointin the way. I looked at her, knew I loved her an knew another minute would turn love to resentment. The flatness, the fences, even her face—beautiful as it was while she slept—I needed to be somewhere else, anywhere else, with anyone else.

Though dreamin tonight when I left, I know she can hear me. She can hear wheat grow.

Here on the edge a town, lights dimmin, darkness outta focus, Pittsburg's cemetery marks passings. Gray, white, black marble stones for no reason other than life doesn't seem so quickly never was, see-through, over. Lookin over a shoulder, thinkin about backtracking, I see the pattern Blue Jean an I fell into. She saw the seed of now in what was then as well as I did, she didn't accept it is the difference.

Zirque (she was in the middle a the dishes) you think it's true you do to other people what you do to yourself?

What makes you ask?

A shrug. Psychology, she said.

A night course she took to be less small town.

She put a drippin dish in the rack. If you lie to yourself, it's easier to lie to people yer with. You think so?

Sounds about right.

From a city divided by a common wall, I wondered is she lookin up at the same moon? (There are two Berlins, not east an west, but one bombed out, left only in memory; one built on those vanished foundations.)

No, it's day where she is.

Buildins gone, bricks left, blueprints an history remain. One Berlin exists only in imagination, the subjective realm a the Hopi on their mesas overlookin the fallin a time like slow dry rain on an earth erodin in a desert wind. They still recall the Red City a the South, destroyed like the bustlin 1930s Berlin of old, but both a them still exist, underneath what we're standin on now though we can't get t'them anymore, the Place a Dreamin maybe its called, the place we crawled up out of like ants out of a hill, each passin minute a grain a sand added, the hill goes up an there's no way back down. So old Berlin some-how reaches out to New York an Paris along jazz wavelengths, reserves a whole dimension for Hollywood imagery (sittin on the U-Bahn subway, a blond German with a duck's ass an divin-board pompadour, a worn leather jacket, James Dean patch that was just a silk-screen shape no detail to its black ink shadow. Dean an avatar, imitation bein the sincerest form a religion). Bridges have caved in but a saxophone goes on squeezin sound from brass, brass echoes against the stone ruins of kristallnacht burned-out synagogue, the temple a window-eyed mask with no face behind. On the Wall, a shadow left in the shape a someone reachin, shot while reachin *What are you looking at,* in spray-painted German, a translation chalked in, *haven't you ever seen a wall before?* Tremblin ephemeral shadows cast by searchlights still whisper past on

[31]

nights, all that's left a the ones scratched onto the wall: 1970–12 shot. 1971–11 shot. 1972–6 shot... so far. You gotta admire they're givin it a go, gotta admire the one's who made it (where there's a wall, there's a way).

In night clubs just underneath the velvet, the fancy gold trim an the chandeliers with diamond-shaped crystals big as horse turds, the bare stained grayin chipped cement remains. A crystalline wind-chime hanging in the breezeless ruins, Berlin night clubs like to let you know Viennese grandeur is founded on the same ugliness as everythin else.

Cafe Orianenberg steel chairs twisted like strung-out entrails only a little more elegant. Everythin tall, elongated, backs a chairs rise up way past your head, as if gravity were less there, an illusion because gravity is more. Pulled agonizin'ly slowly–as if lookin to prolong time here through space–out of original shape. Not so much the back of a chair I was restin against as a cuneiform tablet made to look like cracked clay, the destiny of a city written on it, a thread a tragedy in the tapestry a history. You expect rain t'be thick as engine oil, corrosive as battery acid, smell like asphalt. Even sunlight in those cafes is walled off, shows up in cement-cut squares.

Steel gray light near dawn, lookin at the waterstained pension ceiling–permanent yellowish cloud formation on the grayin white-sigh sky a the faded ceiling–I'd a given anything to be with her then. The mornin light comes in her bedroom on a particular slant I haven't found in any other part a the world, no kitchen has the seasoned smell a hers sunk right into the woodwork, no woman I ever slept with feels the same next to me.

Good mornin Sweetness and Light.

Don't call me that, makes me sound like a cup of coffee.

Yer the fire in my stove, you know that, don'tcha?

Stop it Zirque.

The light in my window.

Yer so ridiculous.

The bulb in my lamp.

I don't know why I put up with you.

Come on, let's head out to the Corner Cafe I want everyone to see how good you look in the mornin.

Mornin passes by in the steam a coffee, the smoke a bacon grease, Big Al sweatin over the grill, Connie goin table to table talkin up a twister Don't come over here with that cigarette she only smokes one but it never goes out not once did I ever see her light up the second one I swear the first never goes out. Then it's a PiCCO malted, nothin Blue Jean likes better. We used to run into Pap now an again, gettin one to cure a hangover Fanshy meetin you here Granges, he'd say as if he had high manners.

Leanin against the fender a my car parked in PiCCO's gravel lot, Blue Jean would work so hard on gettin that malt thick as it was through the straw she'd forget me. A gust a wind and the leaves a September came up around us, a whirlin circle, settled back down in fall colors amber bleedin into red dusted with orange this whole town covered in every moment we ever spent together a drift a fall color over Pittsburg and Frontenac an every breeze that kicks up we remember more keenly while she sits there on the hood a my car wearin my denim jacket the sleeves coverin over her hands just about, every candle lit beneath the stone statue of a saint in the darkness a the old Catholic church on Locust Street gathered right there in her eyes above that malted smile poked through with a red-and-white striped straw, I heard–though he was gone from this earth by then–old Raymond Pallucca, his voice a rusty wheelbarrow Well hello there Rae Anne how you been don't you look beautiful today yer not in a rush I hope you can stay and say hello to an admirer, a little girl she looked so happy, the cold sweet malted slush in her cup all it took, a warm kiss against cold lips, her tongue cold too (that's how we know we're walkin breathin warm-blooded fragments a the universe), an then a little shoppin on Broadway and a greasy burger an thick fries at the 501 drive-up joint where we catch sight a the Duke a Pallucca an Millo Farnetti that old mine mule he lived in Italy on and off twenty years got his picture in the World Book Encyclopedia under journalism, an somehow its evenin already and we drive back home to the quiet a the fields don't need a thing besides her on those cool end-of-summer evenins, everythin its rightful place feelin without a doubt with her huggin herself to me the way she fits to me the way the two of us fit to the whole sweep a the land–every blade a grass bendin past the porch steps, every blackbird call in the deepenin grayin blue, every strip a cloud an shred a light the sky has left can't move a thing half an inch right or left (like touchin the water to get at the reflection it'll all disappear) just hold onto her on that backyard swing, a little countrywestern or New Orleans jazz driftin out from the radio in her kitchen I'm never happier than when I'm with her I guess I can only handle so much before I stop appreciatin it wind up sleepin on rocks for a while to remind me how good it'd be t'get back to a good feather bed.

A shame, the Duke said, you don't leave anythin behind, any more than a boat marks the water by its passin.

It's no coincidence the constellations're named after mythical beings, those old stories a tunnel (studded with bits a the Milky Way) we crawl through to reach a place we feel like we belong, part of a hidden order somehow embedded in our stories told from cradle to grave, grave an earth cradle meant to hold us once again when we're nothin but leather-skinned bags fulla bones an withered organs, curled up fetal, head to knee the next thousand years.

Never even scratched my name in a desk in Pittsburg Elementary best I can hope for when I'm gone I guess is somebody'll save my skull like those African primitives do Where be your tribes now Granges? Put it on a shelf somewhere like the one Pap used t'have, paint it a color to match the room maybe, set a beer next to me I'll catch somma what dries off. Leave off my lower jaw if you don't want me jabberin and keepin you up at night, I'll just sit up there, watch the seasons turn, the light fallin slightly different fall to summer, pale winter light the loneliest for my bones up there on the shelf keep the fire stoked you'll always have a friend exactly where you left him say hello to when you come home.

In the city where I want to live, desire an outlet—a pair a one-way streets—run into each other, I want to set up shop on the corner. Might as well try standin at the core of a nuclear reactor, you say. But there is love an the phenomenon of joined bodies, resonance on another plane. Maybe as close as anyone'll ever get. I hear that's what artists're starvin for. They know existence isn't something you can look up in Websters an have the vagueness cleared up, but they go on tryin, usually cuttin it down to size so you can take it in at a glance.

Veronique said art's a way of lookin at things that shows you somethin you've never seen before but has always been there.

I said, Art's a drunk who drowned one day in a sewer ditch in Crawford County Kansas. She didn't even crack a smile.

All right I said, take an itty bitty piece a nothin weighs nothing with a high-charged name, an electron, gets excited, jumps an orbital, finds itself in a new dimension. Spinnin itself dizzy on the edge it can't stay forever. When it falls, leaves behind a fragment a light. We leave behind writin, a painting, a song, a dance.

Better, she said.

Better than art Veronique, a subtle shift in emotion made solid, given a cold tongue with the fadin taste a malt, imagine that.

I met her in Paris, Bar Sept, a smoky little cave with tables everywhere, dozens a small orangish lights t'give the effect a candles, a collage a magazine photos coverin the walls: sculpted women wearin the latest fashions; bodies a soldiers frozen as if they'd once been flamin wax, hardened, the fire gone out; presidents, politicians makin speeches to admirin crowds. In

[35]

the crowded bar women with fitted looks, a platinum Warhol wig, darkness made visible by wraparound sunglasses, curiously held cigarettes, voices formin words as smooth as shells worn thin by the sea's relentless rhythm (*Ne me le dit pas. Ce n'est pas possible!*) polished lips slipping over glass rims. Stole the bartender's tips t'buy my first drink. A floor down like a dungeon, steep iron stairs an moss creeping through furrows in the old stone walls reminds you high civilization's been there for a while.

Soon as I saw her I invited myself to her table.

She looked at me, straight through me, then turned away as if talkin to the wall. Pale with black hair, sharp cheekbones, uncanny lips which somehow intimated themselves in the shapin a words (you'da been able to see them even in perfect darkness long as you could hear what she was sayin).

Camus and Dean, she said through her French accent, the first real outsiders, modern history begins with them.

How do you mean?

They had—*qu'est-ce que c'est?*—a floating consciousness. In some way above things even while right in the middle of them.

Veronique gave me this theory: You will only meet a certain number of people in your life. You will meet these people again and again whether you try to or not.

Red, the Duke, Pap, Blue Jean, Veronique.

When I came back to Paris, she was her own proof I ran into her in another bar, went home with her that night, too. We didn't always know where to find each other in Paris but always did, middle a the night more often than not.

Night intensifies the difference between shadow and light, she wrote to me, that is why I sleep all day.

Blue Jean calls me Rip Van Granges, thinks I slept my life away, coulda been a this, coulda been a that. But you take rodeo riding I never wanted to make a life of it, or anythin else. This place is nobody's friend, never will be, but you carve outta whatever your knife can cut into somethin you can live with,

your initials, a grinnin god, a back porch. You surround yourself with things a your own doin, somethin a the way a seein
things you've come to call your own. An you make an uneasy
peace with things your blade can't scratch.

You appreciate things more when you've seen a huntin knife
as far inside a man as it can sink an the stare in his eyes as he
gets a look at a place he never imagined he'd be going. If
vudasia (the Duke's word) is the hauntin suspicion yer some-
place you never want to be, that has to be the worst case there is.

I've been close enough.

Only sixteen years old, balmy kinda August evenin, ridin an
old box-type-fender Honda, wasn't doin more than 25 miles an
hour, enjoyin the mildness a the summer drizzle. Picked up my
leg just in time, I woulda lost it cop told me later. All I saw were
the headlights before everythin turned black, reached out in
the center of an endless darkness only to get a hand on somethin as rough an cold as buried coal, the bottom a some earth-
frozen mineshaft I guess only it felt like the bottom a endless
space, this taste like I'd swallowed a mouthful a clay an I called
out with my clay-clogged mouth but there was only my own
echo down there in a shaft a pure black carved outta dusty
Kansas ore. Took a while before I saw off in the distance a
hangin light, one a them old oil lamps burns oil maybe, a miner
come lookin for a fool from way above sea level took a wrong
turn, I called to him Hey, bring that over here, wouldja, help
me get my bearings. The light kept gettin brighter, but the
source was gone an I was surrounded by a thousand suns it
seemed only it didn't hurt my eyes, can you figure? I heard a
voice, Old Man Varanelli's I would swear it was he'd died years
ago in one a the mines, heard him say We're not ready for you
yet. Felt no pain, near floatin in the thick light, that's about
what I was, a fleck a dust trapped in a shaft a sunlight, felt as
good as those Sunday mornins you get up knowin you don't
have to work, the air is real crisp breathin seems more than you
could ask for whaddayou mean yer not ready for me yet? Old

[37]

Man Varanelli's voice came back to me Seems there's somethin you still got t'do elsewhere.

Next thing I heard came from a paramedic We got him back I read in the Pittsburg Sun how I bounced off the Caddy that hit me, off another car (the window was open a crack, I broke his glasses in two as I flew by, ripped off a windshield wiper with the back a my neck), then went 65 feet down the road. Front tire a the bike came clean off, the forks were stuck in a tree (couldn't pull that off again if you staged a couple thousand accidents) paper said I was dead for near five minutes.

Dyin's no fun sure but despair's no carnival ride either. That train station in Italy, a depression thick as the heat the greased tracks scorched by the Italian sun what it smelled like. Futility. Sounds like somethin temporarily outta order, looks like Greek columns standin atop a cliff above the sea, all that's left a the temple a Poseidon. Kids' initials carved in the sun-whitened stone, insects makin the same lonely sounds they do in Kansas you might think Classical architecture makes the difference or bein in another country. But sometimes you might as well be lookin at a fillin station gone to weeds on a dirt road in Oklahoma, a likelihood temples were as common to the ancients as fillin stations and no less useful.

I recall a grand old cathedral, vaulted ceilings high as heaven, glowin colored glass (reminds you holes're poked in the fabric a things, somethin shines through), gold saints an bishops an a sad-faced Madonna lookin a lot like the Mona Lisa, tried prayin in the cavernous darkness, here an there a few candles like lost souls, felt just like I was talkin into a dial tone, no connection. Prayed Blue Jean'd wait for me, wouldn't be lonely, Red'n Earl'd keep an eye on her. But just as I left somehow in the glow–rare purple outta ancient Tyre, fall-leaf yellow, a green near as strikin as Blue Jean's eyes, red on its way to violet, all in cut-gem kaleidoscope shapes–somehow in that illumined gloom I finally saw the larger pattern, bigger than life, floating up there Jesus in the dark stone wall. Felt not so much a faker but a betrayer, a user, hedgin my bets just in case yer listenin Lord.

A room is all I need Blue Jean. One in your house and one in your heart. Not the run a them, just to know I have a place to come back to, your mouth your tongue cold with a PiCCO malted and the smell in your room early mornin (half your perfume, half what's under it), strands a red hair fallin across the side a your face (no alabaster likeness in any museum could measure up) you account for all the sweetness an light in my life. Alchemists of old thought gold was a chunk a sunlight gone solid, if you believe that Blue Jean then yer a piece a heaven fell to earth. Once upon a time with see-through flesh, bones made a brightness, a red-headed kachina with green stars for eyes, come all this way from a home out where Halley's comet could get lost the sun's so small you can hardly see it you landed in Pittsburg Kansas real as the rest of us I watch your breath on clear cold mornings hopin you'll keep me warm keep me company keep me here with you one day I'll be home to stay.

After death finally does us part, I can't say I'd mind bein stretched out overhead like Orion. A man can't ask for much more than that at the end, t'be made into a constellation, t'be pointed at by young lovers in their parked convertible, a signpost to restless travelers, always a part of the ongoing clockwork starshifts in the sky, what makes it familiar like the old compadre you want it to be. You can't live forever, but you can become a universal signpost.

I remember you on our back porch Rae Anne, not far from rustin tracks going nowhere now, blue evening tied around your waist an the season's last sheen grown coppery on your hair. You watch for the things that come with night and I think: what was once (Knossos, Farley's Tavern, my love for you) has always been. And everything, I firmly believe, is still to come.

CADA EDAD TIENE
SU ENCANTO

Sometime around dawn on September 16, 1810, in the Mexican Village of Dolores, Padre Miguel Hidalgo issued his cry for freedom from Spanish rule. The famous call to rebellion has since become known as El Grito de Dolores.

Here, Eduardo will tell you, is the magic: When he wasn't looking, two weeks were turned into 12 years. Abracadabra. He will hold out his black bowler (a magnificently round fit atop his bald head) to show it is as empty as the cavernous plundered tomb of a Mayan king. Then he will laugh.

Twelve years in a hotel room! Who would have believed it?

No less than the Hotel Nacional, which you will see listed in your travel guide–if you have brought one–as one of the cheapest in Mexico City.

Most likely you will have been lured by the limping manager (El General, Eduardo calls him with a salute), who hawks rooms in the tireless voice of a carnival caller This way, this way. The bath water is running is always hot, the rooms are quiet comfortable cheap, the site historic. Here, page 15 of your Baedeker, this is us, El Nacional, built during the reign of Maximillian.

Most likely you will have been doubtful, barely able to see through Mexico City's deepening evening haze thick with diesel fumes to where the streaks of black, the brushstrokes of grays and smears of browns, the darkened stone and painted wood, materialized into El Nacional, squeezed between buildings equally faded, worn, abstract.

Don't be fooled, El General will have said, this was once un gran edificio, the Versailles of hotels, its foundation stones taken from a ruined Aztec temple or two by Los Montez, a family on intimate

terms with Emperor Maximillian, the ill-fated Viennese gentlemen who danced to music fluted by Napoleon III.

Yes, Eduardo will say when you mention the balding manager's extravagant claims, I know you carried all that luggage to
the room by yourself–El General's leg was years ago crushed
when a beam fell on it during an earthquake–but formerly
there was a full retinue of servants (Indians all scandalously
underpaid it is true). And such was the power, the prestige of
the Church in those once-upon-a-time days that clergymen
stayed the night for free.

You will try, but you will not be able to reconcile the velvet-
lined memories of El Nacional–stately oil paintings of Mexican personajes such as Vicente Guerrero, Benito Juarez,
General Santa Anna (of Alamo fame) stolen to the last; hand-
carved chairs with legs bowed as if not able to support the
weight of overstuffed emerald-green cushions; candelabra chandeliers–you will not be able to place them next to the buffet in
need of refinishing in Eduardo's slightly tilted room–

The city is built upon an old lake bed, Eduardo will inform
you, it would not hold still even when Madero rode in
triumphant to end the dictatorship of Porfirio Diaz–streets
shook, buildings cracked, roofs tumbled.

–the balding carpets in the hallway, the dulled paint (unevenly done in the first place) in need of dusting and fresh coats,
the water-stained ceilings, the bare-bulb lighting, the brownish
tapwater (the Victorian clock with wrought-iron hands has
stopped in the lobby but rust marches on in the pipes). Time
is a slow measureless matter of daylight filtering though
the exhaust-fume sky through yellowish shades brittle as
old newspaper.

It's a wonder the rain is not black, Eduardo will say.

On his lopsided buffet–a miracle of warping and water stains
which had once floated several city blocks in a flood–on that
buffet indescribable via Euclidean geometry, admirable to anyone with van Gogh's eye for disproportions, you will notice,

neatly stacked, five or six boxes of Earl Grey Tea.

I would give up Mexico's current form of government, the Republic, Eduardo will say, and live under a restored monarchy to obtain a year's supply.

Then he will smile disarmingly, his teeth yellowed from too much proximity to smoldering tobacco.

A monarchy is rather dashing after all. Not the silliness Iturbide had attempted, appointing himself king—where is the divine providence in that?—or Santa Anna and his ill-mannered clownish followers, no, something with dignity.

No doubt you ran into Eduardo in the hotel lobby which, no matter how musty or poorly lighted, is as securely linked by telephone wire to Cairo, Bangladesh, Jerusalem, Passaic, N.J. as to Mexico itself. You were amused by the pompous air of the manager whom you overheard exclaiming that he will breathe his last breath in the service of his guests.

Viva los touristas!

There, while trying to place a long-distance call—your Spanish is not very good—Eduardo probably took the opportunity to introduce himself and offer his services as translator.

Technology, he likes to say, has a way of dangling the improbable before you only to confound you with an insurmountable detail—language for example.

Anomalous Eduardo Lerma—as old as Mexico City permits men to be—will speak English with an Oxford accent, carry a long umbrella and don his bowler as would any gentleman who has grown accustomed to London's fog. At Oxford University, he will not have failed to inform you, he was another in the long legacy of nobility, possessing a scholar's instinct for well-worded truth, a rogue's predilection for women fragrant with the perfume of willingness.

Of all the things he learned there, the one he would take with him if forced to choose—let us say the planet were coming to an end in a week—is etiquette.

No matter when apocalypse strikes, one must be properly

dressed for the occasion and be sure to utter words that will be remembered.

Resting his creaky back against a chair in the lobby, Eduardo must have directed a comment at the aging manager who steps from past to present, present to past and loses a frame of motion, the continuity, in between–

Digame General, como esta la pierna hoy? Que tiempo pronostica para la semana que viene?

–before inviting you to his room to sip tequila with him.

It is not the best brand, he surely will have apologized, leading the way up a staircase so dim, so humid with years, so badly lit, you will imagine for an instant you are in the catacomb stillness of the temple of Quetzalcoatl in Chichenitza, ascending the breathing wet stone steps that take you to the tiny red idol of a jaguar god, somehow lit in that ancient moss-lined darkness by a lone incandescent bulb.

In any event, tequila is just to make do.

Eduardo would rather a few bottles of a thick Jamaican rum of a color and consistency not unlike maple syrup, an island warmth left in the pit of his stomach.

Yes, rather than repossess all the land taken during the war of the Alamo, I would rather several bottles of this very wonderful rum.

Eduardo will empty his glass with the forlorn grace of a butterfly swept out to sea by mischievous winds.

Oxford, he will say, was a grand experience.

He will pour himself another.

But it was nothing compared to traveling half the length of a country–from Texas to Mexico City–on horseback.

I was a true *caballero*, he will tell you. And talk of the twenty-thousand pounds sterling (quite something in those days) he had with him with which to finish his education. But the first lady who caught his eye on return to Mexico (she had the cheekbones of an Aztec princess) was gracious enough to allow him to reduce that sum by a thousand.

There were other women in other cities–Gaudalajara, Chicago, Vera Cruz, New York, Los Angeles–who were just as eager to eat in the finest restaurants and mingle with the sons and daughters of bankers, industrial tycoons, politicians.

Never the same woman for more than a week or two, no matter how beautiful. They all had to have their turn, don't you see?

He will recall nights spent dancing in domed clubs, twice running into Tommy Dorsey's band and once managing–with a flourish–to get an autograph from Glenn Miller for Louise who bore a striking resemblance to Patty, the prettiest of the Andrews Sisters. The music in full swing, he and Louise danced, two art deco silhouettes pressed against the vault of heaven, the stars wheeling overhead, outdone only by the sequin sparkle of her dress. The world was wondrous unending unbelievable through a full glass of red wine.

What does it matter that twenty-thousand pounds, enough to last a wise man a lifetime, had bought only six months?

Ah, yes, there was *mi padre*.

A hard man locked in another era, enamored of the flint knives of Aztec priests and the hearts bared to them as offerings to the sun.

Sacrifice, Eduardo, there is nothing that more ennobles the human spirit.

Although Padre was descended of a wealthy Spanish family, olive-skinned, his thin mustache perfectly trimmed always, a suit and tie even at the breakfast table, he was the kind of man who could live in a hut with an earthen floor if circumstances demanded, eat corn tortillas for breakfast and again for supper, working in the fields from sunup till sundown, the whole time sprinkling the earth with the salt of his sweat.

Discipline, Padre often said, is what separates man from beast and I respect no man who lacks it. A man must conquer his urges Eduardo. No one is fat against his will.

No, no Father, I beg to differ. A sip of Earl Grey tea at one's leisure is what separates man from our four-footed friends. Wasn't it Shakespeare, he will turn to you and ask, who said even a beggar is in the poorest thing superfluous?

Disinherited, Eduardo did not take well to routine.

What is a man if he cannot take a nap in the sun when the mood so strikes him?

He will admit that even as a child he was too old to change. There was never a time when I would permit myself to be anything other than what I was. Though now I must admit that I have become like the descendant of an Aztec ruler. When we dig subways nowadays, we come across the remains of my empire–I cannot help being reminded. But so many years have gone by that now they come to only so many old stones. And I must live on top of them.

Certain regrets are acquired tastes, sipped at now and again despite their bitterness.

Sometimes (he will rub his brow with thumb and forefinger) my head hurts all the way to God.

You will see him then as he sees himself, leaning over the faucet in the morning for what one day shall prove to be the last time. Like El General, the manager, he too has lost his hair, is not oblivious to the strange smell that is his own, a sourness that no amount of soaping or perfuming can rid him of, the smell of age, the smell he remembers from his grandmother's sweaters when she crushed his child's face to her great stomach, it is in his clothes now (worse, it is something he can never take off) and no matter how many times he sees the sag in cheeks he keeps meticulously shaven, he will be surprised at how unfaithful his memory has been to the image in the dull metal. If he were not so thin– (yes, he will think, his chest is birdlike, is mostly ribs so how did that paunch, a round bloated piñata, get there?) –he would have jowls.

You will see him wandering the halls early in those mornings, steeped in the settled darkness, what seeps through the imperfect joining of night and day, through the ill-fitting walls of the hotel, exposing a body which is a pear in shape, sagging (at its widest) over the elastic waist of his baggy boxer shorts, a clownish sight he would be embarrassed to know you can so easily imagine.

You will see him hesitate outside one of the rooms, hearing as he always does the gunshot he never heard in the first place. He will enter that room, searching the peeling wallpaper of faded flowers until he finds the place—to this day you can see the poor job of spackling they did—where one of the bullets disappeared.

I was a child then, the horse more popular than the car, the Nacional was still quite a place, its owner a meek, spiritually minded vegetarian who got ill at the sight of uncooked meat. A wealthy man with a yellowish complexion, he was very popular with the servants—having doubled their wages—infuriating his wife, Olga Luz who, as it turned out, wanted nothing to do with sallow-faced Frederico (it was the hotel she wanted) and sent her lover to kill the poor man in his sleep. Frederico awoke, several shots were fired, he was killed anyway, and Olga Luz and the lover disappeared for all time.

Leaving their children to war among themselves for ownership. The youngest child, Magdalena the Silken Voiced (and that is not all that was rumored to be silken), the daughter of Olga Luz, was half sister to Wilfredo and Santiago, brothers born of a different mother. She carried on scandalously with Wilfredo, promising herself to him, only to leave him for an unhappy American oil man who spent most of his days drinking tequila and most of his nights staring out at the darkness as if Mexico City were at the bottom of the long-vanished lake, as if he were a body adrift in a tide of unhappy memories. The relationship lasted long enough for her to embezzle to her heart's content and divorce him, cleverly having gotten him to keep the hotel in her name.

By then the Nacional had begun to fall into disrepair.

Spending the money not on upkeep but on her own frivolities—perfumes at a servant's yearly salary per ounce, dresses adorned with the luster scraped from Africa's deepest mines, men she fancied as she aged, whom she attracted with her status and wealth—she found herself alienated from her family, dying at last within the wrapping of her satin sheets, sheltered beneath the hanging lace of her canopied bed—endless looping hours of work for patient women's hands, dark Indian hands. Magdalena left behind a genuine will proven false (A bit of legal magic, Eduardo will say bitterly) which would have made a young man who was no Montez owner of El Nacional.

It was not long after Magdalena ascended like the evil saint she was that the first presidential suite was cut up in a scheme to create more revenue with more rooms rented out more often. This process went on over the years as the neighborhood grew more crowded, yes, one morning you wake up to see clothes hanging in that imprecise zone between two buildings and within a week's time several families have squeezed themselves in, diapers are hanging on cords tied to snapped-off broom handles stuck into the ground, to iron fencing, to a sapling struggling inside a patch of unpaved earth.

On the city's perimeter, entire villages spring up overnight— abracadabra—the new inhabitants praying for a miracle from the Indian Virgin of Guadalupe that the police will not evict them from the harsh land they have claimed, from their rows of shacks leaning, lopsided, unevenly joined. No straight edges (Mexico is a country without reliable geometry). Stakes and ropes hold things from flying off, tarpaper keeps the rain out, maybe, the lucky ones with cloudy plastic windows flapping in the breeze, blankets or no windows at all for the rest. No sewers, electricity, running water, heat, they pray that the diseases of overpopulation do not take their suffering children who play in the dust of the dirt roads and mark their faces with their own dirty hands, who would not be admitted to the city hospitals without a few pesos to get some orderly's attention.

Others live in the city dump, in caves dug into the slopes of piled trash, eyes peering out at you like night creatures caught in the glare of headlights.

Oh these Mexicans are brilliant at improvising, Eduardo will say with a sparkling mixture of condemnation and envy. Look out the window, down on the street, there is the ten-year-old fire-eater Little Lopez, who is discolored from the time he was careless with the fluid, who nearly died when he inhaled. He has gathered something of a collection of thrown pesos over the years, he is better off than Carlos the streetwalker, the wino, who picks through the trash, warming himself in winters at one of the bonfires made of truck tires, burning in the last of the vacant lots—a lucky thing there is so much rising smoke, the gods can't see what has become of their people.

I, I am a perfect Christian, Eduardo will tell you. It is an accident I am here. The Spanish would never have come here if not for the gold. They cared nothing for calendars with a different measure of time nor for a mountainous terrain inhabited by a fierce, dark people whose religion revolved around the sun.

What can be expected of me, living in a country founded on a haunting rumor passing from conquistador to conquistador, whispering of an Indian emperor who had not been crowned but coated in a fine layer of gold instead, who plunged into a lake to wash the glittering excess of royalty from him, sent it to grace the dark bottom, who presided over a city which blinded from a distance so that you must never look straight at it, but always out of the corner of your eye? Whose streets turned up gold on the bottoms of sandals? Whose people are like children, blissfully unaware of the value of what they play with day to day?

These conquistadors came with a strange fever, a sickness induced by the lack of a cold yellow metal, it is an accident they stayed.

Can you blame me for wanting a home in Barcelona—I do miss the sea from time to time—a servant or two, and a small but impressive collection of Picassos?

Instead of Picassos, there were wives—much more trouble though no less beautiful—five of them in all.

My first, Isabella, always thought my father would eventually soften his disposition and reinstate me as heir. She had the name of a queen and the shrewdness of a sewer rat. As the years went by, Padre showed no signs of weakening and she left me for another man.

It was all just as well. At the time I was having an affair with Concepcion, my second wife-to-be. Her voice could shatter glass as easily as her looks ruined hearts. I would go to any length to avoid an argument with her. I remember her so well there is no photograph that could be more faithful, a woman of Spanish Aristocracy with henna-colored hair and her eyes, ah her eyes were the kind could induce men to point revolvers at one another. It is a shame our love was the crystalline variety—beautiful to the eye, but rather impractical, nothing you could dig a ditch with. One day she gave such a yell it went to a thousand pieces. I was still on my way to the another part of Mexico when the echoes died away.

Immaculada accepted me for what I was: a man of simple means with rather extravagant tastes. I met her as she threw seeds to the pigeons outside the Catedral Nacional, stone the color of bad weather, too monumental to be anything but alienating, God's will done on earth, if the masses cannot be fed at least then the pigeons, why should everything go hungry? A doorway to her heart opened during this act, I stepped in, took off my hat, sat down beside her and there I stayed for a good many years. There I still am sometimes. I cannot say exactly why I left her, but she is the reason I put myself up at the Nacional.

He will laugh so strangely you will be sure at that moment—

with nothing of supernatural proportion in sight, no sail of an ancient mariner's lost ship–he has broken with the familiar reality in which forks, knives and trolley buses and television sets are commonplace and we all agree on their uses.

What fantastic irony, he will say and the steadiness of his voice will lift you out of the fear of that unknown pit into which you thought you had descended, what fantastic irony that I put myself up here and not one of the thousand other tawdry hotels in this city.

Because you will not understand, he will remind you of Magdalena of the Silken Voice, the Byronic woman who had carried on with a half brother, whose extravagant tastes and frivolous values began the downfall of the Nacional.

She was among those whom I had enchanted while squandering my Oxford tuition. She was of course, much older than I, but even so, the ruins of empires–Rome, Greece, Egypt, Tenochtitlan–have their own sort of beauty. We were perfectly matched, both well bred, knowing we would never end up in marriage, I using her for her social position, she using me for my youth. She took an extraordinary liking to me, she actually–as far as was possible for her–fell in love with me I flatter myself to think, this queen of an already eroding glorious past.

He will shake his head and smile sadly because you still do not understand.

I am the young man she willed this place to, only to have her half brothers, Wilfredo and Santiago–nearly dead of old age–arrive on the scene with an army of lawyers and disprove the validity of a perfectly valid will. So I was no better off than Mexico with the broken promise of wealth brought by oil, the fool's gold of no new empire.

Here he will dig in the top drawer of the warped buffet and produce a handful of carefully ribboned letters and lavender envelopes–an age of his life meticulously bound–and hold them up as proof.

All in her hand, all signed. It may be these would have swayed the jury in my favor–or perhaps these too would have been discredited, but I withheld them–out of naive faith in justice, out of useless reverence for the unscrupulous dead, out of what is left of *mi padre's* sense of honor.

Returning the letters to their wooden vault lined with silence, he will take out another handful of papers, wave them around with his back to you searching out more papers.

These are how I make my living...

He will produce articles typed in English which one of the city's newspaper pays him a small amount to translate into Spanish.

Without my Oxford English I would be standing next to Carlos smelling of burned rubber during the long winters.

To lighten the mood, he will hold up his faceted tumbler in toast (an excuse to drink more) and bring up the young American from Kansas–a great flat state I am told–and his pretty redheaded wife. He, Eduardo will tell you, his tone taking a shift, was from the land of the strong dollar, he was like those conquistadores who first came here, steel armor gleaming, and saw opportunity spread out before them like another ocean. He had his entire life ahead of him and a beautiful woman who loved him, who would take him by the hand and lead him into it.

Ah, she was so much my Concepcion all over again, her hair more coppery, her eyes as innocent as wide as one of those harmless nocturnal creatures we have in our deep forests. She could not accept the fact that pyramids aren't the exclusive property of Egypt, she could not get over the subway ruins whose ancient stones at night are lit up red-yellow-green for the touristas, are unearthly even to those of us who have seen them like that for a decade, she could not fathom that Tenochtitlan, the throne of the Aztec civilization, is buried beneath the world's largest city.

Don't fool yourself, I said to her, don't bewail too much this ignominious end, the Aztecs were no *Señors Simpaticos,* they overran their neighbors, exacted tribute, made slaves of captives and sacrificed their own people–they occupy a prominent place in Mexico's history of oppressors.

She and her husband–he spent his money quite freely–took me to dinner, bought me a bottle of Jamaican rum, adopted me into their hearts only to leave with a promise to write. (I am ashamed to admit I've since lost the postcards of the great American Midwest and Christmas greetings sent to me over the years. They belong to someone else, to another lifetime. They are gone like coins to the bottom of a dark fountain.)

You will realize then what a rare occurrence you are, that the visitors in Eduardo's tiny room are stirrings out of the past, barely brushing aside the curtains as they come and go. You will feel, inexplicably, a degree of the awful stiffness morning brings to Eduardo (an intimation of what it is like to be trapped in a body trying to return to the inanimate stockpile from which it came), the futility of afternoons checking the empty mailbox, the evening remembrances (eyes closed and tequila fumes beginning to efface perception) of friends whose funerals Eduardo has attended–Alberto Gutierrez who struggled through Oxford with Eduardo night after night in the library and went on to become a respected politician, a portrait of him in his small round glasses now hanging in an administrative building in Guadalajara; Pablo Ribalta, El Torito, the Baby Bull, who had cojones the size of grapefruits and rode with Pancho Villa before he was 12, no bottle of tequila could withstand his onslaught, what a demon he looked in the meager light of a bar or a brothel–his favorite places to be–with his great long mustaches wet with liquor and sweat pouring down his face, his huge white grin in his dark face, strong as a pack mule but his heart finally burst, all that strength but he too is gone; and most of all Vicente Gonzales, a handsomer kinder more open-hearted man never breathed, nor does he any longer his casket having been laid open by

[53]

candlelight the old way in the house not in some parlor, his best suit, his bow tie perfectly tied and *Madre de Dios* even dead he looked better than the tear-glistening faces bending over him. Like Eduardo, you will vainly salute young lovers arm in arm on the sidewalk below who cannot see you, you will invite hotel guests (who always seem to have an excuse ready) to share the bottle. And then you will light a cigarette in Eduardo's honor–in spite of the surgeon general's warning–instead of a candle.

Did I tell you this city sinks close to a foot on a good year? he will ask, hoping to keep your interest. The only steady bit of ground is under the famous Angel Statue, miraculously, if you didn't know better, it would seem to be slowly ascending to the place from which it came.

Yes, this country, once thought to bleed gold when wounded, has proven a dream of dust, far from a source of water now, sitting upon an old lake bed, cut off from the rest of the world now by sternfaced mountains (the sun is hazy on the hottest of days because the fumes create their own weather, their own sky).

And yet they still come, you should see their faces, the *campesinos,* the farmers wearing sandals cut from old tires, bewildered as they step from the bus, used to the emerald green of mountains and the fertile fields they've left, the lowlands and jungles, entirely bewildered. Benito Juarez should never have shown them what was possible. Now every Oaxacan, every Indian who comes to Mexico City wants to become president, transformed by the crush of city life into a diamond brilliance shining through history's darkest moments.

With innocent reverence, they gaze up at the handiwork of our artists who have managed to record Mexico's moments of glory, to turn tragedy into wall murals, life into colors–banana yellow, gunshot-wound red, overgrown green, peasant-earth brown, peon white–they turn blood into paint (their oils dry with the faint smell of rusting iron), and the plastered stone wall that had meant nothing a moment ago—other than you will have to go around it—becomes the wailing wall of a country's soul in agony.

The world will never end—look how much it has endured already without even coming close; wishful thinking an apocalypse—the only mouth we know is the mouth twisted in pain, the mouth gasping for justice—Orozco and Rivera—ah, pain is all we know, the loaded rifle all we respect—Emiliano Zapata taught us that. The painted figures shout like vainglorious Santa Anna who lost his leg to a French cannonball and never let the Mexican people forget his unwilling sacrifice, exclaiming as he asked to be crowned that his last drop of blood would be bled from him in the service of his country.

So now you have seen the New World the Europeans set out for. But which is new? The one of the Mayans or the Aztecs? The Zapotecs or the Olmecs? The Toltecs or the Tarahumara? All older by millennia—not years but another kind of time, more nebulous, harder to measure—than Europe. This is the land of the guttural tongue, the great dead stone cities, the legend that has begun to lift itself out of the ruins, like those surreal paintings in which the images are raising themselves off the canvas, emerging from flat two-dimensional art into the four- or five- or 22- dimensioned actuality we cannot keep track of anymore even if we read the latest cosmological theories.

But in truth, these are things for someone of greater stature to worry about, the next Benito Juarez who may be getting off the bus coming from Oaxaca today. If I stick to my own worries, my own complaints, Eduardo will say, well, they can be counted on one hand.

Aside from a shortage of import items, he will mention a knee which has never been the same since a fall from a particularly unruly horse. He will cite the Nacional's infamously infrequent hot water (one day I threw open a window and

hollered *El Grito Del Eduardo* for a steaming shower). At pre-
dictable times of the year, he has strange dreams he is certain
are somehow linked to what is going on in the mountains,
what does not belong to the city.

A loud uncle with grandiose manners once told me of an
Aztec practice–particularly savage in its imagery–in which
once every 52 years (one year for every week of the solar year)
a fire is turned loose in the chest cavity of a sacrificial victim
and all the pots are smashed, all the used vessels, an out-with-
the-old-in-the-new kind of thing, a resurrection. (I wonder
what kind of coincidence it is that the Pemex building, the seat
of the government oil monopoly, is 52 stories high, a
monument to air pollution. Think of how the terraces of the
old temples built in tiers reflected the Mayan conception of
heaven as a place of levels, Dante would have been proud.)

A miscellaneous warning, like a stray gunshot, he will point
out the window and say: Out there, you must be careful of
coyotes, the kind without fur.

But it will not be these nocturnal coyotes he sees in the
sunless hours before dawn, it will be the Aztec ritual haunting
his poor eyesight. He will be drawn by what is burning, by
the hot orange light, the human face gazing indifferently at
the equally indifferent heavens, the two glassy eyes earthbound
stars with the red gleam of flame in the pit of their black-
hole pupils.

Eduardo will straighten his back against the bedboard, he
will choose his words with the careful desire to be remembered, those things he would say as the clock strikes sounding
the demise of the world that will not end.

There is a great fire burning in Mexico, he will say, beginning
with the tiny ones dousing the streets in woodsmoke, the
cooking fires tended by women in colorful serapes who carry
styrofoam begging cups, Carlos and black-smoke-billowing
truck tires, the oil out of the earth's plundered insides, the
fire roaring inside a hollowed-out human chest–a fire whose

source is at the center of our existence—and the smoke (we pour ourselves into the fire but it is the smoke) that will choke us off in the end, a day as black as the eruption of a fabled volcano that brought about the extinction of some forgotten civilization.

What we need in Mexico is 100,000 years of solitude at least, and no cars or cutting down jungle for farmland and why not a few dinosaurs—the allosaurus, the brontosaurus, the triceratops—to liven things up? No foreigners in the rich plant-infested heat, a heat rivaling the humidity of a woman's erogenous zone, no boats larger than reed-bundle canoes to take away from the distraction of lazy winding rivers in the Yucatan.

For my own part, I would be able to bear the unheard-of inflation of the peso if only I could afford a fine Jamaican rum to go with my Earl Grey tea. What does it matter, eh? We dedicate ourselves to immortality (there is a little Ozymandias in all of us), but we cannot stick around to bask in it, so who is crazy? If you want to build a monument, pile up the things you have done, a grand and determined accumulation of the women you have loved, the dawns you have greeted with reverence in your heart, the times you swam the Caribbean and had the salt washed from you by the sweet water of a violent thunderstorm. Yes if life were made of colors mine would arc across the sky after a good thunderstorm.

Still (he will breathe a sigh laden with cheap tequila) one goes on wishing.

By the time his chin has dropped toward his chest, he will have lost himself in a vanishing city where on every street corner—graced by a stately wrought-iron gas lamp—is a woman in a sequined dress, the slitted pupils and jade green eyes of a jaguar, a beauty he had once danced with, now a ghost of memory made of shifting light standing silently beside the post of a hissing lamp. You will sense that Eduardo has gone off quietly, his stare into the pristine past a portal to the place

[57]

where his lover Magdalena awaits, but he will break the spell by turning to you suddenly.

Ah amigo, Eduardo's eyes will hold the dull glow of the sinister fire burning in Mexico, *cada edad tiene su encanto*. Every age, he will repeat with a finger raised for emphasis, has its enchantment.

Ages in history or ages in a man's life, he will leave you this final mystery to remember him by.

THE NIGHT CRAWLER

"A RING AROUND THE MOON IS SAID TO BE A SURE SIGN
OF BAD WEATHER—USUALLY RAIN OR SNOW. YOU CAN
TELL HOW MANY DAYS WILL ELAPSE BEFORE THE STORM
BY COUNTING THE NUMBER OF STARS INSIDE THE CIRCLE;
IF THERE ARE NO STARS IN THE RING, THE STORM IS
LESS THAN TWENTY-FOUR HOURS AWAY."
—VANCE RANDOLPH, OZARK MAGIC AND FOLKLORE

S HE'S SEEN SOMETHING, HE WAS THINKING, GOT A GOOD
look at it I bet is what fogged her eyes over like that. Rain
tomorrow night, she said, her dark face thin and drawn, a
sweep of badlands, all ravines and wind-worn crags, two blind
niches gouged out for eyes, a jagged rut you had to figure for her
mouth. Don't be out in it.

Whaduzhat mean? He shifted weight in the chair, stirred a memory out of the dry wood that sounded like a creak. Am I shupposed
to melt or shomethin?

Lord, she laughed, I guess it's You I have t'thank for puttin me
down here in the middle a these farmers an fishers an drunks who
decide winter's comin on by the color of a caterpillar.

The drunk, that'd be him. Left out the harelip and club foot—
harelip makes his esses come out wrong, club foot he bobs instead
of walks. Hardly as tall as an eighth-grade boy, five-foot-two, but
I ain't blue he sang when he was gettin drunk enough standing
up was a chore, I ain't runnin. With a six-pack downed, the world
can drown, long as there's another beer comin.

She looked at him with eyes frosted over, two windows in the
dead of winter. Wiry hair pulled back, tight to her head, the sheen of
a beetle's shell. Don't be out in no rain, she said. Fact is, you juss
might melt.

Blind as a bat but she had a sixth sense for light, kept the shades in the house down all the time. A musty wood smell in her kitchen, not many the breeze that blew through her window, lifted a corner of the blue-and-white checked table cloth, a stillness in there you'd think the clock had stopped, up on the wall in the shape of a tea kettle, the hands moved all right but you knew they weren't in step with rest of Frontenac, she couldn't see it anyway what was the point?

Shtay inshide, is that what you're shaying?

Stay outta the rain.

Well what the hell, inshide, outta the rain—what's the differensh?

Don't be out in no rain.

Don't go out t'night?

Tonight.

On account of a little rain? Geez but you're talkin strange t'day... shtay outta the rain... 'bout as meaningful as don't spill shalt on the table cuz it'll bring on a piece a bad luck. Or don't watch a friend outta sight—might never see him again. He rubbed his chin, stubbly, blondish brown.

Art Papish, she said, shaking her head at a schoolboy that wouldn't listen. What is anyone goin t'do with you? Slowly— might've been it took most of her strength to do it—she shook her head again. I guess that's enough for today.

Well, here's what you wanted... Art stuck his hand into a rustling paper bag, pulling them out one by one. A bottle a rum, he said, a box a them cigars you like, an a whole turkey fresh from Pallucca's Market, head'n all.

That's fine. She reached out, put a shrivelled hand on the smooth glass of the bottle. You don't sound so good today, you had a drink?

Not a one, he said.

She knows about the dark circles under his eyes, his eyes trying to edge back away from the light, sandy hair a nest of curls he hadn't bothered to comb out. Somehow, right through the dusty air of the kitchen she felt all the nastiness from last night seeping out his pores. Whatever it was Marano shot him up with, it felt like he was missing his liver, the rest of his insides sliding around in the extra room, his head buzzing all the time, a little dizzy, joints weak as an eighty-year-old's. He'd've loved to heave it all up but he was afraid of what might come out, ugly as an owl pellet—pieces of mice, wadded-up beer labels he'd peeled from long-warm bottles, snake scales, ten years' worth of baloney sandwiches from the Texaco 7-11, chewed cigar stubs, bird beaks, blue pills, green capsules, white powder that burned like the sulphur rained down on those sinner cities back in Time Immemorial, a rat tail, a chicken foot, huge locusts with those cellophane wings twice the length of their fat bodies (downed with a shot riding on the bet), wads of hair and fur—every wrong thing he ever took into his body over the years compressed into a rough ball, booze probably the least of the evils.

You can help yourself to that rum if you want, she said.

Now Risa, you know if I get shtarted on that bottle I won't leave here till I finish.

I guess you'll be goin now.

I guessh I will.

Careful to look at her sideways, avoid those whited-over eyes, nothin left a the irises but a ribbon here an there, couple a swirls a brown, like those glass marbles kids play with, he wished she'd take the trouble to put on some dark glasses.

GLAD AS HELL to be in the open air, not as her dusty kitchen tomb, things incubating in the glue holding down those linoleum tiles, who knows what's growin in the musty basement underneath? Made him feel better to be under sky, plenty of clouds but not a thunderhead among them, all white.

He shook his head. Shtay outta the rain, he repeated. Rot's shettin' in on the boards she's walkin on I think, touch a senility comin on.

Walking, bobbing more like, no car to get him around, it was sitting in his gravel drive, a rusting monument to 1962, a green Ford Rambler splattered with huge white birdshit rain drops, the money his sister sent every month wasn't enough to get it fixed, not the way he drank. Doesn't matter, he thought, I could be in an endless field, my feet know how many steps to take down Broadway before the right onto Fifth Street, hit the Washington Tobacco Store for a couple games a pool, a right out the door, head to PiCCO for the best malted world's ever known, peg-legging all over Pittsburg all day, follow my steps and you gotta map a downtown.

Might as well gimp over past the Duke's house, he thought, see what he's up to. Maybe hitch out to Rae Anne's place later on, or just keep walking, see if I can run into her by luck of luck.

Just the way she moved, her walk down Broadway was enough to stop your blood he wished she'd turn his way, look at him dead on, a full turn of her head, a stretch a two or three sheconds is all, a real heartbreaker she got it all over the other women in town. Used t'follow her into the theater before he knew her, neither a them with anyone t'go to the movie with, watched her more than the movie, the besht place for it–hard to pin down as a dragonfly mosht times, hardly more than a ripple in the air, a wonder when it finally lands, looks at you with enormous eyes, a shine to their green-blue no painter can touch, eyes big as the whole head, a clump a gems carryin around a vision a the world on see-through wings no one can guessh at. Nothin sho beautiful as the blue light on her face, the curve a her nose ends kinda sharp, a blue angel in the dark, green eyes gone violet, the movin shilvery light a heaven on the shcreen, she'd wonder with a box a popcorn in her lap how to get back, how she'd got tossed out into the rough-carpeted seat with everyone else in the first place when she'd had a life on that technicolor screen, 70 mm wide to fit her an Zirque both, but he was off again an she'd gone back to drawin, mostly made-up things–horses with wings, winged dragons, birds you never saw before in your life, all of em with a better place they could get to, didn't have t'call TWA or PanAm for a reservation, just up up an away. To the floatin cities she liked to sketch, islands in the sky. If you could make it up there with someone like her, no reason ever to leave.

When she went to Carol's Corner Cafe, he'd watch her from a hall window up there in the Stilwell, perch on the ledge like a gargoyle, the clubfoot of the Hotel Stilwell.

Wings're what I'm misshin, he thought out loud. Ugly enough I guessh, sit shtill enough sometimes too, no I ain't shtone, but my hangover face'd turn a pretty woman to a pile a quartz, your average ol' nothin-shpecial lady to a slab a gray shale, and her—you can shee jush by lookin can't you? turn her into a sea collection a emerald an ruby an diamond, shilver shkin and bronze hair.

Sitting was good enough, up there on the sill, about as likely to move as a granite block, watching, her name forming like a new heavenly body in his mouth, weightless where he was granite, her name in his mouth while he watched, unpronounced, he wouldn't let it go or it would be gone from him forever no matter how he reached for it back...

No, he could never touch er, not with hands like his, get the shakes sometimes, too big for the wrists they're hangin offa, fulla wiry brassy-colored hair, too much a that too, he couldn't imagine touchin her the way Zirque did, nothin more than a hug she'd send his way now'n again, left a metal taste in his mouth, a tinglin under his scalp, under his skin, a thousand ants crawlin all over him as if he weren't altogether solid anymore, a good wind might scatter his insides like dead leaves out of a scarecrow's unbuttoned shirt. Even in his own dreams (no one else can see or get at or know), the most he does is fall asleep cradled up with her, the way he'd most love to let go a this world, with her arms around him so he wouldn't feel anythin but her. Find him like that a thousand years later, fetal, like those bones in that Italian city Millo talks about, covered over by a volcano, their bones tangled up with one another all those centuries, shettled on a bed a soft gray ash, still holdin onto each other for a thousand years, didn't do any good, they died anyway, but there they are, bones comfortably forever settled in ash all that love comes to in the end.

If he could always see her it would be enough, always be around her, watch her do anything she does, the way she lets her head tilt back when she laughs, her tarnished-copper hair falling long and wavy, the way her smile takes over her whole face, makes you feel like the stadium lights been turned on for you, there you are in the center of everything, the night backpedaling so fast it's about to fall over, that'd be enough.

He brought her things as an excuse, little glass ma-bobs and porcelain do-dads she liked, showed up for dinner knowing she always set for two, her and Zirque in case he showed. He'd sit on the front porch with her and she was glad for the company, he knew, but still a salty bitterness in her mouth because he wasn't Zirque. Never stay too long, didn't want to wear out the welcome, just sat across from her watching her while she talked, rocked herself on the swing seat, scouring the fields with her eyes maybe she'd spot him, like he'd always been there she just hadn't noticed. Other times Pap caught up with her in the Corner Cafe while Carol's sister had Blue Jean's wrist caught in her old woman's hand (tireless as a coon trap), it was all Pap could do to get a few words in under the table, weasel a cup of coffee out of Carol (slip a slug a Old Number Seven outta his flask), sip and listen to them from the booth behind, turned around in his seat, leaning over the back of it with his elbows like a kid without manners.

Pap, up at dawn this morning, cold as the barrel of a gun in winter, stick the skin to it if you touch it bare, knew it was too early for her to be at Carol's, needed a couple glasses of whiskey to get the blood moving.

Lookin out the window, the light was growin, spotted a pale moon, cold round rock up there, white and frostbitten, a high school-age god hurled himself an iceball through space. A new meaning to cold if he could be up there to feel it, him and his pot-belly stove, everything on the whole miniature planet (misshapen like him, only done half way, sh'posed to be a planet but look what happened, got shortchanged in a big way, only gets away with bein so ugly 'cause it gives off a shine), him and his pot-belly stove'd be all the warmth in that corner of the universe, any other life up there'd be attracted to them, come shuffling over to the beacon light, Pap Prometheus and his Amazin Woodburnin Stove.

The skull on a bookshelf, Yorick he called him after a famous skull the Duke told him about, Yorick said, You'd run out of wood soon enough (bein the smart-ass pile a calcium he was), and it's doubtful moon rocks burn.

Just my good luck I'm an earthlin, got this sausage from Pallucca's t'throw in the pan.

They stuff it by hand over at Pallucca's, he cooks it by hand fingers shiny with hot fat no spatula or fork, liked his hands to smell that way. Nothin like shausage on an autumn mornin, sheason a rustlin, nothin shtays shtill, shaddest time a year to go past a cemetery, nothin shleepin peaceful anymore, dead leaves blowin around, wind findin every hollow there is, makin them sing like haunted flutes, whistlin right up through your backbone, always a wind like a shtorm comin, sweepin over family an friends. We put em in leadlined boxes, marble slabs on top, where do we think they're going? Probably should've hung em out on lines, bone chimes, couldn't do a slow dance if they wanted to in those boxes, scratch marks an broken nails I bet if you dug em up, tryin t'get t'each other, should bury the dead naked, let em spread out under the earth, roots lodge between ribs, rainwater pool in the sockets where there used t'be eyes, fingers disappearin one at a time in search a the earth's long-ago, faraway center, might be shome parts that come back up t'the light, feel the autumn wind shoundin like a half-sigh through the burned-out church on Locust Street.

[65]

Autumn time you feel the gapin hole in the roof a the church shomewhere in your shide, makes you pull up your shirt an have a look make sure no one speared you when you had your head turned. And those really cold mornins like this one you don't even want to go out, just fire up the wood shtove, get shausage goin on the cookin stove, warm your hands an watch light come into the sky through the window over the sink curtained pale blue, they float on the breeze in summer, the shapes somehow calling her to mind, twistin in that slow way, a blue lady in the pale curtains.

Yeah-up, nothin but time an sausage grease on my hands it's no wonder I need t'sit around an think a things t'do t'take my mind off shpendin all my time waitin just you and me Yorick, d'ya think she'll come by today?

Doubt it Pap.

Yer jusht a shkull anyway, whaddayou know?

A real one too, not one a those Hollywood fakes with the jawbone attached, somehow Yorick still managed to yap an jabber. Up there on the half-bookshelf, half-display case Granpap built, up there with pottery Zirque brought him back from Gallup, New Mexico, a Darren Harrison fella don't sound like no Indian name but Zirque said he was Zooni-Navaho or somethin, white clay, painted-black design with a couple a insect-lookin figures on there except they got two legs instead a six, humpbacked fluteplayers Zirque said.

Club foot, harelip, a touch of scoliosis, humpback is one thing he missed out on.

Yorick and Zuni pottery, a couple of half-melted candles, a beer bottle with its own porcelain-and-rubber cork wired to it brought back from Amsterdam when Zirque talked him into that, a photo of all three of them on Blue Jean's front porch happy as could be, next to the brass kaleidoscope Granpap made, mirrors make the clustered crystals at the end grind together, new colors, odd shifting shapes, the same old memories getting mixed up, but only so much they can change, the faces and people and places pretty much the same, but the order of things somehow like furniture in a room gets rearranged.

Was Zirque there with ush that time? I thought it was jusht ush two. Way I remember it, I been around a lot more than him, kept after you in the shilver-blue light a shadowy theaters, that brassh tube into memories grindin together, Gramps that's some kinda magic, howd'ya do it? But I gotta tell ya, one a the doors in your shelf is warped, is a heave an a ho to get it to shtay shut. Don't make no nevermind to one-eyed Oshcar, that cat'd rather sleep on top a that than a feather pillow. Time to time he'll look at you an you'll shee shomething older than you're used to smolderin behind his one green eye, shomethin shtraight from the moon they hunt under, the other just a wrinkled pinkish-yellow shocket.

Oshcar whaddayou think? Don't just shit there lickin yer paws, come clean. Am I gonna shee her today, are you throwin in with Yorick or what? You ain't even lishenin you dumb cat. What's the shense a askin a cat ain't smart enough to have two eyes who I'm gonna run into today?

I SURE DO WONDER, he said out loud, rockin forward with each step, on his way to the Duke's house, the afternoon warmed up considerable from the morning smokey with sausage grease, if I'll run into er today.

Otherwise when he got home he'd pull out that T-shirt he'd gotten hold of, slipped off with it one night, kept it in a drawer over a year and somehow never lost her smell, that old cotton trying just as hard to hang onto anything she'd let go. Born again from just a whiff, as clean and innocent and stupid as the first day he looked up at his mamma with a wide-open wailing mouth. A season in the smell of that shirt, her own, balmier than spring, prettier than fall, pain and hurtful desire and death distant long-gone things no one ever heard of. When street lights were just beginning to catch slow fire along

Mckay street where the Duke lived and insects crowded the Texaco 7-11 sign on 69 in a little cloud of swarming living particles and the last of the sun was about gone from the fields out where she lived, he'd've given anything to be coming home to her.

Littlest things get her excited, Chianti in a straw basket, not the pot-bellied bottle so much, but the basket.

Art, she said, that is adorable it reminds me of Italy I've never been there but I've seen pictures in magazines, Zirque promised we'll go one day.

She saved it (you're wrong if you thought it was empty). Some people use a camera, she gets by with pretty glass bottles. All by herself, those insects swarmin around the sign, me in shome bar gettin drunk waitin for who-knows-what, she's pourin into an empty glass from one of her bottles the dinner the three of us had out on the front porch one night.

Zirque dragged the kitchen table out there for the occasion, she'd cooked Italian, baked the bread herself, made shome kinda grits stuff called polenta an a fancy flat round onion-bread no bakery had the recipe for, craysha they say it around here though if old Millo came by cre-sci-a he would go off in an Italiano accent.

Pap brought three bottles of chianti so they could get drunk and laugh at Zirque when he started talking about chiaroscuro those words he brings back from his trips no one's ever heard, thinks he's sho shmart...

She was alone pouring that for herself, the last light of the fields a halo around the bottle, no it ain't right Pap would be the first to admit, but look here Rae Anne it's worse for me...

Alone even when he is with her and Zirque, he was the only one who had to leave after dinner, the two of them home already. He could stand it while it lasted, being near her was enough, knowing she loved what he'd brought, that she loved hearing Zirque tell his stories even though he'd left her two months to go out and get them, Pap's stomach feeling like an overfilled water balloon it was all so damn good he just kept eating, the wine warm good and deep in his guts. It was only after they'd worked the self-timer on that fancy camera Zirque stole or conned or won on a bet, after it got dark, past midnight maybe, all the wine gone the evening gone the night fallen like winter though it was warm, the end always came no matter how good the story, and Pap went off, turning down a ride from Zirque because then Rae Anne would be the one alone, he said he'd hitch, felt like a walk in the balmy night air, the crickets filling up the silence stretched out inside him with their lonely calling t'each other across the dark fields, he need-ed something like that, like the fireflies had, light himself up, make a constant scraping prayer–wing to wish–like the crick-ets, send up a signal Hey over here, gimme a lift into town wouldja? I sure could use one.

Nighttime when Zirque was gone, he'd seen her walking Broadway, the street near empty as the bottles in her collection, breath become mist, a fog out of her mouth, something an angel dreams of being able to do on a cold day. Somewhere Zirque was missing her enough that he felt it too, as mysteri-ous as what held the moon in place, and the rest of this mess which ought to all have flown off in every direction. Love the same, couldn't see how it held them together, but no matter where Zirque went off to, he came back.

I wish he wouldn't sometimes, let her get on with it, but she's waitin, can't help herself. I can't either, I watch over her, wing-less ugly guardian angel she hardly knows I'm alive.

Damn him but shometimes his heart's nothin more'n a chunk a moonglow, pale'n see-through, you'd think it'd warm you up a bit, but what it does, it gives you the shivers. I know there's somethin more solid at the core of it, but it's easy t'lose sight the way he treats her shometimes.

Some nights in the drizzle more like drifting mist he'd seen her, her long red hair covered with it, smeared with light from the streetlamps, and up a block a couple arm in arm, and in some other city maybe Zee Gee was thinking of her, the drifting mist in her was the pain, no shape, it found its way everywhere seeped through her, rubbed off on you when you took her hand, longing and want and need and sadness that smelled of her, yes her.

And there Pap was like something sinister watching, but wasn't him that was a hole waiting to swallow you, was somethin coiled underneath Pittsburg's streets, under the sewers, traveling through them you could almost feel it when you sat still enough, somewhere around two or three in the morning, that strange way things had of going against you, but wouldn't let you close your hand on what it was, and he wondered what was older, the darkness or those old brick storefronts. Bricks pressed outta the darkness, they're the same age, condensed out of it, old partners they don't hold it off like they're sh'posed to, old bricks with Pittsburg stamped right on em, shomethin bein torn down to put up shomethin newer cleaner brighter it won't make any difference. Doesn't even gather itself, this creepin fog under the street, never takes on a shape hairy and slouchin, shomething you can take a shot at with yer double barrel, it's wily all right, like a coyote Zirque'll tell you, a trickshter, a shape-shifter the way Indian gods can be, hard to get a fix on em, you need t'tune your ears in keener than a dog, catch things that don't make a sound. The whole time you feel tattooed, marked, singled out, ain't no wall thick enough to hide behind it always knows where to find you.

THE DUKE OF PALLUCCA, another famous walker, stick in hand, saw Pap on the side of the road, passed out on his feet, bent over, about to pitch forward likely, and started throwing rocks at him. Pap started spinning around in the street looking for where they were coming from. Started coughing real bad, really hacking, staggering so much he lost his balance, fell into a ditch on the side of the road.

Pap what'sa matter?

Papish rolled around some before he stopped and sat up.

I was at a party lash night, me an Marano. He was meltin pills in a jar and shootin people up with em. He asht me if I wanted to go uptown'r downtown. I shaid shurprise me. I don't know what the hell he shot me up with, but he fucked up my week. Pap pulled a flask out of his pocket. Shhhh, don't tell anybody.

A solid drinker every day for 20 years, the Duke couldn't figure who would be surprised, who would think to stop him.

What the hell you doin t'your boot?

Got a piece a cardboard stuffed in this hole t'keep the rain out.

You don't give a goddamn about anything except gettin loaded, do ya?

That an cheap whores.

Come on Pap, walk me home.

The Duke with his favorite walking stick, picked up in Branson, Missouri, a natural branch, a little crooked with an old man's bearded face carved at top, the Duke leanin on the old man's head (Duke could stand to lose 40 or 50 pounds) the whole time he walked.

Had a disconcertin dream Pap, a tooth fell out, I don't like it, someone I know is going to come across harm's way is the old Italian superstition.

Think it'll rain tonight? Risa says I shouldn't go out in the rain.

Don't need a fortune teller to figure that out.

Guessh not. Folks around here think she's a witch.

If she were, she'd turn em into toads. Buncha idiots. They think yer a bad sign, too. Wanna know where you got that skull from they say it's an old gal a yours, yer old lady of old who was usin the back door on you. Earl helped you kill er the rumor goes, the rest of her buried somewhere in the backyard. It's a surprise they ain't called for it to be dug up. With that skull a yours and yer one-eyed cat, you wanderin around burnt-out churches late at night, you sure are a prime candidate for devil worship.

Pap made a noise like spitting out a chewed-off nail. Worst he did was up and down the street beating drainpipes with a stick to sound out the hollows in Pittsburg, get a feel for the emptiness around him, wake up the whole damn town so they know 'cause I'm the only one out at this hour, let them know what they're shleepin on, right under them, crawlin through the sewers, worse than creepin hairy Grendel, I'm goin t'break the silence in so many pieces all the king's horses an all the king's men can't even sweep it all inta one pile. Don't care if I go deaf with the noise, drown in the sound.

Got me arreshted once or twysh, he said.

They took the rope off the bells in the church on Locust to keep him and mischevious kids from ringing at off hours, but couldn't do anything about the drainpipes.

Couple thousand years ago, the Duke said drawing on his endless storehouse of useless knowledge, Chinese used t'bang pots and pans, sticks–probably their own skulls too–when there was an eclipse.

Tryin' to scare off the darknessh or what?

Tryin to scare off the dragon that swallowed the sun. Always worked too.

Scare off the darknessh, now that's a good one, but I guessh there's shomethin to it. Let shomethin know I know, let everyone in Pittsburg–every stamped brick–know I came this way and I'm shtill comin. Ain't got what Risa got, like bats with their echolocatin shqueaks, built-in sonar, God-given, pings off past lives, off events ain't even happened yet, things that ain't solid, and she knows. Me, I'm just bangin away at the pipes, a crossh between Paul Revere an an ancient Chinaman, wouldn't recognize the shape a anythin crawlin through the tube a the night if it shtepped on me along the way.

Hey, saw Cara today.

Now there's a girl knows how t'shuck the poison outta you,

besht in the sholar shyshtem. Till a martian comes down and gives me better, she gets the gold medal. Don't charge all that much either.

Guess you'd be the one to know, bein Frontenac's connoisseur an all.

Well take a good look at me I ain't no Clark Gable why waste my time?

Most everyone is crippled somehow or other, Pap, just happens to show up on you where you can see it.

Pap started hacking again till he spit something up, heavy as an owl pellet from the sound of it.

Shtick to whores I'm tellin ya, Pap said, the ones like Blue Jean are taken no matter how bad Zirque treats her. You an me don't got a shot at them anyway, we can talk an act shweet as can be, buy boxes a roses, we might as well be chasin a feather in a twister. Now whores at leasht you get what yer payin for, no almosts, ifs, buts, I-could-haves—it's a done deal and you don't feel left outta the game, you took a turn, an if nothing else comes your way ever again at least there's that, you don't have t'go t'your grave miserable about misshin out, you won't die wonderin.

A DEEP-SEA MOON LAST NIGHT, the way the clouds covered it, blurred it, striped it uneven, Risa's eye in reverse, glowing white iris up there, swirls and stripes of clouds floating across it, being a full moon it showed through anyway, kind of a halo around it, made Pap think of those firefly fish that glow in the darkness of the world's oceans...

Makes you wonder: What was nature thinkin when she put god up to that? Fish that glow? Inshects like a swarm a shtars risin in the evenin? Glow worms in the dark a caves, no one there to see em, what for? Why all the trouble? An tiny shquid outta deepsea, few inches long, Zee Gee shaid he's never seen one but he's read about em, somewhere off the coast a Japan, light up like a pinball tilt, a real shcratch on the retina, Zirque said. Teeny little reflectors an lenses on em–can you believe? An they put em in tanks, study em but–no one knows why–the lights fade an a little while later, they're litterin the bottom. Never live more'n a few hours in a tank, a mystery no biologist can figure–maybe we ought to tank a few a them and see how long they last.

An what's the big deal about light anyway, ain't nothin when you screw in a bulb, nobody sits around t'gawk an ooh and ahh, it's the background really. Nobody'd give a damn about a shtar if it weren't that the rest a the shky is black, the universe is 99 percent black, dark, empty. It's the ocean depths lit, it's the background that makes the light.

The black is the waitin I guessh, a great sheet've unbroken waitin spent in shilence trapped in this body alone with yourself an no good woman t'ease the loneliness I can't undershtand Zirque at all leavin her like he does. Sure I can see how a trip here an there, a place like Amershterdam formed a shtar kind of in all the waitin, shomethin to look back on. Happens here, too though, that time the three of us took our picture on the back porch, I was happiesht, ain't never going to be no happier, the three biggesht bright-eyed smiles you ever saw, should've died right then and there, keeled over and kicked right in front a the camera.

FEELS LIKE YER WAITIN for somethin to happen but you don't know what it is, like it's just about to come if you hang on long enough, but it never shows up an you don't know what you're waitin for anyway. Wind up passin the time by drinkin– who knows, might need to be drunk when you run into it.

Sittin at home an it seems like you ought to be in a bar because it might happen there, gives you some place t'wait, it's not happenin at home. You can keep company with everybody else who's waitin. Could be a person. Could be an event. A moment different from the last thousand an one that went by no different from the thousand an one before. An under-standin. Of why those shquid die after a few hours in the tank. Why I don't die in mine. A thousand thousand shlimy things lived on, quoth the Duke, and so did I.

What's proppin me up all these years it's gotta be that shomethin's bound t'show up make it all worthwhile, that's what I'm waitin for, that's why I ain't died yet. Waitin because this can't be it, this can't be the whole story. If this is all she wrote, she's the worst author I ever read. You keep turnin the pages because there has to be a happy endin somewhere, at least one that makes sense Ohhh-oh, so that's what it is, I get it now. That's half the reason we bother lookin up at the shky, we're waitin for shomething to drop out, same with every time the bar door opens, lookin up thinkin today, maybe, today.

THE DUKE TALKING about it one night (Pap could barely see his face, only one eye through the cloud of cigar smoke) in Bartelli's Blue Goose Bar, draught beers out of mugs so heavy could've been made out of lead. Zirque there that night, complaining he heard Ozzie was going to close the bar down, going back and forth with the Duke, they didn't always lose Pap, sometimes he managed to hang on, one foot in the stirrup, Zirque and the Duke ahead, going full gallop.

Hamlet was the first modern hero, Duke was saying, trapped in the cages of his own contemplativeness, first one who had t'use his own mind t'deal with his own mind—no stars, no religion, no landmarks, no other way t'navigate.

It's enough to make anybody talk to a skull, Pap said and finished his beer to the foam, his gnome's face mostly blocked out by the thick glass bottom, a halo of curly brown hair around it like some kind of weird flower.

Half our mistakes, the Duke kept up, takin the metaphorical for the literal, the literal for the metaphorical. Course there was no garden somewhere in the Land Between the Rivers, no Gabriel with a hot blade, no apple, no tree. Eden, nirvana, a neverending feast of friends is just the warm moist blanket of the unconscious we were wrapped in, an when mornin came, pulled the blanket off, it ended. Thought rubbed the sleep out of its eyes, looked at itself, an we lost the language a the trees, the spheres, the animals, the insects. We separated out, different, somethin that fell outta the sky, landed here. Death hadn't suddenly been let into the world but now we knew what was at the end a the rainbow an we looked up at where we thought we might've come from—where we imagined somethin might've hidden itself—an asked for a heart to bear all that we came to know, asked to go home again. Click, click, click.

Kansas is a state a mind, Zirque said waving away the Duke's cigar smoke, same as the mythical garden is what yer sayin...

Then whaddo I owe taxes for? Pap wanted to know.

An if you want to find it again, the Duke kept up, go home. Don't bother with a Rand-McNally, use the compass in here, the Duke thumped his chest, not so much a tireless muscle as a place where you either live, or you don't.

There was a strange silence between songs on the jukebox, their voices drifted free in the silence, voices that seemed to come from other conversations, Pap fancied he heard the squeaking of the ceiling fan, a regularity to it, before a rainy sea-wracked Doors song overtook the fan and its overhead time-keeping.

Somehow Zirque got the Duke talking about the Grendel beastie, Beowulf tangled with him without sword or shield, got naked, and you might think well that's a stupid way to face an ogre, but he'd stripped himself of civilization, trying to be only what he was, nothing more, face the hairy man-killer that way, wrestle this thing we're trapped in. When he dropped his sword, there went all the meditations of the Viking equivalent of Descartes, whoever that was. Armored breastplate tossed aside and there went Odin, Thor, the rest of the gods he could've asked to lend an immortal hand. Beowulf was looking to bear the brunt without strength or protection didn't come of himself. Skin to hair, hand to claw, head to horn, find out which of them really had more right to walk this earth.

When they'd about exhausted that vein, the three of them getting up to leave, Pap mentioned living in the blackness.

Who lives in the blackness? Zirque asked.

We all do, the Duke said.

They live in the blacknessh, Pap said whipping his horse up faster, legs snug in place now, an maybe all they're waitin for is a peek at the light, up there, not their own, light out-shide a themselves, not their own, bigger endlessh daylight. Only when they get hauled up there, when they meet the light made them in its image they die, an they didn't know it that what they were waitin for would kill em. Maybe better if they just waited for a messhenger—you know like the poshtman—from the light to come down to them, shee them, appreciate them, bring back a fair deshcription t'his drinkin buddies who're up there in the lethal light, a world an a half away from the darknessh unbroken. The basement a this world, that's where they live, in darknessh unbroken except for here an there a flash a line a light traced out, faded, disappeared, shomethin you remember in your eye, just enough so you can't argue shomethin' came an was there an is gone.

Out of Bartelli's by then, walking west out of Frontenac, a road turned to gravel, sky clear as could be.

All those stars up there pavin the Milky Way, Zirque said, some Indians believe it's a spirit trail you take when you walk on outta this world.

Good way to go, Pap said looking up.

Look at those telephone wires, Zirque was saying, swaying, drunk, they go all the way t'Cairo, Egypt.

Jusht who the hell'd you want to talk to in Egypt anyway? Pap said, still trying to get a fix on where exactly you could pick up the trail that'd lead you above the sky.

You know in Amsterdam it's legal to have the girls right up against the glass, mannequins in lingerie, your own private fantasy wavin t'you an a few Dutch dollars is all you need.

A city's value is directly proportional to its relationship to every other place in the world, Duke was sayin, lookin strange in the streetlight his hair back in neat little rows, in waves as if a wind were blowin or the light was wind but it was just the way his hair was, in stiff waves, his round face angelic under a lamp on Mckay street.

Israfel, Pap called him out of an old Poe rhyme, one to remember well.

Died face down in a rain puddle, old Edgar Allan, didn'ee?

ZEE GEE, THE INFAMOUS Zirque Granges, won a few thousand in a card game way back when, used some of it to buy Blue Jean dresses an such at a fancy boutique on Broadway, tried talkin Pap into Amsterdam.

They had porcelain and gold plumbin when we were still diggin holes in the backyard to squat over, Zee Gee told him as if this were some kind of selling point.

Most a Pap's time watching her. Waiting. Or takin his mind off waitin. Drinking the same as flippin through magazines in a doctor's office. Doin drugs? More magazines. Talked to himself because he always listened.

What the hell?

Made him go to a museum first, look at the paintings by Rembrandt an Rubens, Van der Somebody besides, Zirque tellin him it didn't matter what he knew about paintin, whatever he liked was fine.

One or two weren't bad, couple a bowls a fruit, jugs a wine on the table–hangin one a those'd be a little classier than wax apples an bananas, but couldn't eat either one, that was the main thing, couldn't drink the wine outta that dusty bottle no matter how close t'real it looked.

Picked up from a painting done about 1772, Zirque told him, that Amsterdam ain't changed in 200 years you take away the parked cars.

Almosht as many canals as shtreets, he said to ZeeGee, ain't this shomethin? I never knew.

Red Light District was the big to-do, looked like postcards a Las Vegas, lights an casinos, bars on every corner, in between, too. An there were the ladies in their full-length windows, red glow over the top as if you didn't know, standing there as evening came on, the sun's orange-red light sinking into the cobblestone streets like the blood of a bull slaughtered in the middle a town.

On the second floor, too, Pap said looking up while he was looked down on, almost like the misshes gettin undresshed before bed, shtretchin out for everyone to shee in her nightie. Good oogly-googly but shome of em're sho fat an ugly an nashty, a wonder they don't starve t'death.

On the walls of a shop, a pasted-up picture show. Doggie-like, standing up, lying down, women on women, and–

Gee-zush what is that? Ain't a man, ain't a woman, it's both.

Zirque gave him a word for it, Herman the Dike, was best he could remember.

Hey, is he pishin on her? What for?

Past a longhaired American in an Army jacket selling the show they'd just seen pictures of.

We got muff-divin Lesbians, white girls on black men, black on white, rare parts, used parts, spare parts...

Someone else, some kind of Arab-looking guy callin out: Fom-ee-lee pro-blem? Just thee theeng to feex your marriage!

Stores with toys no kid plays with, plastic dickies all sizes and shapes, things Pap'd never heard of, French ticklers, love bumps, ribbed, ridged, rubber blow-ups, chains, handcuffs and whatnot, enough of it to about make him sick.

Sure I like a whore now an then but who wants to be tied down an pisshed on?

Come on–

Went to a coffeehouse was what they called it, dope den was more like it. Cathedral-height ceiling with beams the size of railroad ties, walls painted yellowish orange with black tiger stripes. Jimi Hendrix, Jim Morrison, Janis Joplin—all Js might've been the trick or maybe all dead—painted bigger than life over the mirror behind the bar. Windows facing the street big enough to hold a vision of Christ in stained glass, but it was just the plain clear kind, hash haze drifting across them from the little round tables, islands in the sea fog of smoke, tiny round tables arranged so that a crowd could fit around them, rolling papers right there in bowls on the tables.

Lightheaded, relaxed, things going in and out of the smoke in Pap's head like a game of hide and seek.

Time to visit a lady in glass, Zirque said taking them back outside, pick a girl, any girl.

A blonde behind a glass door, the kind of beauty could break your heart over her pretty knee, tall as Zirque or close to it.

Go on in Pap.

Nah, she's... she's too good for me, I can't, jusht... look at her I'd be embarasshed.

Zirque walked on over instead. Pap thought he was going pay up, him with Blue Jean waiting at home, damn fool to go in, told her something or other, left her laughing. They weren't out of sight yet when some walking bag of dirt needed a shower a shave a haircut had teeth like a donkey went up to her.

Nah, she wouldn't... Pap was saying and next he knew, that donkey barely fit to pull a shitcart'd gone in past the glass door between the side where people live and the side where there are things out of fairy tales, went into the magic castle through the transparent doorway and the curtain closed.

Hey...! Pap yelled out, started for him, but Zirque grabbed hold of his arm.

Come on now, he said, man paid his money, that's what they're here for.

But him?

Specially him. He'd be lucky to get a dog to look at him with a bone around his neck.

Right past her door (curtain closed, she's at work) they went to an outdoor urinal *You can smell the pissh a mile away* sprang their leaks. That urinal in the dope den was up to my waisht Zee, barely kept dickie outta the water, they grow em tall here.

Pap finally picked one out, a redhead more than half way to gorgeous. Why not they're jusht whores? We make up the rest, just shtupid daydreamin as if there were shtill knights runnin around on horses.

Afterwards, when it was good and dark, had a contest to see who could get his arc higher over the side of one of those canals *Nothin like a good pissh outdoors*. Came out about even. Listening to the stream hit, thinking: Couldn't crawl home in Amshterdam, it'd be shwim or a drown, all these canals you'd think we were in Venice. Always was good at not being where I am.

BY THE TIME HE LEFT the Duke's front porch, couldn't help swinging by Bartelli's, do a little waitin you never know she might come by. Ought to give Yorick a call at home shee what he has to say. Tie a good one on while waitin, buy a few, ship outta the old flashk, save a couple a bucks.

Pap, you keep up the pace yer goin at, yer liable to be bellyin home in a drainage ditch tonight.

Wouldn't be the firsht time.

Crawlin through drainage ditches, countin side roads, more than one way to navigate.

Earl walked in some time before Pap fell off his stool, last of his money gone, nothing left in his flask, dust off the floor on the side of his face, in his nose...

Pap you all right?

Old Earl, 13 years on death row, mighta killed somebody'r other who mushta deserved it but he was pardoned by the guv'nor an no matter what he mighta done way back when he's always good to his friends. To everyone else he's the walkin

[81]

cosmos kinda, don't know if he's gonna shit on you or make you president.

They're lookin for Granges, he said.

Won some money again, did he?

Yeah-up. Fair an square way I heard it. But they want it back.

Earl didn't stay long, just looking for Zee Gee he said.

After Earl left, Pap got worried. What if... maybe they'll try to get hold a her cause Zirque is too hard t'find. Couldn't be nothin worse than that. She's got to know, that's all, maybe get her t'shtay at my place where they won't think t'look, leasht till mornin, then head over t'shee the Duke, he'll know what t'do.

You gonna make it home t'night Pap?

Whrr thrzz a drainidge ditch, Pap nodded, thrzz a way...

Night Pap.

Cold outside, enough to see his breath, but he felt warm from all that drinking, warm and lightheaded, street wouldn't stay put, wouldn't be still.

Risa was wrong. Ain't rain, jusht a little misht, a half drizzle.

Drunk as he was, what with a club foot an all (no walkin stick like the Duke either) Pap fell over. Not much sense in getting up again either, might as well crawl on home, ain't but a mile and a half.

Get home, shober up, hitch on over to her place. Not real likely to get a ride at this hour, maybe shoulda called from Bartelli's... nah, wouldn't want her to hear the new language I shpeak when I'm drinkin like this, wouldn't want her to shee me now.

An Jesush but here comes the rain. Fuckit, I'm hot anyway. Hell wit' this shirt I'm wearin, it's comin off. Howzzat? An the pants next for good measure. Who gives a goddamn? Ain't no money in that wallet anyway, come back for it in the mornin if it don't get washed away, naked as you please, like cold shandpaper againsht my gut this muddy grit but I ain't shweatin no more an don't really care who comes along long as it ain't her. Piece a luck if Earl'd come shcoutin the ditches. We could ride out t'get her after he gets over the shock a sheein me bare assh. Who'da known it'd come down to a drunk like me t'keep her from harm's way? Duke's dream musta been about her, they're sure to come after her. Wish I could crawl faster, half wish I had my pants'n shirt on again, ain't no fun hittin rocks with my elbows, little shtones diggin into m'knees, goddam wet this old sewer ditch with this shtream a goddam muddy water only a half-inch deep but jesusgod cold and nashty got me lookin like shome kinda muddy thing just climbed out an ancient sea, tryin t'get around on land not havin an easy time've it. Work hard enough at it, might get a sweat goin.

Truth is, don't need t'work, thinkin a her accounts f'r all the warmth in this part a the world, hell don't need any clothes after all. Let the whole damn sky come down one long down-pour wash over me, I'll bear up, don't need anybody's help don't need a car, crawl all the way t'her place, make it by shunup, don't want any help, rather do it on m'own, all that hair I got on my body finally comin in handy.

Too bad I don't give off a glow to shee by, dark is dark can't do nothin about it, I ain't no deepshea Japanese shquid, no lightnin bug, can't shee any better than Risa sometimes she's got some kinda light she follows that ain't a fair comparison. Yeah-up, even under the ocean, tons'n tons a water, endlessh dark'n cold, even under all that I could leave a trail jusht like one a them fish, a trail a clothes'n a trail a light, darknessh crushed to black grit, crush the light too, mix em together, a light-dark, dark-light, like you melted down a section a the nighttime sky. I'd be a dishtant flickerin silent shplinter a shtarlight in that pompeii nightdark slag flowin under the world through the sewers, catch you up unawares, preserve you for all time in the strangesht position you ain't careful, make you the talk a the Corner Cafe one mornin.

Man if I could be wonna those fish, they'd find me shtill aglow, why can't I leave a hundred-watt corpshe for her, shomethin pretty? Shquid ain't no looker, but it'll draw oohs and ahs, a regular garden shlug even, if it's got its own halo. Neon Pap they'd call me. Don't want to be no lifelessh bonelessh lump wit' tentacles, pair a eyes starin outta it no grace a'tall t'that. I want t'be shtill glowin when they find me. One-eyed Oshcar tryin t'tell me shomethin all along the way he looked at me outta his good eye the thing yer waitin for kills you, you get t'flare up green-yellow but yer in a sewer ditch no one near but half-drowned earthworms gonna be impressed, leaves you the shapelessh lump you didn't want anyone to see.

Fact is I don't much care long as I leave thish world in a heap a green an yellow makes you squint t'shee, long as it ain't the harelip they remember'r the club foot, long as they say, Pap, he was a night crawler for sure, sewer rat in a way, a gutter ball kinda, a ditch navigator, but he walked the edge a the Milky Way for a while there, left a lightnin trail, couldn'ta missed him on his way outta thish world

SLOW DIVE

NOT INHABITED, NOT REINCARNATED—I DON'T BELIEVE IN these things—not occupying the same place at the same time (physics argues well enough against this); more like two things humming at exactly the same pitch, adrift in a similar underwater reverie, standing on the same numbered square in a game of hopscotch covering all of Paris, Europe, making it even as far as the Dorothy-and-Toto state in America where he comes from.

What does it mean to stand, gawk, reel with *deja vu*, to feel guided, inspired, reborn? And for hundreds of years to blame it on muses or karma or a collective unconscious or something equally plausible? Just this: There is something in need of explaining.

And these musings, do they echo in the moss-grown sewers of Paris? Or dissolve into the ground silence out of which everything came (and if you are overcome by the dramatics of a closed universe, back to which it will all one day crawl)?

Here the silence has taken on the color of deepening evening, a floating gray on top of the failing light—so dense a feather, a metro ticket, *l'addition au restaurant* could be suspended in it.

Yes, even my own body.

Pinned for days on this unmade bed, not like the great-shouldered Greek under the cumbersome bulk of a foolish planet, but by my own marble weight.

Bien. Ca suffit.

Here is the razor, the flame of the candle cold along its edge.

A cheap blade stamped out with no love for steel, one of a hundred-thousand others entirely identical to it, yet this is the one that has been chosen for this game of destiny. It's not death I am interested in–though that is one ending to this story–it's just a way

(The blade sinks in with less effort than I had imagined, draws a rise of warm red out of me, runs cold by the time it begins to drip from my elbow.)

· to goad the universe into making its move. Who knows but I will lose my nerve, call the paramedics before consciousness runs out. Perhaps the police will choose the right moment to kick in the door and interrogate me for what they already suspect. Or Zabere, upstairs, will come knocking for sugar and, finding the door open, will enter. If I do not lift a hand, if circumstances arrange themselves, well then I will have to admit–

Through this tiny opening, ah what a lovely gash in the living stuff of things, your soul leaks out (can you imagine anything so fragile?), hovers over the bed looking at you–a wineskin emptied of wine–sniffs at your foolishness, at premature eviction, moves on. (I must remember to send a cup of this O positive vintage to Sunday's mass.)

Less the pain than the insidious sensation of tearing; no matter how neat, how clean the razor cuts, the feeling of skin being peeled, of being undressed to the bone.

Ah yes, things have begun to move. As they have not for two? three? how many days? Have begun to flow in the manner of time (you do not move through it, it moves through you), and–how did he say it?–time isn't measured by clocks, but by what happens between ticks and tocks, the marks left on the surface of the heart, the contours taken on by memory.

Together he and I do the slow dance of iron-cored planets revolving around a dull blue sun, a Kansas-to-Paris call away from one another but never close enough to touch except on those rare occasions when our trajectories meet, and for a week, perhaps two, a month even, we pull ever so slowly apart–the longer it takes us to pull apart the longer again before we see each other; this is the painful equation describing our movement.

I refuse to come to L'America because that is where she has her strength, a bull rooted to the earth. I am one of those transparent sea animals which loses its graceful shape once out of the water, collapses in a bulbous heap upon itself; what would I do in cowboy boots? Let her come here, under my influence. From the photo I have seen, we three–oh what a conjunction of heavenly bodies who can say what would happen under its jurisdiction? Yes, I have asked him many times to bring her, but she is not like that, territorial, ready to bury her head in the entrails of the nearest trespasser.

She waits patiently for her long-suffering man, but I have walked hand in hand with him down the darkest passages of his longing, left him tired of wallowing in his own semen, sickened by his own voraciousness, full of me, full of wine, worn out by the dream of paradise that enters through the unsuspecting vein, sick of this apartment which in my vampire existence I leave only at night, which smells of a cave–bat droppings, human sweat, scavenger leavings and leftover *croque monsieur* sandwiches, smoke and cigarette ashes, long nights of reverent fucking. Locked inside closed windows, wrapped in dark moods and pulled shades, fermenting in the humidity of the old steam radiator, it must reek to the uninitiated nose, only someone with a bleeding craving would enter.

He knows why he comes to me, though we rarely speak of it, except to ravel it in the sodom-and-gomorrah of myth, mummify the truth that he is here to sink, to smolder, to be sacrificed on the effigy of a primitive god, his steaming insides coiled on the cold stone. I am the woman he forces to swallow his semen, whose face shines with it. He loves with such force it closes in on pain, pushing deeper as a way to rid himself of some ancient curse. Wouldn't he like to die in the moment he comes, every nerve flaring at once, bone blackened from the inside out, a carbon copy of existence for an infinite instant–gone in the same flash that set everything in motion, nothing remaining but the ghostly blue lines he had once traced out, little enough for a mild breeze to carry off, a flimsy negative of everything in him that responded to the calling of his name, of everything he once mirrored.

Instead he has managed some sleight of hand, it is I who have become his sacrifice, impaled on the sharp heat of his desire, he begs to wear my skin after he is done, the rest bitten off, chewed, swallowed to feed his glowing hunger. An Aztec returning to the sun the blood it has lost by killing me, giving flesh back to the stars, sending me to that heaven of strange shapes, broken forms, the unguessed-at sensation, pressed beneath the deep violet liquid weight of nirvana. Jellyfish forms undulate, wave, repeat themselves over and over in sensuous curves. In the shapes of the jellyfish angels a symbol, a sinusoidal tattoo that appears on the face of your lover where there was never before any such thing, on your pale ceiling, in the bright magma of the lava lamp, violet and orange and amber and blue the only colors left to the spectrum.

He wants me but only if he can choose where to put it, almost as often as not above the place nature intended. *Bien,* so long as he uses a part of him–no broom handles, no trick-shop trinkets, nothing battery-run or electric, nothing made of rubber or plastic or wood. Living his own perversion–yes we should, why not? Anything to get that feeling of being plugged into this fantastic creation that is nothing more than charged particles forever in motion, an invisible spiraling dance of infinite becoming balanced against endless destruction in the silence of the vacuum–a Hindu god presiding over fleeting existences–barely time enough to leave more than a lipstick trace on a drink glass, to ask who was she?

And I wonder when I will cross the line from waking to sleeping, from sleeping to unconscious. When my neck will become a curious kind of warm rubber which is as relaxed as water, but does not spill. And from unconscious to never-again conscious, how thin that line, the body dead while the mind floats strangely on, running on exhaust fumes, a new sense of space perhaps, spreading over unfamiliar territory, flashes of electrochemical reactions here and there, ever more distant—an expanding universe of lonely fleeing bits of light—less frequent because the lungs have stopped, the heart is—for the first time since it began its monotonous hammering—at rest, the blood lies in waiting—like the silence of this stagnant room—for the hardening stiffening fossilizing that will make it into something else.

I look to the fluid amber light of the lava lamp—sitting on a small round night table—red globs boiling up, blurbing along, shifting shape, rising and sinking back, huge ruby pearls in honey; they would speak, offer a little friendly advice, if only I hadn't already taken the last of my Windowpane.

In the plastic light of the lamp, a flat-headed stone idol he brought from Mexico, a reclining god, holds a circle of flattened stone, a circle of darkness over its stomach for the deposit of my lover's soft organs. A *chac mool,* one of my bead-ed necklaces hung over him to make him hold up his end of living in my apartment.

Around the *chac,* half-melted candles in colored puddles of hardened wax, on the floor unemptied ashtrays, books lying open, stacked; magazines, letters, notes; papers from the world of pink slips, insurance numbers, valid driver's licenses to satisfy one-digit-following-another demands. The walls are no better, a collage of photographs and postcards, badly repro-duced coffeestained van Goghs and Gauguins and Monets, advertisements and long-legged magazine models, a fresh cut-out of pensive Betty Blue pasted over a woman whose face I am tired of seeing.

There is the smell of something old, the sweat of unending summer nights taken into the plaster, a staleness rising in the old pipes, a fine coat of dust over the wine cellar dampness, over the peeling coats of green and white paint on walls mostly covered by my incessant collecting of images and words, bits of newspaper articles and pages out of books.

The centerpiece in my room, at the foot of my bed beside a white wicker chair, an easel with no painting, just a blank canvas, to coax me into getting started on something.

Ma mere was a great fan of Steinlen and Toulouse-Lautrec, the 1880s night life of a Paris she had never lived in but never wanted to leave, a cabaret on every Montmartre corner, Le Chat Noir, Le Mirliton, La Claire de Lune, smoke obscuring the gypsy singers, the artists hunched over their glasses of absinthe. But Marseilles is where I was born, port city of comings and goings, the oldest in France, who would admit it was founded by the Greeks? Massalia, whose great export to the Gauls—still in animal-hide tunics—wine drunk without water, to the astonishment and revulsion of the Greeks, in this the place I was born, what was given to me while you lived over a bar where I began as a swelling your stomach? What filtered through from downstairs, from the squeaking bedsprings which kept you awake the nights you were not working (oh the things that go on behind the wall and all it takes is this wall for them to go on), the smells that sifted under the door, the Corsican band in the bar downstairs playing a mix of the jazz of American loneliness in its cold lit cities; Island drum sounds which invade the body like a *loa* (the body does not need to dress in Sunday best and invade the church); dry North African wind instruments made to blend with the scraping of the *simoom* across the sand; mournful French songs which have never gotten over the tragedy of death but must make it beautiful, a French god who commanded thou shalt make nothing repellant to the spirit—how did all of this scratch itself on the malleable consciousness of your unborn child? Who can say?

Those puffy lips of yours men admire so much, as if your mouth had just been struck by the back of a mason's hand for that insolent look of yours, yes I have that same insolence, though my face is dominated by my mouth even more, my lips equally swollen, naturally they drift apart during sleep, a recurring nightmare that always dissolves by morning. If I were a little darker I could be cousin to the recurring Kansan in my life, we share a tribe almost he says, why do I keep my hair so short, he asks everytime he sees me, it should hang like the deep black of velvet drapes around the clouded window of my face, formed of rough-cut glass, eyes squeezed a little by the cheekbones, sometimes I am mistaken for Hungarian, a Mongol raider riding through the distant past of my bloodline spreading slowly now into the bedsheets like the lethargic flow of a secret history that can never be known.

You tried to lie, *bon mere*, about being a whore in Marseilles (look at me, I am hardly any better, selling hallucinations and the promise of happiness through the needle), but you cannot lie to me who has inherited your curved talons, your infinite capacity for sinking yourself into things and drawing out, in the midst of pain and blood, the truth. I knew when I was 14 you had only a vague idea who my father was—possibly the brooding one who lived half his life in France, half in Tangier, among the minarets and wild bird shrieks before dawn to honor Allah, unable to decide to whom he belonged. The Australian sailor, about whom you knew nothing, not even a name. O Nameless Father who art in Australia, hallowed be thy namelessness. And the Corsican, a regular at the bar downstairs, in and out of the band, who began to think about me when I was barely 15, coming up late one night while you were out and except for the buzzer old Jacques had hooked up, would have made me his. What a brawl that was, down the stairs, across the bar, out in the street.

What luck to have an adopted *grandpere* who was related to me by nothing at all but I was the shine in his eye as he wiped the bar down at one in the morning. (Perhaps the rumor that he had lost a beautiful schoolgirl daughter to a rare blood disease was true.) He would not even sleep with you those months the rent went unpaid, a cruel kindness, forcing you to bed down with unbathed men reeking of cheap wine and vomit to do Jacques the honor of meeting the bill. Bull-chested Jacques with his furry gray beard and huge forearms, his legendary temper, he told the most riveting unbelievable stories ever concocted in the warmest voice imaginable. He sat me on the bar, his hand in love with my straight black hair (the same as yours) and yours also, thick lips good for pouting, with one pout Jacques would let me have my way, *voila*, the complete works of Hugo, Zola, Flaubert in gilt leatherbound editions as if I were his own granddaughter.

Ah, would the planets have trembled in their orbits, the moon come up a different color if my father–whom you suspect is actually the one–had lain his hands on me? Often I wonder, a man I had never known (Jacques, I never saw him again after you tried to kill him with your great heavy hands, we never shared a full moment of intimacy), would it have been so bad? Only the knowledge of who he was would have made it evil, nothing else. It might have happened naturally, years later, in another part of France, a night-long event when I was feeling partial to musicians or older men missing their teeth, intriguingly tattooed over their whole bodies to mirror the movements of the Zodiac.

There you are, he pointed, on my thigh, a scorpion, when he was in my room and wanted to take down his pants to show me.

No it is only when we know and persist in our perverseness that we end up with a god angry enough to lift entire cities off the earth and return them to it as a slow black rain of hot ash. Even then, who can say it is justified?

What does He know of the human weakness for the perverse or the place evil appetites have in the marriage of a riddle-answerer who killed his father, the death of Hamlet the elder, the sojourns of Zirque Granges in Paris?

It is the Corsican's windburned face (ritually scarred with strange sweeping marks like Arabic writing) I see at night, *de temps en temps*. Exiled from his sunny mild-weathered island in this sea of bitter-cold waters, I cannot help wondering about him. I remember the Freud-type who told me I have confused intimacy with sex he is right, the words are entirely linked in my mind, they cannot be pulled apart without doing irreparable damage. To be intimate, to know, means to have sex for an entire night with him or her, the matter is almost none at all, an entire night, so I do not care to know just anyone, and you cannot know me until you have slept with me. It was living over that bar, I think, that somehow ruined me in this way.

Left me to sit in the stillness of my room, unable to get out of the dark out of which I was born, my blood running into the sheets, mesmerized by the spreading shape, a thing forming as I watch I cannot help this slow dive through the dense graininess of a badly developed photograph tinted violet, bottom an unfounded rumor.

There was too much Basque in you Maman, you passed on the stubbornness to me as surely as these severe cheekbones which dominate my face, a race deposited in the Pyrenees, one of those pools left by the tide, left to dry while the sea retreated ever farther until it was a distant memory, a place like the garden where the first happy hours of humankind are supposed to have been spent, doubted entirely. And this pool of salt water retains the ways of a sea long gone, is salty, no good for drinking, does not fit in, does not want to.

And what is that little flat-headed idol doing over there, on the other side of the bed when I left it next to that volcanic lamp of mine? It's face a little blurry, now there's a shapeless lump on the smooth stone platter it is holding. And why is that lamp a smeared glow, the light a receding spark that has no effect on the expanse of cold underwater blackness surrounding it? Don't those terribly deepsea fish have lights dangling from their ugly widemouthed heads to attract other fish, like the sinking smeared glow calling to me to follow? Ah, never breathe the name of the dead, it distracts them, calls them back, tethers them to this place they would do better to abandon.

This slow thing is a slow dive, the deeper the colder the darker. *Ma mere,* how did you let this happen to your daughter? This slow dive, the way I lived, an endless sinking at three in the morning beneath the streets and sewers of Paris, the trickling water echoing as it drips, mingles with the moldering dead buried in Pere Lachaise. One thing chained to another and all anchored at the nonexistent nadir of a bottomless abyss—heroin and death, the waters of the womb and the deep-sea darkness of unremembered places where nothing can ever be more than intimated, the night of the weeping demons of the soul where you cannot help but wonder why the stars wanted so badly to see themselves (vanity, all is vanity) they spawned an entire race out of dust and opened up a thousand ways to return it to the dust. Why make us prone to disease and the decrepitude of age, why imbue us with a love for needles and the hot white powder in whose glow you see you are just a cage of bone and sinew somehow trapping something of the eternal which childish pre-Renaissance painters tried to show with a halo? The toothless, choleric, redheaded painter who pointed this out also spoke of traveling to the stars as one takes the train to Tarascon or Rouen, but the locomotive is death. If tuberculosis is a first class car to Aldeberan and old age is the light-years-long walk all the way to Rigel (the shining flank of sprawled-out-overhead Orion), heroin must be a slow boat to Sirius.

The coughing whistle of steam from the radiator speaks of rising heat, but no warming from the outside will save me. The radiator is blind and does its blind work like all of what is visible to the eye it operates on a set of principles since the Beginning blind to us *aussi.*

So there is my proof, there was no need to stick myself with a razor, experiment with the tenuous links to what surrounds us, I needed only to think of myself as a corpse and the heat coming up regardless.

Then again, there is the matter of Bar Sept where I met Zirque Granges and he doubted me when I told him–as I had told everyone that night–that my name was Sophie. I cocked my head and tried again.

How about Therese?

Could be he said.

Veronique?

Sounds more like the glass slipper but from the look on your face, I guess I'm wrong again.

Whichever one you like I said, and it was one night in bed he turned to me and whispered, Whatever your name is, Veronique is the one I've fallen for.

Yes, I said, not bothering to tell him in truth I have three names, one name from each possible father, how else can I know who I am?

He puts me on his arm but knows enough to wear a falcon-er's glove. Then sets me loose on the circling winged fears he has and for a moment, an hour, a day, a reprieve. After I've ripped their hearts through their feathered breasts and brought the bloody lumps back to him as proof (until they rise again and again no matter how he tries to outrun them). And she, the other one, the Queen of Blue Jean Babies, the one who takes me from his arm, putting the hood over my head first, the drug which counteracts the side effects of the harsh cure he has called upon.

He wants to keep us separate, his Rae Anne and I, church and state, business and pleasure, good and so-very-irresistibly bad, he who lives like a member of some tribe his life is so unplanned so perfectly a mess that you cannot shake the suspicion something divine has had a hand in it. And the fingerprints of this invisible, where do they show up?

He told me about a drunk in Kansas who used to make it

[95]

home the worst nights by falling into a drainage ditch and crawling, sliding along the edge of near-dawn until it brought him to the creaking wooden steps (paint worn away) of his front porch, except the night he'd collapsed in the ditch and a flood brought him to the foreign field of a neighbor who, astonished at what had washed up on a Sunday morning, shook his head and said it was bound to happen one day.

But when? Pinpoint for us that. The moment when sleep becomes unconscious becomes never going to move, never going to convulse in the throes of an orgasm never going to eat, never going to laugh, never going to squat in an alley at three in the morning and piss out too much beer splattering on the cobblestone and on otherwise perfectly good shoes, never going to *un fois plus* feel the warmth of a man's body against you beneath an avalanche of blankets heaped up against the winter cold in this wood- and coal- and gas- and oil- and memory-burning city.

How much heat do they give off, these memories that are your only evidence of a life lived, set into the furnace in the basement, where they flare up for a second pffFFFT–*fini?* Less substantial than a cigarette, not an ash left, *au revoir.*

They have worked their way–they won't let themselves be anything so useful as oil–into the blood. See, in the shape spreading across the sheet now, clearly the face of my whore-loving father. This doesn't count, you will say, the Corsican may not have been the one, there are no photographs to corroborate my mother, a shadow of the memory of a forgotten existence.

I fall back to the certainty of the time ZeeGee had come to Paris, the third or fourth time, we met under the Pont de Neuilly, gazing stupidly at one another, sodomy and gonorrhea, a pigeon hiding under the bridge where I had also gone to get out of the rain. His face chipped from flint, a neolithic spear-point, dozens of facets all tending toward a characteristic hardness, wet sealskin hair as glossy as your dark eyes, that missing

tooth the space for forgiveness in your smile. You walk sideways around your own life, scavenging claw to mouth as you
go, never wondering what this twisted bit of driftwood you
poke under is doing there–never realizing you are looking at
yourself bleaching in the sun.

In the cafe in Montmartre with four windows (one for each
direction, season, Eliot's Quartets)–famous for having never
seated Hemingway or Eliot or any other *ecrivain celebre*–cleaned
up, insides warmed with clam soup and escargot, fingers shiny
from garlic butter, arguing with three old men about Foucault
and Hamlet and Kafka, looking to me to translate, telling your
stories of the wino-philosopher Lloyd Cruise who, asked by
the cops how old he was, said 99 or 66 dependin on ha ya look
at it, and the Earl of Deathrow, the Polish Kansan, who said
bein ain't no different from nothinness when you been sittin in
solitary confinement for a few years. Who appended onto
Nietzsche what doesn't kill me only makes me stronger, less a
course it leaves me stuck in a wheelchair for the rest a my
natural days.

Only the stubborn one with white hair and a black beret
refused to smile (maybe he never had). Who was confused and
grudgingly listened to what happened to you that day you were
in Gallup, what used to be nothing more than a railroad
stopover in that dustbin part of New Mexico and you came out
of a theater, captivated by a procession of telephone poles
heading crookedly off into the sunset, leaning different ways as
if trapped in motion, the streetlights and red-glare Colonial
Motel sign, the white fluorescence of the Big O Tire shop
strange echoes of the fading glow stretched across the horizon.
The bowing poles, connected by their cables, a line of Apache
crown dancers or Hopi kachinas, branching headdresses made
by the double crosses, the smooth silent orange of sunset in
place of the twisting and spitting of a bonfire.

But that was just a stand-in for a stand-in, you said. You see
these dances and you know you're only lookin at a few bones

a the world which brought this performance on in the first place, an' you try to imagine the whole beast, what it musta been like to inspire those masks, grinnin pop-eyed grotesques somma them, all of em harder to read than Chinese characters.

You are saying we live in an empire of signs, Black Beret offered, knocking his little walking stick on the white tiled floor, and the Eiffel Tower is just another mountain aiming too high like the ziggurat in time-obliterated Uruk.

I don't know, you said, but there's a nebulous tide risin an' fallin in the subterranean mind an' certain things get you to look inside yourself for somethin gone a long time ago, somethin you don't much have time to think about while lunch is being bagged at McDonald's.

Paris will never have one, Black Beret snorted.

The boons of progress are ubiquitous, you said with a smile.

Yes, I agreed, so is bad taste.

But I was thinking about Artur, the drunk in Kansas, the night crawler, how we are all like him, following in the grooves of our habits, our routines and never realizing the very things we trust the most we will one day be buried in. Afraid like no one I know of of death, ZeeGee's hopscotching around the planet maybe his way of staying a square ahead of it. One day it will be his luck that gives out, yes what kachinas are rumored to bring besides rain, it will be a rotted plank between buildings to which he's trusted his weight and destiny which will give out, the *finis* for ZeeGee.

And who do I stand in for? And you Monsieur Granges, are you also nothing more to me? Trace that to its source if you are not afraid, if you do not mind that the answer will bring on darkness at noon, eclipse the sun for all time; if you will not jump off that evil brink, if you will not plunge the nearest cactus needle or sharp stick into your eyes when you discover the answer.

We came home late from the Cafe Quatre Vents and I would have suggested to him a soothing cigarette, but he is afraid of the taste of ashes in his mouth, like the mortality he feels in southwestern winters, New Mexico and Arizona when he smells woodsmoke, a sign to him that it is all burning down—imagine fearing something as formless and hardly conceivable as entropy instead of taking comfort in the cozy triteness of warming his feet by the fireplace and placidly smoking a pipe while reading a good book.

As for his bad sleeping, maybe it is only that he cannot find a comfortable bed. He stands looking out my window which here on the third floor looks down at the bistro across the street, the little Tarot card shop where Zabere tells fortunes for 100 francs—

What are you thinking?

—and is not half bad and makes Zirque laugh with silver stardust eyeshadow on his dark brown skin and silly come-ons. Zabere, if you only knew he could be summoned up during one of your seances if he were only sleeping, never anchored to anything, no not really, except to Pittsburg, that little town he says has as many forgotten pasts as yards of rusting railroad tracks where he is the only one who would risk starvation in Paris to avoid dying of boredom in Kansas and cannot sleep tonight—

What, I asked him, his face streetlit reddish orange, are you afraid of tonight? What do you see in the telephone poles this time?

—in his bed with a sleeping bag for a blanket; I know why he prefers to sleep on his clothes and you might think a hamster has better instincts, but it is the dog he imitates, the dog who has taught a pile of rags to conform exactly to his curled body, a transformation so complete the rags have taken on his musty smell.

I know that the woman waiting for him in Kansas is a bed in the shape of his longing for rest.

To sleep, to rest, this simple mystery of opiates in the brain, for everyone but him. Maybe inspired-inhabited (an unwilling medium Zabere would envy), is what kept him up writing on matchbooks, on envelopes already postmarked, keeping me awake also, mechanically eating one *petits ecolier* after another, wondering who else in this world has just such an addiction to dark chocolate, what is she like how will I find her (perhaps him?) how old is she has she ever given a thought at this moment to my existence?

If you trace the lines as we go from addiction to addiction and plot the points of intersection where our cravings are held at bay, the angry fix an American Poet called it, what you have will be as beautifully formed as the angles in a crystal, as the natural engineering of a spiderweb or the criss-cross of telephone and electrical wires and clotheslines between tenements roping off a bit of alleyway sky.

Heaven has left a wind tunnel in our hearts. And the always-trying-to-fill-it, the always-looking-to-get-there is what leaves us face-down beside the curb, or stretched out naked on the floor, the cigarette burning down to the filter between our fingers, the candle a hardening reddish puddle waiting for our failure to be pressed onto it.

We need an instrument to study the telemetry of our prayers, we worshipers from afar, in time, in distance measured (by that same instrument) from the angel realm to earth, from sunny pleasure domes and a cloud signed and numbered like a limited-edition print, to Pantisocrasy and the Commune of 1871. What can we drop from there to here and what can we take with us and what will be waiting for us there?

And what is to be done with those of us who have an aching for a myth to support our lives, a backbone a world-tree, Yggdrasil whose roots curl like a fist around our troubled hearts, whose leafy branches disappear in the strange horizon where vision blends with the sky lording over it, the pale moon and occasional lumps of burning rock-iron-copper angels who fall through it, gather at our feet as dust that has traveled light years to be stepped on and forgotten except for that one phosphorescent moment when we knew to make a wish before it was already too late. And maybe that is what you are doing up late at night, inventing one, crawling up the backbone as you add vertebra to vertebra, Jacques and the beanstalk, where does it lead and who is the giant waiting at the top? And how heavy are those golden eggs anyway? If we don't want the trouble of using ligament attachments as rungs of a ladder, if we allow it to be watered down (afraid of heights) we paint in oil, we pastel, we draw angels in the air, stamp them out of plastic, print them on comforting cards to send to one another, put them on the tops of Christmas trees, make them in the snow, in mashed potatoes, and compose music to mimic the sound of their wings beating from heaven to heaven.

For a moment music is your salvation, you feel a certain way hearing it, and you want to own it, possess it, bottle it, so that you have cornered this feeling and the needle of your life to follow the grooves, this is what you hope but those times the music refuses to cooperate, fails, you turn to another needle, something stronger. You wander out into the street, tortured hysterical naked, and start to feel how the laughing gargoyles of Notre Dame, a starry sky, the crazy Dutchman's celestial night, a rain-shined street can sink into you, fossilize in the sedentary mind, and how what refuses to crystallize, what remains hallucinogenic, kaleidoscopic and unformed–though governed by unseeable, unknowable rules–is the deepest of all patterns, this I, this me, this peculiar understanding of the sense (or absurdity) of things.

Shall we agree that it is all neither absurd, nor meaningful, neither this, nor that, that it is merely a matter of here it is? That it was merely a matter of time before America fell to worshiping Coca-Cola cans and Warhol restaurant menus, the most easily reproducible, the manufacturable, let itself be led around by a platinum-wigged *pede* whose only form of intimacy is a passion for drawing *les dangs* of men whom he admires?

Man's inanity is heaven's lens.

My favorite dear-departed painter would be scandalized.

In the stone wall around the tiny cottage, he saw an epic struggle against chaos. In the twists of tree branches, the desperate desire to live (I lie here, mocking it). He was certain of the exact color to express the sound of the spoon (lightly stirring coffee) against a kiln-forged cup, but *quel domage,* he turned fate on himself, only thirty-seven. Syphilitic, deep-suffering, redheaded drinker of absinthe, loneliness surrounded him like winter.

Are you moved to tears? And the stars, what would move them, colossal sources of infinite light and heat, what scene of human tragedy would cause a flaming bit of starstuff to fall?

The smallest and the most trivial, the nearest *clochard,* gray-haired Albert the seller of old magazines, face-down in his own vomit. The old woman downstairs who lost her husband in the French Resistance against the Nazis and two sons in Indochina. But not viewed from a distance as Albert is by passing bourgeoisie who are worried about getting their patent leather soiled with pink-colored half-digested wine and bread, rather from a button on the sleeve of his coat, with him through all those years, from fortune to misfortune, and what a story of lost family, the betrayal of his own sons—Albert you used to be so handsome—and the stealing of his wife by an embezzling business partner—who cares? Not even Albert—that he has come to this end, only the button which bids the star look closer and you too will cry.

Look now, who should be at my empty easel but the crazed Dutchman (those are starry nights that were his eyes), a blank canvas attracts him the way a warm living body attracts love, the rod in metallic silvery voice calls to it the lightning, ouija boards attract the mute restless ghosts killed in the French Revolution, my warm adolescent body attracted one of my fathers, this city (the cooking smells in Rae Anne's kitchen) attract my American lover (whose soul was born in a lost Middle Eastern city lying in infamy and dust).

Where are you now?

Under the Pont de Neully maybe.

And even if I had the strength to get up and look for you there, no doubt you would be on your way here by one of your roundabout routes through the Arab Quarter. A Shirley Temple movie. Ah, they've just missed one another in their sleighs, grandfather going up the street she was just on. And so will be my death, no one here, not even Charlie Chaplin Keystone Kops to bumble my experiment.

The judge of all undersea life with a goat's face, his infernal spreading horns twisted like stretched entrails, seaweed beard waving, laughs for me.

I offer him the stare of the retarded, the idiot savant, my fingertips grown as heavy as lumps of iron, this cold leaving them hard to move, clumsy, useless, and my lips locked in a kiss with a gargoyle carved out of ice, his frigid weight making breathing difficult, enfolded in his wings of crystalline dark-ness, of glittering cold, the pins-and-needle feelings pricking my arms, my thighs, the fringes of consciousness, can the bot-tom be so much farther off?

The mad Dutchman's hair is no longer red, his face is tattooed in the flowing mystery of Arabic, *Pere,* what are you doing here now with those strange popeyed fish hovering above your head, above the lava lamp whose red has coagulat-ed in such a way as to show my adopted grandfather's anguished trapped cry, your mouth stretching out of all pro-portion as you rise (ah, such agony, why is there no sound?), Jacques I cannot hear you, the eels like thoughts coil inside me, I am surrounded by a thousand slimy things I am one of them.

Where is ZeeGee? The inset in my life, a smaller photo with-in a photo, exiled to a corner, an overlap, nothing so clearcut as yin within yang, love within lust within sex within sodomy. What bridge in what part of the world on what locust street in Pittsburg, Kansas (there is a Paris, Texas, so I have heard) is he leaning against a building boarded up since Prohibition and

[103]

longing for a yeast-clouded beer in a Berlin cafe where we will be close enough to exchange nightmares? There is more good in him than he realizes and more evil in me than he cares to admit (maybe too in that other woman addicted to *petits ecoliers;* has she even been born yet? she who also lives in a city split by a river, I imagine–the odds are not zero, it's bound to happen). It is a wonder he doesn't feel the clawed grip when I hold him, smell the acrid sulfurous burning.

Who has opened the door of my refrigerator and let in that rush of cold? Oh it is Zabere, the apartment door, Zabere screaming at such a pitch I cannot make out through the thick violet filling my mouth my eyes my ears the words. Did I make an appointment for today? *Zut alors* I forgot. How can you remember a fraction of an hour when the days have slid one into another, a gray slush nightless sunless dayless timeless and now I see it is unconsciously possible I planned this and my answer of course is given in ambiguity, a definite maybe, I should have known.

C'est trop tarde, he is screaming, *trop tarde,* too much blood is lost, I am too blue, what is to be done? He is bandaging me with torn sheets, look at the definition in his skynny lyttle arms, who would have thought all that strength could be called up out of them?

Through closed lids, I hear him, frantic on the phone but I can no longer understand what he is saying, his voice is fading, the room has finally dissolved too.

Oui, oui, y knew it all along, a defynite maybe. but why can't I keep my eyes open, why ys it ympossible not to sleep, and what ys that coming toward me, no, not a dream, something else, a whyspering irydescence as I fall into an abyss y could never have ymagyned yawned below thys world, the whypsering scattered edge of lyght that can only be the soul's desyre to softly burn.

BUDAPEST BLUE

I COULD HAVE TOLD YOU OF PHOTOGRAPHS I KEPT LOCKED AWAY in a drawer of unanswered desires, black-and-whites of you though we had never met, though I had never seen you, so then not you–but yes, you.

Sleep as distant as the memory of childhood I am no better off than a dead leaf, a discarded snapshot curling at the corners, swept end over end down deserted streets, the edges of cities even continents apart always the same near dawn–scattered bird twitters, shadows turning their slow pirouette into brick and stone, the same cold blue-of-drowned-lips appearing in the sky–and I wonder what, besides the brooding shape of Budapest, is silhouetted against reddish amber.

What if I had shown you the photos and you had seen yourself (not you, but variations... a woman with your dark unforgiving eyes, another with the natural arrogance of your downturned mouth, still a third with the inquisitive abrasiveness of your glare when you confront an object with your attention...), would you understand who you are? Or why you were locked in a stranger's drawer?

Haunted by photographic memories, something in me is like film, and having been exposed is left with only the afterimage.

Of you at the Viennese Cafe where we first agreed to meet.

The last time leaving me with a demand: Three glasses of water, you said, in the evening, before it is dark. In a row.

What good will that do?

It will get rid of them.

You never finished, leaving me on the wrong side of a river, bridgeless, wondering how to cross. Get rid of what?

Sitting across from me at the round marble table, the wrought-iron stem holding up its flat petrified bloom, you smoothed the perfectly polished surface with your hand and said, The dreams. You looked at me then, your iris dark enough, liquid enough, to dissolve your pupils. Before I met you, I didn't–they weren't ...

You didn't finish.

Promise, you said, three glasses.

Tomorrow I said.

Good, you answered, pronouncing it more like *gude*.

Standing up, a flip of long black hair, like a sweep of history–horses and darkskinned foreigners atop them, destined to forever change everything–and you were gone, coffee still steaming.

You let me catch up with you later, evening flowing into black. Looking into the Danube atop the Chain & Link Bridge with its stone arches and dormant lions, your lips pursed to spit olive pits, you watched the bats chase them before they silently disappeared into the water, the bats never fooled the whole way.

It's not my fault you are no different from a sultry orange moon floating full and huge over the summer evenings, over the gothic spires of the castle quarter, a moon arisen out of the strange east of this city's origins. No, it's not your fault I was left to burn softly through the night, waking to the faint reek of sleep singed toward daybreak and exhaust fumes sifting through the screen, staining cool morning air.

I saw you first, unable not to stare. You pulled closer to the man you were with (bending to the porcelain figurines in a shop window, oblivious to me). I watched you walk on, your arm linked to his, staring back.

I slept even less that night, walking the city's paved quiet, hardly noticing anti-Communist slogans sprayed on alley walls, a film running through my mind, image by image, your face most of all. Abandoned my apartment in that run-down quarter of Pest, I climbed to the roof and projected my film on the vacuum of the sky for anyone to see, for anyone to take to bed as a blanket, though it would hold off a chill evening no better than a stretch of cellophane, though it was no more real than the faded ghost of a heart outlined in white paint (the names inside it too faint to read) on the wall near Andrussy Street, the brick scarred by bullets fired forty years ago.

You will recognize every film I make by the invisible violence worked on the souls we thought we did not have.

Sleepless through morning, I stepped out of my own film (rough, grainy, its colors skewed to the violets of the spectrum) into the streets of Budapest which had become the black-and-white of newspaper events, had taken on the jagged porcelain clarity of a shattered coffee cup, and saw you at the Viennese Cafe. Alone.

You let me sit down (my hands on my knees where you wouldn't see how unreliable they'd become), but did not look up from the book you were reading.

I don't like Americans, you said turning a page.

I couldn't answer, sitting at the bottom of a tree waiting for another apple to fall (thinking about the impossible odds of looking at one at the precise moment it has at last grown too heavy, the stem too weak, and falls). Afraid to shake the tree, of violating something, I waited in the black-and-white stillness, waited for color—even the yellow of old newspapers—to bleed into a corner of the frame.

Finally you asked, What are you doing in Hungary?

I'm a film student.

Oh. Yes, how interesting. Americans know better than any-one how to spend money on movies.

America is a big country, I said, the grand scale is the only one we know.

[107]

You looked up, this time with an entirely different motive, a different expectation, and asked, Why are you in Budapest?

Tempering my American-ness.

Hm. A snort. Compromise might be worse.

You took a sip of coffee, a bite of a chocolate-covered Grandoletti, offered me the box (I shook my head). And then read to me from your book:

What does it mean that there is a star always in the north? That it has pulled us along throughout the thousands of years of fear and demonic uncertainties? That it burned silently in its perfection of place, unaltering, unfailing?

You looked at me, your face as pale as the morning, flecked with ephemeral freckles and asked Where is mine? The one I can use when the sky is clouded over, when my eyes are closed, when there is nothing to see?

I saw you again at Golgotha, the bar sitting in the middle of a once-Communist street, the name since taken down, known now by rumor as Nagy Street, a good joke on tourists who are like the blind after furniture in the apartment has been moved.

The streets always change their names, you have to know the street not to be fooled, know it on its way into the heart of Budapest, past the other river which still flows, carrying time and Romans and Huns downstream to their final resting place, running past the cathedrals with their vaulted ceilings buttressing belief against the infinite unknown overhead, the source of all fear.

The night, you said, is a place where you can commit crimes, go crazy, be ruined. And laughed hysterically for effect. What am I doing here in this black hole of a bar with you?

I've written you into the script, I said.

Gude, why not?

To you I was one more invader, another Roman, a Mongolian, a Turk, a German, a Russian. The history of Hungary built on the threat of dissolution, the ruined walls of fortresses and rule by foreigners, a country that is a peasant woman of such enduring marble strength, shattered a thousand times, some strange gravity keeps the fragments within reach—an underside of determined jaw, an entire arm braced against annihilation, an eye joined by a single curve to the stubbornly intact nose with the background of a starry night behind. A country whose form is nonexistent yet discernable, an abstract of its Magyar past, the green of its flag, the brown of sunstained farmers' hands, the rich crimson of the fired-upon students who stood in every square before the stern bronze face of a national hero and defied the Russians that October night in 1956. They sit and stand around us, draped in thick sweaters, faded denims sent from overseas (one with blue eyes behind round glasses like those Imre Nagy wore), lift beers to Nagy and the October night the red star above Parliament first went out. Drink something as strong as absinthe, what wells up from under the city making you lose not memory but all sense of time, blowing it up tumorously, so that tanks and chariots rumble along wheel by mechanical gear, and the side of night bulges in an unheard-of direction.

There, standing at a 45-degree angle between the bare brick wall and the floor, nothing relating to anything else the way it should, you told me about one of your favorite musicians who sang that there is a part of us that is too quick flowing too bright too elusive be at home on the earth we have hollowed out and shafted for dusty coal, sidewalked for the afternoon crowds. And it is this we call angel, our grounded desire unfolding the wings, abandoning what cannot escape gravity's pull.

Yes, I've heard that angels have wings, I said, so you must be one of us.

Isn't that sweet, you said, too casually to mean it.

We drank without reserve and spoke as if that bar—badly lit with blue, hung with posters of supposed-to-be-nostalgic movies: *Casablanca, From Here to Eternity, Hiroshima Mon Amour*—had been built on hallowed ground and nothing could touch us for our sins or trespasses or be turned against us. We talked of how I would set my only friend's soul aflame if it would light one unknown corner of the universe long enough to take a clear photograph, how you fear more than anything else waking up in a country where no one speaks the strange language of the Magyars where you cannot make one word out of your mouth understood or find your way home, of the unforgiven older brother who will spend two eternities in the First Circle for doing to you when you were 18 what he had done when you were nine. I admitted that notes I had written to a girl through two years of high school had been passed out to the entire cafeteria (I heard my own tokens of everlasting devotion quoted to me by football players for weeks after) as a way of killing the foolishness I felt for her, but whatever it was that died, I can't say for sure.

We refused to go home, dragging bottles of wine by the neck, winding up under the lion-guarded bridge whose lamps cast over it a faded green, using the Navy coat I picked up for five dollars at a pawn shop in South Dakota to cover the cold asphalt. You taught me that prayer is more than whispered demands, hands pressed together, that it requires more than one person. I learned how it is possible for a tongue to be an Our Father, for hands to restore faith blackened by its own despair, for bone and socket, my body immersed in yours, to be all of Ecclesiastes. You became a river rushing through my mouth, running into an inner sea and what was under the sun didn't matter to us under the moon, under the shadow of that bridge, where a generation could have passed quietly away without altering the rhythm of our breathing.

Almost asleep, your mouth warm against my ear, I felt you waving. I sat up, turned around. The old man who'd watched from a balcony of the bridge, the same one I had seen the other day who'd asked me if I planned to urinate into the Danube, and if so, to do it from atop a bridge, not from the banks, preferably at midnight when the voices at the bottom have begun their incessant muttering. Do you believe that? No, of course not, it's just the tinkling of bones you hear, rattling over one another, clamoring restlessly, tongues long ago rotted out of those heads, twin voids instead of eyes that wanted nothing more than to see grandmothers, lovers, Papa, sons, daughters, wives, drinking companions, the streetcar conductor again. Then he asked me if my *fasz* was large or small, if it fit well into women. And there he was, in long coat and black bowler, waving back.

In the stillness that lies unbroken before the sun has risen, when you scent the pureness of an uncreated moment in the cool air, when it is easy to waver between being and non-being, a flame about to go out, you shifted your weight on the slippery satin lining of my Navy coat, looking down at it suddenly as if you recognized the previous owner (a musician I tend to think who drank a lot of bourbon, I never did before the night I walked into a bar in drafty snow-drifted New York City and ordered one to warm me up), as if you could shake out of its folds dusty songs, torn movie tickets, phone numbers of ex-lovers... you shifted your weight and turned to me.

There are rare elements, you said, which exist only briefly–the memory of the man who wore your coat–and even then only under difficult conditions (at the core of the planet, you know?). It would be easy to think that something as warming... let me see... as warming to the imagination as the pale glow of neon–why not purple neon in a cold drizzle?–has formed between us. But I am afraid that, like the neon, there will be no warmth when I stand beside it, like a cat arching against what it most desires, I will not be able to rub my ache against you, I will come up against emptiness. I think I am better off with Gregor.

Really? I kissed you then; I didn't believe you.

He is not like you, you said, he touches me where I am solid, when I want to be a tree rooted to the floor of my apartment, to a place surrounded by my things–I see them, I can touch them and feel for a moment where I belong. You are the dangerous one, I have no idea what I will become around you.

Yes you do. And every time you cross this bridge, every time you see the river, you will remember.

You turned away, whipping your long black hair in half a witches' circle.

Yes, this is what I become, someone who jumps up from the hard wooden bench in church in the middle of the sermon because she has discovered she does not care for a religion anymore unless she can dress the part.

Enamored of Italians and the Indian Americas where they dance through the piazzas, the plazas, inseparable from their own elongated shadows grown to gothic dimensions they attract other winged dancers in gowns and masks and capes. Like Carnivale in Venice, you wanted to become the mystery even for a wingbeat, otherwise what is the point? (In the beginning there was no neon, no warmth of cat, no reason for prayer. And yet without our asking, every day a new sun–not yesterday's, not last week's–flares into life in the endlessness of endless space.) You wanted to wade into the Danube, waist-high in the river, a Hindu, arms upraised, but I held onto your wrist, afraid of the deceptive calm of the river's surface.

Three glasses of water to wash color from your dreams, you said. With no way to film the film I did not stop seeing, I settled for the haiku of photos, evenings mostly, the luxury of soon-to-be-gone twilight, the acquired taste of bitter foreknowledge. A whole roll with you standing on the Roman wall on Castle Hill, in the weak light falling out of a rain-gray sky.

You attract the black cat, though you prefer the free-swimming porpoise, imagining them to have liquid silver running through their veins, their high-pitched calls for you.

You shook your head at me when I insisted on cat, You have no sense of porpoise, you said and I knew that, yes, we looked at the same thing and saw differently, our hands reaching for each other had proven ghostly, had passed through each other. Yet even when the the word porpoise was in your mouth, you charmed a stray to sit at your feet in that tiny cobblestone street washed with moonlight, to hold perfectly still for the camera.

In your apartment in Óbuda, the weathered stone-block buildings so heavy the streets sag around them, I saw your portrait of Gregor. Even before I was swallowed by the cavernous mouth of your building I knew you lived on the third floor. Three of the balconies bare, the only color from roofgutter to foundation—maybe in that whole quarter if you didn't count the yellow street cars—was the red of whatever you'd planted blooming over the railing of the third-floor balcony. Too small really to stand on, you had to lean out a window to get to it, I knew the first time I stood below it if it wasn't your balcony you'd gotten it on loan.

The stairway, even going up, felt like a descent. Damp and stoney, there should have been moss on the walls instead of that loose collage of hand-made flyers selling cars, advertising student movies, renting out apartments, flapping against their staples in the open-door draft. You were at the end of six flights, cross-legged on the old-soaked wooden floor, amid the reek of oil paint tainted with turpentine. A clutter of canvases, people I had never met peered back at me (the craggy old woman upstairs whose deeply rutted face holds within it a vale of tears), places I knew in Buda and Pest, winding alleys and cafes in a white city I seemed to recognize but could not name. More than anything, self-portraits; one of you in the alley of that white city using nothing but shades of blue, your hair pinned up, a stare that would keep a century from turning.

I saw your portrait of Gregor, as if painted on a surface of water, the tiniest details—no more noticeable than a stray hair—floating in the light, yes more than enough light.

So your style... this is your style, I said.

You didn't look up from your sketch pad, a dozen album covers surrounding you... Robert Johnson, fedora cocked, posing with his guitar; Chet Baker, sleeves rolled up, bent over a piano; Billie Holliday, head thrown back as if the huge microphone in front of her were a serpent that had charmed her, entered her body, made her gasp silently. Not to mention Leadbelly Ledbetter, Bukka White, Mississippi John Hurt, Eldon Sunhouse, Charlie Musclewhite.

It is a style I decided on for him, you said waving a hand at Gregor's portrait but still not looking up, you need to know him to understand.

When I see him again, we'll be like old friends, I said, but wanted to know how Gregor had trapped her attention, how to have my painting on the easel where his sat mute, still, helpless.

You snorted.

I tried to place the voice coming through the speakers, a scratched-up basement recording, the voice grinding the words as they came out, no syllable left unmarked by its rough touch, a black man about all I could pin down.

Blind Willie Johnson, you said. His step-mother threw acid in his face when he was seven years old. It hurts me in a strange way to listen to him, strange because I still like listening. The others, too—

When you paint?

Yes, I like to listen to them when I paint.

Blind Willie singing as if nothing had been taken away, bellowing into the dark unending solitude to break it from the inside out, leave it in ragged fragments like the ancient silence enshrouding creation before creation had spoken its first word. Heaven spread evenly out of reach from where Blind Willie stood, no up or down, directions obsolete, didn't send so much as a tremor through his faith in the unseen.

Blind Willie went on singing, you went on shading with your piece of charcoal, only stopping to reach for a Grandoletti, preferring a dozen or so to a 4,000-forint dinner in Grundel's.

Long as thayz a man, I said, roughening my voice, my accent, long as thayz a woman, thay'll be the Blues.

You stopped what you were doing and looked up at me, skepticism and surprise mixing in your expression, a new color.

John Lee Hooker.

Ah, you said, nodding, yes.

The charcoal began tracing lines, inscribing the blank whiteness of the paper with the face of someone who could find no release, no other way out of the prison of your obscure intentions.

Wrapped in the oily incense of paint, cocooned away in your balconied apartment with the sawed-off voices of black American singers, lost to the cry of the infant abandoned on a sloping Taygetus of garbage, to the incessant muttering of thickset, waistless old Ildiko upstairs who lost a husband in World War II (nothing left but his hat covering a nail in the wall, a black-and-white of him—sharp-boned, thirtyish—in a cheap gold frame) and two sons to the October uprising. Her coffee—heated on the chipped white stove she has to light with a match—is too thick too bitter to be anything but the boiled-down marrow of the dead (it is all she has to warm her in winter). You know almost as well as she, looking out your third floor window, what falls in this rain. How scratches in the thin layer of flaking plaster covering the outside brick inscribe Ildiko's memories. And you have grown crimson flowers to spite the bitter falling drops, each alone in its fall from a place too gray to be anything like heaven, each alone as a sonless widow before the final strike against a cracked wall, the sidewalk, bare dirt or—a stroke of rare luck—your flower bed.

How many times have you looked into stone-faced monuments or stood before the bronze men wearing helmets, carrying swords, mounted on great stallions, their stoic expressions streaked with green, and asked the corroding metal or smoothed stone, was it worth it? Ask Blind Willie Johnson. Ask Ildiko who prays in the living room, whose knees have worn two bald spots in the thin throw rug in front of a sad-faced weeping Madonna painted in oils but shrouded in silver and gold. Mary's painted weeping face in a precious Byzantine shroud like braille to the hands of the faithful (only the face is smooth), framed and hung on the wall above a tiny television set with awkward rabbit-eared antennae almost reaching this image of mourning mounted in cold folds of silver and gold, this face which stares back at her own. It is only one son she lost not two, not her husband too, crucified by the Nazis, and they've put her in churches, she is a saint because of who her son was but a mother is a mother no matter who her son, the eyes don't lie about what they've seen and even with that flat painting of Mary in the eyes you know.

Sketching me (was it me, all along?) while I stood there, telling me about painting and happiness, about rain and Ildiko (who said wars have taken her sons, her husband, yes, but Communism reached inside of her, robbed her of something she'd always believed would live through her death), you handed me a rectangle of cookie, your eyes more on the paper than on me.

A kind of visual alchemy the only thing painting is good for, you said, changing nothing in substance, altering the form only, something more acceptable, familiar, the reason, you reminded me, gods have two legs and eyes and merciful hearts, they are not free-floating energies loose ubiquitously in the ocean of being.

As for happiness it is something out of the corner of your eye, you insisted, you don't go looking for it as if you were mining for silver or diamonds, spending long years of misery for a flashing moment when you can at last exhale, wipe away sweat and say, ah this is what I was looking for.

You looked from me to the sketch to the sketch to me.

Life is a fever, you said, busy again with the charcoal, a burning, a way of turning up the heat to drive out the tedium of nonexistence, but in this city, they are too busy taking temperatures in increasingly minute degrees. Sometimes the dark sanctity of a winter sky makes you a little giddy, the thought of so much space so see-through your eyes go straight to the glowing white heart of the Milky Way, in the cold air you are aware of your own heat. You press your face against a horse stopped with its carriage, the tourists' coachman unsure whether to shoo you with his whip or stand beside you, you join heart to heart with your arms around the horse's neck, your face full of the bristle of its hide, your nose full of its musty animal smell.

Leave him, I said, looking half in guilt, half in anger at the portrait of Gregor.

Yes, you sighed, yes, I'm going to.

And yes, you did, but I misunderstood.

Putting the pad away you stood up, your nose hardly an inch from mine.

Look at you, you said, in this old coat of yours from the Navy. It was never new was it?

I shook my head. Never.

And the night we went to Golgotha, you were missing a button on your sleeve and you held it there with a... she tapped her wrist where the missing button had been on my shirt... how do you call it?

A paper clip.

Yes, a paper clip. Your life is held together with paper clips and the wrong color thread and—what do you say? Glue. My American man wearing away at the edges but he refuses to notice. Because he is always busy looking somewhere else, isn't he?

Not always, I said, trying to see myself as you saw me, but your eyes (the opaque brown of an amber-locked impurity) give nothing back, I knew I was losing something to you standing there, afraid to lean forward, cross the endless inch separating us, afraid to pull back, the fear of letting go deeper still.

Did I ever tell you you are the most disgusting eater I have ever met? The way you put it all together—a bite of your sandwich, a spoonful of soup—achhhhh—all at the same time.

[117]

Fine, I'll only drink around you from now on.

Right here, you said, and touched the corner of my mouth, you have some chocolate. Leaning closer, you used your tongue (the inch nothing to you, the space around you long ago made yours). I stood, my eyes beginning to close while your tongue went over my mouth, slowly and deliberately, as if to give it a new shape, and then, pushing with your tongue, opening what you had just created.

We didn't bother with the bed, though you could hardly step anywhere without knocking over a pile of books, crunching a Big Bill Broonzy cassette, sliding over a Blind Willie Johnson sleeve, squeezing a tube of titanium white or charcoal gray, rolling on a camel-hair brush, smearing a wet palette. We became slippery with color—yellow turned to green with blue turned violet with red turned orange with yellow—and you added to it, your oily fingers smearing my chest with more, lines and daubs until I looked like a tribesmen from New Guinea. It wasn't until after you had locked your arms and legs around me from underneath, squeezed so hard it hurt, not until after you forced me to come inside you, your head thrown back and your eyes closed, your hair around you like a dark halo, that we wondered how we were going to get it all off without taking a bath in turpentine.

Later in the day, I ran into Gregor in the university library, my body a fading rainbow under my clothes, evidence enough for him to put a bayonet into my chest, but he had no idea I knew you and I let the accidental conversation that began continue, and liked him, and liked him all the more because he was a part of your life added to mine and we ended with a drink, Gregor deferential to America, blaming us only for not sending help when Eisenhower had the chance, asking me about New York, shaking his head in disbelief he had never been there, a place where all languages are spoken, all cuisines served, all appetites find what they crave if only you look down the right street. When we left, he had the address of a friend of mine in pocket, promised to make his pilgrimage to the shrine of Americanness in Manhattan and shook my hand warmly and firmly, a bond that had nothing to do with you. Yes, he is exactly like your portrait, his curly blondish hair, passive mouth and narrow eyes open to the better humans we can be, and I knew even then I would like him, but would also, as soon as I saw you again, beg you to leave him.

Yes, I am going to, you told me again in the park, late afternoon, the sun warm for early October.

When?

When we run into him and the three of us are together and I have hurt him so badly he cannot stay in Budapest because the pain of everything we've done here is unbearable.

You pulled me by the hand, pushed me against a tree until I sat down.

I love the Fall, you said. There is just enough cold to remind us we are animals full of warm blood.

You sat on your knees facing me, pulled with your hands locked behind my neck and this time only the statue of King Árpád, who led the Magyars out of the Russian steppes, watched from a distance measured by the first steps of those horsebacked nomads and the last shouts of triumph over the Nazis, the beginning of Communism and its end, the founding of Hungary and our chance meeting.

Do you realize you said, having kissed me quiet, there is no difference between a galaxy and a tree? A falling leaf, a falling star, each has its season. And don't be stupid, of course I know they're just chunks of iron, big rocks burning up, but stars don't last forever either. Everything that holds the leaves to the tree, makes the tree a—how do you say? A complete... thing, well it's the same thing that holds together the galaxy, holds together the part of the universe you can feel, but not see.

But what we can see is what we're stuck with, the only way to cross the distances inside to outside, back again.

Oh yes, how true.

You kissed me again, the cool taste of a wet autumn morning, your sweater rough against the underside of my jaw.

Do you hear that? The singing?

A man's voice, at a distance, passing the time as he adjusted his cap, walked through that clear October afternoon free of Communism.

I like the way men sing, you said, as if they are excited about the world. I think of them collecting things and hunting and disappearing under avalanches of snow.

You ripped up a handful of grass, stuffed it down my red-and-black Rutgers sweatshirt, and jumped up while I pulled out the front to let the grass fall.

Come on, you called, already running, I want to show you something.

Dizzy, out of breath, my head hot and my ears strangely cold, I finally caught up with you at the tram stop. We got on near an open window, pulling out our collars, heat faintly scented with soap rising past our faces.

At your apartment, you pulled me by the hand up the dark narrow stairway.

There, you flicked your fingers lightly, look.

The portrait was shadowed, only one eye visible, half of me in light as harsh and unsteady as fire, the smileless face gouged out of darkness, the strokes straight, swift, severe.

I don't need people to sit for them, you said, I see them better with my eyes closed.

But for me, memory is an out-of-focus photograph and no matter how close I get, nothing is any clearer and always I am left with the maddening vagueness that comes of things that can never be known.

How could you let our portraits sit, side by side in your apartment, two men who would let you be whatever you wanted but didn't want you to be with someone else? Were you really so much the wavering flame about to go out (or flare into a violet only a falling combustible angel could match) that you didn't know which of us you wanted, deciding only for the day, only after you had your cup of morning coffee in your hand? Were you really so double-sided you could not draw out of Gregor the things you loved in me, draw out of me the things you loved in Gregor? Running through the empty early-morning streets of this city with your feathered Carnivale mask we never really saw your face, your gown fluttering around you like moth's wings we never really touched you.

You painted yourself as a memory (who was it that had seen you sitting with your legs cocked like that?) in the alley of a white city you'd never been to (shades of blue, absences, the only colors), and you wondered how you could feel so well the warm wind skimming the Moroccan night, how there could be Arabic music in your heart. Or maybe it was the sing-song of arguing Italians who share kitchens with their animals you wanted to hear, maybe the taste of the salty Mediterranean from southern Italy where there is a pompeii full of old bones uncovered when you brush blueblack volcanic ash from memory.

In whose mind was the look in your eyes, the one you painted from, forever lodged? Whose head did you desecrate–a grave robber with a handful of bones–to find it? Whose thoughts did you roam among, rummage through, to know exactly how he saw you?

Standing with you on the Buda side of the Danube I said, Why don't you go? Go to the city you have painted yourself in?

You Americans. You shook your head. I don't want to be disappointed by a small town, however quaint and beautiful, on some Greek island where I will miss all of my favorite movies and will have to rub elbows in bars with goatherders. I prefer the way I imagine it.

I cannot know what you were looking for, or where between here and sunken cities of a mythical long-ago there is a white city you've never seen, or what the foreign man you will meet there looks like, the smell he will leave on your clothes or the

[121]

whisper of what his pen will write to keep you forever.

Oh you stupid, stupid American. You smiled and took my face a little roughly in your hand. You are that man. I always knew I would meet you, I always knew I would leave you.

It was not Gregor, you said, you had already exchanged goodbyes with him.

(Another prayer is answered.)

It was not a city you walked out of that night, but the underworld you lived in, crossing over the river that flows through it, leaving me on the other side, stranded, without a single backward glance to make me vanish altogether.

I have gone every place we have ever been to see which has lost your shape, hoping to find you in the dawndusks along the steps that lead right into the river, in mist-draped evenings after the rain, in the deepest corners of the bars where we lost track of the flow of words and beer and the Milky Way, under the phosphorescent bridge where the old man watched, outside the iron-and-marble cafe where we first met, along the Roman wall where I exposed a whole roll of film to you, in the park where we sat through an entire season falling slowly past with you as ready as Daphne to trade in your skin for bark your arms for branches your hair for the feathery leaves of a mimosa, willing to die each winter, return each spring and bloom in hot orange flowers (You see? The earth knows without being told when to make a show of what it has).

Just below what the Soviets named the Liberation Monument (the Nazis were driven out)–a towering woman whose arms are stretched above her head, whose back is weightlessly arched, her gown a bronzed national flag frozen in a way to suggest wind, but which is better known as the Reoccupation Monument (the KGB settled in)–just beneath her you can overlook the city. A smoke-stained sky, buildings streaked in black pollution tears, its rhythm starting and stopping to church bells, factory whistles, traffic signals. What I see at this hour are lines of cars unable to move, exhaust fumes joining we-don't-care-anymore breaths in a rasping exhalation that lasts as long as the metallic cold light of this dead afternoon takes to fade finally in the west.

It was the cement-drab weight of this place, the abrasive grays you abandoned. I am the somberness of the way you painted me—in shades of dark, without color (a goodbye I didn't recognize). The immaculate stone of your city scorched white by sun, arches curving across feathery sky, drew you from the cavernous doorways of Pest which even in summer are as dank and cold as if they led to the frostbitten roots of a tree anchored in a bitter netherworld.

I understand the dolphin in you now, which is not a gray fish but a silver mammal, I understand why you left me here in the sluggishness of all this land, only the Danube to remind me, at my feet a mask whose plumes sprout a foot, the almond eyes lined with darkness, a mask exposing a mouth that could form the word that brings into being an irresistible emotion you've never felt rushing through you, the same mouth which holds the runaway river every dead sea lies in wait for.

There is no longer black or white, no longer the silvery green of bird feathers or the flowing reds and desperate yellows we covered our bodies with on the floor of your apartment, no longer the crimson of your hanging garden, no longer photographs that are anything but blue. From the indigo iridescence of long straight hair to the cobalt of horizonless eyes and the pale powder blue of arched lips gone cold in memory, a stillness death cannot approach, petrified by a city living through you, by a city's memory, I stand beneath the arches of your body, running with oily still-life drippings, a woman forever blue, beneath a sky gone violet, as far from me (the street I'm on is a shade of midnight) as the cold, double-moonlit mists of Neptune. The winter-barren trees, the only color Blind Willie ever saw, the bridge where I last saw you (bathed in pale starlight)—all blue.

BRING ON THE NIGHT

17 SEPT. 1:15 A.M. (?)

My skin cold and gloss, metallic in this neither-rain-nor-drizzle hanging mist, the dead-man's feet of this dampness swaying not in the slightest, no breeze. My skin metallic and impenetrable, this Paris midnight is burned at the edges by the lead-blue neon of Café La Lo, stained to the red of a mouth accustomed to cinnamon, a closed record shop's glowing name.

Harsher white from overhead pings off the bronze, a cold resonance to it. Zabere the pede with bronze skin. The French also say pédale, homosexuel, tante, de la jaquette flottante—he whose jacket blows lightly behind him—not much else. It is not the big deal of snow to the Eskimos who have six or seven words for it to distinguish between wet, powdery, crusted, high drifts and so on. Americans must hold most sacred of all the homosexual since they have any number of words and phrases for it—fairy, fag, tinkerbell, queer, three-dollar bill, limp-wrist, homo, fruit, pansy, queen, fill—imagine if my English were up to date.

At this hour, les clochards have emerged from the shadowed hollows of Paris, exhibiting the same regularity as lightning bugs in Provence, that one in a stone doorway with a handsomeness to his white-stubbled face (where did he get his last razor, why didn't he take it to his throat), a slow drop of rain from forehead through eyebrow, down his nose as if this man—too wet to smoke the cigarette he is gesturing for—is being washed away before my eyes. Albert the Ubiquitous, a seller of old magazines and cheap paperbacks with passionate titles, he haunts every quarter of this city I've ever been to, he gets around.

On every corner of this city, a hunchback, a deformity, a quasimodo. Moi aussi, the faggot, Zabere, with bronze skin. Quasimodo, why weren't you a poet? Ugly enough with your clouded eye, your twisted frog's mouth (a harelip, non?); misshapen enough in slumping movement along the cobblestone streets; cruel enough in circumstances; desperate enough in unrequited emotion, but not vicious enough in temperament, not evil enough in mangled heart to give it back to the world in merciless art. All pent up, it became a fabulous lump in your back, a dragging limp, a burden till the day of death. Who isn't looking for his Esmeralda? I can't have her either, we are forbidden by angels with flaming swords so we look down from our bell towers, human gargoyles shitting on passing heads like the pigeons and twisting our stone faces into ghoulish grins. A plaque on you. Hot lead on your heads! Where is our sanctuary? Surely not that cathedral like something a receding tide of time has exposed still standing (to our surprise), an Atlantean artifact, carried forward somehow to the nineteen-seventies, a guardian of a passe order of things, walls whose insides have rotted through, guts and soft organs no more, token of a soul longing to stand outside of itself, to come forth in three dimensions and now, at last, it has fled this astral plane (flying this midnight without its lights) and off to the next.

Ca suffit. On to La La Close.

2:03 a.m.

How strange what separates us from one another is so easily snapped broken breached and yet so rarely. We prefer to go on with our isolation, like dots on a balloon spreading ever farther apart, rubber surface stretching, taking us with it, as the space around us keeps getting bigger, more babies are born, more cities are built, fewer lovers form over the distances—

No, Veronique says, smaller. Everyday the connections are more numerous, deeper, invade your sleep.

Is it that we are not alive at all but simply a desire that has gathered together these bones and my bronze skin. Veronique's brown eyes and black hair. Sartre's bald overheated head, that woman's ivory-white *fingers as she handles the tiny silver spoon in her coffee, in order to act itself out?*

Veronique taps her cigarette into the amber glass ashtray and looks at the gray used-up remainder of the original as if they are on a speaking basis.

What if there are no lights at all in the sky, Zabere asks, just glimmers of desires, hopeful expectation? Just as there are no shapes we didn't project out of ourselves–the cubists made up all those cylinders and triangles and squares occurring naturally–the cold light of the unattainable is what we view through the telescope, speeding away from us at thousands of miles per hour.

Veronique blows smoke through the mandala roundness of her mouth leading to lower things, dark and unidentifiable. There is a separateness that lives within each of us, she says, there is something that exists outside of us, it is true, and wants to go on with or without you–the soul's desire to burn softly eternally on–but without you it is nothing.

And what else does love mean but that you exist? If you walked the planet unloved, if you were buried without mourners, if you howled from the top of Notre Dame at an empty city, did you make a sound?

Thank you so much sweet Zabere for trying to save my soul. (she is rolling the cigarette now between her fingers, a satan with a new recruit, feeling the texture of his sins). If it weren't for you, it's true I would be nothing more than a few photos and what you would have remembered of me. Now stop writing when I'm talking to you.

Just let me finish–

We aim great radio dishes at the sky in the abandoned, most desolate parts of the world, listen to the voice of the Great Beyond for something intelligible and check our mail for the same reason, to see what is out there, aware of us, responding to us, in need of us.

–there.

The pen makes a quiet sound of surrender on the table.

Zabere sips his capuccino through the foamy milk, runs his eyes lightly over the brick walls hung with reproductions of masterpieces tastelessly framed with thin perimeters of silver or gold, a corner of Monet's "Impression de Levant du Soleil" curling down (the glass never replaced) like a layer of night left to expose the blankness underneath. What the city rests on after all.

Look at this city, Veronique says, a mall, a row of windows on the ages.

Blowing smoke, narrowing her eyes, she drives away the stare of a young unshaven man seated beyond Zabere.

Through one rectangle of plate glass we can still be seen fornicating; in another window we still appreciate the latest in fashion, and in that one, the tattoo artists for thousands of years mark us for all time with their art and give us what we need to know who we are every morning on waking (our bodies may have been switched while our minds wandered the passages of sleep more endless than the sewers and catacombs under this hollow city).

A cubist painting, you can step onto any number of planes intersecting, continuous, simultaneous, contiguous, overlapping, coincidental, parallel, incongruous; though some never touch, never even know of the existence of each other, they lie in sight if you just lift your head. A cubist existence, the prostitute (bearing a stunning likeness to my mother) who has never even heard of spending half her straddled money on books like some of these Sorbonne students, who would rather bend over for a pack animal than spend her entire day operating a forklift at the Gillaume Warehouse. This whore of ours has never even taken a museum tour. Here in the same place, we all exist at different levels, oui?

Smiling or wincing through a cloud of smoke she pokes the air with her cigarette. This is your business Zabere my little Tarot reader, navigating between planes for the shortsighted.

Everything is a business, *non?* Zabere looks somewhere past her, at the deep night gathered behind the glass front of the cafe, locking him on the other side. I could have carried the honorific of shaman Way Back When, a well-respected man about town, they would have left me horses, spears, tobacco, wine, roasted cashews and macadamia nuts and great hanging slabs of bruyere cheese I like so well. To have me interpret their dreams or give them a sign for a hunting expedition or maybe a wedding. *Sans doute* the way it is still done in backwardsvilles like Kansas where your boyfriend with the handsome darksome face is growing bored with his life. The penniless rabble there most likely leave a dead fish or maybe fowl in exchange for a reading. Here, I am forced to use a glowing sign, a few painted mystical symbols to give people the appropriate air of the ancient and unknown. And this is why they cannot do it for themselves: they have separated real and imagined, church and state, business and pleasure, work and leisure. Once upon a time there was only living, no word for religion, it was not exiled to Sundays or holidays, it was the gravity that held them to the ground they walked on, stitched their lives together like animal hides, fell with rain on their heads whether they asked for it or not; there was never any collection to take up in its name.

Yes, Veronique says, we keep looking and hoping we will remember.

She crushes the cigarette in the faceted lump of amber where anything could be trapped–her distorted face in miniature, an insect 200 million years old (look closely), a memory, an extinct emotion.

Remember what?

The inside, what it was like on the inside. But all that is left are a few walls and columns–faces like Zirque's with sharp cheekbones, wedding frescoes in Pompeii and Herculaneum, masks worn to Carnivale to intimate to us what is beneath. We work from exteriors on down.

Yes, masks, everything in fact...

Everything—you would hardly believe it—wants to speak to you: the table I am sitting at in this cafe (a compass if you take that coffee stain over there for due north), the bright figures wheeling overhead (Orion to the Greeks, a white tiger to the Chinese, seal hunters lost in the ocean to seafaring Vikings), the cracks in the shoulder blades of animals scorched by fire, your body, an onion, the cards, trees and potted plants, your own mind, the angry red scars—even after all these months—on Veronique's wrists... yes, the great desire in everything is to be heard, to get your attention.

I told you not to write when I'm talking to you.

Un moment s'il te plait.

Oh-la-la I'm surprised I put up with you.

Why can't you wait, exercise more politeness, let a man think—

Is that what you're calling yourself these days?

Oh, enough of that, it's tired, it's old, it isn't you.

Zabere takes a dainty bite of his eclair. Did I tell you I got another call for Andy, the American? He must have a number nearly identical.

Probably.

Or it's some kind of joke Riault is playing on me.

Oh look at that stupid woman with the black beret and the little round glasses, Veronique says, she is probably carrying around a copy of Foucault she has never read. I hate these cardboard cut-out intellectuals.

Veronique, you are too critical, let them have their illusions while they last.

Did I tell you? I heard from Zirque, a postcard of Big Brutus, the biggest goddamn steam shovel this hemisphere is what he wrote I think. It wouldn't surprise me to find out he is here, gotten himself lost or picked up like a wet pigeon by a warm-blooded girl with smooth hands, whom he will subject to his didn't-mean-to-sleep-with-you-on-the-first-night-it-just-hap-pened-that-way-we-fit-together-so-well routine.

Et tu, Big Brutus?

Yes, he has a big brutus all right and knows how to use it or I wouldn't have much use for him would I?

Oh don't tease me like that. What does he need a woman for anyway?

Blue Jean his love is in her kitchen now or will be soon, cutting vegetables as always, naming them: Veronique in Paris, Sonya in Madrid, Ingrid in Bitburg, scattering the parts over the four corners of her frying pan. She sets her table for him, plates as unmanageable as Stonehenge slabs, arranged with the same meticulous attention to position, the only sympathy here is magic.

Oh I'm a better cook than she is I'm sure. And you never cook for him, always it's eating out—

Yes, I prefer not to cook.

What does she know about the crepe? The pan cannot be too hot is the trick—

Every schoolgirl knows that.

—or it won't come out spongy, it will burn and break. Spread it evenly, quickly and it will hang loosely together, a perfect wonder. But this is nothing, it is the sauce—

Go ahead Zabere, Veronique's grin is impish, why not give in to a good woman. I know one or two in Pigale who'll make you shout the names of the 103 elements, forget your own, you will know for certain you're a man.

Doll, *cheri*, I have, you know that, it's not bad but it's not for me. Think how much you adore *men*, you can sympathize. And I thought there were 104 elements. Didn't the Americans just discover a new one?

Made a new one is more like it. It disappeared before they were even sure it was there. Veronique lights up again, waving a hand with three rings gleaming, the extinguished match tracing its path with thin blue smoke.

I wonder about Blue Jean—her real name is Rae Anne, did I ever tell you? How does she live through the never-knowing of her man? Never caring, never expecting, never asking like a good Theravada disciple is what I recommend. The grass of those Kansas fields has whispered something to her while she sleeps. About how to be there season after season, how to let herself die a little, turn brown, save herself for a spring of eternal return when she will feel more alive than the first day of creation.

He never takes her with him?

For a second, perhaps less, a darkhaired waitress in a white T-shirt holds a position nearly identical to the painted Toulouse-Lautrec woman in a red dress, her black hat flaring, erupting with red plumage (she is painted lifesize on the wall beside one of the Cafe's gas lamps, all of the lights gas as a quaint lure in the dark to floating-past late-nighters).

He takes her once in a while, Veronique answers, so he says.

How vicious to be so in need of someone so charming so unreliable so unrepentant.

She can get along without him, no matter how long. He is the one who would wash away—no more than a chalk drawing on the sidewalk—would fade beyond the light if one day she were not there when he returned. He knows it. He is the one who cannot find the strength for the day-to-day of staying, who is afraid of dying, and of himself and of listening too closely to the things Blue Jean hears.

He is—

He wants the stones and bricks and railroad tracks in his ten- or twelve-stoplight downtown to speak his name. No matter when he is dead. He wants his name spoken always and everywhere he has been.

Merde alors!

What is it? Zabere asks turning toward the door.

Je ne peux pas le croire. Look who is here and what he has dragged with him all the way from Kansas.

ZABERE, HOW CAN YOU let him call you that?

Oh it's a thing of affection, really I don't mind, the same way he calls you Blue Jean.

The Creole Queer doesn't sound very affectionate to me. He can be so inconsiderate sometimes.

The brick wall passing is rough canvas for a '50s Cadillac convertible, white and immaculate, driving out of an American past. Bright colors of nostalgia swirl in Blue Jean's head, mix with the memory of Route 69 empty at sunset, of the 1106 Burger Drive-In Zirque and Red and Earl took her to summer evenings, the three men like boys harassing everyone within name-calling.

But this is Paris, where she has never been—a crowd will flock to her at the Corner Cafe, pigeon wings flapping around her—to hear about it. The city where everyone speaks a musically different language and Kansas City isn't such a big town by comparison. Only what about that woman with the tight skirt, the black silk stockings and high heels—

Zabere, is that a man?

It is common in this quarter. A weaker woman, I know, would wish for the Pittsburg quarter but she would miss so much that is not the Eiffel Tower, that is not entombed in the Louvre or mentioned in the travel brochures.

I'm happy to be here, I'm just not used to all this.

Ah, you make me feel like Lancelot taking my arm that way. Avaunt knaves and dogs, the fair lady is with me.

Oh Zabere—

You look *magnifique* today, the black of your shirt sets off the bronze in your hair so well, and your hair is so lovely around your face, it's complemented I mean by those, those flakes of pale red, how do you say-

Freckles?

Oui! What Renoir wouldn't have given to paint you.

Really Zabere—

This way, down the stairs, yes, I have friends in the lowest of places. Here we are.

The man leaning against the doorway is shirtless, just a black

[133]

leather vest, his beard ending in twin spikes, one on either side of his chin (with that beard, his head could pass for some kind of garden tool), foreign looking, dark skinned, he looks like he could give Zirque or Earl a hard time.

The place is filled with racks of clothes, studded leather belts, shoes, boots that reach the knees, earrings as unwieldy as chandeliers, hats and motorcycle caps, the walls hung with film posters (movies she's never heard of), paintings.

Next to each other, there are two women on separate canvases, the work of the same hand—angular lines seen at impossible perspectives (a mirror folded at the back of the eye), the brushstrokes deep, the skin of one midnight blue, the other a marble green. Staring back at Blue Jean, regarding her watchfully, they remind her of—

Yes, Veronique posed for those. When she's not selling a pill to kill boredom or a syringe full of the voices of seraphim singing to the veins, she makes a little extra money that way.

You mean she—

Oh look here. Zabere points to a black-and-white xeroxed page. The explosion of a milk drop in water, magnified and placed next to the mushroom cloud of an atomic blast, inverted and shrunk down. Nearly identical in shape, in evolution.

I gave it to them, Zabere says, as a demonstration. Isn't it strange how perfectly congruous they are? Except that one is inverted, one is the far grander of scales.

Don't that beat all? Rae Anne says looking more closely. When I was a little girl I used to do that with milk. In the sink. And pretend the explosions were real.

Everything that happens happens again on every level, Zabere says. This is a diorama we live in. He winks. That's half my secret to fortune telling.

A woman behind the counter in a black beret, straight black hair, black lipstick, a gold star on her cheek says I saw someone who looked just like you Zabere, carrying on abominably with a prostitute—Get a room! I shouted.

But did he have silver eyeshadow? Zabere asks tilting his head back to set off his make-up better. Did he have sparkles in his lovely hair so much like black wool?

No he—it couldn't have been you, you wouldn't dress that way—but he looked so much like you.

Oh this dress is so beautiful, where did it come from? Blue Jean says sweeping it in front of her, posing in the mirror. I've never seen anything like it.

Too many colors to name, sheer and flowing with enough layers to make it tasteful.

The girl in the black beret who is beckoning with fingers to a green-eyed black cat on the counter says, I once knew a married couple who owned two cats: one playful and fearless, a little *mechant,* mischievous; the other always in hiding, shy. The couple were exactly the same way.

There, Zabere says to Blue Jean, you see what I mean?

ZIRQUE DROPS HER WRIST, shakes his head exactly once, as if that is all it will take to shake loose the bad feeling.

Should've known. Probably at the bottom of one a my sleepless nights.

Almost the bottom of the Seine. The cigarette in Veronique's mouth (for no reason Zirque can think of) is unlit.

I had a dream, he says, I tried to show Earl a picture of us together. But when I pulled it out, I couldn't make out your face. She's pretty Earl, I swear it, I kept sayin an held it up to the light 18 different ways, but your face wouldn't come clear.

What is that you have in your hand?

A bit of paper folded so many times the creases have begun to split, a Bic-pen-and-ink drawing: a snowman, a pine tree, a hardly-more-than-stick woman with long hair and a girlish cuteness to her, looking through one of four quarters of a mullioned window, an X about where the stick-girl's heart would have been.

Veronique puts her cold cigarette into an ashtray. What's that doing in your hand? A charm? A bit of garlic around your neck? She smirks. All right we won't talk of her if it will make you feel better. We will talk about Zirque, trapped being who he is for eternity, tired of being Zirque, distracting himself from himself with a change of scenery.

Slipping the square of paper back in his wallet, he says Sometimes I feel pressed right up against the glass of an extra dimension to this place, pressed up against who I could be in it. Somehow we got the heat a the sun inside us, it wants out but there's no way at all except in the briefest a moments.

A regular Zirque the Dane.

Five thousand years a civilization an we're standin on the same brink worn smooth by generations a footsteps, no further into chaos or godhead, we are no voyant startin at the horizon where our forbears breathed their last. We're crowded like the Persians against the sea the Spartans'll push us into—and we won't be comin back.

What we see when we look in the windows is the same, Veronique says, only the shopkeepers have changed.

To shop, or not to shop, that is the question.

Wasn't Hamlet two people at least? Veronique asks. One mad, one sane? One cunning and driven, protecting the other one, the distant hesitant vulnerable one looking down on it all? What character talks to himself more I would like to know?

Aren't there two worlds at least? The way we live, passin the time granted us here in cafes watchin the steam a coffee rise past our faces, watchin it become the white cloud out of a manhole cut into cobblestone, a mandala of passage, this way, the evaporatin whiteness risin across the dead street at this hour like fog from an underworld.

You belong to one, she to the other.

Can't help the way I love her. She changes the contours a spacetime is what it is.

Yes. And who asked you to?

You told me once I'm not attached t'anythin but it's you,

you're the one—

Love remains after the... after the loved one has vanished, leaving ghost pains, the amputee's complaint. All of our ancient loves, our lost loves, return. Eternally. As pain. As three-in-the-morning mist (you've felt her presence in the stillness of that hour, non?). Another person can... ahh... What touches us once. The sunken impossibly beautiful island city Atlantis. Has always been.

So I've heard.

And what about her leaving you alone with me?

Pretty much permission, he says, though a hard one to figure into the rest a Blue Jean.

It's a thing between her and me, Veronique says, she's made a gift of you to me, *oui?* Though of course to bring it up would break all etiquette.

She'll come back here with what she's bought, sayin wait till they see this back in Pittsburg, but she'll be usin the scarf she's modelling or the shirt she's holdin to cover over what she doesn't want to think about. She won't ask.

Well perhaps this time, I would prefer her.

Can I write something in your book? Rae Anne asks.

Oui, bien sur. Zabere hands it to her with a pen.

After death I think you see things differently, I think human beings become sheets of light, ruffled tin kind of, with colors coming off of them, like at the south pole

—what do they call those lights?

—like the aurora borealis, they are light with black spots where they've despaired in their lives, when they've lost faith and are ready to die, like sunspots. If you could see it from outer space, the earth would be a sea of lights.

That's what I believe.

Ah, oui, Zabere says looking over the handwriting with its deep loops for g's and f's, a flowing hand, almost spiralling in on itself.

Zabere's corollary to Rae Anne's entry: Like stars these people of light get magnitudes and classifications. There, walking by with his cane, a long-ago-collapsed-and-lost-its-great-internal-fire white dwarf. There is Vincent, a red giant (blue stars are the hottest, I know, but I am overcome by the poetic correctness of the color to match his hair). That anti-homosexual—by the look he is giving me—a shrivelled yellow midget. Close.

ZG, THE LETTERS OF OUR first names together—Z, Z—it's almost si, si. *Oui?*

Jamais, jamais Zabere—not a look, not a thought, not me.

Ah well, I couldn't help giving it a try. Veronique is up to the same thing exactly with Blue Jean I'm sure. Would you like a reading?

You got enough Coca-Cola cans here to build a Boeing 747.

Every morning it is impossible for me to get up without having one. You should see me, squinty-eyed in morning light, no matter how dim. I need one to take the taste out of my mouth, sweeten my disposition, to jump start me. It's not the real thing anymore, just caffeine. I'd like the world to sing in perfect harmony with the invisible order of things.

There is a poster of Marlon Brando—draped over the handlebars of a motorcycle, wearing a puffy biker's hat—from *The Wild Ones.* Zabere leans against the wall, says I coulda been somebody, I coulda been a contenda, and sounds so much like Brando, Zirque laughs.

My father tried to make a little man out of me, Zabere says, pushed me into the ring to sink or swim when I was ten. I learned how for three years but I didn't like hitting the other boys—you can imagine—such sweet faces. One named Robert, an American, he was the toughest I'd ever seen. Sandy hair and blue eyes and such a handsome face, but oh he had such a right hand.

Sometimes I wonder what my life would have been like if we had stayed on our tropical island. The memory of the place—it must be from a photograph, I was not even two when we came to France—I remember a wood-and-stone city near the coast, whitewashed houses wavering in the heat, crowded open markets in a flat downtown with nothing over two or three stories, the smell of rotting fish and drying mud in the humid hanging air, all of the flash and color and excitement of a city's facade having gone into the red blouses, the dangling golden earrings, the grand smiles, the bright yellow kerchiefs keeping the sun off black heads—a place where you always feel a sense of hello how are you today, belonging.

What made you leave in the first place?

I was just a baby, an infant, my mother insisted I was possessed—fits of crying lasting through entire nights the way she tells it. When she had the dream of a butterfly trapped inside a hideous warted flower, she was afraid for my soul. Though butterfly is Spanish slang for *maricon* and maybe that's what the dream meant, who can tell they're so unreliable. Anyway, she brought me to my shaman-uncle who exorcised the spirit and got a few bottles of rum for his trouble. Probably I had some bad gas and my uncle is still laughing about it all these years later.

The phone ringing, startles them, makes them exchange half a smile each.

Alo? No, there is no Andy here... Yes, that is the number but there is no one named Andrew, I live here alone—

Zabere shrugs as he puts down the phone. She hung up.

I HOPE YOU DON'T mind the edge of the bed, the wicker chair is already full of things I refuse to put away.

This is strange for me. Her hands on her blue-jeaned knees, her body stiff with trying not to show how uncomfortable she is. I guess I had to sit across from what I've been losing him to all these years.

[139]

Of course, it's expected.

I don't know what good it will do to know what you smell like, to know if he has ever brought the scent home. I've hated you an the rest of them—you especially because you're more than a night's worth of no sleep—I've hated you so often when I was alone in Kansas, but it's so hard now because we're here in person, it's not your fault. I can almost stand it, knowin you. He doesn't even realize after all this time but it's not the unfaithfulness I mind so much, it's never knowing if one day he'll decide not to come back, if he's found something better, forgotten me an all of us back home.

You shouldn't worry, Veronique says, I look after him, I keep him from worse things. There is nothing between us anywhere but here. I have always wanted to meet you. We are, after all, joined through this silly man so afraid of death he cannot sit still, like a child in church. A spacious smile splits open. Maybe he has told you women appeal to me almost as much as men. You're blushing.

Veronique reaches up slowly, traces the length of Rae Anne's eyebrow with the nail of her thumb, sweeps up a bit of coppery hair, wraps it behind an ear, a vanishing moment, the same in which the leaf of a tree whispers against the window until the breeze dies.

In a way, I have always known you, Veronique says, through him, the way he reached out for you but his hand touched me, adjusted himself to the shape of a body he was not used to. Ah, but this kind of talk makes you uncomfortable.

Is that yours? Rae Anne asks standing up, pointing at the easel, changing the subject. Do you paint?

Veronique shakes her head. No. It is set up just in case I ever decide I want to.

I used to draw when I was a little girl. Mostly made-up things—unicorns, trolls, horses with wings, floating islands with crystal cities on them attached to nothing...

She sits back down amid the give and squeal of springs.

Yes, Veronique says remembering a snowman, a pine tree, a little girl trapped by creases of paper, behind glass, tucked inside a wallet a woman holding at her heart a child.

I am surprised you didn't draw something for Zabere's journal.

Oh I couldn't draw what I meant. And the words—well, Zirque is better at that. With words I mean. Itching I don't know where, he puts his finger on exactly the right spot. In one little sentence he says what's been buildin up in me for years. That's how I got into trouble with him in the first place. Rae Anne laughs. He tells the most ridiculous lies, doesn't he?

He remembers through you, Veronique says, through everything he sends you as a keepsake. She leans over slowly and kisses Rae Anne on the cheek. He loves you like nothing else on this planet.

Tingling in the place where Veronique kissed her (it's the buzz licking the end of a battery gave her as a little girl), she asks Does he?

Mais bien sur, you cannot tell you are the only thing he cannot leave forever, the only one at all?

WHAT ABOUT THAT BEATING when I was three, when we lived in a stone house with two stories and my window looked out upon a huge ancient cherry tree, the strapping my father gave me for no reason I can remember, the one that kept me silent for a week, did something go into hiding? Is there any connection to my penchant for le metro, the catacombs, for dance clubs below street level? Close.

SHE KNOWS YOU IN the moment it takes for you to say something, *non?*

Zabere nods.

She sees the love in him—she is drawn to it—and if it were not for that she would have left him a long time ago, though she goes on thinking she can get the rest around this shining core to change.

It is tempting. Knocking an electron or two off lead makes

gold. One little electron.

She reaches down for his hand, lifts it up, noticing something for the first time. She looks at the other one, runs her thumb over the knuckles. What happened to your hand? Did you get into a fight?

The door of Etienne's Citroen, Zabere says, he closed it on me the other night.

But this looks like a toothmark, like you hit someone in the mouth.

But Veronique, me? You know best of all I have learned to walk away from even those men who are most deserving of a good drawing and quartering.

14 SEPT., 3:12 PM
Faggot, buggerer, cornholer, fudgepacker, mud rider, fruitcake, pole-smoker, buttfucker, Creole Queer...

RIAULT WITH HIS CRAZY *red hair said to me—he was wearing his Einstein persona, sparks going off behind his head like Quatorze de Juillet fireworks, he said—I get my inspiration sometimes from a ceiling that has leaked badly over several years—I want to show people there's something going on in a stain.*

No, I told him, it's going on in your head.

His abstracts are nothing at all recognizable, there is no correspondence to a real object. Yes, a stain blown up large, something spilled over. Where is the line drawn in charcoal, the color sch2eme tracing out a connection we'7ve always felt existed between us and what sur5rounds us but had never known exactly how we were joined to it, had never been ab9le to picture, where has it been translat3ed for us into a concrete language we can understand?

QUATRE VENTS—THIS IS THE perfect place for us tonight, *oui?* Veronique's brown eyes shine darkly. A window for each of us. Her smile, meant to be reassuring, rubs Blue Jean ever so snake-scale lightly the wrong way.

When're you gonna let yer hair grow? Zirque doesn't look up, but he's talking to Veronique.

I like it here Blue Jean says, ignoring the bare leg slipping alongside hers under the table. Pittsburg needs one, a real Old World cafe, a little high society.

You'd have to import your customers, Zirque says, running a hand through thick black hair damp with evening's drizzle.

You don't think it would catch on? Something genuine European in our corner of the world? Most of the mining families in Crawford County come of immigrant stock.

Well, I guess if you cooked up hamhocks'n beans insteada escargot you might pull it off.

How can you eat those things, ew! They look like black garden slugs.

No worse than a prairie oyster, go on try one, you'll be hooked. It's just appearances, honey, and a bad reputation in your head.

What's in my head is one thing, what goes in my mouth is another.

Zabere! Veronique smacks his hand. You are incorrigible. Writing even here. On their last night in Paris.

Pardon s'il te plait. It was what she said, it clicked something off.

What? Blue Jean asks.

This bit about what is in your head. Sex is no different, it's all in the mind, 90 percent or so anyway.

Well then you can stop tryin to talk Zirque into jumping the fence, Zabere, Blue Jean says touching her coppery hair lightly to make sure it's still in place, just close your eyes an you can have the time a your life.

Well, it's not quite–

I know what he means, Zirque says. A man can do a thing're two same as a pretty woman an with your eyes closed who could tell? It's the thought a who's doin it–an who it's bein done with. Usin your own hand t'take an example, ain't no good without a major motion picture goin in your head.

The mind is a bottomless pit, Veronique says. Did you know that some mental disorders are peculiar to men and women who are intelligent, who are highly creative? It seems they have unique ways of coping. Most any mental illness is engineered to protect the mind from the tyrannical alcoholic father, from the rape inflicted by your own brother, from witnessing the death of too many loved ones at too young an age, from never having been shown the love any infant needs as much as its bottle. She turns to Zabere. Perhaps *homosexualite* is just such a disorder. You see how many creative people–artists, dancers, writers–fit into this category.

Oh it's not an illness it's something you're born with, like a prick. There it is and most of the world is horrified but you have the audacity to be proud of it.

Sex is a religious experience, Zirque says popping a bloated black body shiny with butter, fragrant with garlic, into his mouth. When it's good. Starts in your head, shoots through your body, then frees you a the spacetime continuum altogether.

Not a religious experience, a religion, Veronique corrects. With witless priests attending.

Sex is part of religion, Zabere says.

Religion is part a life, should've never settled out–the heart is the church the temple the synagogue an should've stayed there.

Religion is a device–contrived, devised; a defense mechanism. So goes the theory posited by Brulliard.

Oh (Zirque's head, hung over his plate, pops up). You mean it got started to protect the mind of Homo Erect For The First Time–not too long out of the egg of the unconscious where it incubated a million years or two–from slipping back into yolky blackness.

I am the one slipping into blackness, Zabere says, I lost four hours today Veronique, I swear it, I cannot trace back where I was this evening, earlier tonight, I lost track somehow.

Mythology came first, Veronique says, using superstitions as tent poles to hold it up, to keep out a night wider than consciousness ever hoped to be, as easily lost in it as a candle in deep space. The mind is otherwise naked, malleable, easily deformed, cratered, broken. Making riddles of the stars, spinning stories to go with how things got to be the way they are, tracing out shapes in the sky with the glowing end of a smoldering stick and getting to know them, hello how are you and be on familiar terms.

Zabere, what do you mean you lost four hours, Blue Jean asks, what happened?

Oh someone here listens to me at least. I mean four hours, just gone...

A way to make caves bearable as much as fire and animal hides, Zirque says, you see it painted in the deepest and darkest recesses, Altamira and Lescaux.

And look, Zabere says pushing back in his chair, looking down at his waist, this belt I'm wearing isn't mine, but I found it in my closet. Along with a shirt I never bought—it's not my taste at all. Who have I brought over? It is either Riault or my memory playing tricks on me.

They threw it, Zirque is saying, his hand almost as dark as Zabere against the immaculate background of the white tablecloth, over their hairy backs like a rough hide to keep off the cold, the hard caress of a rock floor. And their shadows, hunched over an half savage, are thrown on the cave walls at the backs of our minds, by the age-old light a still-burnin beliefs. And once in a while we crouch down—

(Zabere, do you remember the darkhaired waitress at La Lo?)

—and from a distance who could tell?

EVERYTHING SPEAKS TO YOU, the bathroom walls for example, riddled with graffiti. Faggots of the world unite—so that we can kill you all at once. Silly fag, dicks are for chicks (en anglais). The only thing I feel when I kill a fag is the recoil—and it feels good.

[145]

RIAULT HAS GONE TOO FAR this time. He's found my journal somehow, he's gotten in my apartment... all right, I am not attentive to security, I've found clothing not mine–has he moved someone in? And in my journal look.

Zabere hands his journal to Veronique.

Zabere the little faggot whose skin is not bronze at all but more like tissue paper. It's me he's talking about with bronze skin, I'm the one who kept him from being beaten and left for dead by that drunk in the metro. Instead, he was the one bleeding from his mouth and nose, unable to get up. I have to do the hard things while he writes in this journal, I'm the one who is there to take care of him as much as I despise his weakness, his habits, his effeminate taste without me he would be worse off still.

It's not my handwriting, it's similar, as if someone were trying to write like me. Why should Riault try to imitate that? Does he think I cannot tell? This is evil of him, just because I refuse to sleep with him anymore, this is the final straw.

Maybe. Veronique says handing back the journal. Maybe just the penultimate.

...WHILE I PIN DOWN this problem of lan3guages, yes that's it, these thin4gs speak but not always in ways we can understand and we run into problems of interpr7etation, problems–

VERONIQUE, I AM POSSESSED it is certain, my mother was right, there is another soul inhabiting my body, it is the source of the blackouts–

Oh don't be so melodramatic, Zabere. Evil spirits have nothing to do with it.

Non?

Veronique shakes her head.

How can you be so sure?

I finally met this lookalike of yours. Last night, at Bar Dix. She doesn't look up from her sketch, working–unbelievably–on the easel which has been in her room unused for Zabere doesn't know how many years.

Zabere completely loses interest in the conversation, looks over Veronique's charcoal drawing, sees something inchoate but growing–is that a head in there?–taking shape out of the swirling lines, and wonders what demon is coming into full-winged bloom.

So you saw him, he says, no longer distracted. Does he really look like me?

Your very twin.

IT's NOT THAT ALL of creation wanted to turn and look full-length at itself–the stars our heavenly counterparts, of magnitudes beyond measuring–it's just a little warmth the stars were after, a firm chest padded with tickly woolliness to rest the weary head, a little something to ward off the cold and the winter of long nights, that's all.

THE RIVER IS NOT FAR from here, the Seine of polished black glass, a bit of sky (look, you will see the crescent moon wavering in it) flowing over the earth, dividing the city into left bank and right, this side and the other side.

Ah, to be swallowed in shadow, for the four-in-the-morning darkness to close over my head as if I had jumped into the Seine's polluted waters, the stillness unbreakable, a deep long dive into the liquid black, back into inky yolkiness, yes. Like Albert the Ubiquitous, Albert the Barely Conscious, cover me, let the day–when everything is so plainly visible–become extinct. Take away the photographic hardness–the blurring of Impressionism is so much more preferable–yes, bring on the night. Zabere Andre Saint-Martin would like to blend in as perfectly as possible, to be a brick in the red-brick midnight, a telephone-pole sentry along this rainwashed street. Let me run into the sewers, let me become this city, as easily as the Way Back When a shaman slipped into a bear hide and grew the claws of the grizzly–so I will be no more noticed than a cobblestone being stepped on. Let the glow of the streetlight show nothing more than a deluded shadow, a slippery shape–

lessness in the night, *oui,* nothing more than that silently following shadow, sent to hover over me on black wings, protect that inner part of me naked, malleable, easily deformed, yes a dark guardian angel sent in my own image, my very twin.

THE NORTHWEST PASSAGE
a Portolano

"YES, A POWER WE CALL SILA... A STRONG SPIRIT, THE
UPHOLDER OF THE UNIVERSE, OF THE WEATHER, IN FACT
ALL LIFE ON EARTH—SO MIGHTY THAT HIS SPEECH TO MAN
COMES NOT THROUGH ORDINARY WORDS BUT THROUGH
STORMS, SNOWFALL, RAIN SHOWERS, THE TEMPESTS OF
THE SEA, THROUGH ALL THE FORCES THAT MAN FEARS OR
THROUGH SUNSHINE, CALM SEAS OR SMALL, INNOCENT
PLAYING CHILDREN WHO UNDERSTAND NOTHING."
—ESKIMO SHAMAN

THERE IS THIS PLACE. NOT A WHOLE LOT TO PUT ON A postcard, not likely to dot any map showing more than the state. Who knows what arbitrary-imaginary meridian skewers it through? The Duke of Pallucca, walking stick tapping, heading up Crawford Street, past Vacca's Bakery, whitewashed, trimmed in red, red-and-white checked curtains in the windows, a bread-baking operation since the turn of the century, it could pass for a house.

October Kansas winds blowin Lyman Kishpaugh's dry voice around, a muttering from Vacca's, he once found himself a part-time home there among the stone ovens and old-world smells leavened with semolina. Old Lyman with his Depression cap aslant, he could lift a ton, used to say about him, but he couldn't spell it. An awkward face looking like it was having trouble holding itself together there was something about him made you think he was half angel when he smiled, the innocence of a child in a full-grown man, the kids teased him regular as the whistle of the 1 o'clock train on the Santa Fe line.

Carnival left Lyman behind—some say it was a circus—a 17-year-old idiot boy in the strange playpen of a young man's body. God put the strength of a draught horse into that physique a his, but left enough outta his head it was anybody's guess who had more sense, him or the horse. An odd-jobber in bib overalls, time to time on his insomniac walks the Duke heard that straw-dry rustle of Lyman's carried on the wind out of the south, but this time it was the memory of a dream that bellied out the Duke's sails his walking stick for a rudder, sent him drifting up Crawford to take a right at the corner of McKay, down past Pallucca's Market (his cousin Dicky's place). Lyman already old and feeble when the Duke was a kid chasing Yankee autographs, never met Lyman, but that's who it was dropped him through the web of a sticky sleep near five in the morning.

Out of Bartelli's Blue Goose Bar, closed many years, its ceiling skeletal, rafters showing through like ribs, a skylight of sorts letting in sun and moon, star and rain, drifting flakes of snow (Prohibition and the war both over, Augie Dorchy, county sheriff, would cough and clear his throat in the open doorway, summertime, the heat insufferable, and Ozzie Bartelli would get whiskey bottles out of sight, men's hat's would cover glasses, women's purses would swallow them–they were all votes after all–no whiskey in Kansas even then, by the bottle or by the drink, only beer), out of the Blue Goose Millo Farneti emerged, blinking in the late-afternoon sun like it was the mouth of a coal mine or Erebus itself he'd just put behind him. Untamable gray-white hair streaked with black, he had keys to the abandoned Blue Goose where he'd squirreled away manuscripts documenting doings of the comers and goers in Frontenac and Pittsburg, a crotchety Italian monk still speaking all-but-buried Latin, mapping who'd been where with whom and said what, the filing cabinet he used the only furniture left inside the sooty bare brick walls.

"Well hey Ceppo hello what–where, where you headed?"

"Why d'you wanna call me that? Makes me sound like one a the Marx Brothers."

"Well you know youre a, youre just a blockhead sometimes, same as they were."

"Granite slab of a man is more like it," the Duke said slapping his ribs, "upholdin this itty-bitty fair city of ours."

"Yeah awright, awright–"

"What says the Farneti? Yer head gettin any lighter with all that stuff yer dumpin in that file cabinet?"

"Well, I–gee-suss! it hurts sometimes when I take a step the wrong way. I... I tell you, the pain," Millo said, a hand to indicate, "dont just stay here in my hip, it–it grabs the Samsonites an travels down my legs."

"Time's kicked you unfair an unlookin more than once."

"You sure as hell don't say. Waitll–wait–one day youll be draggin a load a years behind you."

"I'm draggin around enough as it is," the Duke said with a friendly pat on his belly. No more than five and a half feet, he knew he went for two-hundred or better, his build solid, squarish (Ceppo all right), deepset eyes and stern eyebrows, only a silvery quickness in the eyes betrayed a forgiving nature, a deep resevoir of calm accumulated over the long walked distances.

Facing east, the Missouri-Kansas line four or five miles distant, Millo was looking past the Duke, down the street where (the Duke knew) he saw immigrant miners hanging off the trolley after a long day's journey into the shiny black boniness of stubborn Kansa earth, the ones who lived nearby hopping off into a ditch along the road like grasshoppers, his Pa among them. Never one for diggin any deeper than a finger in his ear, all Millo said was, "Grasshopper Korner." That, the Duke was pretty sure, was the way he'd spell it, too.

"In New York they went up, piled it against the sky," the Duke said, "here, we tunnelled down, sank shafts."

"And you, youre still in reverse, tunnellin backwards. Klink, klink. *Nunc pro tunc*, that–thats yer motto. Willing to–you wanna trade in pieces of now for bits of then, thats it aint it?" Millo accused.

The Duke shrugged.

"I... you know somethin you–youre lookin a little like an old silver dollar been passed to one hand too many," Millo said.

The Duke nodded. "Never was much of a sleeper." He stepped into the open door of Bartelli's, the early evening sun dimming to an odd glow inside, the groundup years, bits of plaster and wood, fallen laughter crunching underfoot, brittle in the pale gold October light.

Millo, eyeing the shadow of Duke's walking stick on the floor, pointed and said, "You know there, there wuz a Greek in Alexandria, Egypt you know, figured out near 2,000 years before Columbus set sail—he figured out the earth wuz round just by payin attention to the slant a shadows. Blieve that? Came up with a, a fair reckonin of the circumference of the whole goddamn earth besides. Got wind of no shadow bein cast on the bottom of a well at noon on summer solstice in some other city in Egypt, knew damn well well bottoms were in shadow where he was."

"Couldn't keep much from the old-time Greeks," the Duke said. And rapped the jumble of faded-away music and fallen roof shingles with the heel of his stick, his hand capping the bearded old man's face carved into the top. "Gnomon's his proper name," the Duke said, lifting the stick and looking into the tiny petrified eyes, "little on the silent side but a good listener."

"More than you can—more than can be said of most of the people around here."

The Duke looked out a window painted over instead of taped with cardboard, Schaeffer's spelled backwards coming through the beige chaos of strokes.

"You know I came across a photo of Lyman Kishpaugh stuck between a stack of unidentifiables in the basement. Black and white, Jim Morey grinnin in the picture with im, thirties or forties I guess, he's got a smile but it's like he's not used to it, havin his picture taken, posin with a friend. I gave it a spot on my clipboard there's somethin about it."

"If it aint under the sun, its in youre basement, thats my guess."

"It's an illness we've both got," the Duke said, "can't throw anything out."

"You know that–that head a yours got about as much in it as yer basement. No tellin wot you can call up from the vasty deep a memory. I bet–I dont doubt you even know the name a that long-ago Greek–"

"Eratosthenes," the Duke said. "But it's strange what 10 minutes worth of a nap– 'bout five this morning–dredged up, it was him all right–"

"Erastosthenes?"

"Nooooooo." The Duke swatted with his stick. "Lyman. He was pointin, pointin real hard an squintin–he couldn't speak for some reason–tryin to ... I think Lyman knows somethin he was tryin t'spill."

"Lyman never cud–he wasnt a stutterer but, you know, he repeated himself–he–he–cudnt string together more than three sentences straight, you know."

"That a fact?"

"Well here–heres somethin else for ya since its a, a fact-collectin expedition youre on: the last 13 cantos, you know, the Commedia Divina, Alighieri wuz dead and those unlucky 13 were lost. His magnus opus wuddve–theyda likely never swum up from the depths a limbo if the Infernal Italian himself hadnt–hadnt shown up in his son's dream and given latitude and longitude of hidin place." Millo nodded for emphasis. "That–thats the truth as I know it. Might be... there might be something to this Kishpaugh chimera."

"You remember Lyman?"

"Well Lyman, he–he wuz the most insulted man in town. We kids we–we... I regret it now, we threw rocks at him. Called him Chief cuz he considered himself a fireman, chased us off the enjin all the time. Useta howl an bark everytime we saw him, too, I don't remember why anymore, you know–maybe he–maybe he fancied himself some kinda dog ketcher, too. Never caught–no he ran after us a lot never caught a thing he wuz chasin I don't think."

The Duke nodded, considerin what the slant of Lyman's hat might've had to say about the depth of his faith or the circumference of his heart, must've gotten a little thick-skinned after a while all the stones and names thrown his way. Considerin the picture again, the Duke decided Lyman's slow-to-spread smile held no grudges, no bitterness toward the world, knowin he wasn't goin to get much from it–not smilin half as broad as Jim Morey–somehow lettin on that in the little he knows he knows the shot's over in the flash of the camera, realized dimly the most could come of the photo was something to hang in the bakery where he slept, but okay he's still glad Jim wanted to be in it with him and hoped he could keep one to tape up over his cot.

Millo headed out the door of the Blue Goose and the Duke followed him into the paling October light, the darkening sky leaving the streetlights to catch slow fire along Mckay, a due east-west street, takes you through downtown Frontenac, it's lined with lopsided angels–poles with lamps–leaning according to the unfathomable laws governing such things, crooked marchers frozen forever in a procession toward sunset this time of day.

"Well you know gaddammit," Millo said, snapping the padlock on the old Blue Goose Bar's aimlessly silently swirling dust motes behind the painted-over and cardboarded-up windows, "I'm never gonna get back to the–the house I was born in, I cant even make it back to that street I–"

"Don't worry Millo, the trip t'Hades is the same from everywhere."

"I dont care about my body after Im dead, you don't go up or down when you die, I know that, but you might go sidewayz, the point is I wanna live where I came from, I dont rattle around as much..."

Everything unfamiliar a bump that shakes Millo up, even though the house where he's lived many years now is only a couple of blocks away–

"Gaddamnit I know, I know its–its just around the korner but that–thats where creation opened up an spit me out. I haven't been able to–to think about anything else. Id offer the woman who owns it now twice market value, Id–but I know she won't take it and thats the–well, you know that place its–thats the life root."

If Millo could put out a rhizome, he'd grow under the streets and come up in the ten-by-ten kitchen with its black iron stove where Ma used to cook for his brothers and sisters and Pa and him–

"You got the home pull," the Duke said, "like a salmon."

"I'm no, no sale man, cant even get you even to buy wot I'm sayin. You know its that house I–I always understood that that was home."

"You hear about that dam somewhere in New Jersey?"

"Oh geezuss, the one the water backed up–eliminated a whole fukn town. I couldnt take it–it wud always keep me a little off tilt to–t'have that happen here."

Millo the Ptolemy, Frontenac with its coaldust still clouding memory, brick shells of abandoned good times in a hey-day, the streetlamps slanting off while the sun sets, more to him than the minarets of mosques shadowed in moonlit Istanbul, the once-and-future Constantinople, crucible of the Byzantine empire, Frontenac still the center of the universe for Millo he'd come up with an elaborate scheme a cycles & epicycles & whatnot to describe the motion of everything else around this place pitted with mines. How to find the exactness where some internal organ of his maybe is buried, maybe it was that after being born in that house–hospital too long a haul in those days–Ma buried the placenta & umbilical cord underneath the welcome mat, always make sure, like the Navajos do, that he'd come home. Maybe what he needs to do is dig up the whole front yard...

"Wasn't gold the alchemists of old were lookin for," the

Duke said, "was the Northwest passage."

"A little–a little off course for them dontcha think?"

Millo's search for anchorage, for ballast so that he wouldn't wind up a rudderless moth making odd spiral patterns, bouncing off the glass outside of Farley's Tavern over in Pittsburg driven half mad by the soft light inside. Hardly different from Bartelli's Starlit Bare Brick Inn, empty except for what's locked away in there, the aimless motes, cigarette-cigarsmoke wafted off to a place beyond the sunset, a permanent haze that clouds the way for the moon or rising stars or shades still dancing to music no one else hears anymore.

Memory not enough, was what Millo was getting at, not without a person, a place, maybe both, to lend weight to them, bring them back from a lost continent floating on a sea of distant things, a rumored terra australis incognita needed to keep the world from tilting on its axis any further, though really it was Millo needed a counterweight (up from the mines, one cage always full of miners, the other with coal-less shale), coming into the fifth season, Millo talked about it sometimes, four already behind him the way he saw it, it mite not exist, but it shud.

OCTOBER 16, 1762

The company men were generous in their offer and seemed to ask little of the expedition in return. We were simply to provide more extensive mapping of the northerly peninsulas and islands, discover what possibilities of profitable trade among the natives might exist, and essay the populations of animals with valuable pelts. However, had I known the hardships that awaited the crew, I never would have undertaken the voyage.

Vinegar and even lemon juice have frozen solid and broken their bottles. Still harder to conceive, the very mercury of the thermometer has shattered its glass! When crew members open a door leading topside, a dense fog pours down past our feet and gathers on the walls as ice. The crew is never warm. Steam rising from the cook's pots freezes almost immedi-

ately. I fear that we did not stock fuel enough for such a venture and I am considering returning to port.

I am reminded by these conditions of the reports of those intrepid captains who set out in search of a northwest passage, a search which has vexed mariners since Henry Hudson explored the northernmost reaches of Canada in hopes of finding such a waterway as would join the Atlantic and Pacific oceans. Such a waterway, were it to be found, would provide the much sought after short-cut to the Far East for merchants ships issuing from the harbors of Europe.

Yet since the voyages of Captain Foxe, it seems clear that no such passage exists below the arctic circle. Thus, even if one is found, it could be of no commercial value. Foxe himself said even if one were to be discovered, it would be no more than a curiosity. Nonetheless, to many the passage calls out to be found. It seems to me little more than chasing a phantasm which will never materialize on the cartographer's chart.

Far be it from the Octavius and her crew even to entertain such thoughts! God speed to us.

FARLEY'S TAVERN, a hollowed out, lit-up block of brick and glass on East Fifth Street, closer to Locust than Broadway, front window a kind of half-mirror holding the transparent reflections of neon from across the street, a telephone pole with wire rigging, the face of anyone trying to peek in... reaching through at the same time from the other side, light shining off the polished bar and tables set with candles, drinkers hunkered down over their glasses in silent conversation. Peeking in, a clubfoot drunk who wasn't there anymore, hardly five-feet-two, marking the empty stool he used to keep warm, pressing against the glass to be closer to a woman whose loneliness had opened up a whole underworld where her lover left her stranded. There were others caught on the outside, the near-nothing of the air rippled with their mostly emptiness, as fleetingly there as fluttering see-through moth-wings dusted with a vague sense of loss, the near-nothing of the air rippled with their mostly emptiness, breathless weightless longings drawn from the far corners of the night to brush up against the glow leaking out onto the sidewalk which mostly dissolved without getting into the street. Among them, an idiot-man didn't know any better than to always look in on things even in life, never knew Zirque Granges or the pretty red-haired woman who was sitting at a table with him Ain't–ain't she somethin? but he'd've bet his job at the bakery–why he'd–he'd put the whole bakery on the line–that that man's life revolved around her.

The Duke, turning down Fifth, dark settled in, looking forward to a little red wine and conversation, Farleys always waiting for a dropper-by like him to liven things up a bit, the Duke heard the silent sighing, slow exhalations of the exiled, not even shadows anymore, no longer as much as a swirl of dimness in the mellow light, the only way you knew they were there, the odd ghost of a feeling, like the splinter of mourning called up by the dawnlight cry of a dove they were nothing more than early-evening echoes soon enough to be late-night vanishings.

"Well if it ain't the big Pallucca, don't much come outta his basement till the sun's good an gone. Watchya up to t'night? Out collectin rumors, or startin em?"

"'Tis kinda neat," the Duke answered with a half-smile, "when in one line two craft meet."

"Little a both, is that what yer sayin? When it comes to collectin he's like you Blue Jean, comes up with a little bit a everythin from everywhere."

"Savin it all up for the Big Book. If yer lucky Granges, you'll get a page'r two."

"It'll have t'be a big book if you want t'fit me in it."

"What's the Big Book?" Rae Anne asked.

"Millo and I, we're tryin t'keep a record a the shape a things past, a mappa mundi kind of–"

"The Earth's still flat where the Duke comes from."

"–pickin up where others with compass an pen have resorted to pencilin in fantastical-finned sea beasts that never were. Tryin, y'see, t'cut down on the terra incognita floatin loose these days."

"Oh you and Millo—moppa moondy," she repeated with sarcasm, "with all your Italian and this one" –she elbowed Zirque– "with those foreign words he learned one at a time and mostly forgot now, you're gettin just a little outta hand, don't you think?"

"Well Ah'll tell you this," the Duke had smiled at Blue Jean but was answering Zirque, "Ah'm not all that sure the shape to this world is round. Labyrinthine more like, an somma the passages you take the right combination, they get you back to where you started from, same as Magellan—"

"I heard a him—"

"—but wasn't really a circle brought you roundabout."

"Heard about that old-time Greek, too," Zirque said, as he pushed over and made room for the Duke to sit, "think it was Millo told me about im, figured out the circumference a the earth from his backyard. Librarian, clerk or somethin wasn't he?"

"Stamped library cards in Alexandria the way I heard it."

"Where's Alexandria?" Blue Jean wanted to know.

"Over by Fort Scott," Zirque said and got slapped in the shoulder for it but kept talking to the Duke. "He was some geometer—izzat a word? Never left town but he—the figure he came up with, he didn't miss by much."

"Not bad for a guy who never left town."

Blue Jean, in a gray turtleneck (dull compared to her green eyes), her red hair up on a bun, was looking at Zirque, presenting the Duke a profile fit for an ancient temple. "You ought to have taken his example," she said to Zirque, "and stayed at home more."

"Go," Zirque said with a smile, one of his front teeth missing (never did anything about it but somehow didn't look bad on him), "a destination will follow. That's my motto."

"Now where've I heard that before?"

"All right so I stole it from you, y'big Pallucca," Zirque admitted. "Logged enough miles to make it half way to the moon if dead reckoning ain't too much off. You can know somethin by figurin or readin, but to feel it, you gotta—"

"You gotta put your arms around it," Rae Anne said, proving her point, trapping both of Zirque's arms at his sides, warning: "You better get yourself a new motto."

"Shoulda been like the Duke," Zirque said, "racked up that many miles on foot. He's circled the earth without leavin the county."

"Or you could've taken me with you," Blue Jean said, "one'r the other."

"I don't go anywhere anymore an you know it."

"Only took you twenty-some-odd years to settle down."

"First time I stuck out my thumb only got as far as Arcadia, what is that, bout 17 miles north I think, not even outta Crawford County. Wasn't but 14 or so. Done a lot since, though. Almost got myself rolled up there in Indian Country, Arizona, cuz I was dressed too nice, they wanted to mess me up some. But I talked those Navajos into believin I was a relation come distant from a small town in Kansas even though quarter Creek's what I am, had em buyin me beers before I gave em the slip."

The Duke had pulled out a cigar while Zirque was talkin, a stumpy Toscana, had it in his mouth to let the taste sit there for a few minutes before setting it to burn.

"Pyramids in Mexico," Rae Anne said, "now there's one I didn't believe till I saw it."

"And there was that old timer, what was his name? Eduardo, remember? Came from aristocracy but wound up livin in that run-down hotel—the bubble in yer level'd always be off in that place—the whole center a gravity's crooked in that country, specially the politicians."

"He was so sweet," Rae Anne said, "an he had that English

accent an all..."

"Thought I was Mexican, too," Zirque said proudly, "a little on the tall side for the home-grown variety."

"Well, yer dark enough that Creek blood in you—you could pass for a lot of things, Greek, Italian, Mexican—"

"Tell you somethin..." Zirque was waving around a cigarette, a glowing wand that drew disappearing shapes of light in the air, "there are places where there aren't any landmarks, no Kilroy was here, no footprints. Only way to get your bearings—you got to look up, get yourself a star-marker. But it's not always—you can't always know for sure ..."

Zirque Part-Creek slapping the dust off his jeans, could be from the Mojave, could be from the floor of Bartelli's Blue Goose Bar. No tellin. Adrift in a vanishing city he'd never reach for long, inheritor of a restlessness this land is full of you got to figure it's not but a hundred years America's been modernized, carpeted with cities inventing new horizons, what they cover over's a thousand thousand years old, civilization just a layer of dust by comparison, no more than that, an Zirque's a lightning rod somehow, drawing the unrest that passes unnoticed beneath the high-heeled feet of women peeking in the windows along Broadway, the booted men sitting around Carol's Corner Cafe reading about yesterday in the Pittsburg Sun or the Chicago Tribune, eggs and coffee sending spectral steam rising to vanish like the long-ago they were never a part of. The corner where two streets cross as arbitrary as can be if you're not Millo the far-seeing, and he doesn't see more than half a century back, Zirque maybe has some kind of extra sense, without knowing anything about miners or grasshoppers, might every now and then think he hears a Creek hootcall but decides it was only an oddball bird.

"Is that Earl comin in?" Rae Anne asked.

Earl, his hair white underneath a Royals cap, took a chair next to the Duke and pulled a bottle from under his jacket. Hard to tell what was in it, the home-made label (For Use as a

Motor Fuel Only! Contains Lead) no help at all.

"Whaddaya know Earl?"

"Hadda fight, hadda fuck an hadda steal yer girl." He took a sly sip out of his bottle so as not to let on to Farley. "Yer just lucky yer a friend a mind, Granges, can't mess with a buddy's girl. But you know if she gave me one go-round, wouldn't nothin be left a you but a bad mem'ry." He adjusted his baseball cap.

"Oh Earl–"

"If you ain't lookin the part a the Blue Jean Baby Queen, prettiest girl I ever seen–"

"ER-rul–"

"Wondrous fair," the Duke agreed leaning cigar first into the table candle snug in its glass bell, smoke and flame flaring up his wide face looked for half a minute like it belonged to a being dragged down to earth for some kind of fire-lit ritual.

"Ain't nothin like a pretty redhead, specially one with green eyes." Earl shook his head. "Yer a lucky man Zirque Granges."

"My luck was holdin out pretty good till you walked in."

"I'm gonna ignore that," Earl said pointing an imposing finger, his hands big even for a man six-foot two or so, and heavy, cinderblocks when he made them into fists. "An what're you doin here, Pallucca? Ain't you s'posed t'be spinnin webs or somethin in yer basement?"

"Not t'night Earl."

Leaning closer to the Duke he whispered, "I'm goin t'meet Janice later on, Tommy's outta town."

"Now you just said–"

"Shhhhhhh." That same finger he used for pointing making a seam from chin to more-than-once-broken nose (healed a bit crooked but he liked to think made him look distinguished).

"Tommy's one a your buddies, so how're you gonna do that?"

"I'm not gonna tell im, are you?"

"No..."

"Well that's how you do it!" Earl slapped him on the shoulder, slugged out of the bottle he was trying to keep hid behind his jacket. "A beautiful night in Palluccaville, ain't it though?"

"S'posed to get rainy an nasty later on, might even snow they said."

"When're we gonna get the place renamed official? I think Skunk's makin up fliers t'get it put to a vote."

"Wherein the hell's Skunk anyway?"

"Ain't seen im t'night," Zirque said. "Seen his new girl though. Largest living land mammal since Raymond Bauer."

"Zirque...!"

"Jesus what izzit with him and big gals?" Earl lifted the cap off his head, exposing thinning gray hair, settled it back down.

"Mighta left town with er," Zirque offered putting out his cigarette.

"Don't you even talk about leavin ..."

"Yeah Granges, all the times you left this pretty little gal on her own yer lucky I gave her a shoulder t'cry on."

"I'm lucky a shoulder's all you tried to give er."

"That too."

"If it weren't for Earl who knows what woulda happened with that biker in the Pan Club parkin lot," Rae Anne said.

"You are beset from all sides," the Duke said.

"I kinda noticed–"

"And you deserve it."

"Even Lyman Kishpaugh'd've put two 'n' two t'gether by now," Earl said.

"Amazin sometimes," the Duke stabbed at the air with his cigar, "what streets run parallel. You ever run into Lyman?"

"Here an there," Earl said, "but never stopped to say hello that I recall. I ain't as old as Millo y'know."

"Got a lot more mileage on yer face though, don'tcha? Look like you got caught square with everything every ex-gal a yours ever threw your way."

"Granges, yer half as tough as y'think and twice as stupid as y'look."

"My mama knew Lyman," Rae Anne said her voice rising at the mention of a name she hadn't heard in years. "She was just a girl she tried to teach him to read but he didn't catch on too well, he always brought her a flower he was kinda sweet on her, just a big kid is all except he had no mean streak, he used to lose his way sometimes, just forget I guess, which way Vacca's was–it was Vacca's or the firehouse where he slept, I don't remember which she told me..."

The Duke puffed leisurely while he listened, smoke unfurling in slow easy shapes, dissipating soon as they formed–pure capriciousness what they made themselves into–then disappeared cleaner than if they'd never been.

"... and he had a–he had a big ring of keys, probably not one of em opened anythin, but he used to carry em all around she said like he wanted to be a bell ringer, but all he got to be was a key jangler, he'd make noise on purpose with them and start fiddlin with em when he got nervous, he carried a book with him all the time–what was it called? *The Happy Valley* or some such–but he couldn't read much more than the first page, which is what my mom taught him, that book I think was hangin out of his back pocket the day they found him outside the Poor Farm, he'd wandered off and got locked out in the dead a winter and just froze to death right there on the front stoop."

"Found the same way he was left," Zirque said.

The Duke, light from the table candle cutting deeper the lines in his face, making him look a larger version of his walking stick, exhaled thoughtfully. "Whaddaya mean?"

"Well, showed up asleep on Vacca's front stoop in the first place, didn't 'ee? Maybe the smell a that bakin bread is what took him in, an I guess he finished about the way he started–locked out permanent."

Lyman The Key Jangler (his Creek name) gone on to Friskel's House of Dust. Was it he was just confused or was he lookin for somethin those times he went wandering off, his mom or his circus friends, maybe a home he'd had before he got left in Frontenac–?

"Earl how many times I tell you not to come in here with that bottle?" Fred Farley, eyebrows as white as his full head of hair, hawked him from behind the bar.

Earl held both hands up. "Honest injun Fred, you won't see it no more. My buddy Zirque was just gonna buy me a beer anyhow."

"Bring it up here Earl," Fred called. "You can have it when you leave."

"Come on up t'the bar Zee Gee," Earl said pushing out of his seat, "an buy me a beer."

"In the immortal words a Shakespeare, 'I don't hafta if I don't wanna.'" Straightening a leg so he didn't have to get out of his chair, Zirque fished a fin out of his pocket, put it in Earl's hand. "Buy what you want. And get Friar Pallucca–he looks like a monk with that bowl cut a his and that cloak-thing he wears don't 'ee?–a glass a dago red while you're up."

Earl winked at im. "You ain't half bad most a the time Granges."

"Looks like it's gettin cold out, don't it?" Rae Ann asked.

The Duke could see the wind ruffling the green awning trimmed in white, leaves fluttering past, spinning, carried off with no say over where they were going, all of it silent beyond the big plate-glass window.

"Don't know for sure, but after my glass a wine I think I'm goin to head into downtown, see about the waterway connectin *nunc t'tunc.*"

"Back just in time to catch them sellin pure bullshit again," Earl said putting glass of red wine down in front of the Duke. "Them two oughta be married the kinda things they cook up between em."

"Hope you have better luck than to be stuck in ice for years on end," Zirque said to the Duke.

"Well I'll tell you what," Earl said scraping his chair forward, "why don'tcha wish in one hand, shit in the other an see which gets full first?"

Rae Anne tilted her head back, flattened a hand against her chest and laughed, a kind of music that could rearrange your insides, set loose a little dust devil in there, turn everything in circles before it settles haphazardly back again.

"You ever see somma Pallucca's books?" (Earl had aligned himself with Rae Anne, a way of lawfully drifting a little closer to her, a way to keep the other two from leaving him out of the table talk.) "Make a library look ramshod."

"Ramshackle," Zirque corrected.

"Whatever the fuck—"

"Ramshackle don't make all that much sense either—"

"What... the... *fuck*... *EVER*..." Earl said, pounding the table with the heel of his bottle to flatten out each word.

"Your poetic license is hereby revoked."

"I been drivin without it all my life anyway—"

The Duke exhaled a thick stream of smoke.

"So the Two-Flow Way is what you're talkin—"

"Pure horse shit," Earl cut in, "is what he's talkin."

The Duke nodded. "See if I can align myself—rivers a gravity, you know I read about those, move whole sections of galaxies more or less sideways and—and there are invisible rivers down here, too, I think, carry you off it you let em."

"What're you readin these days anyway," Earl asked, "*Goat-Fuckin in Ancient Times?*"

"*The Decline and Fall of the Grand Emporium* more likely," Zirque said.

"Just finished the *Origin of the Specious*," the Duke said, his smile only half visible behind the smoke of his cigar. He tapped ashes into a glass tray. "Fact a the matter is, I got holda some books on English voyages into the arctic, the Crown bent on cuttin across the top a North America, reach the rice, spices, riches a the Far East the quicker. Brits started after their water-way in the 1500s, Henry Hudson himself, the river runnin past

Manhattan named for im, was abandoned by his crew in an open boat after a hard winter up there."

"Guess he had a time of it paddlin back t'England," Zirque said.

Earl shook his head. "Worse than any death row I was ever on."

"Didn't even leave im any oars."

Blue Jean rubbed a chill out of her arms. "That's about the awfullest thing I ever heard."

"Strange thing bein, after Luke Foxe sailed that way 1631 or thereabouts, they knew there was no way t'cut through below the Arctic Circle, the fabled straight'd be frozen solid most a the year, damn near useless. Became an obsession anyway, many a ship locked into ice an never recovered, one named after Foxe was frozen in the ice 242 days, drifted 1400 miles south and east–opposite a the captain's intentions unless back to England was the unconscious desire. The Franklin Expedition worst of all, 129 men not a one made it home, abandonded their ice-wrecked ships but dropped one by one as they walked an Eskimo said, starvation an exhaustion."

"Did they finally find it?" Blue Jean asked.

Duke nodded. "Took near 300 years for anyone livin to map the way but only a modern icebreaker of a ship could make use of it, all those men died for next t'nothin."

"I admire em, though," Zirque said. He nodded his head, finished his beer in silent toast to the frozen bones of lost explorers. "I never did get it down, you know," he said, "just got tired is all."

"Maybe that's the best way," the Duke answered, "quit swimmin upstream, let the current carry you some..."

Zirque's whole life trying to wear himself out, a search for things that would use him up but still leave something of him behind, something to hand down, pass on like a solid old farmhouse on a stone foundation. Stealing cars and smoking herbal brews made every thought into a curveball, nose powders he used to watch the night melt in the white hot glow, chasing after other women and long-distance travelling on a drunken whim done with, he'd finally run himself down, an old dog settled in his musty pile of rags he'd quit twisting around in his sleep.

The glass of wine disappeared while the Duke's cigar burned down to an ashy stump and he lit another and the freezing rain the radio had said might come began to fall, another wine came and Zirque borrowed a cigar ("I'll give you back what's left–"), the two of them buying for Rae Anne and Earl, the four of them talking in a pocket of smoke and wine and beer and dusty amber light, a warm dry corner in the October night, when the Duke looked out the window he saw the cold coming on, icicles giving downtown ragged edges though it was still raining, a weird in-between temperature, he wasn't really looking forward to going outside.

Pushing back in his chair and putting on a long coat given to him by a West Point cadet over his shoulder (he doubts those things have changed since the Civil War), he said "One thing I'll say for you Granges, you didn't hug the shore."

Zirque thumbed over his shoulder at Blue Jean. "She's my homin instinct, or I'd still be out there. Ain'tcha honey," he called over his shoulder. She threw him a glance but kept talking to Earl. Loud enough for her to hear, Zirque said, "She's the sweetness an light in my life."

"Zirque–"

"The kerosene in my heater–"

"You're such a jerk–"

"The car in my garage."

"I'm not going to pay you any more mind. Now what were you sayin Earl–?"

"The bulb in my lamp," Zirque said for good measure. Leaning the Duke's way, Zirque snaked his fingers into the old jean jacket hanging on the back of his chair (the same scrap of denim he took with him while he was off doing fool things that were still catching up with him) pulled out a folded-up square of paper. "She gave me something just in case I lost my pigeon-like powers." A Blue Jean drawing of a woman not much more than the typical stick man except for the hair, a dress, a bit more of a face. "You are here," she wrote and put an X about where the stick-girl's heart would have been.

NOVEMBER 10TH, 1762

For some time now, I have suspected that there is no way out. Sixteen days have gone by that we have been inclosed in the ice. All is bleak around us. No description would serve for the netherlands of ice and snow encountered at these latitudes.

Moreover, what may prove fatal to my crew and me is our failure to imagine more clearly the perils of these waters. Though locked in ice, we make slow progress farther north (and east) as the ice itself drifts in a great pack according to its own inscrutable will. There is nothing we can do. God what great calamity!

It was folly to underestimate the vagaries of arctic weather. How well I know a strait blocked off by ice this year may have been free-flowing water only last season. The maze of navigable waterways and straits, of unfrozen bays and favorable harbors among the islands and peninsulas so often changes that a reliable map would be nearly impossible. And how easily the chance arrangements of ice floes deceive one into believing new bits of land have emerged here or there. Most hazardous of all, perhaps, is the unknown course of the ice stream which circulates through this region in an entirely unpredictable manner and in which we are now trapped.

The first mate has informed me that fire has gone out. God preserve us.

THE NIGHT IS HOLLOW and what we don't fill with a few wisps of light from a neon sign or a streetlamp we fill with unmoored dreaming, imaginings strange as unheard-of sea beasts.

The Duke gets the same drifting-off feeling looking at the webwork of lines on a guilded 16th-century map as he does from the dense criss-crossing of telephone wires and cables, antennas and spun-iron fire escapes downtown. Telephone wires not exactly longitude-latitude, not so neat and systematic, more like plotted courses intersecting with those radiating wind roses. The telephone wires (hung with icicles still dripping though the rain had ended, the sky dried) superimposed on vast chunks of clouds, floating-overhead continents that do not exist. A corner of smooth cloudless sky measured off by the wires and cables, the telephone poles like transplanted masts of wrecked arctic ships, wondrous in their stillness and ice encrustings lavished on them by a frigid place making an offering of itself, breathing on them its own cold cold metal-sharp breath, or maybe all that's visible of ships submerged and frozen in time disguised as asphalt.

A hot water heater on its side, set out for trash, looked like one of those old-time life savers. A tree, branches bent permanent, happened to be aligned with the clouds who'd've thought it could be so loud in its ice jacket, crinkling and creaking as a breeze went through?

That brick building over there filled with light, a bright window against the dark sky near surreal, the crooked world aslant, askew, leanin toward somethin. The very top left corner a the buildin lined up with that star which is lined up with the moon, which is lined up with that telephone pole don't know why but they didn't put a pole in straight on this street they're all leanin one way or another. Whoever planted this pole matched the slant a that buildin exactly. The same force moving through was out tonight, left a temporary trail in the clouds, left that telephone pole to point like some sundial needle.

Fourth Street, Hotel Besse with its thorny crown of antennas, a whole big uneven bunch of em atop its thirteen stories, haulin in signals. Cables hangin off the poles like saggin riggin, sails swept away, useless in this age of electromagnetic waves, wind left to babble to itself (like me) antennas insteada sails, Zirque ought t'be standin stiffbacked among those steel spines, the crow's nest a the Besse, might pull in the music a the spheres from up there, the eternal slappin & overlappin a the ocean a time, might even see all the way to the mythical Drifting Island of Memory.

This small-time city, kind of an accidental labyrinth, the maze a streets & alleys, tangle a streetlamps, traffic lights, TV antennas, criss-crossin telephone wires & electric cables, downtown a reflection in architecture of some part a the mind. Arrangements. From storefronts & storied buildings to the still life of beer bottles (glossed with yellow light), ashtray and crushed white butts (like tiny untended bones) on the table in Farley's, memory becoming a city, remembers by arrangement, the names of a long-ago king's dinner guests crushed by the fallin ceiling recalled by their placement at the table, memory has its alleys & streets and even parks with shimmering ponds at the center where words dissolve, some part of memory feeling without knowing how to say just an electric tingle at back of the neck, some part always under construction, imagination fillin in the gaps, structures within structures, like rooms within buildings furniture within rooms, not repeatin, but unravelin, more revealed beneath. The city evolves, buildings topple, half way fall, new ones go up, some renovated, revamped, some joined, uses altered, new streets added, widened, changed into one-ways, names replaced with new ones. All upon the earlier city a primordial remembrances Jung dug up, its eroded form somehow giving rise to, insinuating, the layout a the new city.

Might be that with Zirque, somethin old in him, some kinda innate get-go, like those baby sea turtles flip-floppin frantic for the breaking vastness a the ocean soon as they hatch, knowin exactly where somethin they've never seen is t'be found. Has he got rigged in him some kinda gyroscope generating a lopsided momentum always carryin him in a direction he's not thinkin about? Maybe he's adrift, carried off at night by the chaos of his own churnin dreams, the rest of us not so unlucky as to have this always-spinning mechanism inside that never leaves calm enough for a good night's sleep (though I ain't much at ease, walkin these alleys & backstreets & Broadways for somethin I missed the last thousand times around, might as well be lookin for the shadow a the moon at nightfall). Might be Zirque's infused with somethin long settled into the land, a magnetism of a kind drawin him along. Maybe a little a both... we're all lead copper aluminum, he's restless iron always pulled at by a pole.

The moon three quarters tonight, the distance nothin the mind can close in on its light reaches across the desert a empty black that is mainly what this existence is, keyholed here and there by a star or an insomniac walkin the edge a the familiar tryin t'peek over, yes empty space mostly, same as the atoms that make up his overweight body solid enough to stop an arrow, solid enough to be held by the fist a gravity to the more solid (but still mostly empty) ground. He wonders how to find his way should he use that moon overhead to navigate or the tiny mercury-vapor moons on their hooded poles (bright as the moon up this close) sparks a dust in the three-quarter eye of a sleepin god. Stars & headlights & a fluorescent sign announcin Crowell Drugstore, the lit end of a cigar that points due east, the source of all light around these parts, all the rest pagan stolen fire, the brief flame jumpin up to grab holda the night before the ponderous darkness brings its inexhaustible weight to bear, crushes the upstart flame. Pillar a cloud by day, star by night. Ain't so easy any more. Now we've even got to deal with the difference between True North an Magnetic North, the one unerring, constant, the other a variable, sometimes northwestin, sometimes northeastin, all dependin on where you are when you take your readin. One found by measurin the elevation of the Pole star, the other by what your compass is doin, uncertainty a snaking wormhole into the familiar: just when we think we know where we are, we drop down through an open manhole cover an come up on the other side a things, not a landmark not a familiar constellation in sight. Or worse, wind up like that happy-go-lucky young Frenchman, Bellot, disappearin in a sudden crack in the ice before anyone was even sure he was gone. Like the Thomas boy, who had all the promise anyone could've ever hoped for in an eighteen-year-old, electrocuted one rainy night.

All right then, Magnetic North... center a the pull shifts dependin on where you're standin or floatin (howsoeverbeit). True North, on the other hand an arbitrary goddamn thing, doesn't exist any more than a straight line on the earth's curved surface.

The strange thing here, town's got its own pull same as a New York, a Chicago, a Far East, due north. Maybe just for tonight Farley's is Magnetic North, on another night it'll be the Pan Club or might be so off-center so as t'get all the way to Frontenac, might even be that ghost bar, Bartelli's, cast adrift backwards in time everybody might be headed over that way, tryin to look past the cardboard & painted-over windows without knowin why without knowing where they're headed might go across the street to the Pool Hall instead, thinking there, *there* is where whatever's to shake loose tonight will do its slow uncocoonin for anyone payin mind enough to notice the Northwest Passage just opened up, the straits are free of ice an mist, time's runnin in both directions but you miss the boat if you're not ice master enough to see the channel's opened up, to see there's a moment of redemption over the horizon, a moment of clarity when we know what it was Pap was up to stripped naked in a drainage ditch where he drowned in six inches a rainwater, a moment when you can see where you should be standin (or flowin) in relation to everything else, the vanishin point is right there—what vanishes at this point being the horizon (you don't need to go any farther) you've found ground zero, the center of stillness where all motion is at rest, where the two are one an from that place the world makes perfect sense, the city your memory has built up fits into the city you're standing in. All the *terrae incognita*–whatever the mapmakers missed–as familiar as the cracks in Mckay Street.

Funny thing is, early on, those mapmakers couldn't agree on a flat, a round, an oval world; debated which end was up–north or east–but they had no doubt there were four rivers runnin through the underworld, no bickerin over the layout a where it is we'd all be headed one day, you might think Friskel's House a Dust one a the doorways but the real way down is here (the Duke thumped his chest), we've all had a peek during a bad night's sleep or a gut feelin, a flash of introspection an we find ourselves spelunking the nadirland we're all carryin around inside us though mainly nowadays we know maps better than the territory, we can draw the country outlines freehand, navigate from here to there a hundred times better than we ever could the maze of our own hearts.

The Duke was standing outside Carol's Corner Cafe, cloudy glass brick on either side of the door, a big window to look out (or in) set in the red brick, Lyman's regular place Sunday mornings, rain or shine. In rain, soaked except for his crew-cut head, that corduroy Depression cap of his heavy with rain water, with oil from his hands it'd been handled so much. A Pittsburg Sun lying on the counter, mainly the pictures he gandered at, a serious look on his face his tongue out lips curled under when he tried to read the local goings-on (a football score put him on his surest footing) he wanted to be like everyone else while he waited for breakfast, taylor ham and eggs every time, sometimes a side of sausage or bacon, it was the grease he loved. Old Mary, shrivelled as cooked eggs left out overnight, his favorite waitress, with those big glasses of hers, she always got him a side of cornbread no charge.

Rainy day shivery, something cold had rolled in out of the north, had drifted invisibly in along with the mist the ghostly chill off an ancestral burial ground of the Kansa (though there aren't any that anyone knows of anywhere near), the streets sunk in a quiet tide of shadowy gray cut with the occasional keening of a train whistle along the Santa Fe line. Lyman with only that hat and an old corduroy jacket worn through at the elbows to keep late October dampness off him, he'd got his corner of late morning smelling of brewing coffee and smoky bacon, he could see people out the rain-jewelled window, on their way in long overcoats, umbrellas up, hats held and heads bent, shroudy figures in the fogginess, as if the shades of people were abroad, detached from owners, a supernatural shang-hai left them in the brick-lined streets of downtown, wandering, wondering, the way obscured, a kind of natural sorcery at work to make a labyrinth of the familiar. Safe inside the cafe, anchored firm to the padded stool at the counter, conversations around him like lazy bees buzzing past settling their fat bodies on flowers on a clear day, a slap on the back hello from George Wilke, smiles, nods, waves from other tables, he was just like them, he smiled back waved and called Good mornin, Mary asking him about work at the bakery, about the Vaccas telling him not to rush through his meal Take your time, just imagine you hear a far-off violin playing something slow and wonderful and the longer it takes you to finish the longer that violin plays, a slow, old-time waltz, those people outside about their business can't hear it and aren't you sorry for them they can't? Before he left, he counted up his change (tongue out), the nickels and pennies to add up to the what he owed, plus a nickel for Mary.

Drawn some nights to Broadway's St. Elmo's neon, Lyman wandered down Fifth, stopped in front of Farley's to peek in at who was there never went in just hovered. What did he know beyond the smell of the bakery or the bells of the fire engines? Was he ever anything more than a child let loose in the carnival of the world, carried along by various rides and conned by barkers Over here, over here my boy, you've got the magic key on your ring yes you do, it opens the door, that and a mere two bits, twenty five cents Lyman for the ride of a lifetime, selling this to a man whose lifetime was a ride he

[175]

couldn't really get off.

Alone in his niche beside the stone ovens, did he sleep sound? When he woke to find no carnival music, no rides, nothing but the dark surroundings of the closed-up bakery the bare bulb he pulled to harsh life with a long string, he tried to read sometimes but couldn't get much past the first pages of that kiddie book *The Pleasant Valley*, a library give-away cover creased, bent from being in his back pocket all the time, a boy and a girl best friends growing up in a Neverwasville without a name where nothing really bad ever happened. Rae Anne's mom taught him did he ever reach for his own mother when he was struggling with the reading, all tongue when he tried to concentrate he wanted to read so badly he just couldn't lift too many of those sentences off the page though he talked about the boy and girl, Robby and Sharon, like they were his friends and he pretended to read the newspaper like everyone else in Carol's when he was really looking at the pictures the way he went through life just looking at the pictures. Bullish strong he could carry a sack of coal like it was full of feathers, could stir a monster batch of dough, the coins people handed in for their loaves had to be worth something because look how pretty they are. Government backin, gold reserves, Marx's Manifesto as far out of reach as Marco Polo's wondrous Cathay which Arthur Stilwell thought to reach with a railroad through Mexico picking up where the Pacific waterway left off.

Weathervane might not be a Kansas invention, though the state is named for the Kansa, People of the South Wind, and there's a steady one kicking up dust on the streets more or less sunup till moonfall, but that kind of directional ought to be a Kansas original, Lyman a kind of human weathervane, no man more prone to the tilt of the earth, the natural lilt carries everything from a Canadian goose feather on up to galaxy chunks, he didn't have much control over anything at all, nor much understanding, his head as light as goose down, his body as solid as a block of ice, swept along like the Octavius, a weathervane for the unfelt gust that doesn't originate in one of the cardinal directions, but maybe up from the well of things, the nadir (a place you'll find on most any Indian compass, along with up, the zenith), keep an eye on him, never much got anywhere unless he got himself carried along, you'll know which way things are blowing.

AUGUST 12, 1775

This day has been witness to the strangest of events I expect I shall see in this lifetime.

It began in ordinary fashion, the hours passing no differently than those of the day before, aye of many days before. We now find ourselves off the west coast of Greenland—well above the arctic circle. With whales scarce of late, the lookouts have been cautioned to keep a keen eye trained on the sea.

The Herald, an icy breeze snapping its sail, made its way through a sea choked with icebergs but otherwise empty. These many tons of ice are shaped as oddly and capriciously as clouds—indeed, as they are as white as clouds, they could have been great clods of heavenly stuff grown weighty and fallen into the frigid waters. It was among these same that the lookouts spied another ship. She was a three-masted schooner that seemed to be adrift and in a state of ill repair. Ropes hung haphazardly from the masts and the sails had been reduced to tattered rags.

I ordered the men to divert our course to intercept the strange visitor that I might hail her. Yet when I made an attempt, I received no reply. Nor was there anyone on deck.

Ordering eight men into a longboat, we rowed to our silent companion in fairly calm waters. The elements had all but worn away the name, but after a moment's squinting in the midday sun, I was able to discern it: Octavius.

When we had pulled alongside, I again hailed the Octavius and again was greeted with a deep and abiding silence broken only by the regular slap of the sea against the hulls of the boats. One of the men crossed himself. The others began to complain, quite audibly, of being so close to such an eerie sight.

I began to lose my temper—superstitious foolishness! What were the perils of an abandoned sailing vessel to those of the arctic region? I chose the four men whom I deemed to be the stoutest of heart and ordered them aboard. Leading the way myself, I took hold of fallen rigging and hoisted myself onto the deck.

THIRD TIME MAYBE he's doubled back up Broadway and come again to the Hotel Stilwell the year Pap died the last it was open. The Stilwell, his haunt, a place to remember well. As famous for bein the grandest built in Crawford County as for old Arthur Stilwell, the millionaire who believed in brownies—benevolent imps that guided his future toward fortune for im. Papish, dead near ten years now, use t'perch like a gargoyle in a hall window a the Stilwell just to catch sight a Blue Jean goin in or comin outta Carol's Corner Cafe, climbed down a drainpipe now an again to sit in the booth behind her knowin all the time Blue Jean's love for Zirque makes up a constellation a longin all by itself, due east where the light creeps into the emptiness of our hearts, points the way, they chase each other, moon and sun in the sky, eclipse the dark moment of embrace. Pap never... unless maybe at the end there, maybe he came on the passage, took him by the hand along the spirit trail.

It ain't all sho easy, the shtreets, shomtimes they move.

"Pap—?"

I mean, don't you remember em bein jusht a shcant different from what yer seein now, ain't they moved?

"Well Pap who'da thought I... I'm glad you left Farley's, nothin for you there anyway you know."

Shome kinda ... Farleyz izh shome kinda—but that ain't the point, the point's the shtreets, I mean, theyre shtill runnin east-west or north-shouth or bendin around shoutheast and whatall, but just maybe they've shifted over a bit. He patted his flannel-covered chest with a flat hand. *The shcrag a land we think's sittin shtill so we can shtand on it, the continents are all afloat, adrift, awash in the world's oceans, the earth itself's ashkew on its axish headin off with the entire sholar shyshtem off in its own direction—what's heavy enough, anchored solid enough, dug in enough, not t'be?*

"Well I... Farley's I guess," the Duke answered, thinkin he might've understood. Pap can't go inside anymore but Lyman... all his life he got left outsida things...

Everything you know, or think you know, it's all heaped up, sittin on the waters they used t'think shurrounded all the land there was, the earth disk shaped back then, shurrounded by the Great Outer Sea of Boundless Extent. Nothin shtays put, memories ain't where you left em when you go lookin for em. 'Less you take the time to arrange em, line em up with yer own personal ashtrolabe so every time you shee Scorpio rising, her shign, you remember Blue Jean and everything she is t'you.

The Duke turned to say something else to Pap, but he was gone, dissolved in a bit of light under a streetlamp, a faint electric hum the only sound.

Habit replaces natural laws out here that's what ghosts are made of routine, still going up a staircase torn down years ago ain't there anymore but what the hell do they know? They ain't there any more either.

THE DECK OF THE OCTAVIUS was deserted. As I had suspected—and feared—the ship's wheel was unattended. We had to choose each step with great care for the planks of the deck were unsound and had been made slippery with both snow and some sort of moss. The Octavius, it seemed, was a ghost ship.

Below decks... ah, there lay the story, frightful though it was. In the crew's quarters lay the bodies of 28 men, all thickly bundled in their bunks against the Arctic cold, all uncannily preserved by that same cold. This time, all of the men (myself included) removed their hats and crossed themselves.

In hopes of discovering what had led the men of the Octavius to this fate, we made our way aft to the captain's cabin. There we found him motionless in his chair, still at his desk, head bent forward, his quill lying beside his hand as though he had gone to sleep at this work.

A film of green mold had crept over the dead captain's face and hands, but otherwise the body–like the others–was well preserved. We tarried with the captain only long enough to confiscate his log and then continued our exploration of the ship.

In another of the principal cabins, we discovered the remains of a woman, reclining, as it were, on the bed. She seemed rapt in some event of great importance. Hardly did she seem lifeless at all but for the shrunken quality of her limbs. Not far from her, the ship's pilot sat cross-legged on the floor, a flint in one hand and steel in the other. Before him lay a little pile of wood shavings. Once more we offered a prayer for the dead and crossed ourselves.

The log book safely tucked inside my coat, I led the way topside whence we returned to the Herald.

Against my wishes (the men already greatly feared disaster might follow us, but would literally follow us were we to take the Octavius into tow) I left her adrift. I watched her, a floating tomb among the icebergs of the North Atlantic, until she was little more than an indiscernible speck and at last, lost to sight.

The final entry in the Octavius' logbook is dated November 11, 1762. Here I feel it only proper to give voice to the dead captain whose log book fate has seen fit to place in my hands:

> *"November 11, 1762. We have now been inclosed in the ice seventeen days. The fire went out yesterday, and our master has been trying ever since to kindle it again, but without success. His wife died this morning; there is no relief."*

Their plight, relived in this passage with all the freshness of the dreadful moment it was written, is indeed poignant. Yet what is astonishing to discover is the ship's location. According to the captain's last entry, the Octavius was at longitude 160 West, Latitude 75 North. I have studied these numbers as Pythagoras must have pored over many a mathematical formula. I called in the first and second mates to be sure of what I had read. There could be no doubt. On November 11, the Octavius had been prisoner of the Arctic Ocean, north of Alaska–on the other side of the North American continent.

Inexplicably, the Octavius had weathered the onslaught of the arctic elements, all the while being pushed ever eastward by the capricious ice stream until it eventually emerged in the Atlantic where we came upon it. Gods above but this ship, with its captain and all hands dead for well nigh 13 years, has navigated the fabled Northwest Passage!

THE AIR COLDER STILL, unlikely to be warmed by the thin light of dawn when it came, the Duke had his mind on how Lyman got left by the blinking twinkling electric-lit now-you-see-it-now-you-don't carnival, washed him up in a place that would take care of him until too old and without family they stuck him in the Poor Farm (name like that gets something for honesty, but you gotta take off for originality), a boarding house since torn down, they gave Lyman a squeaky cot for sleeping and a plug-in burner for coffee, one of those enamelled white cups (black metal showing through where the white was chipped away), a night stand for coffee tin and electric burner, a whistling radiator (nobody shoveled enough coal into the furnace it didn't whistle enough) that made the paint peel along the wall, stained and warped the floor where it had leaked. Sometimes the hot plate was just to keep his hands warm nice folks over at the Poor Farm but his breath turned to wintry mist in his room he went out less and less, wasn't anyone to see anymore, he was lucky to have a place to stay hardly anyone came to visit though he could go into the lounge where it was warmer and play cards or checkers, a brotherhood of the unshaved, the unwashed, the unkept. Mr. Brunges with a bathrobe over his clothes though the lounge wasn't as chilly, an iron-belly stove set on the balding green carpet worn clean through in a couple of places like being in a coal-burning ship's belly, same stained shirt every day pretty much, the robe worn through in a couple places to match the carpet.

In Lyman's room, two nails in the wall behind his cot, one for a big crucifix Father Pat had given him, one for his hat gone flat and shapeless no one knew what was hold-ing it together it was like a wet dishrag on his head Lyman's rough-skinned hand putting it on and pulling it off had worn the corduroy smooth, they used it to cover his face when they found him, about wore through in a couple of places.

Not a one of those keys on that big ring he carried opened the door he tried them all a few must've fit but the lock did-n't turn he was at it most likely better than an hour before he gave up trying the same key two or three times each one seemed a new possibility it must not have occurred to him how really cold out it was how he wasn't dressed for it he should've broken a window but he never broke a thing in his life not on purpose never stole a nickel from anybody either, used to being locked out anyhow ain't much use complainin about it someone'd show by morning curled up against the cold his back to the wind that'd be enough they'd show by morning think on a sunny day in the Pleasant Valley (weren't they all?) he wouldn't mind showing Robby and Sharon the bakery, the big old stone ovens and the warm shelf of stone where he used to sleep long as Mr. Vacca didn't mind they thought he was asleep at first when they found him Don't he look peaceful though still wearing bib overalls and his cap locked out for good this time.

The Duke had walked all the way back to Frontenac, was on his way past town, past the silent houses lined up along the street, it was the insectquiet of the fields he was after. Nothing showed in the eastern sky yet but there was the vague sense the world was growing lighter, darkness giving way (though sleep was no nearer), and he knew he had to keep walking, that the only choice left was which road to walk to the place near the gathered dawn where something was waiting on him to do its slow uncocooning, the straits free of ice and mist, he would have to go no farther, no fur-ther. As he set off, he couldn't be sure (lots of front porches were hung with various types of windchimes), but he thought he heard keys, somewhere up ahead in the near dark, jangling on their ring.

FIRE FROM HEAVEN

"...AND THEIR BEAUTY SHALL BE FOR SHEOL TO CONSUME,
THAT THERE BE NO HABITATION FOR IT."
—PSALM XLIX

T*HE SPEAKER IS LI'SHILAH, A TEMPLE HARLOT.)*

From Gebal in Canaan, Gebal near the sea, he comes.

So long has it been [that] the Chaldeans who study the skies have seen many shifts in the heavens of wandering light [for] it has been so long.

Zedebkiah was he anointed, as the Far-Ranging is he better known. No true dwelling place has he, but his legs are made to go astray. Like a strip of cloth driven by desert winds, he is at the mercy of [the] fierce desires that come upon him. Since the time of his youth has he been thus. Yet his urgings do not master him, nor can they be altogether quelled.

From Gebal near the sea he comes, in whose harbor the curving boats of the Egyptians [are made] to lie low in the water with great trunks of cut cedar. From Palmyra, the oasis city in the sun-beaten desert came he to Gebal, his asses laden with trading goods [...the] glass trinkets and baubles of the Canaanites, earrings and drinking vessels, images of Ba'al, who is beautiful to look upon, no larger than a finger, and His consort, Astarte [...] amulets inscribed with spells and incantations to divert the ill wind that seeks to enter through the open mouth.

By the stars he shall be guided [...] tak[ing] refuge in the shade of

[his] tent during the noon heat.

May Zedebkiah never leave the shade of his tent to wander a night whose sky is empty!

For the vagabond augurs have foretold there will come a night when there shall be no star, nor moon, nothing in the great vault of black overhead. As it was in the Beginning, so shall it be on that night [when] it is said the Chaldeans to the east [who] bear witness to the movements of the heavens shall be left shaking their bearded heads.

For with the coming of the darkness that is like the First Darkness, Zedebkiah shall have no destination. Before the coming of light again to the sky, there shall be no city for him to find.

Yea, long before the sun has risen, it is said there shall come a time of red lightning. Wide-eyed and snorting, our tamed beasts shall take to the plains. Man, woman and child shall fall upon their knees [...] shall make themselves as low as the dust and plead [for] mercy.

Lightning shall strike the watch towers along the walls, lightning shall split sky and earth. The toothless beggar-seer, Jeroaz, has said the earth itself shall open and swallow this city and its dwellers [...]. So too shall all of the work of their hands [be] take[n] back into clay. Yea, the inhabitants of this city, what the Nameless One once formed out of infinite love and the self-same clay [shall be] mere clay again. Hezacham, prophet of the Temple of Ba'al, has seen in his troubled sleep brimstone and ash, hot and black, all consuming.

Who is to be believed? For 10 shekels, the seers will also say the Nameless One Himself will appear at the door of the most humble in the guise of a barefoot sojourner. These same soothsayers will offer the beggar closest at hand a shekel to fool the eyes into believing their prophecy has been fulfilled [and] keep for themselves [the other] nine.

Yet also I fear there is truth in the divinings. Just as the tame beast grows wild before the onset of a thundering summer storm, so something of great weight stirs in the heavens. Jeweled though the unfurled darkness is, there is something that menaces even [the] hard basalt bone of the very earth at my feet.

Yet will I stay. [Not to] goad the Jealous God into making fools or prophets of the soothsayers, but to bear witness to the end of this city—has it not been foretold a hundred times since the laying of its first stone? In dust I would see it lie. I would be visited upon by the wrath of the Vengeful God who has...

(Several lines missing.)

[...] was not expected to live, a wailing infant left to the jackals roaming this city. A mother who broke the bond of all natural things, she I have never known. A simple street harlot, it was rumored no temple would have her and [I] do not doubt it is so.

Mother who has never heard her child's voice, why did you abandon your daughter? Why did you leave her at the doorstep of strangers to be named Li'shilah according to their pleasure? Mother [at] whose breast I was never suckled, mother whose face I have never beheld, I would know why.

Yet it may be that I have indeed beheld your face. Perhaps in the market at the busiest time of day, the midday heat and the dust raised by sandaled feet, [you were] amongst the farmers and traders calling out their prices, the hugely fat bearded merchant who sells fine tunics, the yellow-toothed leather-worker whose skin is as creased and thick as the hides he works, the aged white-haired woman, whose face shines like bronze [who] offers clay vessels baked in an oven fired with the dung of beasts. It may be that I gazed upon you and you upon me, and did not recognize you as flesh of my flesh. It may be I was blind to the eye which looked back into mine and from which mine had come. I did not see in your shape the woman's shape into which I have ripened. Nor did you break the silence between us, but left me to be exiled, joined by blood to no one I know in this city nor in any land, [even] were I to journey as far as distant Shinar. I am left the tomb of no ancestor to venerate. I am left no name that I may know of those who came before me. I will be no more than a hungry ghost when I die, my belly forever empty of sustenance. Set loose among the solid things of the earth, heralded by a howl travelers will mistake for the wind, never am I to know peace even in death.

Mother I have never known, have I not gazed at the bare foot of every woman in this city? Have I not seen those as gnarled as the roots of the olive tree with infirmity and age, seen those missing a great or little toe, those whose age is belied by veins which lie curving beneath the skin like great worms? Have I not searched every harlot's place–the temples, the dens of iniquity, the dark streets and houses well known among sojourning men? For it is said the needleworker has put a snake of dark green coils around your ankle. And upon the other foot, strange symbols whereof no one can read nor understand, but with which you are forever mark[ed]. The unwashed feet of the lowest farmer's wife reeking of dung, have I not seen them? The smooth pale feet of women of noble birth, have I not seen these also? Yet never have I gazed upon the Woman-Of-The-Coiled-Snake. Have I not promised gold to the beggar who brings me to her? Yet there is no word.

Shall I tell you (if you yet draw breath, if you so incline your head to hear) I am become a temple harlot? Yet it is not any coin to make me lie with a man, but the coin of a man who suits me. See, even now I wander the walled garden of a noble. I breathe air perfumed with the scent of dates [so] ripe with sweetness they begin to rot in the heat. Long-stemmed flowers brush against my knees and mingle their fragrance. Servants lie within the sound of the small bell [which] I need only strike to bring one forth. A balcony finds its way around the length and breadth of the garden. That the night may not overwhelm me as I take my leisure in this walled garden, braziers have been set aflame. Braziers which hang as well as those which stand have been set aflame. [F]or so I can afford to choose the men who seek my favor. Yea, pleasing to them am I. At a whim may I set them at one another's hearts [so] that they plot against one another.

Before the eyes of the One True God, those who worship Ba'al come to me. I bid Him watch. Him I offer insolence for the misfortune he has brought to me since I first crawled filthy floors in swaddling cloths. Astarte, consort of pleasing-to-look-upon Ba'al, is my heavenly name, for like that goddess, I couple with the Ba'als of this city, I couple with the men who would be like Him. It is because of such as they and such as I [that] the One True God seeks vengeance. Let it come. As one might gather up an armful of hot coals, I shall embrace it. Let the flesh burn away and the scent of its burning fill my nostrils. Let the pain be as no other pain I have felt before, let darkness cover my eyes.

Does He (God) not see also Canaan, where the worship of Ba'al is all? Has He not looked upon Canaan [during] the Season of Renewal? During the Season of Renewal when Ba'al is said to fertilize the earth, [when] the festivals reach full flowering in coupling upon the flat rooftops, has the One True God not seen them coupling upon the flat rooftops still warm from the sun, the sun which has set? To be nearer His power, Man and woman press against one another. In the sacred groves the devout aspire to be joined by Ba'al Himself, in the sacred groves it is custom for the man to spew his seed upon ground to call Him forth. The Canaanite women, who are grown giddy with wine and [the] strange incense of ground herbs, the Canaanite women lie naked upon the newly planted fields in adulation of Astarte. Fathers are wont to give their daughters to sons for harlotry. Eventimes their own daughters fathers take. Abomination in the sight of He Who Has No Name. For such wickedness shall all of Canaan be destroyed also? Or is the Lord of Hosts lord only over our cities of sin in Palestine?

I have been to the Canaan of festival nights filled with flames as if souls of the departed came again to those hills. Sweet smoke from the scorched fields lay heavily upon the hills like a mantle. Sweet smoke lay upon the hills for the fields were blackened with burning. [So was] the way made clear for the season's crops.

Amid the meticulously tended groves of tall trees, coupling did not cease. Amid the groves I saw women pressed against against rough bark by their heaving mates. [Among] the towering pillars of naked stone also and (the) great obelisks marking the presence of Ba'al, there was no end to the lovemaking. Beside the stone walls, beside (the) carved gods of the spacious outer courts of the temple, men and women lay. Worn with their efforts to arouse the gods of fertility, they lay basking in the warmth of the summer evening, they lay with the cool smoothness of limestone against their bared thighs. To the soothing murmur of the fountain whose waters flowed into a clear pool, I have listened. In those waters man and woman bathe to be refreshed. In those waters, the heat and the dust are washed away, the sweat of labors and pleasures are washed away.

I say that I have been to Canaan and seen the evening fires burning upon that land's hills. In my wantonness I have coupled with those men and worshiped the great mystery of the bringing forth of life. The mystery of the ocean of woman, which a man must enter like a silver fish, the ocean of woman from which new life will be brought forth as by a god casting his net for that which swims, the mysterious ocean of woman I have contemplated.

A child it is that comes of the sea of the womb. Why does woman not give birth to a serpent? A serpent [it is], that enters and begets the child. [A serpent] it was who first lay with a woman. The children's tale of a honeyed tongue and a forbidden apple is given credence only by the foolish. The phallus of God entered her in the enclosed garden. A ruin, no more than a snake-skin husk she was left by His phallus. She [was] left the nearest to heaven living woman has been. Even now a man may make a woman call out His name [for] it is union with Him she truly desires. Her flesh-and-blood husband, who is ever jealous of his own god, she accepts in His stead. Imagine the serpent entering His own creation, His daughter–imagine! The first act of love [therefore] incestuous and profane [...]. It has been an abomination to the priests of the Nameless One ever since. The thickness and length of a snake–O think on that, the screams [to] have come forth to lose her virginity thus. Take heed: It is the king's privilege to first lie with the virgin bride even before she lies with her husband on their wedding night. Who in his heart would believe the ruler of heaven would not do so?

(Several lines illegible.)

[...] the myriad embraces, men whose bellies are covered with black wool, as of the lamb. Against mine, bearded faces have pressed. A sweeter fragrance than many (belongs to) the sweat of donkeys. Yea, ten times a hundred embraces have I felt, yet it is the Canaanite trader whose name has been carved upon a secret place beside my heart. The word [that] enfolds his being lies beneath the rising and falling of my breast. [A] second heart lying in thick darkness beside the first, it is without movement. Yet does it burn as if I had swallowed a cup of flaming oil.

Under Canaan's broad-faced moon, in an alley of the island city of Tyre he stood beside me. The sea god's voice in the winds folded the waves as [if] the sea's surface [were no more than] the bed linens of a sky yearning for rest. In the joining of mouths we exchanged breath and he sent himself forth (into me) to such a depth no crude hand accustomed to the handling of wooden-handled tools nor weighty stones might aspire to reach.

If he is found within these walls, the Canaanite trader whose face is forever marked by the flowing art of the needleworker, the Gebalite who will not dwell in one place, his heart would

[191]

they cut out and throw to the dogs who scavenge the streets of this doomed city.

@@@@@@@@@@@@@@@@@@@@@@@@@@@@@@

(The speaker has been identified as Zedebkiah.)

Day rouses itself slowly from the cradle [in which] it is kept by Night. Below the world still lies Day's bright herald, the Sun, yet is His coming foretold by the darkness which draws back like a tide of the sea. From the east we approach the city, upon asses striding slowly, steadily forth we approach. The towers of rough-hewn stone are but vague shapes, they are but gray-blue shapes in the distance. No more solid seem they than the pale shadow cast by moonlight. Yea, they seem but scattered shadow and dust [as if] no more than a gusting wind would sweep these towers from the sky, as if [they were] no more than a dried and withered mirage.

To this city, I come as one unknown, as a foreigner I come to this city. For my name alone is enough to bring the blade from beneath the robes of my enemies. With me I bring half the Chaldean dozen of asses [to] bear the wares of distant Tyre and mighty Egypt. Asses bear the work of artisans in Palmyra, they bear the goods of the Sea People who sail from an island no one has ever seen in the Great Sea, the Sea People who tell of fish that call to each other as do shrill birds, fish [which] breathe the air.

Wide travelled am I, for am I not called The Far-Ranging? The watch towers of Jericho are common sight to me, the palace of Pharaoh of Egypt with its cities of the dead have I seen. Inside strong-walled Erech, whose grand avenues are the breadth of a plaza in a lesser city, have I walked. In a long-dead king of Erech do I behold my own image, he who is said [to have undertaken] a long journey and held counsel with Utnapishtim the Faraway, Utnapishtim [who was] favored of the gods, survivor of the Flood. If you would hear the story of

Erech's great king, conqueror of the Bull of Heaven, the scribes will speak to you from tablets of baked clay, yea the very words of this great king are preserved upon hardened clay. Upon hardened clay are his thoughts carried forth from the tomb. So have the scribes read:

With my forehead to the forehead of my enemy I have stood, the sweat of his brow running into my eye, its salt bitter upon my tongue. And so it is with this mystery. My double-bladed ax have I brought to bear upon it as if it were the skull of my foe. It is but futility for I am offered an airy target. Its silence mocks me like drunken laughter. It is not to be dealt with by a blade of steel no matter how finely tempered. The blood of kings moves it not. This mystery [which] straddles life and death like a giant bridging a gorge between his great legs, it is not of [the] earth yet it is in the earth, in its stone and flesh, in its soil and bone, in the heavens above it. From the top of Uruk's great ziggurat, have I seen the light of the distant stars shining through it.

And what is this mystery, oh great and long-dead king? He who was blessed by the gods to see the House of Dust where the other kings of the earth had put away their crowns forever, sitting in darkness and silence, for whose hunger there was no meat but clay; for their thirst, only dust. From that unhappy place the greatest of Erech's kings returned to the living, breath still within him, the One Who Saw The Abyss. Yet now even that king, founder of mighty Erech of the strong walls, like many kings before him, that king stands beside Ereshkigal, queen of that House, her face forever sour. What was it he wished to wash from his troubled mind with strong drink? The fate common to all living things would he fain escape, yea, who would not? Yet is there not more? Has this legendary king not also commanded to be written:

Mired in the boredom of hours spent drunk, little more I do than watch the incense smoke rise. I watch the fragrant smoke rise while the dancing maidens dance. By winged fears and cravings I am beset. Always I am beset by winged fears which cause me to question the performance before my eyes. Is there no more than this? Aye, to this city with its crowded streets and markets is there no more? The exchange of one good for another, the clinking of coin on coin, the stamp in wet clay made by the scribe who takes inventory—is there not more than this? How I long to bite into the mystery that lies behind all things, how I long to bite into it as if it were a slab of roasted meat. How I long to let its juice run into my beard. Aye, let my fingers grow sticky and wet with what my teeth have drawn forth! I would learn the art which turns that which is beyond my grasp into a slab of meat. That magic I would learn which turns the ungraspable into the forehead of my enemy.

Of its own accord, my head begins to float. My vision wavers as does the street at the time of day when the sun is hottest. Before strong drink brings darkness to cover my eyes, I choose the maiden most pleasing to me. She dare not refuse the king. The long waves of my hair smell of spiced smoke. I offer breath that reeks of wine. Yet she dare not refuse. Smoother than our finest fabric is her skin. Taut like the legs of the graceful gazelle are her limbs. Her body is perfumed with the scent of the flower that opens itself to the coming season. My breath comes fast. Against my ribs is my heart set so that it echoes within my head. To my sleeping chambers I take her.

When I have begun my thrusting, she lies beneath me. Beneath me she lies not knowing she is not my desire. My frenzy is not for her body. My frenzy is to reach what cannot be reached through flesh. She is become the soul of Erech. Erech's paved streets, Erech's ziggurat, the evening sky above Uruk she is become. My hot seed I send forth. My hot seed that is token of my need to wrap that which is bare in the firmness of woman's moist flesh. If she screams, so much the better. All things are born in pain, in pain we die; in pain creation and destruction, the living and the dead, are joined.

So the great king of Erech has written. And have not the Hebrew prophets said: Everything a man does is for his mouth, and still his soul is not satisfied?

So it is with my restlessness: I am become a common face [among] distant peoples. Unchanged I return to this city and my temple harlot. Yet Ashnanna, my wife, is not a league distant. In that city that begins where the other is dwindled to farmer's huts Ashnanna waits. So close are these two cities, were one to draw breath, the other would exhale; were one to fall asleep, the other would dream.

In the city of Li'shilah, my harlot, I killed a man by the blade of my knife. Though [he was] a thief with his own blade drawn, yet my death is desired by (his) blood relatives. So must I enter the gates (seated) upon the last ass in my train. So [must I dress] in the tattered robes of a slave, so must my feet [must] bear shackles. So must I wait while one of my servants speaks with the armed guards to secure safe passage. So am I forced to be still and know the shame of one who has no freedom.

Through the gates of thick cedar I move forward with my head borne low. My head I must bear low, yet words I see beyond [the gate]. I see words written upon a wall in faded pigment. It [is] yet another fool augury: The days of thy city are numbered.

@@@@@@@@@@@@@@@@@@@@@@@@@@@@@@

(The speaker has been identified as Ashnanna, the wife of Zedebkiah.)
In the distances between the cities of the plains, a storm gathers. Dogs cower in the streets, scenting on the wind [that] the long dead have been disturbed. What was buried and forgotten, once more is exposed. At night their howling does not cease. Sleep is no longer like the smooth-flowing river but is unquiet, like the cataract which falls upon broken rock.

In the narrow place between houses, the cat, who is beloved of the Egyptians, who walks upon the wall which separates night from slow-breaking day, the cat lies in wait. Its green eyes are as twin moons in the thick darkness. Lovers have they have seen, adulterers, the incestuous, the men who lie with other men as though with women, the unhappily born and unjustly buried child, the fears of the man who has waited until the moon has risen to bury a dagger in the heart of another for silver—all this have they seen. And while blood is spilled for coin, while bodies lie locked in carnal embrace, a great wind rises.

Fire and brimstone, it is said, shall sweep these sister cities from the face of the earth. Fire and brimstone shall be brought down upon our heads, it is said, [so that] no man nor any beast within the city walls shall find mercy.

Women heavy with child, who are mothers thrice [before] shall find no succor. Children, whose eyes see the wonder of all things, shall not be spared. The man and woman who have only just come to know love shall die in each other's arms. Or it may be they will die on opposite sides of the city, calling one another's name.

To God who is the One True God, I make prayer. If thy mercy shall not be gained [then] before stars and moon have vanished from the sky, bring to me my husband, Zedebkiah.

For him I wait.

The strength and grace of his forehead [make it] worthy of the carvings of the Egyptians. The fear brought on by the storm riven by lightning, this fear his face blunts. [It is] a face burned with heat and wind. The color of [a] fired earthenware vessel is his skin. His face is the brown of an earthenware vessel touched by red, as if a glowing ember had been placed at the heart of him and warmed the skin. The black of the black glass of the Canaanites is his hair. Into his eyes my love has fallen. Many has been the time I have feared it has disappeared altogether, yet by the look [that] passes over his face I saw [that] the stone thrown into the darkness of the dug well had struck water.

Across his forehead dots of black travel in flowing lines, dots flow as if left by insects engaged in dance to attract one another. The markings on the right are mirror to those on the left [as with] the two wings of a butterfly. More beautiful and terrible to look upon, the needleworker's art has made him. [It is] the path of a soul on its way to Sheol, he has said. By a magus it was divined. [Although] it seems no more than a pattern woven by a rugmaker, it is a map for the dead.

Forever is he marked thus. No hand may remove what has been engraved thereon. His soul, when it rises above his body, will look down upon his face, his soul will understand wither it should go. For mine his soul shall wait, [the] shade of him who was Zedebkiah shall await me. If he dies second, the underworld mazes he will search for me. For he has promised not to abandon me even in death.

Though he has left my side, to me he returns [in] the traces of the distant cities he has visited [which have] settled from his robes. Bits of glass fired by the Canaanites, the dust of gold [which] carries the light of the sun within it, the dust of silver, which carries the glow of the moon. The shells of sea creatures has he brought me. Shells he has brought me that in one moment are shimmering white, but in the next, the colors of the rainbow some delicate magic reveals.

These things I heap in a jar even as the Egyptians are said to store the organs of the venerated dead in clay vessels. Ah, if only I could keep his organs while he were yet alive! Heart and liver, stomach and intestine would I keep, that he would always know his home, that he would never venture far. Hair I am left to gather. The clippings of his nails and what falls from his robes may I keep in a jar. As sacred as the clay vessel that holds the organs of the dead is this jar.

In the corner of our garden, a great black beetle struggles with ants. It is a burrowing beetle, the hump of whose back dwarfs his head. It is a beetle wont to tunnel tirelessly into the earth. [...] I wish this beetle free of the ants for he is like Zedebkiah on his way home, he is like Zedebkiah beset by the many ills that befall the traveler. An ant holding firm one of the beetle's legs—is it any different from a band of thieves setting upon Zedebkiah's caravan? Another ant pulls at the thick black wing—is it any different from a dust storm causing Zedebkiah to lose his way? The beetle is the larger, he does not yield easily. Yet if the beetle is pulled to their mound—see how it is dragged backwards!—he will not escape. Though I favor the beetle in this struggle, yet I shall not interfere. So may the powers choose to speak to us even through lowly insects.

Lord of Hosts, hear my prayer! Across the desolate places of this earth, carry my voice to Zedebkiah. Whisper into his ear. Lord of Hosts, it is to him I call.

Be with me, my husband, when the end is upon this city. Be with me in the time of the red lightning and I shall not fear the wrath of God. Your return shall I await [though] this city is become but smoldering cinders. With the ash my dust shall mingle, yea, [if it is] cast to the four winds, even then would I find you, Zedebkiah. At your sandaled feet I would settle, though you would walk on me as you have walked over this earth these many years. You would not know dust was all that remained of your wife, you would not know (that) this dust had been carried over the desolate places of the earth to be at your feet. You would not know that only in your memory is there that which was our home and she who was your wife.

Do not let it be so Zedebkiah! Be with me in the time of the red lightning.

Ah see, they have gone now, ants and beetle. But wither? Has the beetle escaped? Or is he pulled beneath the mound of his enemies?

Zedebkiah who is my love upon the face of the earth, whom I would follow through Sheol itself, be with your wife in the time of the red lightning. Zedebkiah, be with Ashnanna.

@@@@@@@@@@@@@@@@@@@@@@@@@@@@@@

(Zedebkiah and Li'shilah converse. A narrator also enters the text— though briefly—at this point. The inconsistency suggests the text as a whole is the work of more than one author.)

"Come with me, Zedebkiah, though it may be the eve of disaster. Come below the streets, where we have gone many times in the past, in the shadows where we have kissed, our mouths ashen with the taste of the smoldering leaf."

Zedebkiah, whose body was full of desire, said: "I have not forgotten. For do I not bear the scar of the time we copulated in the embers of a dead fire? A deeper love of the clear sky and the distant sea coiled itself like a serpent around my heart in [that] pyre of a burnt offering. By a coal yet glowing my flesh was burned, [even] as the goat's flesh was consumed by flame was I burned. [Yet] was the pain lost in the ecstasy of coupling."

So narrow is this street [that] no more than two may walk abreast, like a serpent it winds through the dankest of brothels. Among the snake charmer's tent, among the fortune teller's room lit by the hanging brazier, it winds its way. It is home to the gaming stalls where a man may lose a year's wages, where a man may lose so his freedom, for the law makes a slave of him whose debt is not paid. A doorway there is on this street, behind this doorway an old woman peddles the roots of plants with strange properties. These and every other scorpion's nest in the city the street seeks out in its long meandering course.

"Down these steps have you been many times with me, but you shall see a stranger sight than any before. For the corpse of a slave was found washed upon the shores of the Great Salt Sea in whose waters nothing can live. So miraculously preserved by the waters is his body [that] there is no corruption of the flesh but what has been done to him."

(The body of the dead slave has been identified as the speaker.)

"... [what] would Habiru speak? [Of] my mouth, which is flung wide open, locked thus in the stiffness of death? With burning incense have they filled it. Smoke pours forth from my gaping mouth. Blackened is the pit of my mouth that is become a widening hole. Yea, the fires of heaven smolder in the vault of my long-gone breath. Upon a bed of stone I lie,

[199]

like Tiamat I am become. Tiamat, the demon of the foolish Babylonians, [who is] as old as Night, who is Chaos Herself. Tiamat, whose form was horrible to look upon, from whose belly sprang screaming beasts of goats' heads and fish tails, she who opposed the rule of the gods. Marduk, it is said, split her like a shellfish into two parts: half of her bounded the firmament, half he made into the fundament, the solid earth. So it is recounted in the children's story the Babylonians still hold as true. Then should my nether region be planted firmly in earth in hopes [it will] awaken to these callings of the flesh. This, too, is vanity, for the spirit of this withered body is in Sheol already. The remembrances of this flesh, dried out and salt-encrusted, only these remain. What it is to vomit forth, to defecate and urinate, what it is to hunger for the flesh of the roasted beast, to grow mad with the thirst induced by the waters of the Great Salt Sea, these are distantly remembered. For numerous things will they use this body: the mouth to burn incense, the stiff fingers to hang their wineskins, the shrunken abdomen to pillow their heads. Thus am I become like the corpse of the false god, Tiamat.

"An empty wineskin am I, only the smell of wine remains. Here [where] nightly their mouths run with wine. Nightly their mouths take in the smoke of strong herb and exhale it so that a fog of smoke crawls across my withered skin. I see the gap-toothed smiles of men bald with shaving as they lean over me. I see women long-haired and naked. No day or night is there here, only comings and goings.

"Here is come a new one whose face is flowing with the needleworker's art. He accompanies one I have seen before, a temple harlot. Her beauty is of black hair and a fine narrow nose, her beauty is made of the rounded cheekbones of the Egyptian cat and the eyes of the lined eyes of the cat (which are said to see in thickest darkness). Yea, the highest of prices her beauty would command. Into the well of my heart she gazes, into the depths of my heart she looks when she caresses my temple with a warm finger. Yet no voice have I, I have no voice to speak of the fatigue my limbs have felt, the exhilaration which has lifted my heart, the cold grip of death that is like bands of bronze tight around my ribs.

"The temple harlot is not alone in her caresses. A woman of hair as wild as the weed which the farmer plucks from his field, as gray as [the] sky from which rain falls [is] her hair, she sniffs as (would) a dog at my nether region. With fingers given over to leather, she caresses the lower region (of my body) where the hair grows thick. With oil pressed from olives she has anointed me. My toe she has anointed with the juices of her own body. On the stiffness of my toe she grew frenzied and cried out with [the] joy of love. Would that I were alive! For pain and pleasure do not reside in the flesh, but only move through it.

"With the pungent blood that comes of women during their moonphase have I also been anointed. With this blood have I been marked across the forehead and chest. Gnawed upon I have been. I shall be gnawed away, slowly I shall crumble slowly to dust, with fire I shall be consumed. Then shall I truly know the void where no memory dwells, where no thought stirs. The void whence nothing is brought forth. Smoke pours from my mouth as if the fire of a soul yet burned within me. Image of comfort!

"Because they fear the void, also they fear the emptiness of my body. Thus have they given me smoke for breath. Thus do they exhaust themselves with fornication and pleasures of the flesh, wallowing in the fluids of their bodies. So have they replaced religion with worship of the flesh, one for the other. So have they sinned. Like beasts they fornicate on all fours in sight of one another as if their desire were to forget they are man and woman (*human*). Yea, in full sight of the One True God who sees all they fornicate. Breath and sweat make the moist heat between a woman's thighs in this den. In this den is a second womb.

[201]

"Silence they fear. Darkness they fear. For are these not the void? In their fear of the void, they are wont to sting their senses.

"Yea, fear me, you who would cast aside the Commandments and the Sabbath. Neither fear nor joy, sadness nor foreboding, dread nor gladness comes to my still heart [which] is as the discarded pit of the date, hard and dried. I lie as driftwood, as I have lain on the Great Salt Sea, so now do I float. Though on a bed of stone I have come to rest in this den of iniquity, yet do I float on the thick darkness of an eternal night, beneath a city lost to the pleasures of the flesh."

@@@@@@@@@@@@@@@@@@@@@@@@@@@@@

(Zedebkiah is the speaker.)
She sleeps the sleep brought on by strong drink. Amid the smoke of the dried-and-ground plant which dulls the senses and causes laughter to flow like wine. The hours are become a sweet sap, thick and clouded, the amber of burnt glass.

My blood, [which] had been heated even as oil over flame, turbulent with desire, is calmed, as calm as the pool of standing water it is.

In blind arousal, we took one another beside the dead slave whom they call Habiru. The finery of her robes, as comforting to the touch as the soft wool from Anatolia, in blind arousal I pulled these [away]. Beneath the milky white of her robes her skin was brown skin. As light to the touch as the petal of a flower was her skin. To me her mouth opened, as sweet as the flesh of ripened fruit.

Lowering herself upon me she took me into her mouth. Gazing upon Habiru, I regretted [that] his withered phallus would never again rise, no matter the crones who have offered their bodily fluids and vain caresses.

I lay upon my back gazing upon the plastered walls. Upon the walls, plastered smooth, upon the walls bordered in the

blue tile common in Babylon, the hanging braziers offered
their dancing light. Below the blackened ceiling, paintings of
the dying-and-rising god, Ba'al and his consort, Astarte, took
strange life from the wavering light. I looked upon those walls
as my head grew light and Li'shilah's mouth moved upon me.
I saw Ba'al, who was perfectly formed, struggle with Yamm the
water demon. No weapons had he, nor armor nor clothing,
naked he grappled with the sea beast where the waters wash
upon the shore. Into the deep water Yamm tried to pull mighty
Ba'al, there to coil around him and drag him to the bottom
that he might never again see the light. From many wounds
blood flowed from Ba'al, stung by the salt of the water as he
struggled in the waves that lapped at his waist, his own salty
waters pouring from him, his hair matted and crusted.

Upon my back I lay, as if fallen on the field where one army
faces another. I lay as if I had also struggled with Yamm the
water demon. I lay upon the cushions and pillows piled upon
the floor. My limbs grew as light as smoke [while] Li'shilah's
mouth sought to draw the smoke-light soul out of me. Yet did
I feel where Li'shilah gripped my thigh, Li'shilah gripped my
thigh so that I knew I did not drift upwards.

Then did Li'shilah climb atop me, as if I were an ass [she]
mounted me. Twisting as does the flame in a disturbance of air
she lost herself amid her own cries. [In that] burning light did
she seem more beautiful than Astarte Herself. I wished her
beneath me, and (so I) rose up. As do oxen in the mud we
rolled. Her legs she clasped about my waist. Feather pillows
kept us from the cold stone floor. Her black hair heavy with
sweat, her cries grew louder [and] my grunts came forth more
often. Harsh as the hot summer wind which rustles among the
dried-out husks of corn after the harvest was her voice. More
breath was there than voice within my ear. As if in prayer too
deep for any priest to master, Li'shilah, whispered beneath me:
"Deeply, yes deeply. Touch the base of my soul, deeply. Leave
within me the seed of your child." She arched up against me in

the manner of a cat full of fear [and] spoke with more force. "Let your seed come warmly inside the walls of my womb. Come forth into my the depths of my cave. Come into the warmth of my love. Come deeply within me, yea, all of you. Yea, make it so. Already am I mired in my love for you. Already am I wet with desire. Flood this cave that is yours, yea, make of me a warm flood." Her voice came to an end, it was lost within a cry, as [a] trail disappears into a wilderness of desert.

I swayed as if at the edge of a dizzying height, yet did I hold back my seed in order to prolong the ecstasy that comes of the joining of the flesh.

Finally did Li'shilah offer herself up to me as if she were a beast of the field. On all fours was she, her head low, her buttocks raised up. Between her smooth roundness—as if sculpted by the skilled artisan—so did I enter her again. At Habiru's feet we joined as animals join. At the dead slave's feet we revered life more. Reverence was brought on by nearness to the slave whose spirit had gone to Sheol. So too was our pleasure brought to a finer point.

At last I came forth, my seed as milk upon her back. Upon herself she smeared it as if it were a costly oil. In that moment I felt the hands [that] had shaped her upon me. In that moment I knew [such hands] belonged to no earthly thing. Thus do I cast my lot with those who worship the gods, though it is true from season to season does my preference shift now for Ba'al or Enlil, now for the One True God or for Marduk.

No more does Li'shilah mistake the union of our bodies for love than the Hebrew mistakes an idol for the One True God. We are no more than jackals scratching at one another. Like jackals who groom one another [with teeth] that graze the skin, we howl in the pleasure of the deep itch removed. We are as jackals rolling in the heat and dust, biting each other. We but flood our pains with shivering ecstasy. Soon shall we leave each other, as if no more than bones cracked open and gnawed upon. As if no more than bones sucked dry and cast aside.

Yea, for the last time have we coupled. Not again shall I come to you, perhaps not [again] to this city. Not again shall we share the pleasure of entering the passageways of one another's body. Not again shall I be found in the smoke and abandon of these dens.

She sleeps while I lie awake. Though I lie awake yet do I feel [as though] my spirit [has] crawled off to a cool shaded place [...] a snake seeking shadow. The sun lies in darkness [and it] may be [that] what the Egyptians say is true. In mighty Egypt it is said that the sun descends by night and journeys the Underworld. In the Underworld, it is said, He does battle with a great snake. Each night He is the victor. Each morning He rises triumphant. Woe to the world should the sun lose!

Through the night I wander. I crawl the stone streets [for] my lust [has] abated. By the stars I see [that] disaster is held off yet another day. Dry in mouth, as if the leagues of hot sands between here and Palmyra were in it, I wander.

Upon my back I roll, as a dog warding off flies rolls in mud and dust.

In a narrow passage I lie. Here are shops with homes built upon them. One on top of another they are as a hive, stranger [than] those bees make, less orderly than those made by bees. There are stones which are ancient, there are stones ill-fitting and loose. Yet the city piles itself ever higher as more dwellers come in from the fields. Here the buildings [are] so close one may leap from roof to roof. One may [make] his way through the entire quarter without touching the street but only roofs. Here I ponder the rubble of earlier cities. Here I contemplate the old bones and forgotten possessions which lie beneath the streets. Above this alley, garments are hung out to dry. Out of windows, chamber pots are emptied. Here the smell of urine is heavy in the stone. The Moon itself [is] confined by the stone walls rising above me.

Yea, the infinite heavens appear as but a small plot in which star and moon lie buried in blackness. From the bottom of this [alleyway], the sky is but a plot marked off in the vast fields where wheat grows. The city is worn with living. The city is worn with our breathing and sweating, with our fornicating and eating, with our urinating and defecating. Our leavings wash over the stone towers and flat roofs like rain water. Our bones and misery collect on the paving stones of the alleyway. Gathered as thick as swamp mire, yet is it invisible. [An] evil sweetness is held within the foul odor of decay, as of the smell of wounded flesh which has turned black. Here the rankest of thoughts find their birthplace. Murders, incestuous copulations, deeds of treachery; here they lie and ferment. Far above this foul bile left by human habitation, the gods [are] untouched in their eternal purity. Far above this city, the gods float in purity among the stars.

What do They know of the ravenous hungers and fierce desires [which] have shaped me as the ceaseless flow of water, as the endless scouring of desert wind, smooths even the most unyielding stone? These longings I do not understand. The inferior likeness I am of the great king of Shinar who was two-thirds god and one-third man. For here I stand two-thirds man and one-third beast. Ashnanna, whom I call wife, is married to the love I bear her. [It is] a love placed as by the hand of the Infinite at the very center of the darkness that stretches within me. Yea, my love burns steadily as a single star shining in all the blackness of night. Yet also is she married to the hours I spend with Li'shilah. To that within me which will not be yoked as is the oxen, is she also married, to that which refuses the harness [that] allows the rider to mount the horse is she also married.

Would it were as simple a thing as the walling in of a city!

Ah, but these are all unfounded musings, a boat in the Great Sea to the west with nothing to anchor it among the endless waves.

In this gated city, a man is measured. Five times his height the walls lord over him that he may reach no higher. His hand's breadth is the distance he must keep when passing another in the street. The criminal speared at the foot of the wall, the wall whose scaling was beyond him [so] was the boundary of his life marked off.

Within our walls we do not fear the darkness that comes with night. Marduk has slain Tiamat, she who is Night itself. Tiamat who knew no restraint, whose form was horrible to look upon. Tiamat from whose belly sprang screaming beasts of goats' heads and fish tails, bird talons and lions' bodies, she who opposed the rule of the gods. With comfort we look upon the rising walls built to hold off the terrors Tiamat would vomit forth. With comfort do we look upon these walls of stone. Yet does not night undo all that we have built up by day?

@@@@@@@@@@@@@@@@@@@@@@@@@@@@@@@@

(Zedebkiah has returned to Li'shilah, exhausted, they sleep for most of the day. Darkness has prematurely settled. Although the dialogue takes place between Zedebkiah and Li'shilah, the unnamed narrator reappears.)

"This darkness which comes early, like the calf overanxious to free itself of the belly of its mother, this darkness will cover me from my enemies [that] I may return in safety to my house."

Gazing upon the heavens, Li'shilah said: "Not a star is there, there is nothing which shines in this sky."

"It is smooth with clouds," Zedebkiah said. "Yet it may be this is the night foretold. Yea, for what else did the prophets mean when they said neither moon nor star shall give off their light but the whole heavens shall be unbroken black?"

Shaking her head, Li'shilah replied: "A storm is come, nothing more. It may be [that] the destruction foretold shall be no more than a single tower scorched by lightning."

Zedebkiah was not persuaded. "Yet may it also be a storm like no other. It may indeed bring the wrath of the One True God who looks down angrily upon this city and its sister."

[207]

"Then should you fly all the more quickly to Ashnanna."

"What of Li'shilah? Will she stay in this city to await the truth or falsehood of the augurs? Will she not leave this city?"

Li'shilah spoke to him thus: "Once was I saved, once I was cupped by a divine hand of airy flesh. Yea as cunning as the air, [it] lurks behind the storm with all of its force [...]. It leaves behind not so much as [a] path in the dust, it is not heralded by fierce winds [...] So airy [is it] stars shine through it [...]. Yet do I believe in it. A second time will I trust myself to it. I will tempt the prophecies. Not until the time of the red lightning shall I take heed [and] flee this city. Go now to your wife. Do not fear for Li'shilah whose life is as the money of a man in debt, though it is in my own hands, yet it does not belong to me."

Angered, his brow drew itself together. Angered, Zedebkiah answered: "Li'shilah shall I throw across the back of an ass as if she were a sack of corn to be taken to market. For in the time of the red lightning it may be that those who have not fled the city are already doomed with it."

@@@@@@@@@@@@@@@@@@@@@@@@@@@@@@

(A significant section of the text is missing. Zedebkiah has not returned home, but has called upon two friends, Israfel and Gazram. The impersonal and unknown narrator begins the section.)

The house of Israfel was full of the burnt-grain smell of freshly baked bread, round loaves of bread [lay] upon the table. Wine there was also, and cheese newly broken. In corners, shavings of wood lay, shavings of wood lay upon the floor for Israfel was a carver by trade. No fire burned in the pit, there was no fire for the heat of the season was in the house.

The house of Israfel was not all smooth with white lime. Gaps of rough stone there were in the walls. Among the walls' crevices, a scorpion lay hidden. For without words, Israfel had struck a bargain with this scorpion whom he had named

Nebajoth: Israfel would abide it to live with him, he would not crush Nebajoth beneath his sandal, whereas Nebajoth would not sting him while he slept.

Who is the man who trusts the unspoken word of the scorpion?

Zedebkiah sat at the table of Israfel with Gazram the Dwarf. Gazram who ate of the cheese and bread and drank of the wine. A goat tethered in the street called, for something it lacked, a goat called. Nor were dogs quiet in the street but they howled as if agitated.

Israfel placed food and wine before Zedebkiah, but he neither ate nor drank.

To Israfel Zedebkiah said: "There is no hunger within me which bread can satisfy. Nor is there any thirst within me which can be quenched by water or wine."

"Zedebkiah, whom I have not seen in the passing of a season, why have you come to your friend Israfel?"

Zedebkiah answered: "Israfel whose beard is ever in need of trimming, whose hair is ever matted but whose eyes are bright and dart as quickly as does the hummingbird, Israfel whose memory is a plain of clay stamped by the reed of the scribe, is it not you who remember the raid of the Philistines and the tearing down of the southern wall? Is it not you who lived through the drought which withered the fields and left the breasts of women shrivelled so that the children cried for want of milk? Have you not also heard the wandering poets who play music and sing for kings, and do you not swim in the knowledge of foreign places as fish swim beneath the waves? Have you not gathered the images of many gods, of Enlil who is the lord of the firmament overarching the Plains of Shinar, of Thoth the bird-headed god of the Egyptians, of Ba'al Who-Is-Beautiful-To-Look-Upon among the Canaanites, of Marduk whose monument towers six times a man's height in the plaza of mighty Babylon? These are no more to you than the glass trinkets of Tyre. These are as nothing to you for your belief in the One True God is as unwavering as the pillars which uphold the temples in Pharaoh's Egypt. Yet the ways and worship of these gods are known to you.

"Israfel whose staff I used to pull myself up when my infant legs were too weak to stand upon, who took me to the gaming houses where a man may be forced into years of slavery to pay his debt, who made me wise in the ways of men and took me also to the brothels to learn the ways of women, I ask you what is this night of early darkness and sky smooth with cloud?"

Israfel answered: "Zedebkiah, whose face in this city is enough to uplift my heart, I tell you I do not know."

Gazram the Dwarf, who drank wine from a clay jar, said to Zedebkiah: "He who is without the wisdom of the Infinite may read the approach of a storm in the sky."

The words of Gazram the Dwarf, whose head came only to Zedebkiah's shoulder, were of little account to Zedebkiah. Gazram's words went unheeded for so it was Gazram was known to drink more beer and wine than water.

"Yet may this not be the night of which the prophets spoke? The long dead are disturbed, dogs are not quiet in the street but howl through the darkness. My own beasts of burden grow restless. By the oaths we have sworn to another, I call upon you Israfel."

Israfel, who was of great girth, Israfel who liked to lean upon a staff when he walked though he was [as] the caravan mule, though he was as the oxen on whose shoulder the farmer places the yoke for drawing the plow, Israfel asked: "For what does Zedebkiah call upon his good friend?"

"For Li'shilah, who will not leave the city until the time of the red lightning. I bid you show her safe passage beyond the walls before the skies are stricken."

"So shall it be done."

Gazram the Dwarf scratched at his black beard. It was known that Gazram, who scratched at his black beard, desired

Zedebkiah's wife for his own. For was he not betrayed by his gaze when Ashnanna was before him? Did his looks not reveal all that was in his heart? So it was he asked: "What of Ashnanna?"

Zedebkiah made reply: "Ashnanna shall I take from these sister cities. In Gezreel, to the west, shall we five meet [...]."

Zedebkiah the Far-Ranging said no more [but] embraced Israfel the Staff-Bearer and entered the street.

The wind had begun to moan as does the man who grasps at the spear which has lodged in his chest during battle. No one was there in the narrow street but a beggar who held out a hand. This beggar's hand had but three fingers.

To him Zedebkiah said: "You have I seen more than once upon my many returns to this city, to you have I always given a coin of silver. A silver coin then, for your three fingers to close upon."

The Beggar of Three Fingers bowed, but made no word. He who had only three fingers made his way through the street while the wind heaped sand against doorways. Against doorways, the wind heaped sand carried from the far-off desert.

@@@@@@@@@@@@@@@@@@@@@@@@@@@@

(The speaker is Hezacham, a seer and friend of Li'shilah.)

"Thou shalt not lie with a man as with a woman. For it is an abomination." So say the self-righteous. Those who would teach the word of the One True God. Yet what do they know of His will? Hezacham has seen when they have not. Hezacham foresaw the drought of three seasons ago. Hezacham prophecied the coming of the tribes of Philistines [whose] intention it was to plunder this city during the moon of harvest. Now Hezacham has seen the end of this city in fire. The self-righteous, those swollen with importance like the river after the summer rains, they will say it is such as I [who] brought down such wrath from the heavens.

[211]

To hold off the beasts of the field, did we not raise a city? Yet is there not also within each man some of the beast of the field? Is [the wilderness] in each man not held back by walls made not of stone, but by the laws of the rulers? By the laws of the rulers and the pronouncements of the priests is a man's heart constrained.

Evil these twin cities hold, yea, it is so. Yet it is not the men who lie with other men, nor the fornication of nobles with whores. Here is only the bestial appetite sated. In the infant left upon the refuse heaps, there lies wickedness. Yea, in the taking of life in exchange for coin, there lies wickedness. He who wears the robes of the self-righteous yet whose heart is black, this man who is full of sin yet is wont to point his finger at the sins of others, he who calls for punishment for what he himself has done, he is most wicked.

[...s]earch the shadows in this city. All that hides from the sun lies in the shadow of a man. In the shadow of a man, his secret soul is revealed [...].

(Several lines obscure)

Yea, we shall burn for our trespasses. By fire the dagger-wound [shall be] cleansed. Across the flat rooftops flees the assassin, yet he will not escape this fire from heaven, by burning sulphur shall he be cleansed.

To Li'shilah I go now, for the woman [whom] she seeks I have found. Yea, of the numberless sinners who inhabit the Cities of the Plain, of those who have wrought its end, I have at last seen the Woman-Of-The-Coiled-Snake. At last my eyes have beheld she who is Li'shilah's mother.

@@@@@@@@@@@@@@@@@@@@@@@@@@@@

(The speaker is an angel.)

When an angel speaks, it is nothing for the ear, but echoes in the cavern of the soul. From the Great Sea of Darkness on which wakefulness floats, an angel raises images in dream.

Li'shilah, favored of God–for who has greater need of Him than the child abandoned? You spurn the Lord, words of spite you speak. Yea, many is the blasphemy to have issued from your well-formed mouth, yet were you not provided for? Who was it that brought your mother to a woman whose womb was barren, to a man and wife who would raise you in the warmth of their hearts? Reserve the bitterness that rises in your mouth for she who cut the cord which binds mother to child. The day of reckoning for your city is at hand. What evil is done on the earth is [what] man does to man, [what] woman does to woman. Have I not led Li'shilah away from Evil? Have I not lain before her all that is Good? But it is for her to stretch forth her hand. Look you closely, for even as an angel may sometimes have but three fingers, so there are times when a beggar has wings that lift him above the noblest son of the city.

Yet so insolent have the citizens grown that they did not humble themselves before me, before a servant of God they did not humble themselves. Accursed ones! Instead they wished to desecrate a stranger with fornication. Blasphemy unending! Their shoulders they put to the door where I was sheltered, a sojourner in their city. They threatened to break it inward upon its hinges. Fornicaters! They would use me as they would use the meanest beast of the field, as only a temple harlot would offer herself though harm I had never brought them. Yea, I was but a sojourner and stranger to their city. To the stranger in their midst, no hospitality did they show. Citizens of the Plain beware! Look long upon that which you love, for these things you shall not see again.

@@@@@@@@@@@@@@@@@@@@@@@@@@@@

(Zedebkiah approaches his home.)
The smell of the storm that carries lightning within it filled Zedebkiah's nostrils, the taste of copper was in his mouth. What hovered in the air brought forth the howl from the cat,

[213]

[i]t caused the ass to bray and shake its head. So close to his home was Zedebkiah [that] he saw the light from the lamp burning within. So close was he that he saw Ashnanna's shadow pass before the lighted window.

Yet Zedebkiah ceased his walking, the ass upon which he rode he held still. The ass pulled at the rein but gained no mastery over its destiny.

Though Ashnanna could not hear him, Zedebkiah spoke: "I am returned to she who is rain to the thirsting fields and rest to the weary traveller, she who is light to the darkness everlasting. Yet the wind is cold and dry that moves across the plains of my heart. My soul writhes like a snake thrown upon coals. What am I that I have lain in Li'shilah's bed after many leagues of dust and weariness, burning sun and biting wind? After many days of living upon food that is dried up, the withered fig and the wrinkled date, upon strips of meat no better than the leather of the sandal? What am I that I have not returned to her until now? She who waits for me with love in her heart.

"Hers is a beauty that moves through me [as] does a breeze. Unseen to the eye, the wind's passing is made known by the wrinkled surface of the standing pool. So is the calm of my soul like this pool of water. The floating glow of fireflies she is, which boys are wont to chase, the fireflies which are like wandering stars of the evening. What draws me to her is not something to be held as water is contained by the clay jar, as wine is kept within a skin. She is like the short-lived brightness beneath the waves of the Great Sea when many fish that move as one return the sun with their silvery skin. Her breath I feel within [me] when the city is before me, when the city is gray and blue in the weak light of the breaking day [...] when the city is not firm but wavers on the horizon, as if it will vanish in the next moment. Yea, even when she stands before me, she is as an unsteady memory.

"Just as the hot eye of heaven [must] set at the end of the

day below the rim of the earth [and] travel the darkness of
the Underworld before [it may] return to the world, so the
star of wakefulness in a man descends when the gates to the
Land of Sleep open before him. [He is] cast into the darkness
which will one day become the Land of the Dead. The sleeping and the dead, how alike they are. [Each] night is prepara-
tion for travels in that land from which no man may return.
So he must navigate the perils of his dreams [for] one day,
when he travels the Land of the Dead, they will be demons
[...]. [During my] sojourns in foreign places, Ashnanna is the
rising of a second moon. A second moon which lights the
Land of Sleep, she shines in the cavernous darkness of the
soul. Scattering shadows she rises [so that] I will not lose my
way [even] in sleep.

"Yet it is one night and many that a fearful dream returns
to me. In a great desert I am lost, among unfamiliar sands I
wander with the storm upon me. To me I hold Ashnanna
fast, but she is [made of] stone. Upon her back she lies, while
sand gathers against her unyielding robes she lies unmoving.
Of hard marble is her face, its beauty is cold and eternal, it
[offers] no comfort. [As] a monument in the great plaza of
Babylon is she [so that] even her head [is] too large for me to
embrace. In the dust swirling about me, the sky is lost. No
voice is there but the moan of the wind. From her beauty I
draw no comfort, yea, I am to die in sight of it."

Zedebkiah held fast to [the] moment [that exists] before
an event of great importance is to take place. Unwilling to
disturb the peace of his house, he stood unmoving. His
wife, Ashnanna, who went and came from room to room,
he watched.

"Ashnanna, my days of journeying between distant places are
at an end. Have I not purchased land for a new dwelling in the
midst of Canaan? Have I not secured land atop a steepness
which looks out upon the Great Sea? [It is] like the brow of a
god rising from the earth, it is like a god gathering form as He

[215]

ascends. There shall we build a home near the city of Gebal, the place of my birth. There shall I not conduct trade in the port city as does many another merchant? To our house-that-looks-upon-the-sea I shall return daily before the sun has set. Along the length of our house shall there be a columned terrace, a columned terrace of whitest marble. There shall we sip wine at our leisure and watch the ships in the great calm blue diminish upon the horizon. Yea, my soul shall be at ease, shall be as smooth as the sun-warmed marble at our feet.

"Not half a league distant [are] the ruins of Old Gebal, not half a league away are the bones of a city. Only the wind moves now among the columns. The wind makes the sound of a woman in mourning for her drowned husband as it moves through the hollow places of the old city. Here at last I shall lay to rest all that is fierce in my nature [...].

"We shall bathe ourselves in the sea that we may cleanse ourselves of the heat and dust of these plains.

"We shall have the harvest of the sea, what is reaped by the fisherman's net, for the evening meal.

"The mysteries of woman lie in the smell of the sea, [for] it brings forth as does a woman. Nor is there [an] end to the creatures which swim below the reach of the sun, the strange many-limbed crawlers upon the bottom of the Blue Deep. In the Blue Deep [there are] strange water dwellers that lack firmness, [so do] they inhabit shells. Even as a body is abandoned by its soul, even as Old Gebal has been abandoned by its people, so are these shells left upon the shore. The spiraling shell shall find a new home in our house, you shall find them as you walk [...] the cooling waters at your feet.

"I shall be free of the noose of [the] men who have made me an exile in my own city, the gamers and assassins, [those] who loan coin for profit.

"To Li'shilah shall I never return, nor leave word of our house-that-looks-upon-the-sea.

"This night shall purge me of all that is evil. In the fires of this night, all [that is] within me that refuses to obey my will shall burn. The ashen remains shall I cast into the sea everlasting.

"Ashnanna, in sight of the sea we shall at last bring forth a child. We shall walk upon the very Beginnings [?], the edge of the Blue Deep, with our child. [He] shall be delighted by the strange and wondrous things which are cast up by the waters. Our child shall know only the comfort of his mother's arms and the salted breeze which moves across the waters and does not cease."

Yet no more than Ashnanna's shadow did Zedebkiah see. Zedebkiah was kept from his long-suffering wife. Ashnanna was kept from her far-ranging husband for Zedebkiah was struck from behind. Zedebkiah was struck upon the head and darkness covered his eyes.

@@@@@@@@@@@@@@@@@@@@@@@@@@@

In a Land of Sleep darker than any he had ever visited, Zedebkiah dwelt. In a Land of Sleep with neither moon nor star, Zedebkiah lay. At last, the mists before his eyes began to grow clear. The mist began to disappear as on a morning [when] the sun burns away the haze lying across the marshes of far-off Shinar. Yet nothing made itself clear [for] the ground was moving. Upon the paving stones he saw only hooves. Only hooves he saw for he was laid across the back of a donkey as if [he were] a sack of grain. Of the man leading the donkey he saw only sandaled feet. The odor that came of him was of the beggar's quarter. [It was] the odor of long fermentation. Coarse black hair grew upon the legs. The woolen tunic was of a color tainted with filth. The tunic was heavy with mud and the leavings of animals.

The hands of Zedebkiah were bound in leather—tight are the bonds made of thongs of leather! His stomach was in turmoil. Only the pain in his head surpassed the wretchedness of his stomach, the twisting of his bowels. After a time Zedebkiah felt his cheek was sticky as with honey. It felt as if the honeyed feet of spiders clung to it. Old was the taste of blood in his mouth.

Bent upon the back of the donkey, only with great pain did Zedebkiah raise up his head. No more than a glance did he take of his enemy. In a glance a single eye he saw, clouded over as is the Moon on certain nights. A scar as straight as the knife blade, above and below [the eye] was the scar he saw. Then Zedebkiah knew Ramaz, Ramaz who was forever scarred and the sight put out in his eye. Many names had he: Ramaz-Of-The-Clouded-Eye. He-Whose-Dagger-Is-Purchased-For-Coins. Desecrater-of-Tombs. Ramaz Extractor-of-Teeth.

Zedebkiah was afraid [for] it was said Ramaz was a worshipper of demons, it was said he used teeth in his sorcery. For teeth are rooted strongly to the jaw. So it was [when] Ramaz wished a spell also to take root, he offered [the] white dust of ground teeth to his demons. Those teeth which held firmest to the jaw, those made the most powerful spell. Those he coveted most. So would Ramaz seek to cause a man's heart to wither, so would he put a poison into his heart and lodge [it] there forever.

"You are not dead, Zedebkiah, for he who has sent me desire you to pay the blood money for Heroam's death. Yet shall I have your teeth for my own."

Ramaz spoke, but required no answer. He spoke to Zedebkiah as if to a stone stela marking the boundary between nations. Whether Zedebkiah could hear him or not, how could he know?

No answer did Zedebkiah make, for he was weak. Zedebkiah did not lift his head, but gazed down upon a single paving stone. It was covered with the trampled-upon dung of the ass, for within it still was straw. Ramaz's sandaled feet no longer moved. He-Of-The-Clouded-Eye stood as if carved out of marble, his tunic hung still as if a frayed curtain. Zedebkiah turned his head, his head he turned to see Ramaz was gazing toward the skies. With great effort [for] his neck was stiff, he was in great pain, with great effort Zedebkiah looked upon the heavens. The clouds had departed–and behold! No star was there nor the Moon. There was only blackness, smooth and unending.

@@@@@@@@@@@@@@@@@@@@@@@@@@@

(Hezacham has come for L'shilah, but a beggar has given her the whereabouts of her mother and she refuses to leave the city until she has found her.)

"Ah Hezacham, the brothels frequented by seafarers and those who wander the dusty land have I searched. The crowded marketplaces and the smoke-filled dens of iniquity have I also sought out. After all these years, the beggar Tiram has brought word that my mother abides beneath a roof of dried grass. Among the goats and their smells, among the dung heaps she dwells. Married to a farmer, he is now dead and she tends the fields alone."

Hezacham, who wore bracelets of gold upon either arm, whose ears were pierced by golden hoops, Hezacham who was fond of wrought necklaces of colored stones said: "Even tonight I have seen her in her miserable hut, Li'Shilah. He who guards the gate to sleep has pointed his finger to her [...]. I have stood beside [your mother] as she swept straw and dung. Let her be forgotten! For by morning, this city shall be no more. Woman who is as obstinate as the wild ass, look to the heavens. Are they not as black as the First Darkness? Is there star or moon? Why do you not tremble before the wrath of the All-Mighty? Why do you tempt His anger?"

Li'shilah stretched forth her hand, she put a finger to a red stone in the golden necklace Hezacham wore. To him she said: "On such a night is it fitting I find my mother. Let us go to her farmer's hut. It lies beyond the walls, it lies beyond the boundary of the city. It may be that we shall find safety [there]."

[219]

"Li'shilah, these many years have I known you, these many years have I loved you. My love for you is a fire that does not burn, [it] is as [the] love for a sister [...]. For you know that a woman's body stirs no desire within me. Have I not always loved you thus? The morning star of your womanhood was yet faint in the sky when first I took you into my heart."

"Yea, barely was hair grown upon my secret place when Hezacham showed me kindness yet asked nothing in exchange."

Hezacham nodded. "Have I not prevented evil from entering your chambers? Was it not Hezacham who kept the vilest of the temple (patrons) from you? Did Hezacham not show you (how) a noble would pay a thousandfold for such as you? Did you not suck from Hezacham as from a mother, until you needed milk no longer?"

"It is so. These many years have I understood [that] of all the loves I have known, yours is the purest."

"Will you not heed me now? Will you not abandon these cities to their doom?"

"Hezacham, I can not." Li'shilah seized his wrist as if the hand [above it] were the head of a snake poised to strike. "Hezacham will accompany me. Or he will flee from this city. I do not fear what is to come. I do not fear the wrath of the Hebrew god. I go now to a farmer's hut beyond the walls of the city. Do as you will. I will know why motherhood has fallen to such as you."

@@@@@@@@@@@@@@@@@@@@@@@@@@@@

(Some dozen lines are missing. Hezacham is not able to dissuade Li'shilah from finding her mother. Upon arriving, Li'shilah ties her to a post meant for tethering animals—over the protests of Hezacham. Li'shilah is the first speaker.)

"years...

[...in] your looks, graying though your hair is, [though] your hair is as badly kept as the field that lies fallow, that is overrun with weeds, even now do I see mine. Mother, you who call yourself Galata, you who left me to the city, so are you now tied to its fate. You shall bear witness."

Upon her knees, Galata was as low as the dirt, as low as dung. Galata, dressed in worn sackcloth, Galata pleaded with Li'shilah: "My child, free me from my bonds! I shall tell you all, from beginning to end, omitting nothing. I shall be your slave, a servant in your house I shall be if only you will loosen my bonds."

Li'shilah, whose hair was scented with oil, who was dressed in the white pleated cloth of the Egyptians, looked down upon Galata without pity. "Mother who left me with neither a name nor an ancestor's tomb to venerate, you shall remain as you are until you have spoken."

The wind which came from the city was full of the heat of the desert, yea, like the blast of air from inside the potter's oven, the potter's oven which fires the wet flesh of the earth like unto stone, this wind made Li'shilah's heart hard.

"Daughter who is flesh of my flesh, bone of my bone, forgive me. Hardly a child was I when you swelled within me. No father had I but him who used me as if I were his wife even from the time I came only to his waist. I cared nothing for what was to become of me, how could I care for another? Forgive me, for I commended you to the hands of a childless couple, I commended you to the mercy of the Lord of Hosts."

Upon her fingers Li'shilah wore precious rings. Of fine gold were her rings, fine gold (set) with precious stones. She made no answer.

The nails of Galata's fingers were broken and full of earth. Upon her fingers there was no more than a rude copper band marking her bond to a farmer. To her daughter again she spoke: "My child, you were not abandoned. Though I kept myself unknown, still I sent copper and silver so that you were robed, in secret I sent copper and silver to keep the gnawing emptiness from your belly."

Li'shilah stood over her mother who was bound to the earth, whose odors mingled with the dirt. To her Li'shilah said: "And still, these many years later, you have not sought me out, you have never shown yourself. You smell as does the goat, your manner is no better. Even the beast of the field shows affection to its offspring."

"My shame burns ever brighter my child."

"These many years have I known you were a whore of the street, for what temple would have you? My father was no more than a sack of coins. You would not know him were you to lie with him again. Any (one) of a dozen men is he."

Galata replied: "It is not so. A merchant of Gebal your father was. He alone was my consort. Even as I abandoned you, so he abandoned me before you were born."

"From Gebal?"

"To Gebal he returned. A wife he took in Gebal, who bore him a son. Haziran was your father called. No more than this do I know of him."

Li'Shilah gazed upon Hezacham but Hezacham answered with silence. To her mother Li'Shilah spoke: "I know Haziran of Gebal."

"Has he come to you in the temple?"

"To what you abhor you left me, you who bestowed upon me no bloodline."

"My child, forgive me."

"I know of him. Yea, through the temples, through the intimacies of the flesh I know him."

"Ah, that you should have shared my fate and lain with your father!"

"Only through the son do I know the father, through the flesh of his flesh. It is his son who has known me, who has known all the passageways of my body."

No words went forth into the silence. Nor was there any

wind fragrant with the reeds of the field, heavy with the heat of season, for it had stopped. Only the everlasting call of insects there was, the call of insects to one another in the darkness.

Then of a sudden did the darkness fall away. A tongue of orange flame flicked across the sky suddenly and there was day, false and brief.

Hezacham, whose courage wavered in his voice said: "It is the time of the red lightning."

By its light of the false day, they saw two riders. Seated upon asses, two riders came from the direction of the city. Li'shilah saw that it was Israfel the Staff-Bearer and Gazram the Dwarf.

Gazram, who was drunk with wine, spoke: "Greetings O Hezacham, whose anus is flung wide open like the gates of the city and admits men of all lands."

Hezacham answered him: "Greetings O Gazram, whose breath could drop the bird from its perch and wilt even the sturdy tree. May the wind bear your blood to places undisclosed."

Li'shilah asked: "How is it that you have found your way here?"

Israfel answered: "A beggar's tongue is owned by any who has a coin. It is the time of the red lightning. We must leave this place."

"I shall stay. And my mother with me. If the ruin stretches beyond the city walls, let it be so."

Li'shilah bent down to take her mother's face in her hands. Close to her mother's face she placed her own. A finely wrought snake of gold coiled around Li'shilah's [upper] arm looked on with its ruby eyes–yea, just as cold as this ruby gaze was the kiss which Li'shilah gave her mother. Joining her mouth to Galata's, [she] pressed tightly so that they might exchange life-breath, she covered Galata's mouth with her own so that nothing could [else] enter.

Israfel climbed down from upon his ass, saying: "Li'Shilah, you know well Israfel is a man of his word. Even so am I sworn to Zedebkiah to take you [with] me to a place of safety."

Li'shilah released her mother and spoke to Israfel. "Ah Zedebkiah, husband of Ashnanna, he has not forgotten she who is slave to his desires [...] might have been were it not for [...]

(The text breaks off here and what follows is badly damaged.)

@@@@@@@@@@@@@@@@@@@@@@@@@@@@

Ramaz was startled by the smooth blackness of the sky (but) started again for his destination. Only a few steps had he gone before he was beset by beggars seeking coins.

To them he said: "Do you not recognize the face of Ramaz with his clouded eye? Why do you ask for coins when I show neither mercy nor charity to the beggar?"

Yet two of them plucked at his robes, upon hands and knees, begging for copper.

Ramaz kicked one, who fell to his side and covered his head. To him he said: "A curse upon you. May the disease which rots the flesh take your body. May you be exiled from this city and wander the plains with neither rest nor destination."

Yet even as Ramaz attacked the two beggars, Zedebkiah felt his bonds cut. Before him the knife passed briefly and he saw that it was held by a hand that had but three fingers.

Greatly agitated, Ramaz cried: "Begone!"

The beggars shuffled off in the unwilling manner of shades who do not wish to be on their way to Sheol. So the beggars returned to the folds of the city.

Free of his bonds, Zedebkiah gathered his strength [for] he feared his legs would be weak. He was afraid his legs would fail him. With the stealth of the creeping cat, Zedebkiah slipped from the saddle, stealthily he dropped to the ground. Yet no sooner had he begun to run than Ramaz bellowed forth. For a moment, He-Of-The-Clouded-Eye wavered, for a moment he stood, loath to leave his donkey untethered.

To the narrow places of the city Zedebkiah fled, his legs

uncertain beneath him, the darkness confusing [to] his weary eyes. Dizzy, as if he looked down from the height of a mountaintop, Zedebkiah mounted a flight of stairs. An open gate he entered, a courtyard full of scattered stones he entered. Weary of the chase, Zedebkiah reached down until his fist closed upon stone. Behind a wall Zedebkiah hid himself. With all of the strength remaining to him, Zedebkiah, who was hidden behind a wall, struck Ramaz. He-Of-The-Clouded-Eye fell to the earth unmoving.

Zedebkiah returned to the street from which he had come. The donkey of Ramaz had not wandered far. The donkey Zedebkiah gathered and rode with all speed through the streets of the city.

Revelers cavorted in the street. In their voices he perceived no fear of the black sky. What was this sky compared to the sack of coins held aloft by the gamer who had won? For what is there to him but the game? What but wine to the drunkard? To the lecher, the prostitute?

Through the dark streets Zedebkiah rode until he had at last come to his house again.

To him Ashnanna ran but he clung to the donkey. His head was yet a bird in flight without its tail feathers [and] he feared he would fall to the paving stones.

Ashnanna who was anxious pulled at him. "At last you are come home. And so I have waited. How could it be otherwise?"

Zedebkiah slid from the donkey and would have fallen but for Ashnanna.

"Ah but you bleed."

In their kiss Zedebkiah felt himself drawn beneath the waves of a warm ocean. A soothing came to him as to one who sinks into the depths of sleep. Though he was in the arms of Ashnanna yet he felt immersed in the warm salty waters of the Blue Deep. In these waters he did not drown, in these waters where the sunlight is broken into fragments like the shattered pot.

From out of the depths of the waters he spoke: "There is no time. We must go."

Ashnanna answered: "Our horses I have made ready. What is most precious to us I have laid upon their backs."

Zedebkiah looked to the sky, studying it as one who tracks animals in the field. To Ashnanna his wife, to her he said: "There is to be a house near the sea."

[In the sky] light the color of fire flash, the anger of God was the color of fire.

"Come Ashnanna, it is the time of the red lightning."

@@@@@@@@@@@@@@@@@@@@@@@@@@@@@@@@

(Israfel has struck Li'Shilah in the head with his staff and left with Hezacham. Gazram, for reasons which are unclear, stays. Li'Shilah's mother has been left behind also, possibly as punishment for abandoning Li'shilah as an infant. She pleas with Gazram, who, in his drunken stupor, does not seem to realize the seriousness of the situation.)

[Galata s]aid to Gazram: "Will you not loose me from my bonds?"

Yet it was to the south Gazram gazed. [The] towers upon the city walls came forward out of the shadow, beneath the heavens riven with fiery lightning the towers came forward. From [a] wineskin Gazram drank. "So angry is the Lord that he will leave an entire city as ash. Little mercy has He for the wicked, little mercy has He [for those] who walk the same streets as the wicked."

Galata pleaded with Gazram: "Watch if you will, yet will you not cut me free of this restraining leather? I beg of you, loosen my bonds."

Gazram spoke still of other things. "Shall this red lightning smite the cities of the plain? Shall the earth itself open up and swallow them? Who can say but an angel? And shall we not be among those who watch the fall of fire from heaven? It shall be a tale told among travelers for a thousand years to come."

"I beg of you, take what you will, only untie what holds me in place like a goat."

Gazram squeezed the wineskin until no trickle flowed from it. Casting it at his feet he stood over her, for she was still upon her knees as she had been tied. "Farmer's wife," he said to her, "you were once a harlot. Be so again."

He drew aside his garment and his member was raised and swollen. As Gazram's hands were too large for his stature, so too was the staff that emerged from his loins. As badly formed as the root of a tree, so too was it thick. Taking her hair in his hand he said: "Though you are old, yet you were once pleasing to look upon." So saying Gazram entered her mouth. No protest did she make but did as she was bade, as she had done when she took the silver of strangers and fornicated. Ever deeper Gazram pushed into her mouth, yet he was not satisfied for the wine had dulled his arousal. Though she was faithful to his wishes, though she allowed him to use her mouth as if it were the flower between her thighs which blooms with the scent of the sea, yet he did not expel his seed. She began to cry out–though her mouth was closed upon Gazram's root–as the newly born lamb, for it was the time of the red lightning and she feared for her life.

To her Gazram complained: "The wine has heated my desires, yet numbed my senses."

He withdrew from her mouth and pulled away the sackcloth that covered her. She raised herself up that he might enter her. In the light of the false day that lasted no longer than the wingbeat of the bird, he saw that her hips had grown broad. Rounded and weighty her hips had grown, yet there was firmness still [as of] a young woman. As if she were a beast of the field he entered her and she cried out. Her face [was] near to the dust and the dried leavings of animals. The sounds of one in pain she made. [It was] fear that made her cries grow stronger yet Gazram thought it was otherwise and took pleasure from his thoughts. Still his seed did not come forth

[227]

though he grunted like the ox who pulls the plow and labored at the task so that his sweat fell to the dust.

His desires unabated, Gazram said to her: "By your third orifice shall I take you."

Still tethered like a goat, Galata pleaded with Gazram: "Do not tarry, I beg you."

With the very juices that flowed from between her legs did he anoint her anus. Spreading apart her heavy haunches, he thrust his man-root into the smallest of the gates by which he might enter her body. A great cry she let out, as if she were again giving birth.

Gazram said to her: "Squawk if you will, for such is the lot of a woman who has lived by harlotry and broken the bond that ties mother to daughter." And with great zeal he thrust himself forward so that she could no longer lift her head but her cheek lay in the dirt. On her elbows and knees she moaned, she moaned in misery while Gazram plundered the treasure of her forbidden portal and grew frenzied with greed.

In the midst of the pleasure he forced from Galata's flesh he said to her: "Mother of Li'shilah, the heavens move within me."

As one in pain may make difficult reply, Galata said: "Come forth then, spill your libation in the temple you have desecrated, come forth at last."

Gazram said: "Darkness flows into my eyes and my head grows light." With a sigh Gazram came forth and his warm seed flooded her anus. [As] he did so, the horizon grew bright, as if the hot eye of heaven had risen once more. Gazram and Galata saw the sky in the agony of burning, for from the heavens, fire fell upon the Cities of the Plain.

@@@@@@@@@@@@@@@@@@@@@@@@@@@@@

The burning finger of God, an arc of fire from heaven, touched each of the sister cities. As a rising sun on the horizon they became, as red as blood was the destruction. So that

Li'shilah could look no more. Hezacham too was blinded. Only Israfel had turned away for fear of the Lord's wrath.

Bearing the heat of the forge where copper is melted and gold worked, a fierce wind swept forward from the place of destruction. In it lay the black ash of stone walls, the powder of bones ground as finely as incense, the shrieks of the wicked and the fear of those who did not believe the prophecies, the prayers of the old and helpless, the cries of the mother and the innocent child, all made foul with sulphur. Yea, the foulest smell which rises from the swamps to the east could not equal the reek of that evil wind.

Li'shilah and Hezacham turned from the hot ash and sand, from the dust and ground bones, they shut their eyes against them. Yet their skin was burned. They fell upon their knees and covered themselves. Only Israfel, whose long robes snapped about him in the howling wind, did not lower himself. His great weight anchored him as if [he were] a column of stone, though his robes sought to fly from his body.

At last the wind died to little more than a stirring of the air. As dust settles after a horse passes, so the silence fell about them. Israfel was first to speak: "The Cities of the Plain are no more."

The sky had become smooth black once more. To the east there was the glow of a false dawn light where the cities lay smoldering. The smoldering cities were become no more than a beacon signal among the hills of Canaan to announce the beginnings of the spring festivals. In a great column, smoke flowed to heaven. Coiling about itself as if in torment, the smoke flowed to heaven.

Israfel held his staff aloft for–gaze who would–its end was aglow.

"It is Gazram's soul to light my staff so. For he has no other way to bid farewell to his friend."

Li'shilah gasped in wonder at the light around the copperbound staff. Yet it soon faded and there was neither light nor sound nor wind. There was only a great void in which neither Israfel nor Hezacham nor Li'shilah moved forward. The beasts they rode dropped to their knees and would not stir.

Israfel said: "Gazram the Dwarf is no more. So too it is likely has your mother perished."

Li'shilah said: "With their own hands they inscribed this destiny."

Israfel, whose voice was like the sound of stones ground against one another, answered: "It is so. Like the fool who invites blindness to stare full into sun, so for his nearness to God's wrath Gazram has paid." His staff he held up. It was dull, as old wood and hammered copper in the dark of night are given to be. "Gone is the light, on its way to Sheol."

"Ah but see." Li'shilah pointed toward the place of burning where the cities had been. "Are there not two riders approaching?"

risen [...] shades tormented [...] the hot ashes [...].

(The rest of the section is too badly damaged to decipher.)

@@@@@@@@@@@@@@@@@@@@@@@@@@@@@@

(In the final paragraphs, it has proven impossible to identify the narrator. It has been suggested that the speaker is Zedebkiah, although this is conjecture based purely upon stylistic considerations. Israfel is almost certainly the speaker.)

[...] scores of generations beyond the passing of this one will name them the Vanishing Cities. Stone laid upon stone with an eye to iniquity, the din of their markets will be heard in rumor only. It will not be certain whether or not they were built by human hands, it will not be certain whether or not they were destroyed by the One True God. It will not be known whether they were ever but shapes which disappear as the winds scatter the clouds to unknown places in the heavens. It may be [that] the tale of these two cities will be no more convincing than the strange dream a man forgets by the light of day. And yet all cities to come shall be built upon the memory of these that never were.

(The next three lines are illegible.)

And these themselves were built upon the memory of the far-off cities to the east and south, whose foundations were laid by the Seven Sages, which shall also lie in dust.

[...] mirror held up to a mirror–[even as] man is held up to God–echoes again and again in the cavernous eye of the Infinite. [...] no more than the curving [de]sign [...] do we [...] in the snaking tattoo [...]

And so [it is].

AFTERWORD

Unlike most works of fiction, which begin with a familiar disclaimer, this one ends with more or less the opposite intent. The fact is, many of the characters closely resemble persons both living and dead. Notable among the living are Millo Farneti, Earl Kukovich and Stevie (the Duke of) Pallucca. Lyman Kispaugh (that's the correct spelling) is one of those gone to the Kansa earth whom I've resurrected in fiction. It is, however, important to point out that while the characters may, in places, be exact replicas of their real-life counterparts, in others, I've added or subtracted according to what the story called for. (Lyman was nothin but a stick cross when I found 'im-a single black & white photograph & a whole lotta hearsay. I decked him out in shirt & pants stuffed him w/straw as best I could so maybe he's just a scarecrow of what he was in life, but close enough you'd recognize 'im if you saw 'im.) And none of the stories actually happened as I've told them, although there are incidents that did occur (the way the Pan Club got its name for example, although even there I changed the sign from incandescent to neon).

As I've just implied, a good number of the places I've written about either have existed or still do, such as the Pan Club (unfortunately slated for the wrecking ball, last I heard, after a fire), the Gutteridge Pharmacy, Pallucca's Market, Bartelli's Blue Goose Bar and PiCCo (the building remains but it has been closed for years, mainly–I suspect–due to the presence of a more centrally located Dairy Queen). Once again, I may have changed a thing or two, here or there according to what the story demanded. Other sites—such as Farley's Tavern and Carol's Corner Café—are amalgams of similar establishments I've seen in the Midwest (notably Otto's Café & The 311 Club).

These incidents, rumored history and lives overlapping with the stories in this collection were to me much like found objects, more or less scattered among the autumn leaves on windy days and what I've tried to do is put them in a kind of scrapbook... and painted in the background.

Vincent Czyz
Lyndhurst, 1998

ABOUT THE AUTHOR

Born in Orange, NJ, Vincent Czyz earned his Bachelor's degree in English literature at Rutgers University and studied for his Master's degree at Columbia University. He worked at the North Jersey *Herald & News* in Passaic, NJ for two years where he served as copy editor, book reviewer and feature writer. In 1991 he received a fellowship from the NJ Council on the Arts for his as-yet-unpublished novel, *Ghost Dancer*. He was again awarded a grant in 1994 for *Adrift in a Vanishing City*. That same year, *"Zee Gee and the Blue Jean Baby Queen"* tied with Jere Hoar's *"The Snopes who Saved Huckaby"* for the Pirate's Alley Faulkner Prize for Short Story. *"The Night Crawler"* was a finalist for the same prize the following year. Mr. Czyz has resided in Lyndhurst, NJ for the past ten years where he continues to find creative ways to make a living while he writes fiction.

VOYANT PUBLISHING

VOYANT is a virtual publishing house made possible by the proliferation of the internet. The name derives from the term Arthur Rimbaud coined in his famous *Lettre du Voyant* (VOYEUR: one who sees, + SAVANT: one who knows) in which he describes the self-inflicted tortures that await writers who wish to be among the great poets of the age. VOYANT was founded in the interest of literature that values the sentence in its own right rather than as a simple tool for moving a story along. While plain prose meant to be accessible to the most ordinary of readers certainly has a place in the world, it has none here. We do NOT, however, wish to exclude anyone from reading a book published by VOYANT. Nonetheless, we do not think it necessary for writers to reign themselves in, to downgrade their prose for some chimerical "common reader." Rather, we'd like to encourage readers to step up to the plate and take a few swings at pitches from non-conventional writers–no matter how the ball might curve or snake beyond the bounds of readerly expectation.

For more information on VOYANT PUBLISHING, *Adrift in a Vanishing City*, and future VOYANT books, visit us on the internet at:

www.voyantpub.com

For additional copies of *Adrift in a Vanishing City*, please send a check or money order for $10, plus $1 for shipping and handling, to:

VOYANT PUBLISHING
P.O. Box 500
Rutherford, NJ 07070-0500

NJ residents please add 6% sales tax.

CONTENTS

PROLOGUE

SINCE BEFORE THE BEGINNING of time It had been creeping through the passageways. The place was dark as night, but Its eyes were aware of every shadow in every corner, every crack between the stone slabs of the floor. It could discern every odour – odours that alternated between old dust and a new, unfamiliar smell. Again and again It had tried to stand upright, only to end up making Its way, as usual, on all fours.

The sound-making Being running ahead of It on two legs seemed to have realised that even though It was crawling, It was faster, much faster, than the Being itself, which was apparently unable to see well in the darkness. Painstakingly, the Being felt its way along the walls, stumbling occasionally, each time giving out sounds of fury.

Keeping time with Its gasping breaths, Its claws clicked over the stone, which suddenly no longer felt rough and cold, but unusually smooth. Around Its body the space expanded to a boundlessness that chilled It to the marrow. From one moment to the next It seemed to be floating in nothingness, or in one of those dreams that so often haunted It. When It slept, Its world would fragment into colours, images, and grotesque faces, until It started up in terror, Its claws hurting, because in Its dream world It had clawed into iron. It would smell blood and awake in the musty scent of Its familiar low den, where It dozed away Its days. Claw marks lined the grey walls all around It.

And yet this boundless place did not seem to be a delusion. It could not understand the pleasant sounds that the Being had made, but some were familiar and made It feel good. The Being still ran ahead, bent over – running so fast that at last It seemed to fly over the smooth floor, intoxicated by the expanse of the chamber. The world smelled different here – strangely sharp – and all the sounds were bright. When It bent down and ran Its nose over the smooth ground, the Being called It back.

'Come!' urged the Being. It knew this word well, but from the mouth of the strange Being it did not sound like an order, but rather a caress. 'Come, please, come with me!' the voice entreated, and suddenly the Being came back and bent down to It, its embrace wrapping itself around It. It felt the Being's dread, took it up into Itself until Its muscles began to tremble and It closed Its eyes with fear. Garish, strange images bombarded It. Even so, It let Itself be pulled upright. It snarled, because being touched was an unfamiliar sensation – maybe even dangerous. Swaying and bent over, It stood there and leaned on the Being, feeling its racing heart.

'Come with me!' the Being repeated. The smell of skin rose into Its nose, pleasant and strangely familiar. It dropped to the ground again. Whispered, incomprehensible sounds penetrated Its consciousness. But the Being did not seem to hear the creeping and shuffling, now getting louder and louder. Light flickered over floor and walls. The Being cried out, and It crawled backwards, so quickly that It bumped into something transparent, hard, and gave a howl of pain. A voice boomed; there were shouts, footsteps. Something brushed along Its shoulder. For the first time in Its life, It snapped at a hand, but Its teeth snapped together in the air, for in the light It was blind. A dull thud could be heard as a shape seized the Being and threw it to the ground. Sounds of pain and sharp words flew back and forth, and somebody shouted at the Being, which, like It, was cowering on the ground. The Being shouted something too, and then there was another thud.

'Come!' That word again, this time an order. Hissing, It bared Its teeth. Its eyes stung from the light that flitted over the ground, flicked over the smooth transparent object, then suddenly landed on It. It turned Its head and fled. The next moment Its world shattered in pain. Teeth buried themselves in Its neck and shoulder. The Being cried out one last time. The smell of blood enveloped It. Then all was silent.

BLANKA

BLANKA WAS FREEZING. Although it was the middle of April, she hadn't brought a jacket. She had expected to be constantly moving, not waiting around like this in the furthest corner of the lawn on the edge of the forest. The school was an angular silhouette against the night sky. A semicircle of torches set on iron stakes lit up the trees behind her.

Two masked figures in dark cloaks carrying torches had just appeared and taken a second group of students away with them. Now there were just four of them left – two other girls, who had already paired up and, standing a bit apart from them, Blanka and a pale boy with blond hair, someone she hadn't noticed this morning at the welcoming ceremony.

'Looks as though they're being led away to their execution, doesn't it?' the pale boy said, tugging at the zipper of his jacket.

Blanka wrapped her arms around herself and watched the little procession until all she could see was dancing points of light. The last thing she wanted was a conversation. It had to be past midnight and she was exhausted. Memories of the past couple of days ran through her head: the long train ride, the welcoming ceremony, spending her first night alone in her new room in the girls' dormitory wing of the Europa International School.

'If things continue like this, we'll still be standing here tomorrow morning,' the boy commented, trying to get the conversation going again. 'If I'd known we'd be freezing our butts off like this, I'd have arrived a day later.'

The torchlights faded into the distance. 'The guy who showed us our rooms today said the "tour" goes to the orphans' cemetery,' the boy went on. 'The old forest cemetery that used to belong to the convent.' Nervously, he fiddled with his jacket again. 'I bet a couple of the idiots will jump out from behind the tombstones and yell "Boo!" And then there are the stupid costumes. It's all so pathetic.'

Blanka looked at the school building again, trying to imagine the convent that had stood there centuries ago, instead of the existing modern, flat-roofed building with its many windows. The brochure had showed an old drawing of the original building. The only reminders now of the history of this place were the old orphans' cemetery with the Belverina Chapel, and the exhibits in the convent museum. And, of course, all that talk of the pseudo-medieval 'Society of Wolves,' to which only older students could belong. Kid stuff, thought Blanka.

'What subject are you specialising in?' asked the boy.

'Maths – probability and statistics.'

'Oh, so you *can* speak.' He gave a lopsided grin. 'I've registered for the special art course. By the way, my name's Jan.'

'Oh.'

'Am I bothering you?'

'What makes you think that?' she snapped. Even as she spoke, she regretted her rudeness. Ever since her birthday, that cursed sixteenth birthday when everything had gone wrong that could possibly go wrong in her life, she seemed to have forgotten how to talk to other people. Jan immediately fell silent and pretended to study the trees. The two girls moved a little further away so they could text without interruption.

Another half-hour went by in silence before the points of light began to dance again. Five figures were coming over the lawn towards them. Two were wearing wolf masks, and the others wore medieval costumes. One of them glittered bright yellow and red in the torchlight.

'Why are there so many now?' whispered Jan.

'Four to hold us down and one to swing the axe,' replied Blanka.

Jan let out a nervous laugh. 'It may seem funny now, but on the way here I met a university student – he used to go to school here. He told me something about the Wolves that wasn't so funny.'

'Well, clearly he survived the night tour.'

'He didn't mention this masquerade. He just said that the Wolves were all freaks and that I should watch out for myself. They dragged a guy who had messed with them out of his room one night, put him in a sack, and threw him into the river.'

'What?'

'I'm sure he wasn't exaggerating.' Jan lowered his voice to a whisper, as if the approaching figures could hear him. 'It turned out the sack was easy to open, and the river was only a metre or two deep at that point, but still . . .'

Blanka shivered. The night seemed even colder. 'What happened then?'

'He couldn't prove the Wolves had done anything. They all had alibis, and the headmaster at the time believed them.'

'Relax,' said Blanka. 'It's only a tour – in the brochure they make it sound like a tourist attraction. Once around the campus, to the old manor house, and to the cemetery, that's all.'

'Silence! No talking!'

Blanka and Jan spun around. Pointed fangs gleamed in the torchlight, and empty eye sockets glared at them. A tall, wiry boy in a wolf mask stepped up to them. He carried a spear in one hand and his fur cloak was shabby and smelly, as if it had been in a damp cellar for a long time. Something about him made it clear that he was the one the rest followed. Another masked figure, wearing a dark-green priest's robe and an iron mask, had come out of the forest too and now stood beside him. Blanka bit back a disparaging comment – their eerie entrance had had its effect and she wasn't feeling quite so bold. How long might these two have been lurking in the forest behind them? By this time the others had crossed the lawn and they formed a circle around the four new arrivals.

'Who shall we take?' growled the one in the colourful robes. From his belt hung what looked like a long, light-coloured bone in which holes had been bored at regular intervals. It might have been a flute. There was a jingling sound as he sprang forward and gave Blanka a rough shove.

'Hey!' she cried in protest, taking a step back. She felt the breath of another of the masked figures on the back of her neck and spun around. She looked into light-blue eyes.

'Hmm, we'll take those two in the back and this little one,' declared one of them. 'He'll be scared otherwise, all alone in the dark!' It was a female voice, and her costume was modelled on a nun's habit, except for the large stick she repeatedly slapped into her hand. Blanka remembered something. Could she be the short-haired girl who had assigned them their rooms? Around the chalk-white mask, which gave her face a severe expression, some dark strands poked out.

'So, you back there – and you!' thundered the boy who

7

had jostled Blanka, pointing his bone flute at the girls and Jan. As if on command, the others tipped their heads back and started howling, tightening the circle and lifting their torches threateningly.

'Cool it,' grumbled Jan. He adjusted his jacket again and joined the two girls. The circle disappeared as two of the Wolves took their places to the right and left of them. They nodded to the others and marched off with the three newbies across the lawn towards the school. Jan looked back and hesitated for a moment, but when he saw Blanka reaching for her bag as if to join the group, he turned around and caught up with the others.

'Where do you think you're going?' asked the nun menacingly, stepping in front of Blanka. Slap, slap went the stick. 'We can't take more than three per tour.' Before Blanka could answer, the others had formed a barrier in front of her. Involuntarily, she clung to her bag. The tall boy, the one with the spear, stepped out of the line and paced out a circle around her.

'Not so much fun being out here alone, is it?' he murmured. The others laughed, as if on command.

'What do you think you're doing?' asked Blanka indignantly, her voice a little squeakier than she would have liked.

The ringleader stretched out his hand to stroke her black hair. 'A genuine Snow White!' he jeered. Dark eyes shone behind his wolf mask. His voice seemed familiar to Blanka . . .

'I know you,' she said. 'This afternoon you took us through the school. You're Joaquim.'

'Here I'm just one thing – your nightmare . . .' – he paused for effect – 'Blanka.'

'I'm impressed,' she replied mockingly. 'Did it take you long to learn all ten new names by heart?'

'We know a lot more about you,' whispered Joaquim. 'You come from a dinky little town this side of nowhere, read too many detective stories, and want to take psychology at university. You're good at maths – but not good enough for this school. And when we've finished with you, you'll understand why.'

From the throbbing in her fingers Blanka realised how tightly she had been gripping the straps of her bag. The Wolves were silent now – just a wall of mouths, patches of shadow and tongues of flame. They inched closer. The nun gripped her stick fiercely. Blanka forced herself to respond calmly.

'Unbelievable,' she said to Joaquim, looking him squarely in the face. 'You can even read the room assignment lists. When you're all done with your little charade, can we finally get going?'

No one answered. The silence was suffocating. Then the nun brought up her stick, let out a war cry, and leaped forward. The stick shot out so fast that Blanka hardly had time to react. The weapon stopped directly in front of her nose.

'Broken nose,' whispered the nun. Quick as lightning she took another swing and forced Blanka to one side with a feigned blow. 'Rib!' The other Wolves laughed. Blanka's heart was racing, and her knees felt as though they were made of rubber. This was no longer a joke.

'Are you scared?' whispered the boy with the bone flute. 'You should be!'

Blanka gulped. 'Five against one,' she replied. 'Apparently you're the ones who are scared.' The nun sniggered.

Joaquim stepped forward. 'Well, we'll see how brave you really are.' At a signal from him, his followers took the torches from their stakes. They left only one in place.

'We'll come back,' he said quietly. 'And then we'll see who's got the big mouth here. Or are you going to run straight home to Mummy?'

He laughed, turned around, and walked away. Obediently the Wolves followed him.

'Ten minutes, Joaquim!' called Blanka after them. 'I won't wait any longer than that!'

No one turned around.

Blanka sank down onto the cool grass and tried to breathe calmly. It took her quite a while. Not until the Wolves were long out of sight did she begin to feel angry. Why had she let them intimidate her? Clearly, frightening the new students was part of the program. Well, these dress-up freaks would have a tough time of it with her. She wrapped her arms around her legs and laid her head on her knees. As soon as she shut her eyes, she saw her parents' faces. Just yesterday they had taken her to the station. Through the train window she had watched their unhappy, anxious faces getting smaller and smaller. In some ways, it seemed like years ago, but the feeling of loss was still raw.

When Blanka opened her eyes, she saw only darkness. She must have nodded off. The single torch had gone out, it was even colder and her legs had gone to sleep. Dazed, she rubbed her eyes, groped for her bag, and pulled her watch from the side pocket. The crescent moon was partly obscured by light cloud, and in its weak light she could only guess at the position of the watch hands. She had been alone for nearly an hour. Blanka fought against the impulse to howl with rage. The Wolves had simply left her behind! How could she have been so stupid as to wait at the edge of the forest like a well-trained puppy? She hadn't even been surprised when they had taken the torches with them. Of course: they play this trick on the last student, and today that happened to be her. Slowly she stood up and rubbed her stiff knees.

'Idiots!' she snapped. With uncertain steps she crossed the

lawn, heading for the barely discernible buildings. The bushes seemed like shadowy figures lurking at the side of the main path, but the crunch of shoes on gravel was comforting. Finally, Blanka reached the visitors' carpark and ran across the stone path towards the main gate.

Directly in front of her stood the old manor house, which had been built at the beginning of the twentieth century. Today it served as the boys' dorm. Blanka remembered that the girls' dorm was to the right of the manor house, in the same building as the library, and she headed towards the glass structure. The gate was shut – of course. Looking around, Blanka discovered a side entrance on the left, where the bell and the intercom were. She would have to wake someone up to get inside the building. The sensor light came on automatically, startling her. Blanka hesitated, then rang the bell. Expecting a tired, expressionless voice on the other end, she leaned against the door – and nearly fell face first over the threshold. She peered, dumbfounded, into the dark passageway that lay open before her. The door was open! No voice came over the intercom. Well, at least she would be spared the embarrassment of having to explain what she was doing out here at two in the morning.

The passageway led past the bathrooms to the foyer of the library. The glass doors gleamed, black as swamp water. Here, on safe ground, Blanka felt her exhaustion returning. She just wanted to sleep. She felt a draught on her neck. Somewhere around here there must be an open door or window. Blanka stopped and strained her ears in the darkness. Of course she could hear something – everyone heard noises in the dark. This one reminded her of a distant metallic whine. Blanka held her breath and waited. The noise stopped, and in its place she imagined she sensed a shadowy movement to her right.

'Hello?' she called out tentatively. Silence. Surely the light switch must be somewhere near the doors. She bumped her hand against the hard surface, which was closer than she had expected. Her fingers first touched cold glass, then metal, and, finally, smooth wallpaper. At last she found the switch. Fluorescent light flickered on. Reading tables gleamed among deserted chairs.

Blanka heaved a sigh of relief, made her way past the tables, and darted towards the stairs that led to the second floor. If she remembered correctly, the main room of the library was to the right, and to the left were the stairs leading to the dorm.

As she ran, she almost didn't notice the object on the floor – a rumpled coat of some sort. It looked as though someone had just flung it down carelessly. But was there something wrapped up in it? Blanka stopped for a closer look. She noticed fingers poking out from one of the wide sleeves. And half-hidden beneath the turned-down collar, surrounded by dark grey hair, a cheek was touching the stone floor. With an expression of mild amazement, blue, wide-open eyes stared into emptiness.

MADAME LALONDE

HEADMISTRESS MARIE-CLAIRE LALONDE had the situation under control. She had told the young detective to seat himself in the chair nearest her desk, kindly, but so firmly that no objection was possible. The sunlight streaming into the room through the high window was blinding. Every time he looked up from his notebook to ask Blanka the next question, he squinted. Blanka, on the other hand, was sitting in the shaded corner near the door. The armchair was a little too low to be comfortable. The room itself had an air of serious discussions and important decisions. Normally just students would be sitting here, getting a dressing-down from Madame Lalonde. After a sleepless night, Blanka was feeling unfocused and off-balance, but at least she was no longer so cold, now that Madame had pressed a cup of tea into her hands. The detective did not look much more awake than she was.

'All right,' he said finally, putting his pen into his breast pocket. 'I think that's enough for now.' With some effort, he pulled a crumpled card from his well-thumbed diary. 'Here's my contact information.' The chair creaked as he leaned towards Blanka.

'Thank you,' said Madame Lalonde, quickly intercepting and

taking the card. The detective frowned, but made no objection. For the first time, Blanka thought she saw a flicker of emotion on his face. It seemed clear that he did not particularly care for Madame Lalonde. The headmistress did not sit down at her desk again but remained standing, the card still in her hand. Blanka actually felt grateful right now for the commanding manner of this tall, striking woman. The detective stood up.

'If you think of anything else, give me a call,' he said, looking directly at Blanka. 'Carsten Seibold – it's all on your card.' At the word 'your,' which he stressed, he gave a sidelong glance at the headmistress.

'I will,' Blanka managed to say. 'Thanks.'

'Well, then, I'll be off. Take care now.'

When he offered his hand to shake – a hand that poked out of a wide sleeve a little too long – her stomach lurched. She had to force herself to take it and say goodbye. Madame Lalonde was watching the detective's every move intently – as if she was afraid that he might pull out his gun and carry Blanka off. The door clicked shut, and it was over. Blanka heaved a sigh of relief and slid down deeper into her chair. Her fingers were throbbing from the heat of the cup.

'Drink a little more, at least,' said Madame Lalonde. She moved to where the police officer had been sitting. Unlike him, she did not squint, although the sun was shining straight into her face, highlighting every little line. Obediently, Blanka lifted the cup to her lips and took a sip.

'I'm sorry you had to go through that,' said Madame after a lengthy pause. 'And on your very first day at my school.'

Blanka was about to respond but the headmistress continued. 'Well, at least I can offer you the best support we have available. Here at the Europa International School we are fortunate in having close connections with the university. You know, of course, that our optional courses are given in part by associate professors from there. One of them is a very good psychologist, Dr Hasenberg, and he's here at the school at least once a week. So if you'd like . . .'

'No thanks,' said Blanka. 'It's nice of you to offer, but I can deal with what happened last night on my own. I'm just overtired.' Was she coming across as an emotional wreck?

Madame Lalonde frowned. Blanka had the feeling that she was analysing her words, holding them up to the light and moving them back and forth, like a doctor looking at an X-ray. She made an effort to return the headmistress's gaze nonchalantly. Madame's eyes were blue – but an unusual dark outside ring sharply contrasted with the iris. It was a mesmerising, frighteningly intense gaze.

'I'll understand if you want to return home for a while after this shock,' the headmistress said finally. Her voice sounded warm and caring. 'If you want, you can come back in a couple of weeks.' The cup felt like a lead weight in Blanka's hands. Her home flashed before her eyes: her father bent over a radio he'd taken apart, his brow deeply furrowed; her mother coming home from work, pale but moving energetically in the scuffed, sensible shoes that she wore late into the night in the corridors and restaurant of the Mountain View Hotel. The image seemed foreign to her now, and it did not feel like home. She remembered Joaquim's words: 'You're not good enough for this school.' Statements like that shouldn't bother her, not her, the Blanka who was so proud that she never cried. Nevertheless, tears suddenly filled her eyes. She fumbled around in her jeans pockets until she unearthed a crumpled tissue. From the corner of her eye she saw that Madame Lalonde was standing up, and the next moment she felt a hand on her shoulder.

'If you don't feel up to studying after this incident, we could delay your application for six months. You wouldn't even need to reapply – your scholarship would simply be postponed until . . .'

'No!' The word slipped out more violently than she had intended. She would hold on to this opportunity the school was giving her.

To Blanka's surprise, the headmistress laughed. 'Don't break the poor cup! No one wants to send you away from here, least of all me. I'm happy to be able to admit such a good student. I have read your application carefully – you're interested in taking psychology at university?'

Blanka nodded.

'Well, I think you have what it takes. Your determination to stay here, for one, shows me that you're not easily held back.' Madame Lalonde smiled and suddenly seemed very likeable. Her honey-coloured hair shone in the morning sun. 'You know, I was certain you'd stay. I'm not often wrong in my assessment of new students.' With these words, she went back to her desk. Blanka heard the scraping sound of a drawer being opened. Madame Lalonde continued speaking as she pulled out several pieces of paper. 'You're very bright, that's clear. But you sometimes have a sharp tongue, am I right? I think that on the inside you're quite different.' Her eyes were soft and kind. 'I was very similar as a young girl. I'm sure you'll fit in very well here.'

'Well, that's not what the Wolves think.' The words just slipped out. 'Is it true that one night they threw a student into the river?'

Madame Lalonde's eyes turned serious again.

'Who told you that?'

'A new student – he heard it on his way here.'

Madame Lalonde sighed and pushed a loose strand of hair behind her ear.

'Yes, that story's been going around for quite a while – it's as persistent as an urban legend,' she said. 'In all the time I've been headmistress here, though, I've never received a complaint like that. What's more, I can hardly imagine how anyone supposedly kidnapped a student from his room and transported him to the river without being noticed.' She sighed. 'And with regard to the Wolves . . . well, I can't say I approve of everything they do. They have their own special rites, their code of behaviour, and their . . . tests of courage, just like any other student association. They belong to the school as much as the exhibits in the museum and the old chestnut trees in the park. They've been a tradition here for over fifty years.' She smiled again. 'So far, every student has found his place here – as long as they arrive with the necessary staying power. But I'm not worried about that in your case. If you should have any problems with the Wolves, you can always come to me for help.'

Wonderful, thought Blanka. Now I'm a tattletale!

'Another thing I should tell you,' Madame Lalonde continued, 'is that I've decided to put you in with the students in the senior class, rather than with the new students. Caitlin O'Connell will help you settle in. She comes from Ireland and will soon be taking her final exams. She'll be in the adjoining room in your dorm.'

'I don't need any help,' Blanka protested. 'I'm not sick – I just stumbled across a dead body last night. I'll get over it.'

'Of course. But I'm sure you'll like Caitlin. Maths is one of her strongest subjects.'

Blanka looked up with interest. Well, that was different. She drank the last of her tea and nodded. 'That's fine,' she said, trying to smile. 'For now, at least. But there's something else . . .' She swallowed hard and asked the question that Detective Seibold had not wanted to answer for her. 'The dead woman . . .' She saw the headmistress stiffen slightly. 'She broke her neck when she fell, didn't she?'

Madame Lalonde rested her elbows on her desk. 'As far as we know at present, yes, it looks like it,' she said finally.

'Detective Seibold is from the homicide squad?'

'Yes. In a case of a sudden death like this, the first thing they do is check to see if it could have been murder. Especially since we have no idea at all who the woman was or how she got into the building.'

'The door was open.'

'I know. You told Detective Seibold. Well, she wouldn't be the first one to break in.'

'What could she have been looking for?'

'Do you any idea how much one page of our seventeenth-century convent chronicle is worth?' She seemed to be struggling to regain her composure. 'However, it's not our problem. It's the job of the police, and no one but the police, to figure out what happened.' With these words the headmistress shut her desk drawer firmly. There was a knock at the door that made Blanka jump.

'Come in,' called Madame Lalonde, her matter-of-fact head-mistress's voice returning. A tall man entered. When he realised that Madame Lalonde was not alone, he raised his eyebrows. Blanka had seen him before. He was the caretaker, she remembered, a crabby old fellow who looked as though he had drunk too much for the last thirty years. The fine veins on his nose shone red and dark purple. Even so, his sports jacket looked custom-made. Blanka had never seen a caretaker wearing a sports jacket before. But then, did anything at all at this school seem normal?

'The chairs and lamps are here,' he growled. 'You have to sign the delivery slip. And the electrician wants to know where you want him to put the lamps.'

'Of course,' cried Madame Lalonde. 'Blanka, please excuse me for a few minutes.'

Her step brisk, the headmistress left the office. Blanka heard the bunch of keys the caretaker wore fastened to his belt jangling with every step. With no eyes on her at last, the tension began to melt away. Wondering how long Madame might be, she drew back her arm, aimed, and threw the crumpled tissue in the direction of the wastepaper bin beside the desk. It hit the edge of the bin, fell on the floor, and rolled away, towards the chair behind the desk.

Blanka got up and wandered over to the desk. She glanced out of the corner of her eye towards the half-open door, but to her relief she heard no steps. So she ducked behind the desk, grabbed the tissue, and stood up again. So this was what the world looked like from Madame Lalonde's perspective. From here she could see not only the whole office, but also part of the hallway and – through the window – the main entrance and the park. If she had been sitting at her desk last night, she would have seen the Wolves setting out to fetch the new students. Much more interesting to Blanka than the view, however, was the stack of papers on Madame Lalonde's desk. Blanka noticed a drawing that looked like a branching geometric diagram. Only when she stepped closer did she realise it was some sort of family tree. She set down her empty cup and leaned in to get a better look. Instead of names, abbreviations were entered, as well as symbols that looked very scientific. The principles of association were easy to recognise: connections were shown by two interlocking rings. To Blanka, it looked like the intersection of mathematical sets. Each intersection formed a child – and in one place, even two children. 'Dr Florian Hasenberg' was noted in shorthand at the edge of the page.

Blanka heard the sound of jangling keys approaching. She jumped, and stumbled over something soft and shapeless. She caught herself before she fell, grabbing the edge of the desk for support. She shook off the object that had caught her foot.

It was a light-coloured leather bag. She bent down quickly and pushed it back to where it had been leaning against the desk. The leather was as soft as a suede jacket and in good condition, though clearly not new. Something on the flap caught Blanka's eye – interlacing initials burned into the leather: an 'M' and a 'J.'

The next moment Blanka was sitting in her chair again, her heart beating wildly. The headmistress and the caretaker entered the room a second later.

'Mr Nemec will take you to your dorm now. Blanka will be rooming with Caitlin O'Connell for the time being.'

The caretaker studied Blanka and then nodded. His glance travelled to the desk, as if drawn by a magnet. Blanka blushed furiously. Her cup was right beside Madame Lalonde's documents.

The telephone rang.

'Lalonde,' the headmistress answered. Her expression was matter-of-fact, but then her glance fell on Blanka, and her voice became friendlier. 'Of course. Just a moment, please.' She smiled encouragingly at Blanka. 'It's your father. He says he can't reach you on your mobile.'

Blanka jumped up and shook her head. 'Tell him I'm fine and I'll call him. Please!' For a few long seconds she looked imploringly into Madame Lalonde's strange eyes. There was an unfamiliar but not unpleasant feeling of closeness. Madame Lalonde hesitated briefly, then nodded and took her hand off the mouthpiece.

'Come with me,' grunted Mr Nemec. He turned around and jangled out of the room.

CAITLIN

CAITLIN CAME FROM THE IRISH COAST, near the town of Dingle. She did not fit the stereotype of the red-headed Irish girl at all, but had short brown curls and green eyes that shone like light-coloured malachite. The introductions were friendly, if a little cool, but after Mr Nemec left, Caitlin seemed relieved and gave Blanka a genuine smile.

'Welcome to your new kingdom.' Caitlin motioned towards a narrow bed, a desk, and a chest of drawers. Not exactly smart, but not uncomfortable either. Through the narrow window Blanka could see the visitors' carpark, and she glanced at the hill behind it, where the orphans' cemetery was. A shiver ran up her spine.

'The rooms in this building were originally a lot bigger, but since we keep getting more and more students, they had to renovate this old teaching wing,' said Caitlin. 'The rooms were divided in two – and most have this connecting door. Some of the students moved their chest of drawers to block the door, but Jenna – the girl who moved out of here three weeks ago – and I usually just left it open during the day.'

Indeed, in the middle of the wall to the left was a simple

wooden door. Blanka finally put down her heavy backpack and suitcase and followed Caitlin into the next room. It was like entering another world. A colourful patchwork quilt covered the bed, with a well-worn stuffed toy crocodile stretched out on it. Around the window was a string of red heart-shaped lights, and the whole wall was covered in photos, cards and mementoes, all pinned to the wallpaper with drawing pins. One was of Caitlin with two boys who had the same green eyes as she did. They had their arms around each other and were laughing into the camera. 'My brothers, Aidan and Paul,' said Caitlin with obvious pride. 'And in this picture here, that's my little sister, Kathy. That's my Mum and that's my Da, and that's my friend Deirdre. When I've finished here, I'm going to Trinity College in Dublin. Deirdre's going to apply, too. Maybe we'll even be able to get jobs as teachers at the same school.' Her words echoed in Blanka's head. Caitlin's room intimidated her – so warm, cosy and safe. There were presents from her family everywhere. You'd never know that her door led out to a hallway lit by fluorescent lights and not the living room of her parents' house in Dingle.

'Don't you have any photos of your family?' asked Caitlin, when a little later Blanka pinned a poster of the solar system onto her wall.

'No,' said Blanka, a little too abruptly.

'Or of your boyfriend?' Caitlin eyes twinkled. 'You must have one!'

Blanka pressed her lips together and shook her head. That was all she needed – her roommate reminding her about Alex.

'Sorry. Did I say something wrong?' Caitlin wasn't giving up. 'Did you two break up?'

'What else do you want to know?' Blanka snapped. 'My shoe size?'

It was supposed to sound like a joke. Caitlin looked at her thoughtfully but didn't ask any more questions. Blanka choked back her tears, unpacked her things, and began her new life.

It was not quite as easy as she had thought it would be. As soon as she closed her eyes, she saw the woman in the rumpled coat. That first night in her new, much-too-soft bed, Blanka several times caught herself running her fingers down her neck, lost in thought. How bad did a fall have to be, to break your neck? Even after all the noises from the neighbouring rooms and hallways had died down, the formulas, numbers, and calculations that normally sent Blanka off to sleep weren't working. Counting did not help, either, nor did visualising imaginary numbers, which flared up briefly in the darkest corners of her imagination and then faded away again. Not even the thought of her problems with her parents could distract her from the woman with the grey curls. Her face kept coming back, her lips moving as she tried to tell Blanka something. Blanka went over every detail of this stranger's face in her mind, someone she had only seen for a few moments. It seemed important to picture her alive. She had a dimple in one cheek – it must have looked nice when she smiled. But her forehead was furrowed with worry lines. What had brought her to the school library? Blanka couldn't shake the memory of that hand poking out from its sleeve – the hand of a grown woman, with fingernails chewed down to the quick, like those of a nervous thirteen-year-old.

Despite the investigation, the new semester at the Europa International School began as planned. Only the library was closed. Every time Blanka looked out her window into the carpark, a police car was there. And for the first few days, Blanka was a novelty for her fellow students. More than once she noticed students poking one another and nodding towards her. But she didn't have much time to feel annoyed.

Her course load was very heavy. At times Blanka envied Caitlin for having already made it through most of her studies, with just the final exams to go. The hours in class seemed to fly past, but the mountain of books that she apparently had to master before those first few preliminary exams in a few weeks did not get any smaller.

Although there were a number of mandatory subjects that scarcely interested Blanka, the course in probability theory was a revelation. The professor, Dr Kalaman, gave the impression of being strict and brilliant, and every sentence he uttered was absolutely clear. He said he came from Austria, but his ancestors came from Mogadishu. Blanka followed him readily along the paths of histograms, frequency polygons and distribution function, though she stumbled on some of the newer concepts and spent many hours at her desk after class trying to catch up. For the first time in several weeks, she had the feeling that she could at least make a grab at the fluttering, flyaway fabric of her life and hold on to it, if only by one corner . . .

Caitlin was amazed to learn that when Blanka was studying, she was completely oblivious to the ringing of the phone in the hallway – a piercing noise that the residents of the student quarters, many of them plagued by homesickness, could hear through the walls even in their sleep. Blanka's father managed to reach her once, but the conversation was stilted and carefully friendly, which ruined Blanka's mood for a whole day.

Whenever she was outside, Blanka would surreptitiously look over at the groups of older students who liked to hang out at the entrance to the cafeteria, but for the first few days she did not see Joaquim or any of the other Wolves. At the end of the week, however, she noticed Simon Nemec entering the cafeteria with a tall stack of papers. A girl from Caitlin's volleyball team walked towards Blanka with her thumb pointing back over her shoulder.

'Did you hear?' she asked casually. 'They've figured out how the woman died.'

Blanka set off at a run. From some distance away she could see students crowding around the bulletin board in front of the cafeteria. A girl protested as Blanka wedged herself in beside her. She felt elbows in her ribs, but finally she was at the front of the crowd and could read the photocopied newspaper article. 'The dead woman was identified as 54-year-old Annette Durlain from Brest, in Brittany,' a student standing beside Blanka read aloud. 'Her passport and luggage were found in a locker at the railway station. On the afternoon of her death, the woman had visited the convent museum at the Europa International School with a group of tourists.' In several places Detective Seibold was quoted. 'Why the woman was in the Europa International School at night has not yet been determined.' Her death, the article continued, had definitely been caused by a fall down the stairs. The investigation had concluded that no one else was involved.

'So it was an accident, after all,' said a boy squeezed in next to Blanka. Bewildered, Blanka let herself be pushed back until she was again standing apart from the group. An accident. The word sounded all wrong, as if someone had said 'afternoon nap' but really meant 'coma'.

Blanka thrust her hands in her pockets and began to walk away. Beside the entrance hung a sign announcing the new schedule for tours of the convent museum. In this school they really did not waste much time on dead strangers.

'Hey, Blanka!' Although she had run a fair way to catch up to Blanka, Caitlin was not out of breath. Her curls were still wet from the shower. 'I just heard.' She grinned and pushed her hair off her face. It seemed to Blanka that her roommate still bore the scent of magnesium powder and the worn leather balls from the gym. 'That means they'll open the library again tomorrow,' Caitlin continued. 'Thank heavens. I was starting to think I'd have to study shut in my little room right up until the exam.'

Blanka stopped abruptly. 'Is that all you lot care about?' she snapped.

'What's the matter?'

'It's a miracle that anyone has even noticed that she was a person, not just "the dead body," or the reason you can't go into the library.'

Caitlin looked at Blanka in astonishment and then held up her hands. 'Sorry – I didn't realise you were taking it so much to heart. What on earth do you expect us to do? Hold a funeral service for her?'

'That would be better than nothing.'

Caitlin pulled a face and shook her head. For the first time, Blanka saw anger flash in those green eyes. 'Blanka, you know I'm not a monster. But . . . well, the woman was here and had an accident. That's tragic, and terribly sad. But . . . life goes on for us – school is hard, the demands they make on us are even harder, and when you've taken your first exam you'll see that we can't afford to waste even a single day. That's just the way it is. I'd like it to be a bit less stressful, but it's not.'

Blanka stared at the ground. She really wanted to snap at Caitlin, to tell her to spare Blanka the lecture, but she took deep breaths and restrained herself.

'I'm not stupid,' she said quietly. 'Believe it or not, I've already noticed that classes are still being held. But I simply can't see . . . she was in the museum in the afternoon – but she died after midnight. What was she doing in between?'

'Presumably chasing ghosts,' came the dry reply.

'What?'

Caitlin spread her arms. 'Maddalina of Trenta,' she said melodramatically. 'Her witch's robe is hanging in the museum.'

'And?'

'She haunts this place. I don't want to give you nightmares, but there have been students and teachers who have sworn that someone was following them. Some even claim to have heard the poor little orphan children crying. Then there's the groaning, scraping, howling – the whole deal.' Caitlin rolled her eyes and continued, 'If you only knew how often someone or other who's into witchcraft stands in front of that glass case as if it were a shrine. Once a woman from a society that called itself "New Witches" tried to hide in the museum so that she could spend a night beside Maddalina's robe. Crazy, huh?' She laughed. 'Man, they should come to Ireland some time and spend the night in some castle ruins.'

'The woman was going to hide in the library until dark and then go down to be near the witch's robe in the basement?'

'She was just unlucky enough to learn the hard way that the stairs aren't lit up at night.'

'I'll say. Isn't the museum locked up?'

'Yes, of course. But other people have broken in, or tried to pick the lock.'

Blanka fell silent. The dead woman had not had any tools with her, unless she had hidden them under her coat. Blanka let her gaze wander back to the notice with the opening times of the museum. Let it go! whispered a very sensible voice in her head. Just do your homework; the rest is none of your business. Blanka listened to this voice for two or three heartbeats, then came to a decision. So, this place is haunted, she thought. And Annette Durlain simply fell down the stairs?

STICK DANCE

AFTER THESE EVENTFUL DAYS, the weekend seemed to Blanka to be an island of tranquillity in a stormy ocean full of strange dreams, dreams in which Annette Durlain came to her and tried desperately to tell her something. On Saturday morning the school building was deserted, but outside there were people everywhere. A constant stream of cars turned into the visitors' carpark; parents and brothers and sisters arriving for a weekend visit. Blanka felt a stab of sadness when she saw a girl run up to her father and hug him. She looked at her watch. Four more hours until the tour of the convent museum. In front of the manor house, where the boys had their rooms, the first tourists were already being led through the buildings. One group was admiring the columns on either side of the doorway, which gave the building a temple-like appearance. People pointed up at the stone statues, imposing women who gazed at the people below with solemn faces. Blanka hitched up her backpack full of books and set out for the park bench by the chestnut grove. Caitlin had been right about one thing: nobody here could afford to waste even a single hour. Blanka would have to sit the first preliminary exam, in history, in two weeks. The books weighed heavily on her shoulders as she passed the open sports fields. The May sun had long since burned off the morning mist. The orange all-weather tracks glistened, and the area that served as both soccer pitch and athletics field was deserted. Blanka picked up the pace, walking briskly along the hedge that marked the front edge of the sports fields. A *thwack*, sharp as the crack of a whip, interrupted her thoughts. The sound came from the right – from behind the hedge she heard another *thwack*. A throaty, long drawn-out cry pierced the air. Blanka tightened her grip on her backpack. She hesitated before cautiously approaching the hedge. Slowly she stretched out her hand and pushed a few of the branches aside. Part of the lawn came into view, and a spiralling piece of fabric. She leaned further forward and looked through the gap, almost losing her balance. Terrified, she recoiled. A branch snapped back over her fingers. Suddenly it all came back: the night in the park, the stick whistling past her face, the fear – and the dead woman. Blanka took a deep breath and wiped the beads of sweat from her forehead. Coward! she scolded herself. Curiosity won over fear. Her heart pounding, she stepped closer to the hedge again.

Without the masks and furs, the Wolves did not look nearly so threatening. Joaquim was practising doggedly. He landed every blow perfectly. Reluctantly, Blanka had to admit that she admired his co-ordination and quick movements. His partner, a blonde girl, dodged Joaquim's swing deftly, springing aside. Two other Wolves joined the circle and hemmed in Joaquim – as if to capture him. It seemed to be the enactment of an ancient, ritual-istic story. With narrowed eyes, Blanka observed the two newest fighters – a gaunt blond boy and a pale boy with his hair tied back in a ponytail. Was he the one who had worn the iron mask? A fifth fighter, one Blanka hadn't noticed at first, was a girl with freckles. Her movements seemed rather playful and dance-like. She avoided the thrust of Joaquim's stick, twisting away. Her copper hair streamed behind her; she twirled around – and hit Joaquim in the shoulder. A dull thud. Blanka winced involuntarily. The blow had landed! Joaquim bent over in obvious pain. Stunned, he stared at the stick dancer. In an instant his face reddened with anger. She returned his gaze and stood still. The other Wolves seemed to have been turned to stone. Blanka held her breath. The game was over. The wind blew away Joaquim's words, but Blanka could follow what was happening, just from watching him slowly straighten up.

The red-haired girl grasped her stick firmly. She took a step backwards and slammed her weapon onto the ground. She shouted a retort, but all Blanka caught were the last few words: '. . . along with it any more!' Blanka pushed further into the shadow of the hedge, until her shoulder was brushing against the wall of green. Leaf tips tickled her cheek.

The dark-haired girl stepped forward and whispered something to the redhead. The other two Wolves just stood there, uncertain what to do. The redhead shook her head violently. The blonde girl tried to touch her arm in a soothing, conciliatory gesture, but the redhead snapped at her and shook off her hand. Strangely, all the noises around them seemed to have disappeared. Blanka could no longer hear any laughter, any twittering of birds, not even the rustling of the chestnut trees.

The redhead left. Joaquim turned, his shoulders drooping, and watched her go. Through the gaps in the hedge, his face was framed with green leaves. It bore an expression that Blanka would never have expected. He looked frightened.

The Wolves' eyes met in silent agreement. Blanka swallowed.

She would have liked to jump out from the hedge and warn the girl to run, but it was too late.

They shot into action simultaneously – four against one. The redhead skilfully parried a few strokes, but then she screamed and went down, gasping. Her freckled face distorted with pain. Blanka could see a bright red mark on her right upper arm.

The Wolves stood before her in battle formation. Blanka was afraid they would attack her again, but they suddenly let their weapons drop. Joaquim licked his lips, concentrating. The redhead gazed up into their dark faces, at a loss as to what to do. She grimaced, then howled with rage. Finally she stood up, retrieved her stick, and turned away.

Running with the heavy backpack wasn't easy. Blanka was panting by the time the carpark finally came into view again. Her desire to study had completely left her. To avoid the sports fields, she had taken the long way back, going all the way around the manor house. The last thing she needed was to be discovered by the Wolves. Spotting a couple of tourists, she felt a little better. She would feel even safer when she was back in her room. She looked up to her window in anticipation. The day seemed colder all of a sudden. The sudden crunch of gravel startled Blanka, but she suppressed the impulse to run. Certain it was Joaquim behind her, with his fighting stick at the ready, she turned around.

The redhead was clearly as surprised as Blanka. She jerked to a halt. Her sports bag hung from her left shoulder – and she was also carrying three practice sticks, each one a different length, under her left arm. Blanka noticed the welts on her right arm, already turning blue. Now the girl raised her injured arm and wiped her mouth and nose with the back of her hand. Her eyes were puffy, as if she had been crying all the way from the sports fields.

'What are you doing here?' she asked quietly.

'Studying,' Blanka answered promptly. 'And you? What did you have to do to make the others let you go?'

She indicated the welts and the girl flinched, as if she had just received another blow on the same spot. 'I saw what happened,' Blanka said softly. 'They're pressuring you. Because you don't want to keep doing something with them, right?'

The girl cast a venomous look in her direction. 'So, now you're meddling in our affairs?'

'Interesting that after that beating you're still talking about "your affairs". What was it you didn't want to go on doing?'

'That's none of your business.'

'Does it have anything to do . . . with me?'

Without warning, the girl's arm flashed up. Before Blanka could figure out what was happening, a stick was flying towards her. Instinctively, she reached for it. Her palms hurt from the impact, but she held the stick firmly in her grasp. Her mouth went dry with shock.

'Good reaction,' remarked the girl, putting down her bag. Blanka could see an airline tag and read the name on it: Sylvie Kay.

'What was that for?' she asked.

'The stick's heavier than it looks, isn't it?' This was true – and Blanka realised how powerful Sylvie's delicate-looking hands must be, to swing the long stick so quickly.

In one smooth move, the girl laid the two other sticks down on the ground, picked up the shorter one with her left hand, and swung it once in a graceful circle over her head.

'It won't help to run and hide,' she said seriously. 'If you want to stay at this school, you'll have no option but to fight.'

'Against you lot? Why should I? I have nothing to do with you.'

Sylvie laughed bitterly.

'Nothing at all,' she said, and pulled her arm back, ready to take a swing. Blanka recognised that it was a slowly executed practice move. It gave her enough time to snatch up her own stick and parry the attack. Sylvie's stick cracked against the wood of her own, and Blanka could feel the jarring in every joint of her fingers. She stepped back and let her stick drop.

'I don't want to,' she said firmly. 'I'm here to study.'

Sylvie curled her lip scornfully and leaned on her weapon.

Blanka decided to meddle some more. 'You should report it to Madame Lalonde,' she said. 'I don't know what it is you don't want to do, but they have no right to beat you up. If you want, I can tell her what I saw.'

'Madame? Phew, now I feel so much better,' answered Sylvie, her voice dripping with sarcasm. 'Make no mistake about it. She can't stand losers. She's very nice, sure, but try going to her and showing her you're a problem case or a coward. There's no room for those at an elite school. Have you ever wondered why two-thirds of the students don't pass the preliminary exam?'

Blanka gripped her stick harder. Two-thirds?

Sylvie gave a little laugh when she saw her face. When she continued, her voice sounded hard. 'Just so we're clear here: no one "beat me up". When you practise, you get bruises. Understand?'

Almost before she was aware that Sylvie had moved, Blanka noticed a sharp pain in her lower arm.

'Are you crazy?' cried Blanka. It had not been a strong blow, but her skin was smarting all the same. Before even being conscious of what she was doing, she had snatched up her stick and attacked. Sylvie parried the blow with an expert, almost lazy, movement. Blanka had trouble reacting, the stick whistling through the air so quickly. There was a thwack. The crossed sticks hung in the air.

'That's better,' said Sylvie. 'You have good reflexes. When I can only use my left hand, like now, you could even make things difficult for me.'

Blanka lowered her stick and dropped it at Sylvie's feet. 'It's not my thing,' she replied. 'You're really all crazy.'

'Your decision. But in that case, be sure to lock your door.' Sylvie laughed. 'In fact, you'd best lock all the doors you can find.'

'Oh, I assume that Joaquim will break the door down if he needs to.' Blanka did not quite manage the scornful tone she'd been aiming for.

'Who's talking about Joaquim?' asked Sylvie quietly. She gave Blanka one last superior smile and picked up the sticks. 'Have fun on the tour,' she said, leaving a dumbfounded Blanka standing in the carpark.

About twenty tourists crowded around the door of the basement museum. Most of them were leafing through the brochure, not much different from the one included in the information folder for new students. Here too there was a diagram of the foundation of the old convent, and an aerial photo of the orphans' cemetery. Realising that the dead woman had also waited at this door,

Blanka felt like a thief slinking into a forbidden room. Gingerly she ran her fingers over the red mark on her lower arm – soon it would turn into a bruise. The Wolves were planning something, of that she was sure. The society was not as innocent as Madame believed. And how had Sylvie known that Blanka wanted to take the tour? Caitlin was the only one she had told about it. Would Caitlin . . .? Blanka shivered and pulled her jacket sleeve down to cover the red mark. Beside her two tourists were talking quietly in rapid French. A huge camera lens dangling from the man's neck was aimed directly at Blanka. Seldom had she felt so exposed. When a rhythmic jingling approached, all conversation died. Blanka moved inconspicuously behind the French couple.

Mr Nemec came around the corner and looked over the group of tourists. He recognised Blanka immediately and raised his eyebrows. In the fluorescent light of the hallway, the old man seemed like a ghost: his cheeks looked sunken and he had uneven stubble where his razor had missed. Silently, he moved past the group and opened the door.

The room they entered in single file had a low ceiling, and the walls were panelled in light, sweet-smelling wood. The parquet flooring was so old that in some places it had bowed under the weight of countless footsteps. The colours of the various types of wood used for the parquet made a pattern of curved geometric figures in which Blanka could not help immediately seeing inter-sections and ellipses. Columns divided the room into a small main area and a walkway surrounding it – the architecture was probably supposed to be reminiscent of a convent's cloister. The tourists fell silent and looked around, awestruck. Along the walls stood rows of glass cases containing exhibits. On the wall opposite the entrance hung the impressive fragment of an old door, the original entrance to the convent, decorated with an intricate carved relief. Of the twelve apostles who had once looked out at every visitor, six remained – the left side of the door was missing.

Mr Nemec was not a gifted tour guide. In a monotonous voice he reeled off the information. 'In 1641, Maddalina of Trenta took over the leadership of the Belverina Convent. Most of the documents from this time were destroyed after the witch trial and the dissolution of the order and its orphanage that followed it. The only thing that remains is a part of the original transcript of the trial of the Abbess. In addition, the Maddalina von Trenta Foundation managed to buy back from private owners some of the art treasures that once were used in the convent. Like this monstrance, for example.'

He indicated a display cabinet. In it stood a vessel decorated with a striated design in gold.

The French couple leafed through a tiny dictionary. A younger couple were whispering together and smirking about Nemec's slurred pronunciation. Blanka looked at the caretaker and came to the conclusion that he had probably been drinking.

'And here you see the witch's robe,' he continued. 'Maddalina of Trenta wore it during the interrogations.' With these words he turned a switch on the wall. The effect was well calculated – a murmur ran through the group. Blanka shuddered. In the display case a worn, coarsely woven robe was illuminated. Almost invisible nylon threads held it suspended. In the places where the dress had rested on collar bones and breasts, metal coat hangers shone through the threadbare fabric and somewhat suggested a body shape. It looked as if an invisible woman was wearing the long robe. Where the feet would have been there was paper covered with cramped writing – the transcript of the interrogation, as Mr Nemec explained. Another light went on, lighting up an iron mask with horns and iron slits instead of eyes. It bore a remote resemblance to the mask that one of the Wolves had been wearing that night. 'Note the needle near the mask of shame,' continued the caretaker. 'It was used to test witches' marks. If an accused prisoner had an obvious birthmark or mole, their accusers stuck the needle into it. If the accused felt no pain and did not bleed, then it was declared a witch's mark.' Nemec smiled coolly at the Frenchwoman, who was staring at him open-mouthed. 'This original needle here, by the way, is a mechanical masterpiece and was clearly intended to deceive. When you press on it, it retracts into its shaft – no pain, no blood.'

Blanka tried again to imagine the dead woman standing on this same spot. Had she read these words? And, if so, what had they meant to her? Blanka wondered if she, like Blanka, had looked at the transcript of the interrogation and tried to decipher the interlaced letters:

'. . . He Ask'd Maddalina of Trenta [if she] Her Self had been Qveen of the Witches there [at the Witches Dances] amongst Witch People and Feends.'

Trying not to let Mr Nemec see her, Blanka pulled out her notebook and copied the words down exactly as they were written. She looked several times to be sure that 'Feends' really had two 'e's. Just as she was finishing, a tingling sensation on the back of her neck made her lift her eyes from her notebook and look around. At first she was scared, because she thought she saw the boy with the sun-bleached hair from the Wolves, but then she breathed a sigh of relief. It was only a tourist, one she had not noticed before. Tall and gaunt, this tourist had buried his hands in the pockets of his leather jacket. His fair hair shone in the light of the display case. He was looking at the vessel in the other case – but his interest seemed feigned.

Blanka quickly turned back to the witch's robe, but this time she did not look at the exhibits but rather at the reflection in the glass. She could make out the French couple behind her, who were staring over her shoulder – and to the left stood Leatherjacket. She guessed him to be about eighteen. He did not look like someone who would willingly spend his free time viewing historical exhibits. And she was right: as if he had been waiting for her to turn away, he turned his head to look at her again. In the reflection, she could make out his serious face and narrow, curved lips. With a strange intensity he examined Blanka from head to toe, as if memorising what she looked like. She stepped to one side, avoiding his gaze. 'Who's talking about Joaquim?' Sylvie's words rang in her head. Uneasy, she stared at the glass panes of the case, which had been sealed with silicone. Had Annette Durlain stood here too – observed by a stranger? Blanka noticed that in some places the silicone seemed new – transparent and untouched, like fresh icecream. A tourist moved closer, jostling her a little. Gratefully, she crouched down, half hidden behind the glass, and examined the hem of the witch's robe. She noticed something right at the bottom. She frowned and leaned a little further forward. Near the frayed hem she could make out a dark spot. It must be a rust spot, but with a bit of imagination one could say it was blood.

DREAMS

THE SOUND OF THE KETTLE WOKE Blanka with a start. Her T-shirt was sticking to her body and she was trembling. The reading lamp, which she had turned on last night, was still on. The dream had been even worse than those of previous nights. The woman in the rumpled coat seemed to desperately want to tell her something, but she was prevented from doing so by Joaquim. He was roaring, lashing out with his fighting stick. For a moment Blanka thought she could still see the iron mask of shame that had whispered secrets into her ear; then this image disappeared too, leaving her alone in her damp, twisted sheets.

Her maths book lay on the floor like a bird with its wings outstretched. She heard the birds in the orphans' cemetery and slowly started to realise it was morning. She thought it odd that she couldn't detect any movement in Caitlin's room. Only the water bubbled, as if the kettle had been turned on by a ghostly hand. Usually Blanka could hear the patter of Caitlin's feet in the darkness and then the gurgling of water when she tipped the mineral water out of her bottle into the kettle – she never used tap water for her tea.

Blanka glanced over at the connecting door, which was open just a crack. No movement. With a click, the switch on the kettle snapped to the 'Off' position. The bubbling stopped. A moment later she heard the beeping of Caitlin's alarm, which she set on weekends too, so she wouldn't miss breakfast. Light showed through the crack under the door. Relieved, Blanka followed her roommate's steps as she went over to the kettle. A second later she could hear Caitlin pouring water into cups. She rolled herself out of bed.

'Oh, good morning!' Caitlin always looked especially nice in the morning. Her cheeks were rosy and her tousled hair as yet untamed by gel. She opened her eyes wide in astonishment. 'You look awful! Are you sick? Your eyes are all puffy.'

Blanka forced a lopsided grin. 'Headache,' she said. 'So now you have a remote control for the kettle?'

Caitlin reached for the wall plug and passed Blanka a bizarre-looking little box attached to the plug. Blanka sat down on Caitlin's bed and turned it over in her hands.

'Radio-operated timer,' Caitlin said. 'Jan installed it yesterday while you were in the museum.'

'Jan who?'

'You know who he is!'

'The guy in my year?'

Caitlin nodded. 'He's nice,' she said, with a knowing grin.

'Since when do you bother with children?'

'Children? Jan's nineteen!'

Blanka looked up from the timer switch, shocked.

'Really? He looks about fourteen! How many times did he have to repeat a year?'

Caitlin stopped laughing. 'Ask him yourself! By the way, he told me he thinks you're quite nice. I think he was disappointed you weren't here yesterday.'

'Really? Well, I think he's kinda weird – why would an art freak build switches like this?'

'Like I said – ask him yourself. It's OK to talk to people, Blanka!'

'Yes, you're a good example of that!' It slipped out a little too sharply and Blanka regretted her tone immediately.

'What's that supposed to mean?'

'Did you tell Sylvie that I was going on the basement tour?'

Now Caitlin was really mystified.

'Was it a secret? No, I didn't tell Sylvie. But a few of the girls on my volleyball team knew I was going to be alone in the room because you were going on the tour. Why are you interrogating me?'

'I'm having really bad dreams.'

'Don't change the subject – what's going on?'

Now Caitlin's voice sounded sharp. Blanka realised that she had gone too far. Resisting the urge to start screaming at her roommate, she pulled herself together. 'Nothing,' she muttered.

'Don't try to fool me! Since you went on that tour yesterday you've hardly said a word.' Caitlin sat down on the edge of the bed and passed a cup of hot tea to her. 'I'm serious, Blanka,' she said more gently. 'I'm not trying to tell you how to run your life, but you don't seem happy. Is there anything I can do?'

Blanka looked at her roommate thoughtfully. She really looked worried – and Blanka's mistrust suddenly seemed quite unfounded. Embarrassed, she pushed her hair back behind her ears and starting telling Caitlin what she had been waiting for.

'If I tell you – will you promise you won't try to persuade me to go to Madame Lalonde?'

'It's the Wolves, isn't it? Are you having problems with them?'

'They seem to be having a problem with me.'

She told Caitlin about what she had seen at the sports fields and some of her conversation with Sylvie. She didn't say anything, though, about Sylvie's warnings, her bruised arm, or the strange boy in the leather jacket.

'So that's it,' said Caitlin, relieved. 'Why didn't you tell me yesterday? – you would have slept better last night for sure. I already know about the argument. It was about the medieval festival. Every August, the city puts on a medieval market and the Wolves usually give a demonstration of stick-fighting. Sylvie doesn't want to take part this time, so she backed out. Too much stress from schoolwork.'

'And so they beat her up?'

'Listen, the Wolves have their own rules and they sort out their disagreements amongst themselves.'

'Yes, that seems to be the way it is at this school. Everyone has to look after themselves.'

'And only someone as prickly as you would say that,' responded Caitlin with a smile. 'You think everyone's out to get you. You don't notice that there are people here who like you, and you won't let them near you.'

'And the rest of you seem to see nothing at all – a woman falls down the stairs and dies: so what? A student is hurt, just because she wants to back out of the medieval troupe: so? They have their own rules. Is there anyone here who cares about what happens to other people?'

To her surprise, Caitlin put her arm around Blanka's shoulders. 'I care about what happens to you,' she said. 'It's just that this isn't like other schools. Here we all have to learn to solve our own problems. It's hard at the beginning, I know. But just to reassure you: yes, the Wolves are crazy. Some, by the way, are also quite nice. Tobias – the boy who goes around in the musician mask – went out for a while with Jenna, the girl who lived in your room.'

'And?'

Caitlin laughed. 'What do you want me to say? That he forced her to howl at the moon with him? That's rubbish – the Wolves are simply a society, nothing more. Jenna and Tobias had an argument, and he broke up with her. But that certainly wasn't the Wolves' fault – more Tobias's, because he hung out too often with a girl from his chemistry class.'

'And Joaquim?'

'Good athlete. Sometimes rather arrogant. And he has a short fuse – like yesterday. But it's not your job to protect Sylvie. We all have to make our own decisions.'

'How many Wolves are there altogether?' asked Blanka, after taking all this in.

'Joaquim, of course. Tanya, Tobias, Martin and Sylvie. That's the core group.'

'Is there . . . a blond boy in the group, one who wears a leather jacket?'

Caitlin frowned. 'Hmm . . . not that I've noticed. Maybe among the "newbies," but in any case they're mainly there for the stick training.' Her face softened. 'Listen, I don't think the Wolves want anything from you. Even what they did on the first day – it was nothing personal. They always pick on one student to tease at the beginning. If I were you I wouldn't worry about it at all. Just hang in there for a couple more weeks. And if you're still being harassed, then come and tell me, OK? I promise I won't go running to Madame.' She looked at Blanka directly. 'And one day you'll have to tell me what your mother did that was so terrible that I always have to make excuses for you when she calls.'

Blanka winced. 'You think I've flipped for sure, don't you?'

Caitlin laughed and gave her a friendly push. 'At first I was afraid you had,' she admitted. 'Madame's great, but because I'm the student president she makes me take on the problem cases. But anyone who's been through what you have would have bad dreams.' Caitlin yawned and glanced at the clock radio. 'C'mon! If we hurry, we'll still get breakfast.' She jumped up and opened a drawer, which squeaked in protest. Blanka took a sip of tea and stared into the amber liquid. It smelled of orange and vanilla.

The library was supposed to reopen on Tuesday morning. Blanka was so impatient she could hardly focus on her class. As soon as the bell rang, she snatched up her things and was the first to leave the room. Today the hallways seemed particularly long. The other students made a beeline for the cafeteria, but Blanka turned down the hallway that led from the biology labs to the main entrance of the school, and from there she quickly crossed the grounds to the library. Above the high double door hung a plate of brushed steel, engraved with the school's motto: *Porta post portam* – an invitation to strive to open more doors of knowledge. Blanka stepped through the door into the open air. Suddenly she felt a hand on her shoulder. She turned around, terrified.

'Sorry,' panted Jan. 'I didn't want to frighten you – didn't you hear me calling you?'

Blanka took a deep breath. 'No. What's up?'

He reached into his pocket and pulled out a crumpled piece of paper.

'From Mrs Catalon. You left in such a rush that you didn't hear her calling us back in. Worksheet – due the day after tomorrow.'

'OK. Thanks.'

Jan watched as Blanka folded the paper and absent-mindedly pushed it into her bag.

'So?' he asked. 'How are you?'

'Fine. Why?' Was this going to be a friendly chat, classmate to classmate?

'Caitlin said you . . . were asking about me.'

All of a sudden Blanka caught on, and nearly groaned aloud. Two lonely souls who were destined to find each other. What a clever plan of Caitlin's. Somewhere far down the hallway the last door clicked shut.

'Actually, I was just asking about that timer you built for the kettle.'

He was neither surprised nor disappointed. 'It's nothing special. I cobbled it together in class.'

'Are you taking a shop course, too?'

Jan grinned. He still looked fourteen, though he had a new haircut.

'No, only the art-project course. It's called "Back to Metropolis". We're building a model of this silent film town.'

All at once he became serious again and looked around anxiously. He stepped a little closer to her. Blanka noticed that he was no taller than she was. 'Actually . . . I wanted to tell you that I'm sorry I abandoned you during the midnight tour. I really thought you were right behind me. If I'd known they were going to just leave you there, I would have gone back again.'

'It's OK,' Blanka replied. 'Don't worry; it'll take a lot more than that to intimidate me.'

Jan looked at her doubtfully. 'I hope so,' he said. 'They don't seem to like you particularly.'

'Well observed. Are you really nineteen?'

'Yes, that's right.'

'Why are you only in the tenth grade?'

'Is this an interrogation?' he asked, annoyed. 'I was out of school for a while.'

'Were you . . . sick?'

'Yeah, something like that.'

'And now you're interested in art.'

'Actually just in clay.' He grinned, leaned in closer, and whispered, 'I didn't have such a great kiln at home.'

He gave her a wink, turned on his heel, and headed down the empty hallway. Blanka's mobile started to vibrate in her jacket pocket. She took it out and saw it was her mother. She sure didn't give up easily! Blanka stared at the display until the phone vibrated for the fifteenth time. Then she turned off the phone, jammed it back in her pocket, and wiped her eyes on her sleeve. The bruise on her arm hurt. Once again she felt that dull sense of emptiness.

The library walls were dark from the powder the police had used to check for fingerprints. A note on the glass door warned that renovations were in progress. As Blanka entered the foyer with its reading tables, her stomach lurched and she felt as if she was on a rollercoaster. Every trace of the dead woman had been eradicated. The stairs and the steel banisters had already been scrubbed cleaned, and the stone floor shone. Blanka stared at the spot where the woman had lain, and fumbled in her backpack for an unnecessarily long time. Finally she plucked up her courage and slipped past, eyes lowered, keeping as far away from the actual spot as she could.

The first-floor library was, like the school, bathed in light, and its glass walls and brushed steel gave the rooms the appearance of a modern office building. The chairs were designed ergonomically and the reading lights looked like the outstretched arms of robots.

Feeling like an intruder, Blanka filled out her application for the language lab and got her user card for the computer workstations. She could feel her notebook with the notes she had made about Annette Durlain pressing against her. She stepped close to the glass facade that looked down onto the broad staircase and reading tables below. To the right of the drinks machine a few students were using some of the small tables as a cafeteria. A blond boy wearing a leather jacket was not among them. She contemplated the spot at the foot of the stairs. For a moment, she imagined she could see the outline of a figure, and shuddered. How could Annette Durlain have fallen so awkwardly down those stairs? She had landed on the floor right beside the banisters – wouldn't she have automatically grabbed on to them to catch herself? Blanka looked around, and when she was sure no one was watching her, pulled out her notebook and sketched the stairs. She drew an outline of Annette Durlain's body, indicating its position as far as she could remember.

Behind her loomed seemingly endless aisles of steel shelves. Slowly Blanka turned around. 'Languages,' she read on a sign, and behind it 'French III'. A library full of school books. Annette Durlain had hidden here for seven hours. Blanka pushed her pencil back into her bag and began walking down the aisles, imagining Annette Durlain seeking out a spot to hide. It wouldn't have been easy. The shelves stood at right angles to the wall and you could see right through them. Even in the corner seating areas there was hardly anywhere you would be invisible. A narrow door led to a staircase, but it was locked. Not likely that Annette Durlain had had a key. Again and again Blanka took out her notebook and noted down the corners that offered some protection from view. At the far end, a wide door was ajar. Blanka ignored the 'Private' sign and slipped into the adjoining room. It smelled of old wood varnish.

It was another room full of books. Blanka walked up and down aisle upon aisle. Freud's works were here, and other psychology classics, such as the theories of C. G. Jung. Blanka noticed the worn carpet and stopped short. Some of the shelves were on casters – and one of them was slightly out of place. There was an obvious hollow where a caster had once pressed into the carpet. Quietly Blanka dropped to her knees and peered out over the spines of the books. Behind them there was only a wall – but was it possible to push the shelf aside and hide behind it?

She struggled to pull the shelf forward. She could only move it forward a centimetre at a time. The result was disappointing. The wall behind it was freshly painted. She could see a remnant of masking tape on a light switch. Obviously the shelf had only been moved because of the renovations. Blanka sat down on the floor and contemplated the lower rows of books on the adjacent shelf. 'The Mechanisms of Selected Psychotropics' was the title on the spine of one of the thicker ones. Carefully she pulled the book out and began to leaf through it. Hundreds of technical terms. If you believed them, you could imagine man as a chemical construction kit. You just had to balance the substances, the hormones, the serotonin, the flow of adrenalin; everything followed a plan that could be figured out. Grief was quantifiable. Or was it?

She shut the book with a snap and looked up. She could hear something! She sat motionless and listened until she could make out the sound – sniffling. And it was coming straight from the next aisle. Blanka crawled closer to the bookshelf. Through the gap left by her book she could see dark jeans. Something jingled, a knee appeared, then the gap went dark – and suddenly she was staring into Simon Nemec's face.

'I thought it was you,' he said in a husky voice. The strong peppermint smell of his breath did not quite cover the smell of alcohol. He disappeared and emerged again around the corner. The sports jacket that he always wore was rubbed at the elbows and looked shabby in the harsh noon light. Caught in the act, Blanka stood up.

'What are you up to?' he snarled.

Blanka gripped her notebook firmly and flashed an innocent smile.

'Research?' she said quietly. 'Aren't we allowed to be in the library?'

Silently they regarded each other. Nemec's eyes were slightly red, as if he had a cold.

'There's no reason for you to be in here. This is part of the reference library, for the faculty only.'

'Where does it say that?'

'In the library rules, which you have obviously not read. And what about the sign saying "Private"? Did you read that?'

Blanka felt her confident smile melt away.

'I call this snooping,' said Nemec. 'And don't think I didn't notice that you were at Madame Lalonde's desk. Do we understand each other?'

Blanka's heart sank. The look she gave Nemec must have looked pathetic, for it elicited from him a grim smile. Hesitantly, Blanka nodded.

'Good.' He leaned further forward and indicated the notebook that Blanka was still holding tightly. 'And be grateful that I don't confiscate your notes,' he said. 'I bet I'd find a few things there that have nothing to do with your homework, eh?'

Only now did Blanka notice the fresh bandage on his right hand. 'What did you do to your hand?' she asked quietly.

Nemec folded his arms and looked down at Blanka. 'Slipped. Working on the renovations.'

'Are you left-handed?'

'Why do you want to know?'

'Usually right-handed people are more likely to injure their left hand.'

'I suppose you think you're very clever,' he said. 'If you really want to be clever, then you'll quickly return to the students' area.'

The dreams still came like thieves in the night, creeping up to her bed and entering her brain. Instead of the witch's robe, sometimes it was Blanka's mother in the display case now – a sad wax doll. She wore the red-and-white uniform of the Mountain View restaurant, which always made her look a bit too pale.

Annette Durlain, in her loose-fitting coat, was standing beside the display case. A face was reflected in the glass – Blanka had expected to see Nemec's features, but to her horror she realised it was the boy in the leather jacket. She did not dare to look to the left, straight into his eyes. Instead, she watched in the reflection as he reached inside his jacket and pulled out a gleaming witch's needle. It looked like a dagger. Blanka cried out and ran to the display case, but a wall of heat stopped her in her tracks. Her mother's features began to melt and dripped like skin-coloured wax onto her uniform. Blanka called out, but her voice sounded creaky, like a door. Suddenly a red-hot sun shone beside Blanka. It had a face and looked like an ancient copper engraving come to life. The rays flickered and only then did Blanka see the lion. The beast was gigantic, as big as the sun. Blanka stumbled backwards and bumped into a hot wall. The lion crouched and sprang. Its claws drove into the sun, and it buried its fangs in the glowing sphere, biting into it as if into prey. The pungent smell of beast and soot was everywhere. The boy in the leather jacket raised the needle dagger. Annette Durlain doubled up in terror. The sun screamed.

Blanka jerked awake and felt for the light switch with fingers slippery with sweat. Nothing happened. The room remained a black hole. Only the sound of the switch on her reading lamp, which Blanka kept flicking, disturbed the silence. Obviously the bulb had burned out. Blanka wiped her hands on the sheet and stared into the darkness. She spent a while just trying to breathe calmly.

The silence in the dorm was oppressive. Blanka threw back the bedclothes and felt her way towards the door, her knees shaking. Luckily she had only pulled the blinds down halfway the night before. Gradually she could make out the outline of the chair, the door, and beside it the lighter patch of the overhead light switch. When it clicked she closed her eyes tightly, expecting a bright light. Nothing happened. A power cut – now, of all times! Uncertainly she reached out again to feel her way back to her desk, hoping her keys were there. Yes. The keys clattered as she pulled them towards her and fumbled for the little LED flashlight attached to the chain. Through the wide gap between the blind and the windowsill she could see a strip of the carpark. She gave a start and stood still, not breathing, her keys in her hand. Someone was standing down there, half turned away from her.

Blanka leaned forwards over the desk. The jagged edges of the keys dug into her palm. She was dreaming. She must still be dreaming! Below the window stood Annette Durlain. The figure just stood there – black and shadowy, barely distinguishable from the night-grey gravel of the carpark. Blanka squinted in an effort to make out the outline. The blurry shadow seemed to be changing shape. It could be a woman in a coat, yes – but suddenly the phantom almost looked like a man in a dark cloak. Nemec? she wondered. The Wolves? As if it had felt Blanka's gaze, the phantom jerked its dark head back and looked up, right at Blanka's window. At the same moment Blanka felt as if she had the vision of a cat. It seemed quite logical that she could now make out what it was wearing – a nun's habit? She felt rather than heard a voice reverberating deep within her, like an echo. There were no words, just a feeling, a certainty that something lay ahead for her – a battle, a . . . danger? A shadowy black arm rose into the air, as if the phantom was waving to her.

Blanka darted to the side so quickly she banged her shin on the bed. The thing could not possibly have seen her in this dark room. Nevertheless her heart was beating wildly. She waited several minutes, which to her seemed like a whole day, and only then dared to take a careful look out the window – from the very edge, so she could pull back out of sight quickly. The figure had disappeared. Only a glimmer caught her eye. Perhaps it was a glass shard reflecting light from somewhere. And there was something that might have been a burning cigarette. Blanka sank onto her bed and pulled up the covers. Now she was sure someone was outside her door. Joaquim and the others – and Leatherjacket, who was waiting to drag her to the river. Maybe he *was* one of the Wolves. She got up and crept over to the door again. Once there, she laid her ear against the wood and listened.

Of course she thought she heard a scraping noise. The door handle felt cool to the touch. Then it moved under her hand. Someone was pressing down the door handle! Blanka pulled her hand away as if she had burned herself. Breathlessly she watched the handle moving. Someone was checking whether the door was locked. The keychain fell out of her hand and landed on the carpet with a soft clink. At that moment the lights came back on. Startled, Blanka recoiled and crashed into the armchair near the door. It was many thousands of heartbeats later, it seemed, that she dared to reach out her hand for her umbrella, to use as a weapon if necessary. But the door handle was not moving any more. Quietly Blanka picked up the keyring and unlocked the door. Umbrella at the ready, she flung open the door. In the empty hallway the digital display of the wall clock flashed and then jumped back to the time: 3.48 a.m.

SAINT APOLLONIA

BLANKA HAD CONSTRUCTED A MOUNTAIN of books at her spot at the reading table in the library. Yellow Post-its stuck out from the pages. In two days she had to hand in her biology project, and tomorrow she would write the first preliminary exam, in history. History did not worry her, but now that her biology teacher, Mrs Catalon, had left action potentials and nerves behind and moved on to genetics, Blanka felt as if two years of material had been squeezed into four weeks. She leaned back and peered through the aisles to the computer workstations. In twenty minutes the library computer that she had booked would be free. A blonde girl with buck teeth was there now, clicking through a database. Sighing, Blanka bent over her notes again and read through them for the hundredth time. She had to make it! There were no two ways about it – if she wanted to stay at the school, she had to pass the preliminary exams. But the words refused to find their way into her head; they slipped from her grasp and faded away. It was impossible to concentrate. Again and again she felt as if she were holding her door handle, and when she closed her eyes, the phantom waved to her. Again she ran through all the possibilities she had thought of so far: it was Leatherjacket, and her eyes had played a trick on her in the dark. He had Annette Durlain on his conscience and in the convent museum had selected Blanka to be his next victim. Or was it Tanya, acting as lookout while the other Wolves tried to get Blanka out of her room and drag her to the river. Or – Maddalina of Trenta?

'Ridiculous!' whispered Blanka, putting her pencil down. She rubbed her eyes hard and red stars exploded behind her eyelids. Her thoughts ran in circles: Annette Durlain and Leatherjacket, Leatherjacket and the Wolves, the Wolves and Joaquim, Joaquim and Blanka . . . nothing made any sense. And yet she had the feeling that there *was* a connection. Exhausted, she pressed her palms to her eyes. She saw the grey-haired woman going down the stairs, step by step. Annette Durlain turned around and looked up at Blanka. In the shadows her face looked like a mask. She smiled, opened her arms wide – and fell backwards. Blanka gave a start and opened her eyes. In the library all was silent. Exhausted, she stood up and went over to one of the wide, half-open windows. The fresh air felt good. From below she could hear the jubilant cry of a volleyball team, then a short blast from the referee's whistle. Blanka leaned her hot forehead against the windowpane and gazed at the path, and the hedge alongside it. She had to talk to Sylvie – as quickly as possible.

A figure walking along the path slowed, then stopped. Hastily Blanka pulled back and then carefully looked out of the window again. She needn't have bothered; the person could not possibly recognise her from down there – the tinted glass facade acted like a mirror. The concentrated and furtive look with which Leatherjacket was surveying the building disturbed Blanka all the more. He had turned up his worn collar as if he were cold, and a cigarette drooped from the corner of his mouth. After a minute that seemed to last for ever he went on his way and disappeared from view.

She only felt safe again when she was back at her reading desk behind the stacks of books, which separated her from her surroundings like the walls of a fortress. She was about to pull the thick biology text towards her again when she stopped short. It was no longer open at the same place. Some passer-by must have caused a draught that had turned the pages. Then she looked at her other books. The sticky notes had disappeared, or had been set at different places in the books. An important reference work on genetics had disappeared. With a sudden sinking feeling in her belly, Blanka quickly lifted up the top page of her notes. Empty pages grinned mockingly up at her. She sprang up and looked around. Some students had left. Behind her, at the computer, stood the girl with buck teeth, packing up her things. Blanka sank down onto her chair and looked over her books again. One of them she had definitely not brought to the table. It was thick and slightly yellowed; its title indicated it contained legends of the saints. A paper protruded from between the pages, obviously marking a passage. She opened it. The passage described the martyrdom of Saint Apollonia. 'All Apollonia's teeth were knocked out by her cruel torturers.' Blanka swallowed hard and looked at the figure of the martyr, who was holding forceps and a tooth in her hand. Someone had used a pencil to underline the words 'knocked out'. But what frightened her even more was the fact that someone had coloured the saint's hair black, which made her look strangely like Blanka.

Caitlin nearly dropped her soda bottle with shock when Blanka rushed into the room. Blanka did not even show any surprise at seeing Jan sitting on the bed.

'What's wrong?' cried Caitlin, jumping up.

'My project's gone!' gasped Blanka. 'Stolen!' She spilled out the whole story. Jan listened for a while in silence, then stood up and went out without a word.

'Somebody's just playing a trick on you.' Caitlin said soothingly.

'Bullshit! Someone's very serious about this. And this place marked in the book – that was a threat!'

'Blanka, calm down!'

'I don't know if it's Joaquim or not, but someone is trying to scare me off. Perhaps the guy in the leather jacket is part of it, too.'

'What guy?'

'He's been watching me. He might even have been below my window one night recently.'

'When?'

'The day before yesterday. There was a power cut,' said Blanka. 'And . . . there was somebody in the carpark. In the middle of the night. He was staring up at our window.'

Caitlin made a face, obviously sceptical.

'It's true!' persisted Blanka. 'I didn't tell you, but he was standing down there as if he was looking for something.'

The pause that followed grew uncomfortable, and Blanka already regretted telling Caitlin about it. Caitlin looked at her closely. Blanka could almost read her thoughts.

'I didn't dream it,' she said with emphasis. 'Someone was there.'

'So what? Maybe he was at the disco and was coming back late from town. Maybe it was the boyfriend of one of the girls in our building and he was throwing stones at her window.'

'At four in the morning?'

Caitlin pressed her lips together.

'Think about it,' she said finally. 'Who was in the library? Joaquim?'

Blanka shook her head.

'Another of the Wolves?'

'No.'

Caitlin was silent.

'You don't believe me, do you? You think I'm crazy.'

Caitlin hesitated.

'Yes, of course I believe you,' she said slowly. At that moment Jan came flying back into the room and threw an armful of papers and books onto the bed. Papers fanned out in all directions.

'This was at your seat.'

Bewildered, Blanka stared at the papers. They were her notes.

'They were gone,' she stammered. The look Caitlin and Jan exchanged spoke volumes.

'And where is the book about saints?' she asked, getting worked up. 'I can prove it to you – someone drew a picture of me. That was a threat!'

'There was no book about saints there,' said Jan calmly. 'I even looked under the table.'

'And the other books? Look – the sticky notes have all been moved around.'

'Hmm,' said Jan. 'You come from a very respectable neighbour-hood, don't you? Where I come from, people often give themselves an advantage by making life difficult for the competition. You're lucky your notes are still here.'

'That makes no sense!' said Blanka.

'If you ask me it does,' replied Jan, 'Don't leave your stuff lying around like that. Obviously you're not coping too well with the stress here.'

Caitlin dug him in the ribs. Jan grinned apologetically and grabbed his jacket.

'OK, got it,' he said. 'See you!'

There was an uncomfortable pause while Jan's steps retreated down the hallway. Blanka took her notes and leafed through them page by page.

'There!' she cried. 'Two pages are missing – and of course it had to be the ones with the classifications, and the whole of the bibliography. Who would take the whole stack and then put everything back except for two pages?'

Caitlin stood up and smiled at her reassuringly. At this moment Blanka hated her 'student-president' smile. 'Have another look,' said Caitlin. 'Maybe you forgot to take those pages with you, or you've put them in the wrong place.'

'Do I look as if I'm senile? I had them with me!'

'Do you know how you've seemed to me for the last couple of days? Like someone who's from another planet. Not only do you insist that we both lock our doors . . .'

'There's a reason for that!'

'What reason? Do you think someone's creeping around at night taking things? Geez, Blanka! Come back to earth!'

Caitlin folded her arms. Her smile had faded. Blanka sank onto her desk chair, snatched up her keychain, and looked for the drawer key. She tore the drawer open so roughly that all her notes slid forward, landing against the front edge of the drawer. Furiously, she took out the papers and binders and threw them onto the bed. Caitlin watched in silence as she searched through the pile.

'No notes,' said Blanka finally. 'I didn't leave the two pages here.'

'I've had enough,' said Caitlin. 'If you really think the Wolves want to throw you into the river or scare you away, then we should go to Madame Lalonde right now.'

'Definitely not,' snapped Blanka, standing up. 'Not a word to Madame! Or I might as well just go straight home! Promise, Cait?'

Her friend looked at her doubtfully, but finally she nodded. 'Promise. Hey, where are you going?'

'To look for Sylvie.'

'Sylvie? She won't be back for ten days.'

'What? Why?'

'Her mother's sick. She went home,' said Caitlin.

'Well, what a coincidence.' The words had slipped out before Blanka could stop them.

Caitlin's green eyes flashed. She looked as if she wanted to shake Blanka to make her see sense. 'She got permission and even registered her absence in the office. And this morning she took a taxi to the station. Doesn't quite have the appearance of a violent death, does it?'

'OK, OK,' Blanka snapped at her, jumping up. 'Don't worry – the lunatic with the persecution complex is now going peacefully to the library to get her jacket!'

Nothing had changed there. Once more Blanka went over every step in her head, trying to remember who had been in the room. Buckteeth was now sitting in the reading corner, busily making notes. A few other tables were empty, and Blanka wondered whether members of the Wolves might have been sitting there, and she had just not noticed them. Everything was the same as usual, except that she felt a threat lurking in every corner. With a shiver she left the room and went to the bathroom. As she was reaching for her jacket, she noticed a figure standing behind the big glass wall on the second floor. Simon Nemec was standing right at the edge of the hall, between two shelves, where he could not be seen from the cafeteria. He just stood there, staring at the stairs. His face was red, and the corners of his mouth hung down like those of a sad clown. He raised his arm and wiped his eyes with his sleeve. It took Blanka several seconds to understand what she was seeing. The old caretaker was crying.

LA BÊTE

THE HALLWAY IN FRONT OF THE school offices was deserted. Nervously, Blanka stood in front of Madame Lalonde's door and waited. The message she had found stuck to her door after school was now limp and crumpled, she had handled it so much. The last time she was in this hallway, she had not noticed the big map of the world that filled up almost all the space between the two doors. It was dotted with innumerable tiny flags. Each blue flag represented a student, and each red flag, a teacher. The names were printed on them with black markers. Marie-Claire Lalonde came from Alsace and many students came from Austria, Holland and Germany. Blanka's chemistry teacher came from London; other teachers came from France, Poland and Slovakia. But there were also flags near Odessa and in Kiev. Blanka's gaze wandered towards Spain, to a little flag in Madrid. 'Joaquim Almán,' she read.

'Ah, Blanka, come in!' said Madame cheerfully, as she opened the door. Head down, Blanka went in and sat down. The headmistress studied Blanka intently. She made her way back to her desk and folded her hands in front of her.

'I've asked you to come here for a special reason, Blanka,' she began, coming straight to the point. 'Well, actually for more than one reason, but I hope I can explain the first quickly. Your roommate – Caitlin – has brought to my attention that there is some friction between you and some of the older students.'

Blanka's eyes opened wide in disbelief.

'Before you get annoyed with Caitlin – yes, she told me. As you know, I asked her to keep her eye on you, to make sure you're settling in all right.'

'By telling you things about me behind my back?'

'At our school, it's customary for the older students to watch out for the new ones.' Madame insisted. 'Caitlin was worried about you, that's all. I understand you believe someone stole your papers in the library?'

Blanka tried to sink lower in her chair. 'I'm missing two pages of notes,' she admitted hesitantly.

'And what makes you suspect that it was members of the Wolves?'

Blanka was speechless. Caitlin had really spilled the beans. Finally she cleared her throat.

'Not really suspect,' she said, 'I just have the feeling that the Wolves don't particularly like me, that's all.' Had she said that carefully enough?

Madame Lalonde stood up and went to the window. There was a brief pause. Blanka caught herself nervously kneading her fingers again. For a moment she was tempted to tell Madame everything – about Sylvie's warning, the nightmares, and her suspicion that Annette Durlain's death was not an accident. But she knew how it would sound. 'You don't belong at this school,' echoed Joaquim's voice. But perhaps the headmistress would believe her. She swallowed hard and searched for the right words.

'Basically, I believe that everyone is responsible for choosing her own way.' Madame spoke again, and Blanka had to listen. 'This also means that everyone looks after her own affairs and is aware that classes at this school can be somewhat harder. Later, at university, or working in a big firm or somewhere, you'll find that the Europa International School has prepared you well for professional life and the . . . pitfalls of a career.'

Blanka closed her mouth again. Sylvie was right. Madame was tougher and less compassionate than she seemed – but also more successful and clear-sighted. Right now Blanka would have given anything to please her and to satisfy the school's demands.

'Regardless,' continued Madame, 'we'll look into the matter: question students, find out who was in the library at that time, speak to the staff . . .'

'No,' said Blanka in a firm voice. 'No – it was my mistake. Next time I'll watch out for my belongings better.'

The appreciative smile that Madame gave her made her feel as though she had just been knighted.

'Good. So that's that,' said the headmistress. 'Let's get to the second point.' She briskly opened a drawer, took out a folder, and laid it on the desk so that Blanka could see the cover page.

'Your history test, marked,' said Madame. 'Look at it at your leisure.'

Blanka stood up and picked up the folder. Through the transparent cover the mark looked like 30 per cent. That must be a trick of the light! Incredulously Blanka turned back the cover. It was no trick. Blanka read her name at the side and ran her eye over the first few lines of the test. It was her close handwriting, rather too small – but the answers were not the ones she remembered writing. Errors had crept in, and she had obviously completely missed two questions, although she was sure that she had read them all carefully. She continued to leaf through. Every red mark was like a physical blow. She even found the place where she had made a mistake and had crossed out the first letter of the line. It was clearly her writing. Was she going mad?

'Well?' asked Madame Lalonde.

'I . . . I don't know. Yesterday I thought . . .'

Blanka's throat felt as if a hand was closing around it. Just don't cry! Not now! If she admitted now that she was going mad, she'd be put on the next train and sent home, that was certain. And nothing could be worse than having to go home.

Madame Lalonde sighed and suddenly looked tired. She pinched her nose, as if trying to get rid of a headache.

'As you can imagine, it isn't only my decision whether you stay at this school,' she said quietly. 'And only the best can stay here. You may be a genius in maths – but if you don't make more effort in the other subjects, it won't matter.'

'I know.'

'However, you still have the chance to make up for this poor result on the next two tests,' continued Madame. 'The next couple of weeks will be quieter for you anyway, since the senior classes are sitting their exams. Use this time to catch up on what you have missed. I hope you will make more effort in future. If there is some other reason you are not able to concentrate on studying for these exams, you must tell me. You know I really want you to stay.'

The intimacy between them was suddenly back. Blanka felt as if a warm hand was stroking her hair; it was a strange feeling that confused her and at the same time gave her strength.

'I believe you are very talented, Blanka. You have a scholarship from the Maddalina of Trenta Foundation – make something of it!'

Blanka felt a little guilty when her mother's tired, washed-out face flashed before her. She would never have encouraged her like this. She had not been happy that Blanka was going to a boarding school – even at their parting she had hardly said a word. And during the whole journey to the school, Blanka had been expecting her phone to ring, but it had remained silent, dead, like the unspoken words between them.

'But I actually called you in because of something quite different,' said Madame. 'As you know, here at the Europa International School we make use of our contacts with the university as early as possible. We offer students who are already interested in a particular field of study a very special program. They can work with professors in their chosen area in a mentoring project for a period of eight weeks. That means they are introduced early to the basics of their future field of study and can get a real sense of what it entails. At the end of the project they receive a comprehensive evaluation from their mentor.' Her smile became wider. 'I was able to persuade Dr Hasenberg that you should approach him regarding such a project. Provided, of course, that your average improves – but I have no doubt in that regard. What do you think?'

Blanka took a breath and nodded, dazed.

'Wonderful!' cried Madame. 'Then write this down: Thursday, 5 p.m. You know where Dr Hasenberg's office is? He'll be expecting you.'

Blanka had only just got back to her room when there was a knock at the connecting door. Caitlin could not hide her feelings. Her cheeks burned as she attempted an apologetic smile.

'Well, well, Sherlock Holmes in person,' said Blanka coldly.

Caitlin's smile turned into a rueful grimace. 'I'm sorry, Blanka – I didn't think Madame would make such a big deal of it.'

'How dare you tell anyone about my private affairs?'

Caitlin's face went even redder. 'Madame caught me and asked me all sorts of questions.'

'Do you have any idea what you've done to me? I look like a hysterical idiot!'

'She really pumped me for information,' insisted Caitlin. 'But she could have asked anyone. Take a good look at yourself, Blanka. Obviously the thing about the dead woman has taken more out of you than you realise. Plus I'm always having to make excuses for you to your parents when they call. What's that all about?'

'I don't want to talk about it,' snapped Blanka. 'That's the last time I'll ever trust you! I'll never tell you anything ever again.' She grabbed her jacket and stormed past the flabbergasted Caitlin into the hallway. Head down, she hurried down the stairs. As she walked, she looked at her watch – if she hurried, she would just catch the bus into town. All she wanted was to get away from here! She ran around the corner – and crashed right into Jan. With a loud clatter his bag fell to the ground. Screwdrivers and bits of metal poured onto the stone floor. Jan went deathly pale at the sight of the metal entrails of his bag.

He turned on her. 'Why don't you watch where you're going?'

'I could ask you the same thing. I'm trying to catch the bus.'

He cursed and bent down to quickly pick up his equipment. Reluctantly, Blanka helped him gather his things. She held up a little pair of pliers.

'Give them to me!' he said through gritted teeth. 'You don't want to miss your bus. I'll deal with this.'

Blanka nodded and jumped up. She left the school building at a run, gravel spraying at every step. She headed for the bus stop and did not stop to catch her breath until the school grounds were far behind her. The running felt good, but as she neared the bus stop, she saw the bus driving away around the bend. Too bad. Feeling uneasy, she looked back. Glass sparkled in the sun. The building crouched there as if lying in wait, and the elegantly curved crossbeams of the facade looked like a malicious grin. Her mobile rang. Caitlin's number lit up on the display. Reluctantly she turned it off. On a whim, she decided to walk into town. Somewhere between three and five kilometres – she could manage that.

But soon after she set out it started to drizzle. Blanka hunched her shoulders and walked as fast as she could. Cars zoomed past her, and then she heard the sound of a motorcycle approaching. Out of the corner of her eye Blanka could see it slow down and then accelerate again. It disappeared around the bend with a loud roar.

Nearly an hour later she was there. The road led to a residential district on the outskirts, and as she reached the bus stop a local bus came along, which she took into the old town. The town was quaint: a square in the middle, a medieval pillar commemorating the plague, a bit of unspoiled old town, with ever more modern areas surrounding it like the growth rings of a tree. The most impressive things were St George's Church and the huge university buildings, which stood near the centre.

The rain had stopped, and in the sun of early summer the medieval facades of the houses were glowing like an old painting. Tourists sat in the cafés, their cameras on the empty seats beside them. Students were cycling or ambling towards the university for afternoon lectures, backpacks on their shoulders. Blanka followed a group of them along the little street to the market square, stopped to contemplate the gentle face of Mary atop the medieval pillar, and then hurried to catch up. Two streets later they were at the university. Blanka stood still and watched them crossing the square. A broad staircase led to the entrance. Longingly Blanka watched the students disappear through the heavy wooden door. If she did not manage to improve her marks, this door would be closed to her. A feeling of loss hit her, although nothing had changed yet.

A metallic flicking sound brought her back to reality. She looked to her right. A few feet away stood Leatherjacket, lighting a cigarette. A flurry of wind blew through his blond hair and tugged at the turned-up collar of his leather jacket. A black crash helmet sat on his backpack, which was plonked on the ground.

'Hello, Snow White.'

Without a word she turned and ran back the way she had come. At the end of the market square she looked back. He was not following her. When she reached the centre of town, she was still almost running, her hands balled into fists in her jacket pockets.

He was standing, breathing hard, in front of one of the cafés, waiting for her. For a moment she was confused. Had he flown? Looking sheepish, he held up his hand.

'Hey, I'm sorry about that,' he said. 'That was pretty stupid of me. I didn't mean to scare you.'

'How did you . . .'

'. . . get here? Short cut. Through Pelargus Alley. My student residence is there – it's quicker than going the long way around via the market square. I thought you were going back to the bus.'

For a while they looked at each other. Blanka noticed that he had grey-blue eyes and he looked as if he hadn't seen too much sun recently.

'My name's Nicholas,' he said finally. 'Nicholas Varkonyi.'

'You seem to know my name already. You've been spying on me – I saw you at the school.'

He smiled nervously and shrugged his shoulders. He couldn't hide his feelings any better than Caitlin. With this observation, some of Blanka's confidence returned.

'That's right,' he said. 'I've been spying on you, because – I have to talk to you, please.'

'You're one of the Wolves, right?' she said challengingly.

He frowned. 'Interesting you should say that.' He looked

around a little too casually. 'Can I buy you a cup of coffee? I don't want to discuss this sort of thing out in the open. La Bête is over there.' With an ironic smile he added, 'There are lots of people in there. And it has windows, too.'

Blanka still hesitated, but when a few raindrops fell on her face, she gave in. She reached into her jacket pocket, though, and turned her mobile back on.

Someone had gone to great lengths to furnish the café in the style of old black-and-white movies. Grainy photos of movie stars hung larger than life above black lacquered tables. In the central picture a prince with a cat-like predator's head was depicted in front of a fairytale backdrop. In a niche hung copper engravings of sea monsters, werewolves and flying fiends. Nervously, Blanka sat down and waited. She did not take off her jacket and shook her head when Nicholas asked her if she wanted to order anything. His nervousness was infectious. Funnily enough, she felt as if she were on a first date with someone who did not know how to impress her. His movements were precise, but agitated. With a practised gesture he shook a cigarette out of the pack and, like a magician, let it skip over his fingers before lighting it.

'Do you have to do that?' asked Blanka.

He looked at her blankly, and then to her surprise promptly took the cigarette and stubbed it out in the ashtray in silence. The paper tube burst, and tobacco trickled out of it.

'So, what do you want?' she asked.

Nicholas took a deep breath and moistened his lips. 'First I'll answer your other question – no, I'm not one of the Wolves. I'm a student here.'

'You look pretty young for a student.'

'Is eighteen too young?'

'That depends – did you graduate early from the Europa International School?'

'What do you mean?'

'Well, they graduate a year early there – and because of the optional afternoon seminars, you can take an assessment exam when you start university and skip the introductory courses. It saves time.'

'No. I've got nothing to do with your school. I'm new here in town, like you.' He hesitated before continuing, choosing his words carefully. 'I don't exactly know how to start. Your notes disappear, books go missing, and funnily enough, you're always the one who gets the wrong information. Sometimes tests you've written disappear, and your name vanishes from a sign-up list. Does that sound familiar to you at all?'

Blanka folded her arms and leaned back.

'That's what they're doing to me, anyway,' added Nicholas. 'I don't know about you, but I'm just waiting for the tripwires on the stairs.'

'It sounds familiar,' admitted Blanka after a while.

Nicholas's face seemed to light up with relief.

'But what are the Wolves doing at the university?' asked Blanka sceptically.

'A lot of Europa students go on to attend this university, as you know. If they were members of the Wolves when they were at the school, they stay in the society while they're at university.'

'I see. And what do you want from me?'

He hesitated, as if searching for the right words.

'Well,' he began finally, 'I thought we could form a sort of self-help group – and do a bit of research. But I'm not a student at the school and have no access to the Wolves' notes.'

'And you're looking for them at night in the visitors' carpark?'

He looked at her blankly. 'I have no idea what you're talking about,' he said.

Blanka gave him a suspicious look and did not reply.

'So, are you in?' asked Nicholas after a pause.

'Do I look like someone who snoops around and puts her graduation at risk? No way! Find someone else!'

She was about to get up when he grasped her wrist. His fingers were cold. 'You don't seem to realise that you'll definitely ruin your graduation if you keep walking into their traps. They want you out – just as they want me out. And they're serious.' He reached into his backpack, took out a book, and threw it down on the table. 'I heard you were looking for a book about saints.'

Blanka sank back down onto the chair. She had to make an effort to take the book and look under the letter 'A'. The portrait of Saint Apollonia looked up at her – with Blanka's hair. Even the underlining below the words was still there.

'A fairly clear threat,' said Nicholas. 'But you wouldn't be able to prove anything. There was no book about saints listed in the library catalogue, was there? You can never prove anything against them.'

'How do you know that?' whispered Blanka. 'And you knew that they call me Snow White.'

'Oh,' he said, leaning back. 'No magic there. It was actually supposed to be a joke.' Surprised, she saw that he was blushing slightly. 'Well, you have such fair skin. And with that black hair, too . . .'

'Don't lie to me,' hissed Blanka. 'How do you know about the book?'

'Someone told me.'

'Who?'

He put up his hand defensively. 'Believe it or not – the story got around.'

'And where did you get the book?'

'I simply looked in the theological department.' Nicholas

smiled and drummed his fingers against the table. But his smile faded. 'You don't trust me.'

'Just before the book surfaced, I saw you in front of the library. Who's to say you didn't put the book there yourself?'

'No one,' he replied. 'You only have my word. I was looking for you that day in the library, because I wanted to talk to you. You see, there's something else.'

He leaned forward. 'When I was in the train on the way here, somebody told me the story about how the Wolves threw someone into the river.'

'I know that story. So?'

'It really happened, nineteen years ago. It was a student – and he drowned.'

'What?'

'An accident,' Nicholas continued quietly. 'If you want to believe that. Anyway, they were never held responsible for it. No one was accused. Strange, don't you think? And I'll tell you something else. It was you who found the dead woman a month ago, wasn't it?'

Blanka stiffened. 'That's right.'

'Do you believe that Annette Durlain's death was an accident?'

Suddenly Blanka's mouth was so dry that she could hardly get out her answer. She looked directly into Nicholas's eyes. 'No,' she replied.

He half smiled and then nodded. 'Me neither. Did you notice anything? Anything at all – was there any sign of an injury?'

'Just read last week's paper. There's more in it than I know about her. Why?'

He played with his lighter. 'Promise you won't blab? The story's a bit – delicate. If it comes out that I've talked, I'm toast. You won't tell anyone? Deal?' He held out his hand to her.

Blanka wavered, but eventually shook his hand.

'Good,' he said, putting his fingertips together like a professor. 'Officially she stumbled and fell downstairs – an accident. And I also know the story about the crazies who are so fascinated with witches they want to spend a night beside the witch's robe. It might even be true. But there's one detail that could turn the whole thing around.'

'She didn't break her neck?'

'Oh yes, she did. Only ... she had a wound – just over two square inches. A piece of skin was missing.'

'A wound – so what? That doesn't prove anything.'

'It happened after her death. Not very smart, huh?'

Blanka held her breath. She felt as if the café was rocking. The movie monsters seemed to be smirking.

'How do you know that?'

He pointed at his chest.

'Medical student,' he said. 'Orderly at the Institute of Forensic Medicine, reports lying around, gossip in the waiting rooms.'

'You go snooping in reports that are none of your business?'

'No, I photocopy the reports.'

There was a short pause, and Blanka suddenly felt cold. Up until now, her suspicions had only been a game in her own mind, but now it was becoming frighteningly real. Could it really be murder?

'The Wolves,' she said quietly. And mentally added: Or Nemec?

'Do you think it's possible that they have something to do with it?' Nicholas asked.

'They're students. Why would they kill someone?'

'To get rid of witnesses? Greed? Or revenge? It might have been a commission for someone else. We'll figure it out. So, are you in?'

Blanka shook her head and jumped up.

'Where are you going?'

'Away from here!' she replied sharply.

'What's wrong? Was it something I said?'

'You have to go to the police!'

'I don't trust them. Didn't you read what it said in the paper? No one else was involved!'

'Ever heard of undercover investigations? Quite likely the police have known about your discovery for ages and just want to give the murderer a false sense of security.'

Nicholas held up his hands in a conciliatory gesture. 'Fine, end of conversation. But please take time to think about it. At the university there's no documentation on the Wolves, and I don't have access to the documents at Europa.'

'I won't think about it at all – I'm leaving.'

'Can I call you? Give me some way to contact you – the school number, or whatever you like.'

'No.'

He tore a piece off the cigarette pack, scribbled something on it, and pushed the scrap over to her.

'My mobile number. Please just take it with you, OK? Just in case.'

STIGMA DIABOLICUM

THE WHOLE CLASS WAS SUFFERING WHILE Mrs Catalon tried to scratch out a particularly beautiful diagram on the board with a squeaky piece of chalk. Today Blanka was finding it more difficult than usual to follow Mrs Catalon's explanations. For the first time in weeks she felt wide awake again. The heavy fog that had wrapped itself around her thoughts had disappeared. With her pen she scribbled little circles and arrows in the margin of her notebook. Simon Nemec had been weeping – would a murderer weep for his victim? Or was he crying because he had known Annette Durlain? And Annette Durlain – was there really a connection between her and the Wolves? Blanka could hardly wait for the bell to ring for lunch break.

The few students who came from the town and lived at home jumped onto their bikes and rode away, not to return until just before three o'clock for afternoon classes.

Blanka ran to the library building. She was in luck – the computer stations were free; only a few of the older students, like Caitlin preparing to sit their first final exam in three days, were scattered around the room, hunched over their notes. Blanka sat down at a computer and logged on. It took forever until she could enter her keywords in the search engine: 'Simon Nemec'. Not a single hit. Annette Durlain did not exist on the Internet either – not even on the French pages when she added 'Brest' to the search. Under 'Joaquim Almán' there were just the results and tables from sports tournaments, but Blanka did find several pages for a certain F. Almán. She called up the picture search function and waited. Three pictures appeared – and Blanka immediately knew he was Joaquim's father. Sure, he was balding and wore round glasses, but the facial expression, the mouth and the eyes were identical. The photos all came from charitable institutions he was involved with, but none of the articles mentioned how he actually earned his money. Blanka printed out a few pages, then called up the library's online catalogue and entered 'Maddalina of Trenta'. That got 28 hits, of which she was immediately able to eliminate 24. The last four were interesting, though: printed copies of the convent chronicle, as well as the complete records of the witch trial, a short history of the school – not much more than a booklet, written in 1961 – and also an essay about Saint Belverina. Something, at least. Under keywords for the town history she found only current directories and school yearbooks. Blanka noted down the location of the books and started a new search. Using the search word 'Wolves' she got 159 hits in the biology department. Once more she limited her search, combining it with concepts like 'student association', 'society', 'Middle Ages', the name of the town – and landed on a single book. It was the same book, the one that told the history of the school. With a sigh of relief, she shut down the program and looked at her watch. She still had time. Caitlin's fellow sufferers hardly looked up when Blanka went over to the checkout desk.

'I'd like to see these, please,' she said to the library aide behind the counter, a student whose hair shone with a harsh orange tone. She was probably earning a bit of extra cash by working in the library. 'N. Kuhlmann' was printed on the badge on her shirt collar. Wrinkling her brow, she studied the information Blanka had scribbled on the notebook.

'If that's an M and this scrawl here is 49, then we have the book in the stockroom. We only lend out books like that when there's a reason for it. What do you need it for?'

'History essay,' lied Blanka without hesitation. She bit her lip. Would it work?

'Oh, I see.' The student smiled. 'You should have said that straight away. Then I need a note from your teacher. Do you have it with you?'

Blanka gulped and shook her head. 'I wanted to suggest the topic and do a bit of research ahead of time. I'll get the note tomorrow and bring it in.'

N. Kuhlmann frowned and looked searchingly at Blanka. 'You're the new girl, aren't you? The one sharing a room with Caitlin O'Connell?'

Blanka nodded and prepared herself for the next question. Instead, the girl pushed a form over to her. 'Here, fill the card out. I'll get the book for you.'

'Thanks,' said Blanka, surprised. 'I'll bring the note tomorrow, then . . .'

The student stood up and waved her hand dismissively. 'Don't bother,' she said. 'As long as it's OK with Madame, then it's fine with me.'

The convent chronicle had been photocopied page by page – grey shadows indicated that the original had been yellowed or dirty. Only a few pages were reproduced in colour. Black writing ran over a yellowish-brown background, and from time to time there was a page with splendidly illustrated initial letters. With an effort Blanka could decipher quite well the lines composed in German. In a footnote, a well-meaning translator had translated the Latin lines into clumsy German. Unfortunately the writing was so small that within half an hour Blanka's neck was as stiff as if it was made of wood.

The convent had been home to the order for nearly 150 years. It was named for Saint Belverina. Blanka already knew her picture from the museum. 'Belverina was carried off from her home in England by the Vikings and sold to the court of the king of Neustrien as a slave in 641,' Blanka read. 'Held in high esteem for her wisdom, she rose quickly to high rank and was particularly fond of the children of the court. After the king's death, Belverina became advisor to the ten-year-old heir to the throne. She acquired great wealth, and with it she endowed orphanages and founded convents. Around 675 she was cruelly murdered following a conspiracy by the aristocracy.' The description went on to say that Saint Belverina had been considered the patron saint of children up to that day. A dog sat next to her as a symbol of loyalty. Well, that was interesting, but it didn't really give Blanka anything to go on. The dog had little to do with a wolf: in the picture it looked far more like a deer sitting on its haunches. A few pages further on, Blanka discovered inventories relating to the convent's housekeeping. At the time of the witch trial, eleven women had been living in the convent. The last entry was made in February of 1651; on the following pages the translator had written a summary of the witch trial. Blanka snapped the book shut and looked at the clock. Ten to two. If she wanted to finish her physics homework before afternoon classes, she'd better hurry.

She bent over her backpack and packed up her books. Only now did she notice how quiet the library had become. No more rustling of paper, no clearing of throats, no footsteps. Blanka looked up and froze. Joaquim was standing in front of her. All the other students had already left. Even the student at the checkout desk was gone.

'Hello, Blanka,' said Joaquim. His smile was no warmer than a snowball.

'Congratulations,' she replied. 'You've managed to memorise my name after all.' She hoped he could not hear her heart hammering with fear. 'Where are your gorillas?' she asked, as the pause grew longer.

His eyes had the warm colour of dark amber – a strange contrast to his harsh manner. He was pale and looked tired. 'Who do you think you are?' he said quietly.

'Who do you guys think you are?' she returned.

'Good students,' he answered sharply. 'And a loser like you simply comes along and snatches up a mentoring project. Do you know that you usually have to be in your second year at the school to get one? And then only with an average of at least 80 per cent.'

'Who told you about it?' she replied calmly.

'Hasenberg,' came the answer. 'He's my mentor. That is – he was, until yesterday.'

Blanka was dumbfounded.

Joaquim looked at her with hatred, his lips pinched.

'It wasn't my idea,' she answered. 'I didn't know anything about the rules.'

'I won't let anyone stand in my way.'

'Right. And the best way to manage that is to steal my notes. Very clever, Joaquim.'

'Did you tell Madame that bullshit?' he hissed. 'I'm beginning to understand! You lying bitch!'

'Hey, watch what you're saying!'

He lowered his voice to a warning whisper. 'Oh, I'm really frightened.' He took a step forward and stood so close to her that she had to tilt her head back to look into his eyes. 'Are you going to go straight back to Madame and cry on her shoulder?'

Blanka drew back, bumping painfully into the edge of the table.

'Careful,' he said. 'Something might happen to you.'

'I wouldn't be the first,' she said with an effort.

'And that alone should make you think,' he replied evenly.

'What do you intend to do? Beat me up like Sylvie?'

Her question did not disconcert him at all. Amused, he half smiled. 'We don't beat people up. At most we remind people of their proper place.'

'Leave me alone!' she hissed, pulling away from him. With all her strength she hit him with her backpack full of books. He groaned, and his hand shot forward, but Blanka ducked under his grasp and ran. In the passageway in front of the door she nearly crashed into the aide, who sprang aside with a shocked cry.

From the painful throbbing in her jaw, Blanka realised that she had been gritting her teeth the whole time. She tore open the door and dashed towards the stairs. From the floor below her came the subdued murmur of voices. Just the big staircase, then she would be among people! A blow came from the side, knocking her legs from under her. While she was still falling, she had the sudden thought that it could not have been Joaquim. The stairs flew towards her. Everything seemed to be happening in slow motion – she felt as if she was seeing with Annette

Durlain's eyes: she was aware of every single step and could see with absolute clarity that any moment now she would fall down them. Something wrenched her shoulder painfully and pulled her back, then two arms wrapped themselves around her and dragged her into the alcove by the stairs.

'That nearly went wrong, Snow White,' said Tanya mockingly.

Dazed, Blanka looked up at her. Her shoulder still hurt – Tanya had twisted her arm behind her back. A practice stick pressed against her throat.

'Turn down the project!' said Tanya softly and very clearly. 'If you don't, I'll make sure you do. And I guarantee you one thing: it'll hurt.'

'You won't get away with this!' Blanka said through gritted teeth.

'Wanna bet?' replied Tanya.

A whistle pierced the air. Joaquim appeared, out of nowhere. The colour drained from his face when he saw Blanka at the top of the stairs. Suddenly he just looked helpless and frightened.

'That's enough,' he said hoarsely. 'Let her go.'

Abruptly Tanya loosened her grip and removed the stick. As quickly as she could, Blanka crawled away from the stairs; not until she felt the solid wall did she begin to stand up slowly. Joaquim and Tanya stood face to face.

'You're going too far,' he hissed at her.

The girl stared at him uncomprehendingly. 'But you said . . . Why . . .?' There was disappointment in her voice. All at once Blanka felt she could see right through Tanya. What else might she do for Joaquim?

'Because,' came the gruff answer. 'Leave her alone, OK?' Not deigning to look at Blanka, he turned around and walked away, his shoulders seeming to bear a great weight.

Tanya gave Blanka a look that was hurt and vindictive in equal measure. She lowered her voice to a whisper. 'Just don't get any silly ideas. No one will believe you.'

'Madame will!'

'Madame needs money. Joaquim's father isn't just the chairman of the school foundation. He *is* the foundation. What do you think is more important to her – her school or someone like you? Who are you, Blanka? Some loopy bastard whose parents threw her away like garbage?'

She picked up the other practice sticks and hurried after Joaquim. Blanka watched her go, stunned. A wave of nausea hit her. For a moment she thought she was actually going to throw up. She sank to the ground, wrapped her arms around her knees and sat there, trembling.

For the first time she was glad that Caitlin was not there. It was easier to cry when no one was in the next room. Blanka was freezing, although it was nearly 32 degrees outside. It was Tanya's last words that had hurt the most. How did she know so much about Blanka? With damp fingers she searched the side pocket of her backpack. Finally her fingers found the soft, torn edge of the cardboard. There it was – Nicholas's number, scribbled down on a bit of his cigarette pack. Blanka clasped the scrap in her hand. Should she call him after all? In one bound she leaped up, locked the door and the connecting door to Caitlin's room, leaving the key in it. The phone rang exactly eight times before someone picked up.

'Varkonyi.'

Blanka hesitated. 'Hello,' she said finally.

'Blanka?' His delight at getting her call made her feel good. 'That's . . . to be honest, I didn't think you'd call!'

'I didn't either, until just now. Where are you?'

'Pelargus student residence, in the kitchen. My job doesn't begin till four. And where are you?'

She hesitated. 'I just got back from the library,' she said vaguely. There was a pause.

'And?'

'Nothing there about the . . . Wolves. But I'll keep looking.'

'I see.' Another pause. 'Blanka – is everything all right?'

Blanka took a deep breath. For a moment she was tempted to tell him everything, but then she swallowed and forced herself to speak calmly. 'Sure. Nicholas, you asked me yesterday if I could imagine that the Wolves could have had anything to do with Annette Durlain's death.'

He said nothing.

'Well,' she continued. 'I can imagine it – very clearly.'

She heard a click in the background and imagined Nicholas playing nervously with his lighter.

'Blanka?'

'Hmm?'

'If anything happens, call me – I can come to the school any time.'

'That's not necessary.'

'Are you sure? Yesterday you didn't sound as if you had a cold. Or as if you'd been crying. Did something happen?'

'Listen, Nicholas, I don't need a protector. I'll get the information for you – but stay out of my business, OK?'

'And you listen to me,' he replied. 'I'm no psychologist, but I don't have to be, to see what you're like. You want to do everything

84

alone – heaven forbid anyone should help you! Isn't that right?'

'None of your business, Mr Freud.' Furious, she hung up. All the same, she felt a little better.

Shortly before midnight the light in Caitlin's room finally went out. Blanka waited another half hour, then crept to the connecting door, stuffed her bedspread into the gap under it, and sat down at her desk. The light from her bedside table lamp illuminated a yellow rose, a gesture of reconciliation from Caitlin. The rustling of the pages of the chronicle was so loud in the silence that she was sure Caitlin would wake up.

It was all over quickly. From the first accusation to the point when the last little heap of human ashes had blown away and the convent had become known as a place to be avoided – a place of the Devil – just about three months had passed in 1651. Nevertheless, the 'witch police' had had enough time to do their work thoroughly. It had all begun when the novice Maria and two of the older orphan children had been accused of witchcraft. It was said that they used magic to bring rain, ruined the harvest, and visited a plague of mice upon the mill after a dispute with the miller.

Maddalina of Trenta, Regina Maria Sängerin, a deputy prioress by the name of Katharina, and other nuns were on the second list. The accusation quickly spread to the convent's employees – the gardener Hans Haber, a cowherd called Georg Kastellus, and others in the convent's service, such as Theophrast Mittenmann and Bernd Gerber Halgfuss. Altogether twenty-four people had been arrested and charged, of whom six were 'witches' children', boys from the orphanage that was attached to the convent. At the 'witch trials' the chronicler had apparently let his imagination be his inspiration:

'Carried Out the Old Familiar Witch Trial with Regina Maria Sängerin, in Accordance with which She was Thrown into the Water with Bound Hands and Feet, Whereupon she Floated like Balsa Wood, in Addition Hildebranter Klara was Put upon a Large Scale, at Which it was Remarkable that this Big, Fat Woman Weigh'd Less than an Ounce.'

Blanka pulled her notebook out from under the book and noted down: 'water trial – drowned student?'

The most extensive account given by the clerk documenting the proceedings was that of the abbess's interrogation. The prosecution and questioning of the six 'witches' sons' was also documented most meticulously. They were accused of using magic to cause harm and of contributing to the desecration of the communion bread.

'The Millers Daughter was Infected and Lam'd by the Witches Children Standing Accus'd.'

Reference was made to a '*stigma diabolicum*' being tested on one occasion. The end was the same for all the Belverina nuns, the convent's staff, and the orphan children:

'. . . and All Witches and Conspirators will Receive Eternal Fire for Their Sins.'

Regina Maria Sängerin and the fat Hildebranter Klara were the first to be chained to the stakes in the pyre. The public celebrations went on for more than two weeks. The last one was the 'witch queen', Maddalina of Trenta, who met her death in the courtyard of her own convent, before the eyes of those who a few weeks before had been her friends and acquaintances. The documentation of the case ended with the last of the clerk's footnotes:

'When They Examined Her Cell, They Found a Robe of Fur, Which She was Wont to Wear When Going Out to Her Customary Witches' Dance.'

Blanka stopped dead. A robe of fur – that did not fit. Except for this detail, it was a classic trial, and if you discounted the over-exuberant imagination of its author, it seemed almost impersonal. Blanka leafed back and skimmed each page again. She saw again the words '*stigma diabolicum*'. To be sure of the meaning, she read the explanation in the footnote: 'A mark, usually in the form of a birthmark, that the Devil makes on the body of a witch.' In Maddalina of Trenta's case, the devil's mark had been low on her right hip. Blanka looked up from the book to her alarm clock. Half past one.

Despite the late hour, Nicholas picked up at the first ring. His voice sounded breathless, as if he had been sitting beside his mobile the whole time, waiting for the call.

'Nicholas?'

'Yes!'

'We have to meet. Preferably first thing.'

'Sure.' He sounded infinitely relieved. 'Have you found something?'

'A *stigma diabolicum*,' she said.

THE EXECUTIONER'S SWORD

SHE RECOGNISED HIM RIGHT AWAY through the café window, despite the distance. The tension in his posture made him stand out, even without his leather jacket. Suddenly she was simply happy he was there. Today he was wearing a black T-shirt that emphasised his thinness. His cigarette smoke danced in the slanting rays of the afternoon sun. Except for Nicholas and an older lady reading the paper, La Bête was empty. Most people were sitting in the ice-cream parlours in the market square. Tourists crowded around a tour guide like a swarm of bees around its queen, turning their heads respectfully towards the pillar and to the church tower, looking for all the world like a well-rehearsed ballet corps. Nicholas seemed to sense that someone was approaching: he looked round before Blanka could call out to him. He quickly stubbed out his cigarette in the ashtray and stood up.

'Hello! Thanks for coming.'

They shook hands formally and sat down. For a few uncomfortable seconds they just looked at each other. Nicholas's eyes were like a stormy sky.

'You don't look as though you've had much sleep,' he remarked.

'Nor you,' she returned. For a moment she was tempted to tell him about the incident on the stairs.

'Anything new at your end?' she asked instead.

'Yesterday my anatomy books disappeared without a trace and they have no record of my registration for a seminar.' He swore. 'That means I might lose a semester.'

'Do you think they're watching us right now?'

She could tell by looking at him that he felt uncomfortable sitting there – carefully he looked around and shook his head.

'It doesn't look like it right now. Come a bit closer!'

She slid her chair closer to his, so they could talk without being overheard. The clerk behind the counter smiled to herself as she watched the couple whispering. Sitting so close to someone was very unusual for Blanka. Suddenly she realised how much she had kept her distance from the people around her in the last few weeks. Nicholas's hair smelled of shampoo, and a blond strand was falling over his eyebrow.

'*Stigma diabolicum*,' he whispered. 'What's that all about?'

'Just a guess. Maddalina of Trenta had a birthmark. And the dead woman in the library had a piece of skin missing.' She leaned further forward. 'Did you read in the autopsy report where her wound was?'

Slowly he let his hand slide to his right side, indicating a spot just below where his belt sat on his hipbone. Blanka nodded. 'Just like Maddalina!' she whispered. 'I don't know the shape of her birthmark, but do you think it could have been a brand, a tattoo, or something like that, rather than a birthmark? Let's assume that the dead woman had the same mark as Maddalina of Trenta.

Then her murderer could have removed the piece of skin so that no one would know she had belonged to a . . . group.'

Nicholas had turned pale. Blanka said nothing as he took out a cigarette with a nervous gesture. He forgot to light it, however.

'Then brace yourself,' he said. 'Because I found something out, too – the autopsy report has disappeared.'

'What!'

'I wanted to copy it today – and then I saw that it had been changed. There's nothing in there about a missing piece of skin any more. Just her broken neck and a few scrapes. The police aren't investigating it any more, Blanka. The case is closed – officially, it was an accident.' In Nicholas's eyes the café window was reflected as a light-coloured rectangle, its sides curved outward. 'That means,' he continued, 'that there may be more people involved – a doctor, or even several doctors, who are hushing up a murder. Maybe even the doctor I work for.'

Blanka watched his hands as he played with the cigarette, twisting and twirling it, until he finally put it back into the pack. 'Let's go,' she said quietly.

A little later they were walking through the town park. Some students had strung a volleyball net between two trees and were trading volleys vigorously. Blanka and Nicholas crossed the lawn in silence and sat down on the park bench by the duckpond. Blanka pulled her knees to her chin and stared at the mirror-like surface of the water.

'The student who drowned,' she said after a while. 'His death may be connected with the witch trial. In the record there's an account of a trial by water. It could be a ritual – maybe a punishment, or even a test of courage that got out of hand. We have to get a list of members of the Wolves. All the names listed since the society was founded. If we look hard enough, I bet we'll find the name Annette Durlain. The student associations must have all the old yearbooks and photos in their meeting rooms . . .'

'Don't waste your time,' Nicholas interrupted her. 'They don't have meeting rooms. And no local bar, either, where the Wolves have a regular table. They never use a room, not even the Carnival Association. There are just the minutes of meetings in the Oliver O'Deen room below the student cafeteria, where the upcoming training plans are discussed, and the cost of costumes and new flags for their part in the town's medieval festival, but strangely enough, none of the Wolves have actually met there at those times.' He leaned back. 'At least, if you can believe the schedule by the cafeteria, where the university theatre group books the room for its rehearsals, too. Unless, of course, the Wolves held their last official meeting with a play rehearsal going on in the background.'

'So, no meeting room,' said Blanka. 'No information in the school library or at the university, no history. Just those dumb costume games. They make fools of people with their Carnival Association nonsense. And I have a feeling that this isn't just about the Wolves. There's something else. Something . . . something I don't get . . .' She had talked herself into such a fury that Nicholas looked at her in astonishment.

'What do you mean?' he asked.

Blanka thought about the phantom, her nightmares, and Simon Nemec weeping.

'I can't describe it exactly,' she said evasively. 'Something threatening.'

Now Nicholas was looking at her so uncertainly that she decided to change the subject, and quickly. 'Forget it. Somewhere there must be more information about the Wolves – maybe in the town museum? I've read that there's an archive there.' She looked at her watch. 'I still have an hour and a half before my afternoon class. What about your lectures?'

Nicholas hesitated. 'Well,' he said finally, 'if we leave right away, it'll be OK.'

The town museum was next to the old town hall. It was an unprepossessing modern building that looked out of place beside the town hall's half-timbered facade. Blanka and Nicholas pushed past a group of Japanese tourists, who were looking up at the clock in fascination, waiting for the chimes that rang every hour.

In the museum it was cool, and they could smell new stone and fresh paint. The interior rooms looked as though the building had originally been intended as a gallery. Soft light fell through circular skylights of frosted glass. The exhibits were displayed on modern steel and glass structures. There was a section with artifacts from the Bronze Age, Roman coins, and the plaster cast of a horse skeleton. Blanka almost had to run to keep up with Nicholas. Drawings of Celtic warriors and gleaming lance tips flashed by. The coolness felt good, although the sudden temperature change left Blanka dazed.

'That's the way to the Middle Ages and early modern times, over there,' whispered Nicholas.

Blanka nodded and followed him through the reproduction of a city gate. At first glance the exhibits looked like those in the convent museum. Here too were a monstrance, embroidered altar cloths, and golden goblets for mass.

'At the back there's a model of the original convent,' said Nicholas softly. His steps made hardly any sound on the smooth grey floor. Blanka went from one display case to the next, finding craftsmen's seals and documents, portraits of guild elders, spinning wheels, and a cradle decorated with inlaid silver which was enthroned like a work of art on a steel pedestal. At the end of the exhibition room she found a small passageway. Obviously the architect wanted to create the atmosphere of a journey of discovery, for the passage came to an unlit dead end.

Blanka went closer and squinted to read the text. 'Special Exhibition,' she read on a poster. 'Witches, Hangmen, Torturers – 1 March to 31 August.' Wondering whether to wait for Nicholas, she looked around, but he was nowhere to be seen. So she entered the passageway alone and went towards the shadowy corner. A worm-eaten door came into view. In front of its square window was an iron railing. Only when Blanka was standing directly in front of it did she realise that it was just a photograph on the white door. Blanka pressed down the handle, entered – and was standing in the middle of a torture chamber. Straw rustled beneath her feet, and the walls were formed of roughly hewn blocks of stone, like castle walls. Imitation torches lit up the room. The glass cases, in which the flickering light was reflected, were the only reminder that this was a museum. Blanka wiped her forehead – despite the cold, she had broken out in a sweat – and looked around. Not all of the exhibits were from this town: some were on loan from Tübingen, Rothenburg and Münster. The prize of the collection was an angular reclining chair whose seat and back were covered with iron spikes.

Just as Blanka was about to turn away, her glance fell on an exhibit in the corner. It was a jagged sword with a very straight, not too broad blade. To its right hung a yellowed document. Blanka moved closer and read the write-up. The sword had belonged to Johann Georg Feverlin, town executioner until his death in 1654. A small thank-you note indicated that the sword now belonged to the family and had only been made available to the museum for the duration of this special exhibition. The document said that Johann Georg Feverlin had given evidence of his qualification to be town executioner on 5 September 1646. The date was interesting – the hangman had lived in the town at exactly Maddalina's time. The name of the family who had lent the sword to the exhibit was, however, not noted. Blanka took out her notebook and wrote down the dates. A few steps on she came across documents that looked familiar to her – that's right, they were parts of the documents that she had read yesterday. Page by page she skimmed through the interrogation records. Nothing new, she established after a while, disappointed. The same sentences, the same sequence of events, the same gaps. Finally she had reached the photograph of the page of the record that lay in front of the witch's robe in the convent museum.

'. . . he ask'd Maddalina of Trenta [if she] Her Self had been Qveen of the Witches there [at the Witches Dances] among Witch People and Fiends.'

Disappointed, Blanka stood up, tipped her head back and massaged her painful neck with her right hand. Then she stopped and read the words again. 'Fiends,' it said. Not 'Feends,' like at the museum. As she tried to leaf back through her notebook much too fast, a page tore with a horrible noise. There it was – the sentence she had copied down letter by letter in the school museum. It was identical to the one in the photo – except for the spelling of this one word.

Blanka was so absorbed in comparing the original and the photo that she did not notice at first that there was someone else in the room now. Not until she heard breathing did she press the notebook to her chest and instinctively hide behind the torture chair. The smell of furniture polish and old wood assailed her nose.

It was Nicholas, of course. He had his hands in his pockets and was looking around with a concerned expression. Blanka cleared her throat and stood up. Nicholas jumped. 'Man, so this is where you are!' he said.

Blanka beckoned him to come closer. 'Take a look at this!' she whispered, pulling him towards the wall.

Nicholas compared the sentence on the notebook with the photograph several times and whistled softly through his teeth.

'Either the original document at your school is forged, or the document that was photographed,' he confirmed.

'I had the feeling yesterday that the chronicle was incomplete. It all seems too smooth – like a model trial for a textbook on the witch hunts. But in one paragraph it mentions that Maddalina of Trenta had a fur mantle that she supposedly wore when she carried out her devil's rites. That just doesn't fit the picture. I have a feeling that an important part of the documents is missing . . .'

'. . . and at the very least, that there are two versions of the interrogation record,' said Nicholas, finishing her sentence.

They found the only pictures and documents that referred to the Wolves in the 'Town History' section. The whole wall was set up like a page from a gigantic family album. The photos were in simple frames and showed the town in different periods, the turn of the century, after World War II and in the 1960s. Naturally, the manor house had also been photographed – before it had been renovated it had looked like a dark grey temple from a silent movie. In addition, there was a framed list with the names of the people who had made donations to support the restoration of the old buildings and the orphans' cemetery. The cemetery had been protected as a historical monument for nearly fifty years. Among the sponsors, a Dr Almán was listed – of course, Joaquim's father was an active supporter of the school and surely also of everything belonging to it. Blanka read through the list, name by name, until she came across one at the bottom that she knew only too well.

'Carsten Seibold,' she whispered. 'That's the policeman who questioned me after I found the dead woman.'

'That doesn't prove he's connected with the Wolves – it just means he gave money for the restoration. But it could well explain why the investigation was dropped so suddenly.'

Nicholas indicated a row of small pictures. They were photos of the town's associations and institutions – the Vintners and the Beautification Society, the group that promoted traditional costumes, and the Music Association. Finally, almost beside the door, there were about a dozen photos of the Wolves. The earliest dated from 1955; in them the costumes looked heavy and roughly sewn. Over the decades the costumes changed, adapting to the fashion of the day. In 1972 the nun's hair was in a topknot and the man wearing the wolf mask had sideburns. The silent faces seemed to smile at Blanka and Nicholas knowingly.

'They look like a harmless Carnival Association,' said Blanka, with disappointment.

'Last try,' Nicholas murmured.

In the entrance hall the museum employee was bent over her keyboard. She did not notice the two visitors until Nicholas cleared his throat. Fascinated, Blanka eyed a huge wart near the corner of the old lady's mouth.

'My name is Klaus Jehle,' said Nicholas. 'From the university newspaper, *Attempto*.' He pulled out a laminated card and showed it to her. The lady raised her brows. 'I'm doing some research for an article about the medieval festival,' Nicholas continued, 'and I'm particularly interested in the history of the Wolves. I didn't find anything about it in the museum.'

The woman glanced at the card and her expression became a little more friendly.

'You won't have much luck here.'

'Don't you have archives? You have the original documents of the city library here, don't you?'

Regretfully, the lady shook her head and reached for a pen and paper. 'We have pretty much nothing on the school history or the Wolves here.' She scribbled a couple of names on the paper and searched briefly in the computer before adding the phone number. 'The best place to look is the university library – or better still, at the Europa International School. I'll give you a couple of names.' She smiled at Nicholas, the wart wandering in the direction of her ear as a result. 'Say hello to the lady from Mrs Nyen. Or you could ask one of the Wolves directly.'

'Good idea,' said Nicholas without the least hint of irony. 'Thanks a lot.'

He hid his disappointment well, but Blanka could not resist asking another question.

'Why don't you have any of the original documents?'

Mrs Nyen's smile became cool. 'Well, if you had read the museum's history on the third floor carefully, you would know that, unfortunately, the archive was almost completely destroyed by an electrical fire in 1954. Luckily the school had copies of the convent documents as well as a few original pages of the convent chronicle.'

'Thanks very much,' said Nicholas, taking the paper. 'I'll bring you a copy of the article as soon as the paper comes out.'

Out in the lobby they were hit by a wave of heat, a taste of what awaited them in the market square.

'Since when is your name Klaus Jehle?' asked Blanka.

'Since the real Klaus, who lives on my floor, lent me his ID. Hey, what's wrong?'

Blanka had come to a halt. She gave Nicholas a suspicious look.

'I just feel less and less sure about what I should believe,' she said. 'Are you lying to me? You're a journalist, aren't you?'

Nicholas's mouth fell open. 'Where were you brought up?' he asked, annoyed. 'The gulag? Why are you so suspicious?'

'I just want to know where I stand.'

He swore, turned, and left her standing there. The museum door swung shut in her face. Blanka reached for the steel handle and pushed against the door with all her strength. Relieved, she saw that Nicholas was standing on the steps. He did not look at her as she ran down to him.

'What do you want me to show you?' he shouted at her suddenly. 'Passport? Student ID? University registration?'

'No, I just wanted to know . . .'

He shook his head vigorously. 'It'd be nice if you just believed me.' With these words he pulled out his wallet and took out a photo.

'I'm not a journalist. If my father had any say, I'd be a stone-mason like him. This is him, in front of his business, in Hemmoor, in northern Germany.'

He held a picture out to her. A thin man stood in front of a workshop, smiling into the camera. He had hardly any hair left on his head, yet the similarity was amazing. Nicholas turned the picture over.

'Sandor Varkonyi,' it said on the company stamp.

'My father comes from Kecskemét in Hungary. Can you imagine what it costs him to send me to university here? I'm not going to let the Wolves take that away from me.'

'I'm sorry. I just thought . . .'

'Exactly,' replied Nicholas ironically. 'You think – that's the problem. You think far too much!'

He put the photo away and studied the piece of paper the lady at the museum had given him. 'Mrs Klaas – that's the librarian at the university. I talked to her last week, and she couldn't help me. What about this name?'

Blanka looked at the paper. 'Natalie Kuhlmann. That's the student who's responsible for the library stockroom at school. And I've already gone right through that.'

'Not much help,' remarked Nicholas.

'There's still the hangman.'

'What hangman?'

'In the special exhibition there's an executioner's sword. It belonged to the hangman Johann Georg Feverlin. He lived at exactly the time of the Belverina witch hunts.' She lowered her voice. 'It said on the notice that the sword comes from a private collection. We have to be able to find out who it belongs to – maybe a descendant of the hangman. They might know something about it, or they might have some documents from that time.'

A smile flitted over Nicholas's face. He nudged her appreciatively. 'Not bad!'

'Do you think the wart lady will give us the address?'

'You can be sure of that!' Nicholas took out his wallet and put the paper into it. When it flopped open, Blanka noticed several hundred-euro bills.

'Did you win at Bingo?'

Nicholas quickly closed the wallet. 'Something like that,' he said apologetically. 'I cashed a cheque today. Do you have any idea what a room in the Pelargus residence costs?'

He caught sight of Blanka's watch. 'Don't you have to go to class? If you hurry you can catch the 3.30 bus.'

Blanka slung her backpack over her shoulder. 'We'll talk on the phone!'

'Be careful!' he called after her. 'And call me – no matter how late it is. My mobile's on all the time.'

'Same here,' she called back.

ENGRAM

THIS PARTICULAR THURSDAY, NOT EVEN Dr Kalaman could lure Blanka into the realm of probability theory. Unable to concentrate on the lecture, she leafed through her notes. 'Sylvie' was underlined twice in the margin. In a few days, when she'd returned to school, Blanka would have to get hold of her.

Blanka had not seen the other Wolves since the incident on the stairs – and in the evenings she not only locked her door, but also pushed the back of her chair under the door handle.

'What on earth are you doing here?' Caitlin called out, when Blanka came into the room after her afternoon seminar. 'Don't you have that appointment with Dr Hasenberg?'

'Oh, crap!' Blanka turned on her heels and ran. It was two minutes to five when she finally reached the language labs. Taking two stairs at a time, she raced up to the third floor. She ignored the stitch in her side and knocked.

Dr Hasenberg had light brown curly hair and looked far too young to be a university professor of psychology. Blanka guessed he was barely thirty. 'Right on time,' he said, pretending not to notice how out of breath she was. 'Come in and sit down!'

The room was sparsely furnished – the two blue armchairs could not do justice to what could have been a cosy sitting area. A heavy, black-lacquered bookcase took up almost a whole wall. Behind its shiny glass doors the books looked like the sad inmates of a glass institution. Hasenberg simply did not belong in a room that exuded this aura of sober administration. The door to the next room was ajar, and behind it a secretary was tapping away at a computer.

'Water? Orange juice?'

'No, thanks,' said Blanka, trying to breathe normally. Dr Hasenberg poured himself a glass of water and sat down, facing her, mimicking the way she was sitting. Blanka nearly grinned. Was he copying her posture to make her feel he was trustworthy?

She crossed her legs the other way and folded her arms.

Hasenberg gave a faint smile. 'Madame Lalonde tells me you want to take psychology at university?'

Boy, he was definitely getting right down to business. 'Yes, that's why I'm taking Dr Kalaman's extra maths course.'

'Statistics will be a great help to you,' he said, putting his fingertips together, the way Nicholas had in the café. 'Why did you decide to go into psychology?'

'Why did you?' she countered. There was a pause. Blanka felt uncomfortable. The psychologist did not give the impression that he liked his new student much.

'More or less by chance,' Hasenberg replied finally. 'I had started to study medicine – until I realised that even a doctor is nothing more than a psychologist – or a shaman, if you will.' The keyboard in the next room chattered quietly, making Blanka feel drowsy. She was still out of breath. The notebook with the cues she had written down for the conversation was in her bag. She had to gain time to gather her thoughts.

'You mean a doctor must also be a good psychologist, and vice versa?'

'It certainly can't hurt,' replied Dr Hasenberg. 'But I believe that neither a psychologist nor a doctor can heal the patient. He heals himself. The rituals and symbols are the important thing. No matter whether it's a shaman's mask or a white coat, a spear or a stethoscope – it's trust in the healer's abilities that heals the person. How long have you wanted to be a psychologist?'

'For ever,' replied Blanka. The lie slid over her lips with amazing ease. In fact, she had only picked 'psychologist' after learning that she would have a better chance of winning a scholarship if she had a definite career goal in mind.

Hasenberg nodded. 'Have you done any serious work on it?'

'I've read a few essays – on Jung.'

'Good. I would like to give you a list of books today, to work on over the next two weeks. You don't have to memorise them, don't worry, but you should read them carefully and think about them. We'll talk about them at our next meeting.'

'And then you'll decide whether you want to be my mentor?'

'We'll both make the decision. Look at this as an opportunity, not a duty. You are interested, aren't you?'

Blanka thought about Tanya's warning and stuck her chin out defiantly. 'Of course!'

'Good. Do you have any questions?'

'What's your specialty?'

Dr Hasenberg leaned back. 'Trans-generational research,' he said. 'Which simply means examining the mechanisms that control a family over generations and exposing their interconnections. Members of a family are often beholden to each other, or mutually dependent, in unseen ways. Because of this, some problems or events occur over and over again. If a grandfather died in an accident, it sometimes happens that there are more accidents in the next generation. That's just a general example, of course.'

His voice was pleasant, almost soporific. Blanka's lack of sleep was becoming noticeable. The whole office seemed enveloped in a restful aura as soft as cotton wool. 'You might say that we pass on not only our genes but also our tragedies and strokes of fate,' he continued. 'We remember things for generations, if only subconsciously. You must not interpret the moment: you must look for the pattern.'

Blanka suddenly became aware that she had become so tense that her temples were throbbing. She was starting to get a headache. Dr Hasenberg's words frightened her. She saw her parents before her eyes – and behind them, threatening shadows, phantoms, reaching out for her. Hasenberg's hands were relaxed, holding his glass; he looked somewhat like a saint. His smile seemed to be a mask. When he looked directly at Blanka, however, she thought she saw a flash of annoyance in his eyes. He lifted his glass and drank deeply.

Blanka cleared her throat. 'I . . . I'm more interested in clinical psychology and . . . psychotropics,' she said.

'Ah! The organic approach: accountability, neurotransmitters in the brain, biochemistry – also an interesting subject,' he conceded readily. 'That's the great thing – every scientific discipline ultimately serves to research the human spirit. If you decide later that you'd rather be a neurologist or biochemist, you can track down engrams, for example.'

'Engrams?'

'They're the traces that important events leave in the brain. You can track them and in that way research the way consciousness and memory work.'

'Yes . . . that sounds interesting.'

He twisted his mouth into a cool smile.

Blanka thought of Joaquim. 'Did you have connections with the Wolves when you were younger?'

He looked at her, bewildered. 'What makes you ask that?'

'I'm just interested. I'm writing an essay about the town's history. Earlier you talked about shamans and healers. If you know all about shamanic rituals, you must know some things about the Wolves, too. They have a long tradition, after all.'

'I'm afraid I can't help you there. I took part in the procession just once, as a flag-bearer. When I was sixteen or seventeen.'

'So you went to the Europa International School?'

'Yes – and I went to the local university, too.'

'Do you know what the costumes mean exactly?' Blanka's questions continued. 'The masks, the fights – they must all have a symbolic meaning.'

'Not a very spectacular one, in psychological terms,' said Dr Hasenberg, suppressing a yawn. 'The wolf is an archaic animal. In many cultures people believe that they are descended from the wolf and connected to his spirit. He's a totem animal. Our wolf's clothing here is probably just a remnant from heathen times, like the carnival masks in the area you come from.'

Dr Hasenberg smiled faintly, looked at his watch, and stood up. 'Good, Blanka. I'll just find that list of the basic literature for you.' With these words he took a printed sheet from his desk drawer. Then he leafed through his diary. 'Two weeks, same time?'

'Yes . . . but . . . There's something else.'

'Do you have another question?'

'What's going on with Joaquim Almán? I don't want to take his place away from him.'

Dr Hasenberg stood up abruptly. 'What makes you think that's what's happening?' he returned frostily. In the next room the typing had stopped.

'Isn't Joaquim in your project?'

'Whether and for what reasons other students have terminated their project early is not something you should worry about. Leave those decisions to us. You're not taking anything away from anybody.'

Blanka still felt as if she were trying to keep her balance on a swaying tightrope.

Dr Hasenberg looked at her thoughtfully. Every trace of kindness had left his face. 'I'll be honest with you, Blanka. If it were up to me, I would have delayed your mentoring project for at least a year. But Madame Lalonde is convinced that you can organise your time well enough to manage it all. She thinks very highly of you – even though your grades at present are far below expectation.' That hit home. 'But I too believe,' he continued with a civility that sounded forced, 'that you have what it takes. Here is your list.' He gave her the sheet of paper. 'Don't be surprised when you find works on there that relate more to philosophy, or even physics. I like to give my students a global perspective. And there are also books on the list that aren't on the open shelves. Please ask Mr Nemec to find them for you – he knows where the reserved books are. Today if you can.'

Blanka thought it was odd that Mr Nemec was in charge of the special collections, but she had already begun to suspect that he was far more than just a caretaker.

In exactly one hour the students would head to the dining hall for the evening meal. But right now the hallways were so empty that school seemed no more than a memory. Blanka's steps click-clacked on the linoleum floor. Hasenberg and Nemec, she repeated mentally. What do they have to do with each other? She ran down the stairs, turning towards the language labs. She had never noticed that slight echo before. She could hear her steps just a split second later. It sounded as if someone was running after her. Blanka stopped. Now it was dead silent again. Quietly she went on. The echo was still there. And there was something else – a click, but not of heels. Abruptly she stood still again and listened. Directly behind her someone took another step. Blanka gripped her pen like a weapon and swung around. The hallway was empty; she could hear nothing but her own breath. Carefully she took a step back, then another. There – someone or some-thing was sniffing the air, as if it was trying to find Blanka's scent, and then there were three clicks, one after the other. A presence surrounded her, so close it felt as if someone was standing directly in front of her. She imagined that a breath brushed her hand, and she screamed. The sniffing stopped and Blanka was there alone, feeling as though an icy wind had taken hold of her.

'Did he tear you to shreds?' asked Caitlin. She was lying on her bed in the middle of an avalanche of books. The day after tomorrow she would sit the first of her final exams, and even

Caitlin, always so relaxed, was pale at the thought and had no appetite.

'Hardly,' replied Blanka, throwing herself into Caitlin's reading chair. She was still freezing, and when she rubbed her lower arms she felt goosebumps.

'And?' her friend persisted, without looking up from her books.

'He gave me a list of books I need to get from the library.'

'Oh, then they're sure to be special books that you can only get from Igor.'

'Igor?'

'Nemec – doesn't he remind you of Frankenstein's servant?'

Gradually Blanka was finding her way back to reality. That presence – it must have been a draught, she told herself, just her imagination playing tricks.

'Let's see!' said Caitlin, stretching out her hand for the list. Blanka hesitated a moment too long. Caitlin frowned and let her hand fall.

'I've had this!' she cried. Her green eyes flashed. She jumped up from the bed and went over to Blanka. 'How many times do I have to tell you I'm sorry? I didn't mean to dob on you. I'll never talk to you about your nightmares again, though I worry, and you talk in your sleep. And I'll be a good girl and lock my door so you'll feel safer. But it doesn't matter if I do – you don't trust any-one, do you?' On edge, she ran her fingers through her hair and sighed. 'Sorry,' she said softly. 'I didn't mean to attack you. It's just . . . I'm very wound up because of the exam, anyway. And I'm not very good at handling this strange atmosphere between us.'

Blanka had never seen Caitlin in such low spirits. Nicholas's words came into her head, and she was ashamed of her distrust. 'Sorry, Caitlin. No more bad moods.'

Caitlin visibly relaxed and smiled hesitantly at Blanka. She was just about to say something else when her mobile rang. Blanka went into her own room. She lay down on the bed and closed her eyes. She could hear Caitlin's muffled conversation through the door. She couldn't really hear much, but it didn't sound as though Caitlin was talking to a member of her family. A few minutes later Caitlin stuck her curly head through the door. Blanka had never been so relieved to see a smile.

'I'm meeting Jan in the library café,' said Caitlin. 'Do you want to come to the library with me?'

Today all the reading tables were occupied. With a dull feeling in the pit of her stomach, Blanka looked around for the Wolves, but could not see any of them. She could look down into the café area through the glass facade behind the bookcase containing the dictionaries. Caitlin was sitting with Jan at a table, beaming. The two of them obviously had a lot to talk about. Blanka watched them for a while, then plucked up her courage and went to look for Simon 'Igor' Nemec. Her secret hope that he wouldn't be there was dashed. She had scarcely left the languages section when he approached her. A sharp peppermint smell wafted towards Blanka. At least his eyes weren't red today.

'Dr Hasenberg's list?' he growled, before she had said anything.

She nodded and held it out to him.

He glanced at it. 'Don't need it,' he said, waving it off, and indicated to her that she should follow him. She observed his stiff shoulders, which looked as if he was trying to hold his ears shut with them. He led her past the psychology section; they passed physics, metaphysics, and biology, came to the history section, and finally reached a corner of the older part of the library, the same area Nemec had chased Blanka out of at their last meeting. Nemec stopped and started taking books from the shelves. He seemed to be following a well-practised routine. How many students' hands had these volumes passed through before hers?

Nemec piled the books up and set them down on a shelf near the psychology section. Then he grasped a broad wall of shelves and simply swung it aside. Blanka's mouth fell open. So! There *was* a door behind the shelves – she had just been looking in the wrong corner when Nemec had caught her. The door was hardly visible, mind you, as it was wallpapered like the wall. Nemec pulled out his keyring. His fingers trembling slightly, he picked out a flat key and opened the door. Behind it yawned a black hole. A faint smell of leather and dust reached Blanka's nostrils. A hideous fluorescent light blinked on, flickering. Nemec stepped into the room and let go of the door handle. With a harsh creak and then a whine, the door closed behind him. Blanka grabbed the nearest bookshelf and held on to it tightly. Like a flash photo, Blanka suddenly saw herself in the foyer of the library a moment before finding the woman's body. There was just darkness – and a sound. This sound. A moment later Nemec came back out of the little room.

'Here,' he said, heaving the whole pile of books into her arms. The bandage on his right hand did not look so new any more. At the sight of his sinewy hands Blanka imagined these hands killing Annette Durlain. Don't flip out, she warned herself. The noise just meant that someone else as well as Annette Durlain must have been in the library. Nemec – or someone else.

'Have you been doing the museum tours for long?' she asked.

Nemec's eyes were watery and yellowish. To her surprise, he smiled at her fleetingly. 'A quarter-century,' he answered. 'And it doesn't get any more exciting as the years go by.'

'Do you still remember some of the visitors?'

'You mean Annette Durlain, don't you? No, kiddo. Do you think I notice every face?'

He sighed deeply and suddenly looked like nothing more than a pitiable old man who had somewhere, somehow, lost his grip on life.

'So you didn't know her?'

He shook his head wearily.

'So why are you so sad?'

'Life is sometimes enough to make you weep, don't you think?'

Blanka lowered her gaze and looked at the topmost book. On the cover was a stamped picture: a lion that had bitten into a sun.

'Is . . . this book really on the list?' she asked in a weak voice.

'Of course.'

'What's it about?'

'The lion that ate the sun,' he said. 'The magic symbol for the philosophers' stone. It's a book about Faust, who practised the black arts, and his experiments in alchemy.'

The load of books pressed heavily on Blanka's hips as she ran down the stairs to the exit. The evening sun had laid a golden veil over the grass and bathed the manor house in an insubstantial light that nevertheless emphasised its sharp contours. With quick steps Blanka ran along the wall for a little way, to a place where there was nothing but ivy and stonework. Here she took time to catch her breath. Her fear of the Wolves, which made her anxious and irritable inside the school building, disappeared out here as if by magic. Relieved, she took out her mobile.

'Nicholas, it's me!'

'Why are you speaking so softly? Where are you?'

'Behind the manor house – I needed some air.'

'I was going to call you in a second, anyway. The museum lady got suspicious and won't give me the Feverlin address. I spent nearly the whole evening in the Internet café, but the Feverlins I found there don't seem to be the ones we're looking for. Tomorrow I'll get on the phone again.'

'You can save yourself the trouble.' She lowered her voice to a whisper. 'I know where Annette Durlain was searching. I'm sure now that she wasn't alone in the library! And if I'm right, we may well find the chronicles that are not supposed to exist.'

'Where?'

'In a special little room off the library. I just don't know how to get in yet. The room is locked and I don't think it has a window.'

'Got it,' said Nicholas. 'Time for Plan B.'

SHADOWS

CAITLIN WAS TOO NERVOUS to drink her morning tea. Her pencil case fell out of her hand for the third time, as she checked to see if she had all her pens and pencils, and whether they all worked or were sharp.

'What's the first subject?' asked Blanka.

Caitlin rolled her eyes. 'History – two hours. Then a break. Then oral exams in French and Spanish. And then this afternoon, physics.'

'I'm sure you'll write the best answers ever and get into Trinity College Dublin with flying colours. You can do it!'

'If I do the exam the way I feel, I'll be back home in Dingle in a week, applying for a job washing up at O'Reilly's. Thanks all the same!' Caitlin hugged Blanka in a brief goodbye and grabbed her bag. The next moment she was gone. Blanka heard voices in the hallway and fast steps disappearing into the distance. The morning's tensions fell away, and her weariness returned. She rubbed her eyes and crept back into bed. She still had ten minutes before she had to leave – and while she was listening to Mrs Lincoln's explanations about new aspects of English grammar, Caitlin would be sweating over her exam paper like the sixteen other examinees. Other duties awaited Blanka, however. Above all she had to get used to the idea that tonight she would be risking her future at the Europa International School. She must be crazy. Nervously she looked at her alarm clock and checked her calculations. Seventeen more hours until she would meet Nicholas. The timing was perfect – all the teachers and students were concentrating on exams. Nicholas and she could not have hoped for a better distraction. She closed her eyes and imagined the route she would take tonight.

None of the Wolves appeared the whole day. That surprised Blanka at first when she was at her reading table in the library, but then it occurred to her that some students must have been assigned the task of making sure the exam area remained quiet. Blanka tried without success to concentrate on her homework. Today the formulas and diagrams looked like cryptic signs, whose meaning she could scarcely remember. The lack of sleep and the dreams worried her. I just have to hold on for one more day, she told herself. The answers were almost within her reach. A haggard-looking Caitlin rushed by on the floor below. She was following five other students, who looked just as tense. As if aware of Blanka's gaze, all at once she looked up. She beamed and gave a thumbs up.

The minutes were creeping by, more slowly than Blanka would have thought possible. For an hour she had done nothing but stare at her mobile and the clock. Luckily Caitlin had been so exhausted that despite her nervousness about the next day's exams she had gone to sleep quickly. Finally the numbers changed. One o'clock. Quietly Blanka got up and slid the phone into her tracksuit pocket. Without making a sound she opened the door and slipped into the hallway. Because she had spent the last hour in darkness, her eyes had adjusted to the gloom; she could make out the doors to the other rooms and the glass door at the end of the corridor. Somewhere a toilet flushed; light shone through the crack under a door. Blanka hurried on, leaving the girls' quarters, and fumbled her way down the stairs. The alcove under the main staircase was dark. Blanka stopped at the place they had agreed on and peered into the shadows.

'Nicholas?' she whispered. A scraping noise answered her. Heart pounding, she stood still, her right shoulder pressed against the cool stone of the staircase. Then she heard someone clearing his throat quietly. Blanka was so relieved that her legs nearly buckled. 'Nicholas!' With clammy fingers she felt for the tiny flashlight that she had taken off her keychain.

'Nope,' said a voice. Blanka jumped back; the flashlight slipped out of her fingers and hit the floor. 'If you stand there, anyone in the park can see you through the glass. Come with me!'

'Jan?'

A shadow rushed past, beckoning to her. Blanka felt for her flashlight. Something clicked in the darkness, then she heard a snap that sounded like something electric turning on. A badly oiled door hinge creaked softly.

'Come on!' hissed the voice. With knees of jelly Blanka started to move. The door to the map room, which was usually locked, was open. The next moment a flashlight flashed on. A cone of light moved quickly over rolled-up maps and battered cardboard boxes. Blanka blinked. Jan too was wearing a long T-shirt and trackpants that bagged around his legs.

'In or out!' he said.

She gulped and went into the room. The door shut with a snap. Jan put the flashlight on a shelf and set a bag down on the floor. It rattled.

'What are you doing here?' whispered Blanka. He laughed, half asleep, and rummaged in the bag. Blanka looked at his tousled hair. The crumpled T-shirt he was wearing was probably his pyjama top. He took something out of the bag that looked like an electric toothbrush without its brush attachment.

'I see,' said Blanka sarcastically. 'You're planning to move in here.'

Just then her mobile vibrated. In trying to take it out as quickly as possible, she almost dropped it.

'Is he there?' whispered Nicholas's voice.

'You sent him here?'

She heard his sigh of relief. 'Thank God! Then it's working out all right – listen, I can't get away. But Jan knows what to do.'

'You're not serious! God damn it, couldn't you have told me before?'

Jan laid a warning finger on his lips.

'Sorry,' whispered Nicholas, genuinely contrite. 'I swear there's a good reason. I'll explain later.'

'Fine. Then have a nice evening!' snapped Blanka, pressing the 'Off' button on her phone. The display went blank.

'Well, I guess dear Niki gave us both a surprise,' said Jan, yawning. Again he bent down and rummaged in his bag. 'What sort of a key did Igor use?' he asked.

'Why do you want to know?'

Jan held up the toothbrush. 'Universal key,' he said quietly. 'But I have to know what attachment I need.'

'The toothbrush is a key?'

Jan nodded. 'Door-opener. Of course I beefed it up, otherwise the rpm would be too slow. You can use it to brush your teeth, too, of course,' he added ironically.

'Flat key,' said Blanka. 'About as long as my little flashlight here, with lengthwise grooves.'

'Standard security lock,' said Jan, adding mockingly, 'Ah well, just as secure as the other doors in this building.' Fascinated despite herself, Blanka watched him select a metal attachment and slide the remaining steel pins into the baggy pockets of his jogging pants.

'You really built that yourself?'

'Sure – I also built the radio control for your kettle, remember?'

'I thought you were an artist.'

'What do you think I do in the art room – mess about with clay? No, but first of all, the art room is further away from the bedrooms and the caretaker's apartment than any other – and second, there's a high-powered kiln there.'

Blanka shivered. 'And your toothbrush works on a security lock?'

'Sure – you just stick this attachment into the keyhole and turn it on. The vibration turns the steel barrel and – click! The door's open.'

'Why build something like that?'

Jan shrugged and pushed his bag under a shelf. 'I have a thing about locked doors.'

In the light of the flashlight he actually looked nineteen for once. For the first time she realised how strong he was.

'You missed two years of school. Were you . . . in a home, or something?'

'Reform school. One year for grand larceny. I lost the other year because I failed.' He smiled sweetly. 'Hey, cat got your tongue?'

'No . . . I . . .'

'Ah, you didn't expect that at this venerable school? Never heard of the quota?'

'The scholarships for disadvantaged students?'

Jan laughed softly. 'No one would ever put it that way, of course – sounds too much like discrimination. If you look at it like that, Madame bought my freedom, yes. I was surprised myself that I was so good at physics. It was a chance to get away from my stepfather. But of course, here I have special conditions. All the parents had to sign a form saying they agree I can be here.' He smiled ironically. 'Yours, too.'

Blanka was flabbergasted. 'And Caitlin? Does she know?'

'Sure,' he replied shortly, adding rather crossly, 'At least she didn't make as big a deal of it as you.'

'Why did you . . .'

Jan rolled his eyes and raised his arms dramatically. 'Oh, God, not that question again,' he whispered. 'Why? Why? Because . . . nothing's easier than breaking into cars. Because it brought in money, because the weather was good. No idea. Because I'm a loser? You tell me – it's your specialty, isn't it, explaining to people what makes them tick.'

'I can't be much of a psychologist. I thought you were just a coward.'

'Oh, you're not far wrong there,' he replied calmly. 'I am pretty cowardly. But a door is only a door.' He tugged nervously at his T-shirt and looked at Blanka pleadingly. 'You won't tell Cait anything about this little outing?'

'I promise,' replied Blanka. 'As long as you don't tell her either!'

'Let's shake on it!' They shook. 'Let's go, we need to hurry.'

'Wait a minute,' she whispered, gripping Jan's arm to hold him back as he reached for the door handle. 'Nicholas and you – how do you know each other?'

'Nicholas is a really good guy. Medical student with money. We really only know each other by sight. His motorbike is a heap of rust. I soldered a few connections for him and gave him some information – about you, too.'

'So you were the one who told him about the book of saints,' Blanka said. 'What's he paying for tonight's action?'

Jan clicked his tongue and shook his head. 'That's classified information! But the book you want seems to be important.'

It felt spooky, walking at night in the hallways that she knew only from the daytime. Jan went ahead with such a sure step that it seemed he could see in the dark. He often had to stop and wait until Blanka had felt her way along the walls to him. He led her to the library via back stairs that Blanka had never seen. With a click, the door opened under Jan's expert hands and they entered the library from a side wing. Moonlight shone through the blinds and threw a pale net of light over the reading tables and shelves.

'Which section is the door in?' whispered Jan. Blanka got her bearings in the gloom, recognising the crooked bookshelves containing the dictionaries, and felt her way further. Finally the wall with the door gleamed ahead of her. With their combined strength they pushed the bookshelf aside. Jan knelt in front of the lock. For a moment the light of his flashlight flashed on, then went out immediately. There was a click, then a fast vibration, which seemed to Blanka as loud as a circular saw. Frightened, she looked round, but nothing was moving. With a dragging noise the door opened inwards. Quickly they slipped into the room and closed the door behind them carefully so it would not creak. Immediately the fluorescent light came on. Jan took his hand off the light switch.

'There's no danger – there are no windows,' he whispered, smiling at Blanka's horrified face. His eyes were gleaming. He looked around the little room eagerly. If Blanka had wondered before what could make Jan risk losing his chance to prove himself, it was clear to her now that he lived for moments like this: for control, secrecy, the feeling of simply being able to go where no door could block his way.

'That's a lot of books,' he said. 'I hope you know what you're looking for.'

The room was bigger than it seemed at first glance. What made it look so small were the deep bookshelves, in which two rows of books stood one behind the other. Right at the back sat an ancient copy machine. Blanka could not make out any logical order. The place looked like the brain of a crazy scientist who could not distinguish between what was important and what was not. A few book spines were decorated with gold writing; others had been new a decade ago but had now taken on a brownish-yellow tinge. Blanka's gaze fell on a row of yellowed chronicles and yearbooks. On each book cover the year was given: the first said '1649–1700.' On the next book it was '1701–1750,' continuing in the same way up to the year 2000.

An hour later Blanka was close to despair. She was finding only statistics about the locality, lists of houses, the accounts of various associations and trusts, the dealings of the volunteer fire brigade, and whole bundles of copper engravings. No sign of the convent's history – and no sign of the Wolves. Tirelessly she searched row after row. Again and again Jan had to suppress a sneeze as a cloud of dust went up his nose. Painstakingly they made sure they put the books back exactly where they had come from, matching them up with the marks left in the dust. Finally, when they had got to the medical reference works, Blanka put her hand on a thin, worn booklet with a binding of firm cardboard. Carefully she pulled it out. The edges were already curling and the book was coming apart. Blanka laid it on the floor gently, knelt before it, and began to leaf through it page by page.

'Here's something!' she whispered. It was a Wolves' club record book – only three years old, but better than nothing. When she started reading through it, however, she was disappointed. All the expenses for new costumes were listed in excruciating detail, and bills from a carnival store were stapled to the edge. Then there was a training schedule and choreography for the stick dance. The last entries were the members' names and contacts at the local Carnival Association.

'Crap,' she murmured. 'That can't be right.' Again she looked through it page by page, but there was nothing to help her. Here and there someone had scribbled something in the margin – had maybe been chatting on the phone and doodling on the booklet. One of these artists had tried to draw a human figure. Blanka leaned closer over the booklet.

'Jan,' whispered Blanka. 'What do you think this is?'

He knelt down beside her and looked at the drawing.

'Boobs,' he said. 'Someone must have been drawing his girl-friend.'

'And below it – what's that?' Blanka pointed to a symbol that had been partially crossed out.

'Hmm. His girlfriend must have had a tattoo. Do you need the picture?' Blanka nodded. 'Better get the names, too.'

'Do you have a digital camera with you?'

'No.'

'Shit,' said Jan, just like Caitlin when she was having a bad day. 'Nicholas was going to bring the camera. But wait a minute – we don't need one!'

He'd already jumped up and plugged in the copy machine. Humming, it began to warm up. Blanka got to her feet and looked round at the door.

'Somebody might hear that!' she whispered. Jan waved the idea aside.

'Don't worry. It won't take long.'

'And the counter? What if someone notices that the counter has moved?'

Jan half smiled. 'Abracadabra,' he said, taking out a match. 'It's an ancient machine. It has a mechanical counter, no digital stuff. All I have to do is interrupt the meter pulse.'

Blanka watched uneasily as Jan opened the front panel of the copy machine, removed a metal coupling from the counter mechanism, and jammed the match into position. After copying the booklet unhurriedly, he took the match out again and draped the cable exactly the way it had been before. Blanka took the small pile of pages and quickly stuffed it under her T-shirt.

When they turned the light out again, they were both completely blind. Their fingers met by chance in the darkness, and without a word they held hands as they felt their way forward together. Moonlight gleamed on the metal arms of the reading lamps, and gradually the tables and chairs emerged from the darkness. The shelves towered in the aisles like stone giants. Metaphysics, Physics, Chemistry: Blanka counted them off mentally. Together they slipped between the shelves into a side passage. There they had to separate so they could walk in single file.

'Wait, Jan!' she whispered.

He stopped and turned around. 'What?'

'I'm going back to my room via the main stairs. It's ... shorter.'

A shadowy shrug. 'Fine,' he replied quietly. 'I'm going out the back way again. See you!'

He ducked down and disappeared into the darkness. Blanka waited until his stealthy steps faded into the distance. Then, legs like jelly, she followed Annette Durlain's trail. Had she found what she wanted in the room? Had she taken it and had it with her on the way to the stairs? Blanka took a deep breath and crept around the shelves. She took four, five steps towards the main stairs, then froze. The sound of a footstep behind her stopped instantly. Blanka hesitated, then turned around. Since when had there been a chair in this aisle? Straining, she tried to see more clearly. No doubt about it, the chair ... was standing up! The chair legs left the floor and the whole thing became a swaying shadow as tall as a man. Nemec? Blanka heard a scraping sound, then the phantom moved. Strange breath flowed through the gaps in the bookshelves like smoke. Over the top of a row of book spines Blanka could see the figure turning around, and a shadowy head turned towards her. Her body reacted instinctively. She rushed towards the door. Too late she realised that the figure that jumped out at her the next moment was her own image in the glass door. Without knowing how she got there, she found herself between two rows of bookshelves again. Her muscles hurt. Book spines dug into her shoulderblades. Then something hit her head. Her knees gave way, and everything went black.

Had it been one of her bad dreams? Dental enamel shone in the moonlight. Warm saliva was dripping onto her hand. A stinging pain pierced her scalp. She struggled to open her eyes and felt for her bedside lamp. But all she found was the metal base of a book-shelf. In the darkness she opened her eyes and saw the pale eyes of the phantom staring at her. The next moment it was on her. A hand covered her mouth and stifled her cry. A ray of light appeared from nowhere. Dazed, she blinked and did not try to defend herself when someone laid a hand on her forehead. It even felt good, because the pain lessened. 'You're dreaming,' murmured a voice, and she sank back, relieved.

The next thing she was aware of was the library's scratchy carpet against her cheek and the moonlight still shining in between the slats of the blinds. Dazed, she looked around and a wave of shock hit her. What she had taken for dripping saliva was her own blood – at the hairline her scalp was throbbing, and when she carefully felt the spot, she felt a small cut, which was already forming a scab. Presumably it had come from the book that had fallen on her head and now lay on the floor, a little off to the side: *Shakespeare's Collected Works, Volume IV*. She must have bumped into the shelf, and the book had fallen down and hit her head. The cut on her temple was from the corner of its hard cover. She touched her T-shirt and heaved a sigh of relief. The copies were still there!

She had to struggle to get to her feet and put the heavy book back on the shelf. Then she headed for the stairs, legs shaking, expecting at any moment to hear a voice behind her ordering her to stop.

Maybe it was because she was still dazed: when she entered her room, she stumbled over the chair that she had earlier placed beside the connecting door. Before she was back on her feet, she heard Caitlin's sleepy voice. 'Blanka?' Light appeared under the door, and the next moment the door swung open.

When Caitlin saw Blanka, she opened her eyes wide. 'Oh my God!'

'Shh!' said Blanka. 'Calm down! Everything's OK.'

'Everything's OK? You're bleeding! Where've you been? Who did this?' Then Caitlin suddenly put her hand to her mouth. 'Did . . . Joaquim do that?'

'No,' Blanka said, exasperated. 'No one did anything to me – I tripped.'

Someone banged on the wall.

Caitlin lowered her voice. 'You tripped in the middle of the night? Don't bullshit me, Blanka – you have shoes on, and you don't sleep in your tracksuit! What did they do to you?'

'No one did anything to me!'

Caitlin surveyed the cut, and the strands of hair all stuck together. 'That's enough,' she said. 'We're going to Madame, right now! Something's going on, and it's clear that you can't deal with it alone.'

'No way!' Blanka grasped Caitlin's wrists. 'Listen to me. If we report this, I'll be thrown out. The only thing that will help me now is an alibi. I can't tell you what happened, but it's possible that Nemec will knock at my door in a few minutes, and then – please! – tell him you don't think I've been out of the room.' Beseechingly she went on, 'Something big is going on, but I can't tell you everything. I'll go to Madame as soon as I have more proof. Please just trust me.'

Caitlin broke free and stepped back. Thoughtfully, she rubbed her wrists and looked at Blanka.

'Proof?' she asked suspiciously. 'Of what?'

'I can't say.'

'I'm your friend!'

'Are you?' The words slipped out. Instantly she regretted it. Caitlin looked as if Blanka had slapped her.

'You still don't trust me,' she said. 'What do you think I am? Do you really think I want to make you look bad to Madame Lalonde? God, there are better ways I could've done that! What would be the point? I just want to finish school here and go back to Ireland. That's all.'

Blanka's silence made Caitlin angrier.

'You can't imagine anyone simply liking you, can you?' she hissed. 'What do I have to do to make you trust me? Some sort of proof?'

Blanka raised her head and looked Caitlin in the eye. 'Your T-shirt,' she said, gesturing towards Caitlin's hip. 'Pull it up.'

Caitlin stared at her as if she had finally lost her mind, then she crossed her arms, took hold of the hem, and pulled the T-shirt over her head. Angrily she flung the shirt on Blanka's bed. She stood there, dressed in just her underwear. Her skin was flawless. 'So?' she asked, stretching her arms out to the sides. 'What are you looking for?'

Blanka picked up the T-shirt and gave it to Caitlin. She felt foolish. Yet at the same time she was extremely relieved.

'I thought you might have a tattoo,' she said apologetically.

'I see,' said Caitlin sarcastically. 'Well, I don't. So now are you going to tell me what happened to you?'

Blanka considered how much she should tell her. Finally she pulled out the copies with the names. Quickly she told her about the threats by the Wolves and about Nicholas, who was having the same problems she was. She did not tell her about the forged autopsy report or her meeting with Jan.

'And tonight I was in Nemec's book room, to find out more about the Wolves. But there was someone in the library – I think Nemec saw me. Maybe he's reporting it right now. If he is, tomorrow I can pack my bags and go home.'

Caitlin's eyes had narrowed to slits. 'So you broke in – into a room that has a security lock?'

Blanka held her breath.

Caitlin suddenly looked as if she'd bitten into a lemon. 'Shit!' she said. Without looking at her friend, she went into her room and slammed the door behind her. A few seconds later Blanka heard her on the phone. She was whispering, but still, Blanka was glad she was not in Jan's place.

MADDALINA OF TRENTA

BLANKA LAY IN BED IN THE DARK, expecting to hear a knock at her door at any minute. The cut, which she had doctored herself as well as she could, had formed a scab, but it still throbbed with every beat of her heart. Six o'clock passed, then seven, and nothing happened – and finally, at quarter past seven, Caitlin headed out to her next exam marathon, her eyes puffy. Blanka switched her mobile back on. Eleven missed calls from Nicholas. Just as she was about to call him back, the phone rang in her hand.

'Thank God!' cried Nicholas. 'Did everything go according to plan? Why didn't you call?'

'Because I'm lying in bed with a cut on my head, and today they're going to throw me out – I'm not sure, but I think Nemec saw me.'

'A cut?'

Although she was furious with him, it was good to hear him worrying more about her than about Nemec.

'Someone knocked me down.'

'Who?'

'Shakespeare.'

Nicholas hesitated for a moment. 'Your first class doesn't start for twenty minutes. Let's meet!'

'No!' she cried, and then immediately lowered her voice. 'No, I'm fine, a book just fell on my head. I hope your excuse is just as original.'

'Look out of the window,' he answered dryly.

Blanka got up, ignoring the slight dizziness that hit her as she did so, and gripped her mobile between her shoulder and her ear. It was hard work pulling the blinds up in this contorted position. Morning sunlight bathed her face. She blinked and looked towards the carpark. She would have recognised those hunched shoulders anywhere. When he saw her waving to him, a relieved smile spread across his face. 'Well, at least you can still stand,' he said. 'And now look what happened to me last night.'

There was a rustling sound as he put the mobile in his pocket, bent down, and rolled up his right pants leg. A bandage came into view. His entire shin looked like an abstract painting in a wide variety of red and blue tones. Nicholas put his mobile to his ear again. 'Damn road,' he said, shrugging. 'On the right-hand curve near the last traffic light. I was on my way here. A car stopped and took me to emergency.'

'Welcome to the club,' replied Blanka dryly.

'Luckily the bike still runs,' he said. 'What do you think, when can we meet?'

'I don't know. I . . . I'm wondering whether I should go to Madame.'

He stared up at the window in silence. Blanka heard his breath at her ear.

'We have next to no proof,' he reminded her. 'And what if your policeman really is involved in all this?'

'I know,' Blanka replied sharply. In the pause that followed, she noticed him nervously lighting a cigarette.

'You choose,' he said finally. 'Tell the office, and we're busted. Then we probably both lose our place in this town. Or we finish this.'

They looked into each other's eyes across the distance.

'Anyway, there is one piece of good news,' he said quietly. 'I, alias Jehle, have an appointment tomorrow with a lady whose dead husband's grandfather was called Heinrich Feverlin.'

Really, nothing could go wrong. The three of them left the school after breakfast on Saturday and crossed the carpark. It was a hive of activity. Car doors opened, and parents got out with big bags and packages, handing their sons and daughters the promised jacket, books, or pile of CDs. The air shimmered with family, but today Blanka had no time to let it ruin her mood. She kept an eye open for Simon Nemec. He had not been in the library, and no one had spoken to her all day. No teacher had summoned her with a serious expression to the office. It was spooky.

'Stop tugging at your hair,' whispered Caitlin to her. Blanka only now noticed that she was playing with the strand that she had combed over the scab and bruise. Jan walked beside Caitlin in silence, like a dog that had been whipped. The tension between the two of them was so unbearable that the air around them seemed charged with electricity. At least Caitlin's exam had gone very well. In the evening she had checked and figured out that she had answered eight of the ten questions correctly. Now she felt confident – and furious with Jan. The day would be anything but a romantic outing for him. Three abreast, they crossed the carpark in silence and headed towards the bus stop. As always when she left the school, Blanka felt a heavy weight being lifted from her shoulders. Rounding the corner, heading towards the gate, she nearly bumped into Madame Lalonde.

'Oops!' said Madame. She was wearing a dark-green suit that emphasised the colour of her eyes, and she had a small suitcase in her hand. When she saw Blanka, a smile flitted across her face. 'Oh, Blanka – good morning!'

'Good morning,' answered Blanka and Jan in unison.

'I'm glad I met you. I saw on the schedule that once again you're not going to see your parents?'

Blanka nodded and suppressed the urge to smooth her hair.

'We're going to the pool,' Caitlin said in turn.

Madame raised her eyebrows. 'Too bad. If I'd known sooner that you had plans ... I'm going to Brussels until Wednesday, but I've asked Dr Hasenberg to speak to you. There's a lunch here today. A few of the other psychologists from the university will be there, too. I thought you might be interested in joining them.'

Blanka had the feeling that the headmistress had found her out. Her swimming bag lay in her hand like a lie as heavy as lead. And the fact that Madame was leaving her here with the Wolves and Simon Nemec made her even more uneasy. Caitlin hooked her arm through hers.

'Thank you for the offer,' said Blanka finally. 'But I haven't even started to read the books on the list Dr Hasenberg gave me.'

Madame Lalonde laughed. Blanka realised that she looked tired and had dark circles under her eyes.

'Whatever you think. You're right – we stuff you full of enough knowledge as it is. Caitlin can tell you all about that, can't you, Caitlin?'

Caitlin smiled a little too nicely. A taxi door banged. The driver got out and opened the trunk, and Madame dropped in her case. She waved goodbye to Blanka and got into the taxi.

'What's she doing in Brussels?' whispered Blanka to Caitlin.

'As far as I know, she's giving a presentation on the concept of the school and looking for more backers,' replied Caitlin.

Jan looked at the taxi as it drove away, interested.

'Well, you seem to be well in with Madame Lalonde,' he said.

So far, thought Blanka gloomily.

Nicholas was waiting at the bus stop as arranged, a motorbike helmet in each hand.

'So that's him,' murmured Caitlin to her. 'Now I get it!'

Blanka was annoyed to realise she was blushing. 'Thanks for the alibi,' she said briskly. 'I'll be back by five.'

'We're late,' grumbled Nicholas, passing her the helmet. 'Let's see – is that where you got hurt?'

She nodded silently and let Nicholas move closer and brush her hair off her forehead.

'Ouch,' he said. 'That was a big book. Do you think you can get the helmet on?'

'Sure!' He looked at her for a moment that seemed to last for ever, and then smiled at her. She took the helmet and carefully put it on, while Nicholas got onto his motorbike. It took him a while to manipulate his injured leg and settle into his seat.

It was a strange feeling, climbing onto the bike behind

Nicholas. Without asking he took her hands and pulled them towards him, until she was holding him above his hips. The motorbike lurched just once, then the centrifugal force pulled her backward, and they roared along the main road, heading out of town towards the west.

The trip took more than an hour. It was more than 60 kilometres on the highway to the next large town, and then the route continued through several villages. Each was smaller than the one before. The roads got worse, too, until finally Nicholas and Blanka were driving on something only slightly better than a cart track. A sign saying 'Kosrow' was rammed deep into the ground.

'It's number four, High Street,' Nicholas said, once he had taken off his helmet and shaken his hair, which was soaked with sweat. They looked around and saw a white house.

The woman who opened the door to them did not look at all like a grieving widow. She had a deep frown line between her eyes, and curly hair dyed blue-black. Blanka guessed she was fifty. She wore dark red lipstick that matched her red-and-black blouse. Nicholas smiled at her winningly.

'Good afternoon, Mrs Meyer,' he said, holding out his press card. 'Klaus Jehle. We phoned you. This is Martina Huber, who's doing an internship with us.'

The woman's face lit up immediately. 'How nice. Do come in.' Her soft voice was unexpected in view of her severe appearance.

They followed Mrs Meyer through a long, narrow hallway painted a discreet blue. Colour photos looked down accusingly on the intruders. There was a peculiar smell coming from the living room. As soon as Blanka entered the small room, she realised where it was coming from: on the walls hung dozens of stuffed animal heads and birds. She could see deer, chamois, the head of a wild boar, and several pheasants. African masks made of wood had been hung between them – a strange contrast to the modern, leather-upholstered furniture and glass cases.

'Would you like some orange juice?' asked Mrs Meyer. Nicholas thanked her and nodded, which gave them time to survey the room at their leisure.

'Oh, you found the masks,' said Mrs Meyer, coming back into the room with a tray. 'Yes, my grandfather-in-law, if you can say that, travelled a lot – he was a sailor and lived in Africa for a long time. My husband . . .' the short pause was almost imperceptible '. . . inherited his estate about twenty years ago.' She smiled and put the tray down on the glass table in front of the sofa. 'Help yourselves! Are you both students at the university?'

Blanka shook her head. 'I'm still at school, but I want to be a journalist.'

'Oh – what school do you go to?'

'Lessing High School in Ammring,' Nicholas answered for her.

'I don't know that one. My stepson from my husband's first marriage used to go to the Europa International School. It's not far from the university. An excellent school – you should try to get in there, Martina.'

Blanka cleared her throat. 'I thought about it. Maybe I'll apply next year.'

'Do that. It's a once-in-a-lifetime opportunity. My stepson went straight from there to London, where he studied Business Administration. Mr Sandor, the headmaster at that time, really did a lot for us. As a thank-you, my husband gave the Maddalina of Trenta Foundation some of the original documents from the estate.'

Nicholas and Blanka exchanged a quick glance.

'What exactly are you taking at university?' Mrs Meyer turned to Nicholas.

'History,' he replied promptly. 'At the moment I'm looking at the history of the town in the seventeenth century. That means I'm working on part of your family history.'

'My husband's family history,' Mrs Meyer corrected him seriously. 'Well, as I told you over the phone, I'm not sure whether my papers will be any help. It might make more sense for you to ask the Foundation directly. But I'll be happy to show you the documents that I could find, anyway. You've already seen the executioner's sword and the hangman's certificate, of course.'

'I'm sure you can help us,' said Nicholas, beaming at her. 'Thanks so much for going to so much trouble!'

Mrs Meyer smiled. 'I was tidying up, anyway. The house is going to be sold soon. I've brought out everything I could find from that time, but there's not much: just a few documents and photos. My husband and I never bothered about the papers. Oh well, see for yourself whether you can use them.' With these words she got up and went into the hallway. They could hear a drawer opening in the next room.

'So, once again no original documents,' whispered Nicholas. Impatience made him sound curt. The masks and glass animal eyes seemed to stare at them as they waited. Finally Mrs Meyer came back into the room, carrying a package with envelopes and papers in plastic covers. Right on top lay a worn notebook.

'Here,' she said, laying the bundle on the coffee table. 'These have been in the attic for more than twenty years. My husband just couldn't throw anything away. Take a look at them, and if you need anything or have any questions, call me – I'll be next door in my study.'

They thanked her and waited until she had left the room. Then they fell on the papers. The dust made Blanka's nose itch; it stank of mice and old wood. Mrs Meyer was right – there was not much there. There were a few ancient banknotes and with them several documents to do with the purchase of farmland in the nineteenth century. In the envelope there were numbered photos showing various town buildings around the turn of the century. Blanka recognised the facade of the university, the old town hall, several streets in the old town, and finally the manor house. Impatiently they worked their way through the more recent documents. Copies of passports turned up between older papers. Finally Blanka reached for the notebook. 'Heinrich Feverlin,' was written on the first page. 'That must have been Mr Meyer's grandfather.'

The paper was so dry that it seemed it would crumble into dust at the first touch. Every page was closely written in a cramped hand but was nevertheless legible. Obviously Mr Feverlin had used the notebook for his household accounts, to record his monthly income and expenses. More than thirty pages contained only accounts. Blanka leafed through further and gave a start.

'Nicholas! Here's something!'

He came so close to her that his hair stroked her cheek.

'He copied the hangman's records before he gave them to the school. The original records!'

Johann Georg Feverlin had been an honest man, and God-fearing too. On every page he praised God so many times that after three pages Heinrich Feverlin had started to use just abbreviations to note them. Maybe his belief in God was all the executioner could cling to in 1651 – after the Belverinas' trial. Putting heart and soul into it, he had recorded one interrogation after another, every disturbing detail. In his version Maddalina and her nuns were not the kind of witches who called up thunder and hail. They called up something much worse.

Nicholas brought out a digital camera.

'Thus did Bernhard Haussman Kohlbauer Swear before the Exorcist that on April 24th Evening He was on the Way to his Field, the Which Lies only Two Versts from the Convent, When He Saw the Devil in the Shape of a Terrible Monster Creeping out of the Walls. The Beast Hiss'd and Disappear'd with a Dredful Roar.'

Bernhard Kohlbauer was not the only witness. The same evening several farmers in the area said they had seen the monster. Johann Georg Feverlin also mentioned the reports of other eyewitnesses, who swore that flames had shot out from the body of the beast, its face was misshapen, and it was drinking sheep's blood. The first 'witch stories' circulated: people saw lights in the convent at night, and some of the orphan children who lived in the convent became sick with a fever. And so people set out to look for the monster. They didn't in fact find the beast in or near the convent, but the convent burned down anyway – only the walls and the main building remained standing. Gradually there were more and more rumours about the nuns, until a mob set out to search the ruins.

'They Found the Chalices with Powder and Unguents that They were Accustom'd to Use When They Did Go Out,' Blanka read. 'Of Which More Stickes with Wild Grotesque Faces and a Flute of Human Bone, on Which a Piper Might Play.'

The camera clicked quietly as Nicholas photographed page after page. Finally, the two nuns had to face the accusation that they had consorted with the Devil.

'Regina Sängerin did Admit on July 16th that She had even Wish'd to Conjure Up the Monster with the Piper.'

She would not admit who the musician was, and so the convent's male employees also fell under suspicion and were interrogated soon afterwards.

'It was Claim'd that Hans Haber was a Witch Piper and Did Pipe on the Bone Flute.'

'That's the gardener,' said Blanka. 'I've read about him. And here it mentions Georg Kastellus, the cowherd, too.' Fingers trembling, she turned the last page.

'We did Drag the Witch Qveen onto the Windlass and When We Saw Under Her Shirt Her Bare Body, It Had the Mark of the Devil . . .'

The next section was furnished with a symbol that Mrs Meyer's stepfather had carefully copied from the chronicle.

'. . . a Mark of the Devils Wooing, Burned On with His Kiss.'

'That's the mark,' said Blanka.

The mark looked like a wolf's head, its fur feathered out behind it like licks of flame.

'And some of the orphan children had it too,' Nicholas added. 'Look, here's the charge against them.'

'The Millers Daughter was Infected and Lam'd by the Witches Children Standing Accus'd.'

Two of the 'witches' sons' were garrotted and then burned at the stake. Blanka and Nicholas read the final sentences with bated breath. Nicholas lowered the camera. 'I don't believe it,' he whispered. Maybe the hangman's writing in the original documents had been shaky; his words, which his descendant had neatly copied, reported a great commotion and ended with the sentences:

'The Witch Qveen and Two of the Others Accus'd Disappear'd. My Servant, Who was Guarding the Prisoners, Awaken'd Lam'd, Without Mark or Injury.'

At this point the records broke off, as Mr Feverlin's grandfather noted matter-of-factly. At the bottom of the page was the date the copy had been made: 7 September 1924.

Blanka and Nicholas looked at each other.

'Maddalina of Trenta was not executed.' Nicholas said what they were both thinking. 'She got away – and the gardener and cowherd with her.'

'And for some reason that's supposed to be kept secret,' added Blanka.

The sound of the door opening made them jump, and quickly they turned around. Mrs Meyer came into the room. 'Did you get anywhere? Oh, Martina – don't you feel well? You're quite pale.'

'No, I'm fine,' replied Blanka, hastily reaching for the photos. 'We found a picture of the old manor house at the Europa International School.'

'My husband's grandfather was very interested in the building. Apparently it was haunted.' Mrs Meyer laughed. 'At that time he belonged to a group that was interested in hypnosis and ghostly visions. But apparently he didn't meet enough spirits there.' Now she looked almost mischievous. 'Other than perhaps the alcoholic variety, I imagine. Anyway, after the war the Maddalina of Trenta Foundation bought the building, set up the school, and also restored the old orphans' cemetery. If you like I'll ask my stepson. He probably knows more about the school's history.'

Nicholas leaned forward to take the photo. As if by chance his glance fell on his watch.

'Oh, goodness, it's getting late,' he said. 'Mrs Meyer, thank you so much for everything. I think we have enough information. You were a big help.' Without further ado he jumped up and reached for his helmet. Blanka smiled at Mrs Meyer apologetically. It felt rude to break away so suddenly. A few minutes later they were sitting on the motorbike, waving goodbye to Mrs Meyer.

'Send me a copy of the article!' she called after them.

The lazy afternoon sun hung low in the sky. Nicholas accelerated and Blanka tried not to think what would happen if they did not make a corner. Not too far from the road the river meandered back and forth. When they were still a few miles from the town, Nicholas reduced speed and turned off onto a cart track. Silently they dismounted and walked to the river bank. There they laid the helmets on the ground, sat down beside each other, and looked at the water.

'OK,' said Nicholas after a little while. 'We have Maddalina, the piper Hans Haber and Kastellus the cowherd, who were supposed to be burned at the stake.'

'And several orphans,' Blanka added.

'And don't forget the monster.' Nicholas continuing her line of thought. 'Let's look at the Wolves: they have a nun, a piper, a witch, a girl – and the wolf.'

Blanka nodded. 'And Joaquim plays the monster.'

'Do the Wolves know the true story?'

'Of course,' hissed Blanka. 'The original chronicle about the witch trial wasn't burned. Someone wrote a new version – that's why the trial seems so superficial and peculiar. And, so no one could check to see if it was genuine, that same someone burned the supposedly original chronicle – except for a few harmless fragments that it's impossible to figure out the whole story from. The rest are only copies. I bet the Foundation is behind it.'

'Falsifying history,' Nicholas concluded. 'Now we need to find out who was in charge of the town archives of the Foundation before the fire.'

'Not only before the fire,' Blanka replied. 'The Wolves have never ceased to exist since Maddalina's time. It's just that no one knew about them until the official founding of the society. They were there the whole time – and they were always involved with things that were illegal or were far ahead of their time.' She cleared her throat and quoted: '"The miller's daughter was infected and lamed by the witches' children." That could be through hypnosis or suggestion – perhaps with the help of drugs. Experiments like that used to be considered the Devil's work. But the nuns were interested in that sort of thing and obviously knew what they were doing. And in Feverlin's notes it also says that in Maddalina's time chalices and tools were found. Maybe they were tools for making gold. Alchemy – a prohibited science in the Middle Ages. You could be charged with witchcraft for practising it.'

'I understand,' murmured Nicholas. Blanka stared at two ducks chasing each other on the water. She felt sick at the thought of going back to the Wolves' lair today.

'Blanka, what's wrong?' Nicholas's voice broke into her thoughts. Only then did she notice that she had balled her hands into fists and tears were running down her face.

'What's wrong?' Nicholas repeated softly, but she could only shake her head. He did the only thing possible in the circum-stances and laid his arm around her shoulder. For a while they stared at the water, until Blanka came to a decision.

'Nicholas,' she said. 'I have to tell you something.'

She began at the beginning – with her conversation with her parents on her sixteenth birthday, which had led to her running away in the middle of the night, until she had realised at the bus stop that she had no money and no idea where to go. Then she told him about Alex, who had broken up with her because he did not understand what had changed her so much. She told him about the scholarship that had been advertised at her school, about the exam and her move to the Europa International School. Finally she came to her nightmares, in which Annette Durlain was warning her, and her suspicions about Nemec. Last of all she told him about her latest meeting with Joaquim and Tanya.

'Why didn't you tell me this before?' asked Nicholas. 'I'd like to take these guys and whip them within an inch of their lives. They haven't tried anything like that with me so far.' He pulled her closer to him. 'And now you're feeling guilty that you didn't defend yourself, right? For God's sake, Blanka!'

'As far as your parents are concerned,' he said softly after a while, 'even if they adopted you, they're still your parents. Or don't you think so?'

'Yes. But since I've known, they seem so foreign to me. How could they pretend all those years that . . . I feel as if they've been lying to me my whole life. And they wouldn't have told me in a hundred years if I hadn't happened to accidentally find it out myself. I don't even know who my real parents were.'

'I know who mine were,' said Nicholas. 'But it's no help, either – because they're dead. At least you're not alone.' He hesitated before continuing. 'My mother died when I was five. She was very young – just twenty-six. And my father . . . just a few months ago.'

'I'm so sorry,' whispered Blanka.

Nicholas made a dismissive gesture and looked at the river. 'I should have told you ages ago. Sorry I didn't tell you the whole truth.' He cleared his throat. 'I . . . don't want sympathy.'

Blanka bit back the questions that were on her tongue and fell silent.

'Dammit, where were you?' Caitlin berated her. 'I thought you'd driven into a ditch somewhere!'

'I'm sorry!' Blanka slipped quickly into the room and threw her unused swimming bag onto the bed. 'We went to the Internet café in town afterwards to look something up.'

'Your mobile was off.'

Blanka fished her phone out of her jacket pocket. 'The battery needs charging,' she said contritely. 'I didn't hear it beeping.'

'Did you find anything out?'

Blanka nodded, went over to her friend, and took her by the shoulders.

'Caitlin, could you call Jenna? The girl who used to be with Tobias?'

'Jenna?' exclaimed Caitlin. 'What does she have to do with it?'

'I have to find out whether Tobias has a tattoo on his hipbone. Jenna must know – unless she did nothing with him all year but pick flowers.'

'You want me to ring her right now?'

'Please, Caitlin. How else can I find out? Should I drill a hole in the shower walls? Or spill coffee over Tobias's pants and hope he undresses in front of me?'

'No,' Caitlin said dryly. 'I really couldn't be responsible for that.'

Then she folded her arms and gave a lopsided grin. 'Hmm, the Wolves have a tattoo. So I guessed right. You really believed I was one of them?'

Shaking her head, she went into her room, got her mobile, and looked up Jenna's number.

'Jenna? Hi, it's me, Caitlin. Listen . . .'

A moment later Blanka took the phone. Jenna's voice sounded far away and a little disembodied. Quickly Blanka explained to her what she wanted to know. Jenna hesitated.

'Do you want something from Tobias?' she asked sharply. 'I'd advise you to keep away from him.'

'I just want to know if he has a tattoo.'

Jenna hesitated again. Blanka bit her lip impatiently.

'Yeah, he does,' Jenna replied in a drawl. 'It was sort of a test of courage for being accepted into this group . . .'

'A test of courage?'

Another pause.

'Yes. They tattooed the mark on each other. With an antique needle. He showed me once. Pretty sick, huh? And right where it hurts most.'

'Between the hip bone and the belly button – a little closer to the hip.'

'Yes. How did you know?'

'What does the mark look like?'

'It's a profile of a wolf's head, with shaggy fur and this kinda creepy tongue. Why do you want . . .?'

'Thanks, Jenna!' said Blanka quickly, returning the mobile to Caitlin.

I T

I HAD FOUND THE PRESENCE – there was no longer any doubt; it was here. The strange and yet so familiar Presence, which kept slipping away from It and which It felt compelled to chase after. Its thoughts were calm, and Its claws throbbed under their crusts of blood. For too many hours It had been floating between images and stone, crawling in circles, constantly agitated by the colours which It could feel and smell like tormenting waves. But now all was still, except for the strange smell nearby. They were breathing in time with each other! It enjoyed the sense of breath flowing, felt the strange warmth, and could hear the comforting sound of blood pumping.

It took Blanka a long time to realise that she was not dreaming any more. The room was dark. She had not fully closed the blinds, so the pale grey of the carpark light shone through the slats. Her blue jacket, hanging on the door, looked like an intruder standing in a threatening posture. She had dreamed of a hypnotist, she remembered, closing her eyes again. And about masks. Beside her something was breathing.

Breathing deeply, It soaked up the scent of the long black fur. Its eyes took in every shadow. No light dazzled It and no colour caused It pain; there was just an angular object on which something was lying, something that smelled dry and a little sharp. When It looked more closely, It recognised what the others called 'Payper.' It was spiteful – it cut. Near the entrance to the cave hung a limp being with two empty arms. It was blue, light blue.

Blanka opened her eyes again and stared into the darkness. Strangely, she was reminded at this moment of her grandfather's farm dog. He was a very old dog and stank pitifully of musty fur and a little like a damp stable. When she blinked, the images from the first part of her dream flitted by again. What she saw terrified her – dirty children whose horror was burned into their eyes. She looked round – and found herself in a dungeon. It had to be a dungeon, as she was sitting among the children. She could see traces of blood on the walls where their fingers had scratched. And then it was there again – the wolf's mask. 'Joaquim!' she murmured, twisting in her bed. The image moved with her. She blinked to get rid of it, but it stayed before her eyes like a nightmare that would not leave its victim in peace. The Wolf raised his hand and removed his mask. She prepared herself for Joaquim's scornful grin. But it was Nicholas. He looked at her seriously. 'At least you're not alone,' he said, reaching for her throat. She let him touch her and he did not betray her trust. Gently he stroked her skin. Blanka felt for his hand and recoiled – hard crusts of blood scraped her palm like a rasp. She reached out to Nicholas's face and felt matted hair.

She sat up with a jerk, eyes opened wide. Something was breathing beside her in bed. Caitlin? was her first thought, but then she noticed the smell. A dark, blotchy crack yawned where the mouth should have been. It moved, getting wider and wider – far too wide for a human smile. In spite of the darkness, she could see its teeth.

She did not know why her throat hurt and why the light was shining in her eyes. It was not until she ran out of air that she stopped screaming. She could feel her jacket pressing into her back and realised that she was standing with her back against the door, staring at the empty bed. Where the thing had lain, there was nothing – just a bulge of pillow that in the darkness had looked like a body lying down. The chair blocking the door handle still stood where she had put it the night before. Caitlin's worried face appeared. With one glance she grasped the situation.

'You were dreaming,' she said. 'It was just a dream.'

The light went on in the hallway and footsteps sounded. There was a knock at Caitlin's door. Gradually the sleepy faces of the students from nearby rooms appeared at the door. They hardly listened to what Caitlin was telling them. Instead they were eying Blanka as if she was crazy.

SECRETS

BLANKA WOKE UP WITH A PLUSH CROCODILE in her arms. It took her a while to realise that she was lying in Caitlin's bed. Her friend had puffy eyes. Presumably she, like Blanka, had lain awake in the dark, listening.

'How do you feel?'

'Better,' murmured Blanka. Anything was better than lying next to a breathing something with teeth. After Caitlin had gone to take a shower, Blanka got up, too. Nervously, she went to the connecting door. She had to force herself to open it. Her bed was just as she had left it last night. She was sure that it had not been a case of night terrors, nor a dream. The strange presence had been real. She must call Mrs Meyer – she would be able to find out more about the ghosts that haunted the old manor house. Quietly, Blanka found her clothes and tried to sort out the debris of the previous day. Before she left, she took her copies and documents and put them in the bottom of one of Caitlin's desk drawers. She took the key with her. There would be time for explanations this afternoon.

There was no sign of any of the Wolves. For days now they seemed to have been swallowed up by the earth. Jan waved to her once from a distance, as they passed each other in the hallway on their way to different classrooms. Blanka did not go to the physics room to make the call, instead finding a corner in the empty stairwell and pulling out her phone. She misdialled twice before finally getting through.

'Meyer,' a quiet, strange voice finally answered. Blanka was so confused that she nearly gave her real name. She caught herself just in time.

'Good morning. This is Martina Huber, from the university magazine,' she began. 'I'd like to speak to Mrs Meyer. We were there yesterday. It's about the article . . .'

In the pause that ensued, Blanka heard the woman at the other end take a deep breath and clear her throat. 'Mrs Meyer . . . is not available,' she said in a hoarse voice.

'Should I try again later?'

The woman hesitated again. 'No . . . you . . . Mrs Meyer . . . died last night very suddenly, of heart failure. The police were here and the doctor is just filling out the death certificate. I'm her neighbour. If your notes are still here, you can pick them up at my . . .'

Blanka hung up and clutched the phone to her chest. Mrs Meyer, slim and vigorous, barely fifty, dead of heart failure. This thought was as strange as the next was terrifying: who had known about their visit to her? Only she, Nicholas, Jan and Caitlin. Could Jan have been bought off by the Wolves?

As if her thoughts had echoed throughout the building like a warning siren, she saw a group of students coming around the corner. Tanya! She was talking to another girl, but she could turn her head any minute and see Blanka. Blanka slipped towards the wall. A door handle dug into her hip. She felt for it and fled into the room. The sharp smell of floor cleaner pierced her nose. Holding her breath, she waited until the students' voices faded into the distance. Only then did she dare to turn on the light. It was a storeroom with a cleaning cart. A clear bell announced the beginning of class. Blanka picked up her mobile with damp fingers.

'Caitlin . . . Loans Center . . . Nicholas . . .' She went through the small list of phone numbers. After a brief hesitation, she pressed the key. She was enormously relieved when someone picked up.

'Hello, Mama?' she whispered. At the other end, the answering machine came on. Blanka fought back tears as she listened to her mother's voice. As always, it sounded gentle and rather monotonous. It felt good to hear it, although longing suddenly overcame Blanka and left her feeling even more lonely. She hung up without leaving a message and called Nicholas.

'The subscriber you are calling is not available at present,' said a tinny female voice.

Blanka did not deliberate for long. She rushed into the hallway and ran.

The bus into town seemed to take forever. The whole way, Blanka felt she was being watched. Several times she turned around, but there was only an old man so engrossed in his newspaper that he had probably missed his stop. Finally the door opened with a hiss. By the time she reached the residence in Pelargus Alley, Blanka was gasping for breath. She tried Nicholas's mobile one last time, giving full rein to her worst fears: Nicholas kidnapped or killed. She could not find his name on the list at the entrance to the residence, but then she realised that it was only for mail. Nicholas's parents were dead. Presumably he had no one who wrote to him. She remembered that he lived on the third floor, so she ran up the stairs. Music boomed in a narrow hallway. Blanka went from door to door. Not every door had a name on it: some students had made their mark with posters or a cartoon. At the end of the hallway, she reached a small kitchen, where a student in shorts and a crumpled T-shirt was spreading jam on a piece of bread.

'Hi!' called Blanka. 'I'm looking for Nicholas Varkonyi!'

The student turned around slowly and squinted in her direction. After a few seconds Blanka's questions seemed to register with him.

'Nicholas? Don't know him. But if you mean Niko, he lives one floor up, number 319.'

Niko was not Nicholas and did not know anyone of that name. No one knew Nicholas. He did not exist – his description did not even come close to any of the students living in the residence. After half an hour Blanka was in the kitchen again, pale and shaking.

'Hey, sit down a moment,' said the student. A bit of jam was stuck to the corner of his mouth. Blanka sank down onto the proffered chair and nodded, as if in a daze, when he asked if she would like a coffee.

'Is he your boyfriend?' the student asked politely. 'It sounds like he's really taken you for a ride.'

The sympathy in his voice frightened her. She realised that he was right. Nicholas had lied to her. But why? Feverishly she ran through all the possibilities. He'd moved and hadn't told her. He'd given her a false name . . . the name!

'Klaus Jehle,' she said. 'He writes for the *Attempto*. Does he live here, at least?'

The student raised his eyebrows and wiped his mouth. 'At the other end of the hallway – there's a dreamcatcher on his door.'

Blanka abandoned her coffee cup and rushed out of the kitchen. She hammered vigorously on the door. To her relief she heard movement on the other side of the door. Bedsprings squeaked, something clattered, and then the door opened. A young man with long black hair was looking at her.

Blanka hesitated. 'Hello,' she finally managed to say. 'You . . . you're Klaus Jehle?'

He folded his arms and looked at her seriously. 'That's me,' he said laconically. 'What's up?'

'I'm looking for Nicholas. Nicholas Varkonyi.' Her courage failed her when she saw him wrinkle his brow. 'It's about the press card for the *Attempto*,' she added.

Finally his expression brightened. 'Did this Nicholas find it?'

'You lost it?'

'Yup. A month ago. Or someone stole it.' He looked at her suspiciously. 'Tell me more,' he demanded. 'What do you want from me?'

'Nothing. Sorry, I made a mistake.' She turned and ran off.

'Hey, wait!' She heard Klaus Jehle's voice behind her, but she did not turn around. Standing in front of the residence, the sun blinding her, Blanka rubbed her damp hands and looked around. Pelargus Alley with its small half-timbered houses and the historic cobblestones looked like a picture frozen in time, a facade behind which a chasm was opening. The face of the dead woman appeared in it – and now Mrs Meyer's features, too. Blanka had to lean against the wall so as not to lose her balance. She wanted to scream. Damn it, how could she let someone fool her so easily!

The manifestation last night – had it been a warning against Nicholas? Now even the dream with the mask was beginning to take on meaning.

She was in danger; that was the only thing she was certain of. Nicholas was wearing a mask – but what was behind it? Desperately she dug through her pockets for money and found some notes. Too little to simply go to the station and buy a ticket home. The day after tomorrow Madame would return from Brussels. It was time to put the cards on the table. Suddenly it did not matter to her whether she could stay at the school. She just wanted one thing: to be safe, to run away and hide, to forget the disappointment and fear. Just then her mobile rang. Nicholas. Rage filled Blanka. Her fingers hurt, she pressed so hard on the 'Talk' button. 'Leave me alone,' she hissed. A few passers-by turned to look at her.

'What's wrong?'

'I've just left your residence. Think about it.' With satisfaction she heard him struggling for breath.

'Listen . . . I can explain.'

'Never call me again!'

'Blanka, wait . . . Please! I've discovered something else. We've got to . . .'

The display went dark. Blanka had turned the mobile off.

Finally the bus rounded the corner. Blanka, who had found a quiet spot on a park bench in the shadow of a house, jumped up and wiped the tears from her face. She avoided looking across at La Bête, where Nicholas and she had talked for the first time. Brakes screeching, the bus stopped and breathed out with a hiss. The next moment Blanka heard panting behind her. Someone laid a hand on her shoulder. Blanka whirled around and lashed out. Nicholas stumbled backward, his hands pressed to his face. Blood was dripping between his fingers. Behind Blanka the bus drew up. For a moment she saw herself turning on her heels and rushing over to it. It stopped, she got on, and left – from the back window she could see Nicholas getting smaller and smaller, finally disappearing altogether. But the moment passed, and she was still standing in the same spot.

'Oh shit,' groaned Nicholas. 'Do you have a handkerchief?'

Blanka shook her head. Strangely, her anger had melted away. What remained was only fear. Nicholas cursed again and pulled up his T-shirt to stop his nose from bleeding.

'Don't tip your head back,' said Blanka.

He glowered at her. 'Thanks very much,' he mumbled from under the corner of his T-shirt. 'Damn it, if I'd known you'd hit me so hard . . .'

'Then you'd what?' she replied sharply. 'Would you have pushed me in front of the bus?' He looked up aghast. 'Is that what you did to Annette?' she cried. 'Gave her a push?'

'Hey, are you crazy?' he roared.

She pulled back from him and balled her hand into a fist. 'I don't know what sort of game you're playing or who you are,' she continued more quietly. 'But you're not Nicholas – and you don't live in the residence. And I'll bet no professor has set eyes on you at university, either.'

He groaned and suddenly looked crestfallen. 'You're right,' he admitted. 'Except for the first. I really am Nicholas.'

He reached into the breast pocket of his motorbike jacket and got out his wallet. His driver's licence looked genuine. 'Nicholas Varkonyi,' it said. His birthplace was given as Kecskemét. And it was true too that Nicholas had turned eighteen just a few months previously. 'Please let me explain,' he entreated. 'I've been wanting to tell you for a long time. And there's something else. I called Mrs Meyer's house today. She's . . . dead!'

Blanka, still suspicious, took another step backward. 'I know.'

Confused, he wrinkled his brow, then looked around as if he was afraid someone had followed him. 'Give me five minutes in La Bête,' he begged. 'On neutral ground.'

'You lied to me! The whole story about the Wolves making your life difficult was a lie. You bought my trust with lies!'

She hated herself for sounding so pathetic. Ashamed, he bowed his head.

'Yes, that's true,' he said, almost inaudibly. 'You seemed so . . . hard to me, Blanka. At the beginning I didn't like you very much. You were so cold. As if the world wasn't good enough for you. I was just trying to find a way to approach you.'

'Well, it worked very well.'

'I know. I'm sorry. I didn't want to involve you any more than I had to – five minutes, Blanka. Please!'

Nicholas pressed the wet cloth the waitress had given him onto the back of his neck. His red nose glowed in his chalk-white face.

Blanka leaned back and folded her arms. 'One minute's already gone,' she said.

'OK, OK,' he snapped. 'Can't you drop the arrogance for once?' He pulled himself together and continued, 'I'm not a medical student. I just said that so you'd talk to me. I had the feeling you'd be able to tell me more about the school than Jan. He said the Wolves wouldn't leave you alone and so I thought . . .' He sniffed, then shrugged.

'So, a journalist after all,' said Blanka.

He shook his head. 'I only finished school last year. And then my father got sick. I looked after him – we have no relatives left, just his distant cousin in Hungary. We lived there for a while.'

He cleared his throat and searched for the right words for a long time. Blanka waited while he discarded the cloth, absently fumbled around in his cigarette pack, took out a cigarette, and lit it.

'My father had a stroke,' he said hoarsely, blowing out the smoke. 'He didn't make it. He died one day after my eighteenth birthday.' Again he cleared his throat and blinked a few times too many.

'Well . . . I had to clear out the house. And I found letters there from my mother. I was five when she died. But I can still remember her laugh. She was a storyteller. Until I was three I believed she was really the Queen of the Clouds and she had fallen into my father's workshop when her horse threw her – and then the next year I was convinced my father was a globetrotter on the run and she was a Persian princess. She described to me in great detail how my father had carried her off from the palace of the black Sultan. All these stories are almost more real for me than my actual childhood.' He took a pull at his cigarette and then stubbed it out again. 'She made me believe that we had to hide from the Sultan. That was the only reason we lived in Hungary, and my father had a moustache, so that he wouldn't be recognised. Ever since I've been capable of thought, I've felt as if I'm being followed, and I've tried to keep a low profile. Crazy, huh? She had thousands of stories like that – but I don't know who she really was.'

Blanka was still not sure whether to believe him. 'And the letters?' she asked.

Nicholas seemed to wake from a daydream.

'The letters, yes. She'd got to know my father when he was living in Budapest and she was on holiday there. For a while they wrote to each other, and then she came to join him in Hungary.'

'Did they get married?'

'She didn't want to, although he often asked her. She . . . she'd been married before, to a man she'd known when she was still at school. The marriage was very unhappy. I found out why from one of the letters.'

Nicholas looked as if he'd suddenly come down with a fever. His eyes were glistening. After a pause he continued. 'Shortly after her wedding she nearly died,' he said quietly. 'Because – because her former husband beat her up. When she left him, he threatened to follow her and kill her, wherever she went. She wrote all this to my father – and I didn't understand till a couple of weeks ago why she was always so sad and restless. I think she really spent her whole life hiding from this man. Maybe not well enough.'

'Nicholas . . . that's terrible.'

He nodded and took another cigarette from the pack. 'She was always frightened something would happen to me. After I'd read her letters I noted the return address and went there. I just wanted to know where she came from and perhaps speak to people who'd known her. Well, I found the address, but a married couple had been living in the house for thirty years. They'd never even heard of my mother. I kept looking, but I didn't find her. It was as if she'd never existed.' He sighed. 'And then I had one last idea,' he said. 'In among her letters there was a photo. I sat down at the computer and searched for buildings that looked like the one in the background. And I found it. Then I sold everything I'd inherited and came here.'

'That's why you have so much money.'

'You'd be amazed what's possible when you hand over a ten-euro note. The pathology assistant finds hidden files, Jan builds tools and acts as a spy, and even the cleaning lady at the police station knows where to look. But nothing helped. I still don't know who she really was. She's not on any register. But I came across another name.'

'The student.'

Nicholas nodded. 'He drowned at exactly the same time my mother was here.'

'Show me the photo,' begged Blanka. He hesitated for a long time. He seemed to find it very difficult to allow her a glimpse into his life. He took out his briefcase again. Carefully he opened a side compartment and took out a small photo. The colours had faded. Blanka thought she felt a crackling between her fingers as she took it. She looked at the picture and understood. The walls of the manor house had not been restored and painted in a light colour like today, but she would have recognised it among thousands of buildings. But much more interesting was the girl standing in front of the house. She was wearing a school uniform like the ones Blanka had seen in old pictures in the museum. Light blonde hair fell to her shoulders. She looked serious and a little grim, her smile only for the photographer. Nevertheless you could see that she had a dimple in one cheek. In her arms she was carrying a light-coloured leather schoolbag, with two initials burned into the leather.

'How did your mother die?' whispered Blanka.

'She went to Stockholm to visit a friend. She drowned in a ferry accident.'

'Was her body ever found?'

He looked at her in amazement, turning even paler. 'No,' he said. 'After ten years she was declared dead.'

'What was her name?'

'Klara.'

'Klara Varkonyi?'

'Klara Schmied. She insisted I take my father's last name. Blanka, what's wrong?'

She hitched her chair closer and put her arm around Nicholas. 'Listen,' she whispered. 'I really hope I'm wrong, but I've seen this bag before.'

'Where?'

'It was on the floor in Madame Lalonde's office. The day after . . . the dead woman was found.'

His eyes were open so wide that each iris looked like a perfect dove-grey marble. 'That means that Madame has the same bag?'

'That means it may well have been one and the same bag,' Blanka corrected him. She hated herself for having to tell him the truth. 'It means they may well also have been the same person – your mother and Annette Durlain.' She indicated the photo lying on the table in front of them. 'I can't say if the face is the same. But the dead woman had blue eyes – and a dimple here. She had dark-grey hair, but hair can be dyed. She didn't want to be recognised when she slipped into the school as a tourist.'

Nicholas did not seem to have been listening to her properly. Bits of tobacco fell onto the photo and Blanka noticed that he was crushing the cigarette in his hand. 'That's impossible,' he said. 'The dead woman was fifty-four. My mother would only be forty today.'

'Forged passport – false date of birth. And of course she made herself look older – a good disguise.'

'No,' he whispered. 'No. It's impossible. I . . . The autopsy report . . .' Then he pushed Blanka's hand away roughly and dashed out of the café.

Blanka pulled some money out of her jacket pocket, slammed it onto the table, and ran after Nicholas. To her relief he had not run away. He was standing a few paces away in a side alley, leaning against the house wall, breathing heavily. A few steps, and she was beside him, grasping his shoulders.

'Let's walk a bit,' she said. 'Show me where you live!'

The place Nicholas was really living in was far less comfortable than the student residence. It was on the edge of the old town, in a huge, unattractive apartment block. Nicholas stumbled through a narrow back door and dragged himself up a never-ending staircase. His room was nothing more than a small attic with a crooked window. There were two suitcases on the floor and a hotplate was perched on an upside-down cardboard box in the corner. The sun had turned the little room into a furnace. Blanka immediately went over to the window and with some effort pushed it open. Nicholas sank down onto the mattress under the sloping ceiling and buried his head in his arms.

'It's impossible,' he said finally. 'That would mean – that my mother was still alive when I came to town. We may even have walked right past each other in the marketplace . . .'

'Nicholas, perhaps I'm wrong,' said Blanka softly.

'The woman in the photo looks like the woman you saw?'

Blanka gave up trying to be reassuring. 'I only saw her for such a brief moment – I can't say for certain. But I'm almost sure it was her. I'm so sorry!'

'Why didn't she ever let me know she was alive? Even after my father's death . . .'

'She must have wanted to protect you. Don't forget the tattoo – she was one of the Wolves. She even staged her own death so she couldn't be found. She didn't want to get married and she insisted you take your father's name. She herself took the name Schmied, a name that's very common. In other words, she did everything she could to cover up all traces of you and any connection between the two of you.'

'She could have had the tattoo removed.'

'Quite likely she tried that. Jenna told me that the Wolves do their tattoos by hand – that usually means they're much too deep. The mark is often still clear even after the tattoo has been removed. The Wolves, at least, were able to recognise the mark. Did you never notice a tattoo or a scar?'

Nicholas had calmed down somewhat. His face set, he sat staring at the wall. After a while he shook his head. 'I was only five! When we went to the lake, she wore a swimsuit. No, I don't remember seeing anything.'

Dust particles danced in the sunbeams, and from outside the noise of the street reached into the room. Life went on, unmoved and uncaring. Blanka felt as if she were trapped in a block of ice.

'There's something in this school,' she whispered. 'And it's not just the Wolves – they seem to me to be possessed. Don't think I'm crazy, but I'm beginning to think they practise witchcraft. Think about it: for centuries the Wolves have been experimenting – first with alchemy, then with hypnosis. But always here. Maybe it's a ritual site.'

'And my mother's bag is in Madame Lalonde's office. That means she is involved.'

Blanka thought for a second, then shook her head.

'The way it looks to me is that the police are in on it – and a couple of the doctors are involved, too. They officially declared the murder to be an accident. If Madame knows about that, it would make sense for her to hide the bag from the police. And also, she's trying to find new sponsors for the school right now. If Joaquim's father has something to do with the murder, that would make sense, too: she'll get the school's financing in order before handing over the evidence.'

Nicholas ran his hands through his hair. 'We'll break into her office,' he said dully. 'Today. I'll call Jan.'

'No!' said Blanka, almost shouting. 'That would be too danger-ous. If the Wolves killed Mrs Meyer, then they'll be watching me all the more closely now. No, we'll wait until Madame comes back.'

'Do you really think that's a good idea?'

'It's just two days.'

Nicholas looked at her doubtfully. Finally he nodded in defeat.

'I'll sleep here,' she said. 'I wouldn't be able to get a wink of sleep at school. Is it OK with you if I go to the school one more time? I'll just get my things. I'll be back in an hour.' She sat down on the bed beside Nicholas and hugged him. He hesitated for just a moment, then hugged her back.

'No more secrets.'

'No more secrets,' whispered Nicholas.

A hazy, colourless sky behind the school gave the effect of a black-and-white photo. Today the buildings looked terrifying in their modernity. After hesitating briefly, Blanka entered the school. Inside, her steps quickened until she was running up the stairs to her dorm. Surprised faces flashed past her. Finally she was at her own door, searching frantically for her keys. She didn't notice the envelope until she had unlocked the door. The school's office stamp was emblazoned on it. Blanka tore the envelope open and read the letter. A summons because of unexcused absences. In her room, everything was as she had left it. She had expected to find her drawers ransacked. With a sigh of relief she looked at the clock – Caitlin would not be back for an hour. Blanka pressed down the handle of the connecting door and went into her friend's room. She looked around in disbelief. Caitlin was gone. Not only Caitlin – everything that had belonged to Caitlin. The bare mattress lay on the bed. The chair, desk, and dresser stood abandoned against the wall. The little pinholes in the walls from Caitlin's posters and pictures were the only evidence that she had ever lived there. For a strange moment it seemed to Blanka that her friend had never really existed. She pulled her mobile out of her pocket and switched it back on. Before she could dial Caitlin's number she saw there were ten beeps, telling her she had missed a lot of calls. All of them Jan. Heart thudding anxiously, Blanka waited for Caitlin to pick up. There was a click, then a mechanical voice announced that the subscriber could not be reached.

'Damn!' The word slipped out. Her eyes filled with tears. She reached into her pocket for a tissue. Something fell out and landed on the floor with a clatter. The key to Caitlin's desk. Blanka sniffed back her tears, picked up the key, and went over to the drawer. It was still locked. The key turned easily. Blanka pulled the drawer open. It was empty.

She could see that it was Jan calling. However, when she picked up, she would never have known. His voice sounded thin and worried.

'Blanka! At last! Did you talk to Caitlin?'

'No – I don't even know what's going on. Her things have gone, and . . .'

'She didn't pass the exam.'

'What?'

'It's on the list on the noticeboard. I thought she wasn't answering her phone because she was frustrated, but then someone in her class told me she left this afternoon.' He paused, struggling for breath. 'I don't believe it – she didn't even say goodbye to me. And that she didn't pass . . .'

'Can't be true,' said Blanka, finishing his sentence.

'Where is she?'

Dead? thought Blanka. She rushed out of the empty room, slammed the connecting door shut, and leaned her back against it. Now alarm bells sounded in Jan's voice. 'Blanka, are you crying?'

'Of course I'm crying,' Blanka snapped. 'I dragged her into this – damn!'

'Dragged her in? What do you mean? Are you in your room? I'm coming right over!'

Blanka slid down the smooth door and wrapped her arms around her knees. After the shock, it took her a minute to think of calling Nicholas.

'I'm sure she didn't fly back to Ireland just like that, without telling anyone,' she stammered into the phone. 'She must still be somewhere in the school.'

Nicholas thought for a moment. She was amazed that he could remain so calm.

'We'll look for her – tonight.'

METROPOLIS II

'TAKE THE LAMP,' WHISPERED JAN. When the flash-light's beam flitted over his face, Blanka could see his cheeks glowing. He was screwing an adapter onto his lock-opener, while Nicholas, following his instructions, unrolled a cable. Nicholas was limping a little. When they had climbed in through the chemistry lab window past the alarm system, with Jan's help, he had stumbled and knocked his injured leg again. It was now 2.30 in the morning. It had taken Jan more than half an hour to disarm the alarm system at the door to the office area. Finally the door opened with a hum. The equipment Jan was using today was not a small door-opener – it was a strange-looking machine that bore some resemblance to a mixer. In the weak beam of the flashlight Blanka saw wires and the uneven surfaces of small soldered metal plates, holding various connections.

In single file they crept along the passage leading to the head-mistress's office and the staffrooms. They stopped in front of Madame's door. Jan nodded to them and indicated to Nicholas to plug in the cable.

'Are you sure we need to break into her office?' he whispered. Blanka nodded.

'The school archives are in her room – and there's a connecting door to the school office.'

'But Caitlin won't be there.'

'No, but we need a starting point. There must be a floor plan or a calendar there. Something.' And, she said to herself, maybe there's also some trace of Nicholas's mother. Jan wiped his hand over his forehead and pushed a pin into the keyhole. The machine hummed again, then there was a screeching noise.

'Shit!' whispered Jan.

'What's wrong?'

Carefully he pulled the pin out again. A scratch gleamed in the metal.

'Wrong key,' he growled. He reached into his pants pocket and took out a much stronger pin.

'Don't be scared,' he said softly. 'Something's going to break in a moment. Move back.'

Obediently, Blanka took a step to the side. The next moment there was a loud hum, then there was silence, until they heard a dreadful grinding noise. The door swung open. Blanka stared in horror at the hole and the splinters of wood.

'The door's broken,' Nicholas stated.

'So what?' Jan turned on him. 'I'd like to burn the place down with them in it! They've done something with Caitlin and you're worrying about a door?'

Nicholas raised his hands. 'Hey, calm down,' he said. 'Don't yell like that here!'

Blanka stretched out her hand and laid it on Jan's shoulder. 'It's all right, Jan. We'll find her.'

He nodded and wiped his hands on his pants.

'Are we going in, or what?'

'Yes. Let's go!' Blanka decided. Like shadows they flitted into the office and pushed the armchair in front of the door. Nicholas let down the blinds. Only then did they dare to turn the little flashlight back on. The beam of light roamed over the bookcases and was reflected in the glossy bindings of thick books. It was not long before Jan had the first of Madame's desk drawers open. The headmistress was an exceptionally tidy person. Everything, every sheet of paper, every pencil, was placed meticulously. Blanka felt guilty snooping around. They found only notebooks containing accounting records, receipts for books on financial management, and a copy card.

'To the office,' whispered Blanka. In the dim light Nicholas's face made her think of a wax death mask.

In the office they had a lot more to search through. Mountains of files and loose papers were heaped at the edge of the gigantic table. Blanka brought out the second flashlight and began sifting.

'Maybe we should start with the computer,' said Nicholas after a little while.

Jan, who had been searching a desk drawer, stood up suddenly, bumping his shoulder against the desk chair.

'I've found something,' he hissed. In grim triumph he held up a folder. 'Here!'

They crowded into the light and stared at the long rows of numbers.

'According to this list, Caitlin got an even worse mark in mathematics than Michael Cline,' Blanka declared.

'They've killed her!' Jan burst out.

'Don't jump to conclusions,' said Blanka, pulling Jan up by his arm. 'Quick, into Hasenberg's office!'

She did not want to admit that she was beginning to lose heart.

She felt even more nervous as they entered Dr Hasenberg's domain.

'What are we waiting for?' whispered Nicholas. Jan grabbed his machine and plugged it in. Here the search was more difficult. Inside the cabinets were more compartments, each with its own lock. In most cases they were special locks, and Jan, cursing, tried different pins until they finally yielded to the steel teeth of his lock-breaker. Blanka found dozens of sketches that looked like geometric diagrams. She recognised them easily – they were family trees. Behind her she heard the crunch of a pane of glass breaking. Jan swore quietly.

'Blanka!' The stifled cry made her turn around quickly. Nicholas was standing in the middle of the room. At first she thought he was swaying, but then she realised that it was the flashlight, which he had put down on the table. It was rolling back and forth as if drunk. It was not until the beam of light slid back that she recognised what Nicholas had taken from a compartment of the shelf with the broken glass.

'The bag!'

Dazed, Jan squinted into the light. 'What sort of bag?'

'The proof,' replied Nicholas bleakly. Blanka could see his face crumpling. She jumped up and went to him. The bag still felt soft and almost familiar. Together they laid it carefully on the floor. 'M. J.' Nicholas quietly read the initials aloud. 'There's the clue to her real name.'

Blanka resisted the temptation to reach out to the clasp. The bag belonged to Nicholas now. Gingerly, he touched the front. His fingers left dark marks in the suede. The clasp opened with a soft clink. Nicholas turned the bag over and emptied it out onto the floor. The dead woman had not carried very much around with her: a knife with an ivory handle and an old-fashioned 35-mm camera. Nicholas popped open the case and shook his head. 'No film,' he whispered. In a side pocket there were several sheets of thick paper. Nicholas unfolded them and laid them on the carpet. Carefully he stroked them flat.

'A map. Do you know what it's of?'

Blanka slid over to Nicholas to look at the map so quickly that her knees grew warm. It was the floor plan of a huge building. Only one room on the east side seemed vaguely familiar to her. It was outside the building, separated by a long passage. A few lines indicated stairs.

'The single room is the basement of the museum,' she said quietly. 'This square here is the display case with the witch's robe. And the small square is the piece of the old convent door that's hanging on the wall.'

'A door?' whispered Nicholas.

'The door behind the door,' Blanka amended. '*Porta post portam* – the school's motto. The door leads to a building underneath the school.'

Nicholas laughed softly and shook his head. 'You were right,' he said hoarsely. 'The school, the teachers, the students, it's all just a sham. Madame and the scholarships, the teachers – all puppets in a puppet theatre. The real world lies below the surface. And my mother knew that.'

'Hey!' came Jan's sharp whisper from the other corner of the room. 'Take a look at this!'

Blanka and Nicholas jumped up together. Jan slapped a transparent folder onto the table. Accusingly he shone the flashlight onto it.

'Here's Caitlin's test. Not marked. I bet it was an A+.'

'The mark behind the mark,' said Nicholas. 'The door behind the door.'

'Someone must be damned good at copying handwriting,' said Blanka. 'Perhaps the same person who wrote the new version of the convent chronicle.' And, she added to herself, wrote my messed-up history exam.

The back stairs that Jan used to lead them to the convent museum were steep and narrow. When they entered the hallway again and Blanka saw a red light blinking, she nearly gave up hope. 'This one's a really big alarm system,' she whispered. 'There's one like it in the town museum. Do you think you can deal with it?'

She could not see Jan's expression, but she could tell by the way he shrugged his shoulders that he was up for the challenge. Without another word he took something out of his pocket. There was a click, and then the red light dimmed, finally going out altogether. The flashlight went on. Astounded, Blanka looked at Jan. 'You have a remote control for the alarm system?'

'And for the video camera over the door,' he replied.

'And what's on the tape now?'

'The still image of an empty museum,' Jan replied dryly.

Blanka and Nicholas were amazed when they saw Jan walking in as if he were following his daily route to school.

The witch's robe glimmered eerily in the beam of the flashlight. The overhead light snapped on. Blanka and Nicholas recoiled, huddling against the wall. Jan, who was standing by the light switch, looked at them in amusement.

'What's wrong?' His voice echoed. 'Nobody's here – it's hermetically sealed. So it's OK to have the light on.'

'You come here a lot, do you?' Nicholas was pale. Blanka took his hand, which felt cold and dry.

'Could be.' Jan went over to a piece of wood panelling that had an almost invisible groove cut around it. Skilfully he took hold of it and lifted up a flap. Thick cables and power meters came into view.

'The school's main junction box,' he said. 'Do you see the ceramic fuses?'

Blanka was wide-eyed. 'The power cut we had the other day,' she said. 'That was you?'

'Only happened once,' he replied. 'Then I had it under control. What door are you talking about? The old ruin back there?'

The fragment of the old convent door on the wall towered in front of them like the jagged, blackened tooth of a dragon. Blanka had to force herself just to touch the ancient wood. Nicholas and Jan gripped it by the edges.

'On three,' commanded Nicholas. The door creaked a little in its iron brackets but hardly moved. Then, when their hands were getting slippery from sweat, it started to move with a screech. The whole time Blanka had the feeling that the wooden apostles on the door were eyeing them reproachfully. Once she even thought she heard a thin cry through the wall – Caitlin's voice? The screech became a squeak as the door suddenly slid out of its supports and swung to the side, surprising them.

'A hinge,' Jan confirmed calmly. 'And a hydraulic system. Man, we only needed to lift it and push!'

Amazed, Blanka and Nicholas looked at what should have been wall. Instead there was a narrow metal door.

'The door behind the door,' whispered Blanka.

'Not a chance,' Jan said, with a professional glance at the lock. 'Latest-generation security lock. I can't open that with my master key.'

'Does that mean we have to give up?' Nicholas asked angrily.

Jan's eyes flashed. 'Does it look as though I'm giving up?' He cracked his knuckles, staring at the lock as if it was his enemy. 'For this I need Metropolis II, from the art room.'

The features of the floor plan were firmly fixed in Blanka's memory by the time she finally heard footsteps and a rumbling sound. She jumped up in relief. She had spent the past quarter of an hour sitting with her back against the wall, memorising the floor plan. Only the centre part was drawn properly – she could not tell whether the passageways indicated at the sides led to other rooms or were just exits. Nicholas's red face appeared. Together he and Jan dragged a machine into the room. It looked like something out of a science-fiction film. A tangled mass of cables and stiff hoses hung over Jan's shoulder. Carefully they set down the machine. Nicholas stood up and stretched his sore leg.

'The thing's made of lead,' he groaned.

'Steel,' Jan corrected him. 'It operates at 3000 psi. If it was lead, the cables would fly all over the place.'

'So it works on pressure?'

'Of course. You know the jaws of life that firemen use? This is the same principle. An electric motor using 400 volts AC and an oil-pressure pump that creates pressure. You can open pretty well anything with it. And as it's a hydraulic system, it hardly makes any noise. I've tested it several times on the furnace power supply.' He reached into his pants pocket and pulled out a cylindrical piece of metal. He quickly pushed it into the keyhole of the main door of the museum and used a small key to lock it.

'Special plug-in lock for security locks,' he explained. 'Without this key no one can open the door. We don't want any surprise guests coming into the convent museum tonight, do we?'

After Jan had unscrewed the front and side panels of Metropolis II, the block looked like a car battery with levers and a cylinder screwed onto it. Blanka looked over at two hydraulic pry bars that were vaguely reminiscent of a pair of scissors. Jan reached for the thick cables and pressure hoses. Calmly he began to hook up his machine and to attach the power cables underneath the ceramic fuses. Nicholas sat down beside Blanka and passed her a cloth in which several hard objects were wrapped.

'I only have my pocket knife with me,' whispered Nicholas. 'But I'm sure these'll be better – they were in the art room.'

Shuddering, Blanka looked at the sharp blades of the box-cutters sticking out of the cloth.

Jan noticed her worried face and grinned. 'Nothing can go wrong,' he explained, indicating his Metropolis machine. 'The motor turns itself off if necessary. Idiot-proof. Give me a hand, Nick!'

It took a couple of minutes to position the machine properly in front of the door. With intense concentration, Jan jammed the pry bars between the door and the steel frame.

'OK!' he cried. Blanka expected at any minute to hear an ear-splitting explosion and then to feel splinters driving into her back. Instead there was an ugly metallic grinding sound. Shortly afterwards the door, bent completely out of shape, swung open. Nicholas whistled appreciatively.

'There really are stairs,' whispered Jan.

The smell emanating from the narrow stair shaft of the secret passageway was reminiscent of a deep cellar where wine bottles indulge in their dusty dreams of Christmas parties and clinking glasses.

Blanka could not help thinking of Caitlin, tied up and mistreated, being dragged into this sepulchre. She picked up a box-cutter in her right hand and the flashlight in her left. At every step the papers that she had slid under her T-shirt in Dr Hasenberg's office rubbed against her skin.

Blanka counted each stair. Behind her she could hear Nicholas breathing fast. From one stair to the next the air grew cooler. The passage walls seemed to be getting closer and closer together. Blanka imagined she could hear the echo of her own heartbeat. Finally the end of the stairs came into view. Calves aching, they entered an even narrower passageway. Blanka closed her eyes, mentally tracing their route so far, working from the approximate distance and the number of stairs, and relating it to the length of the passageways on the floor plan.

'Thirty metres straight ahead and then right,' she said quietly.

The passageway was so narrow that they could only go through in single file. Blanka went first, trying not to think about what she might meet. The passageway was panelled with wood and smelled of fresh varnish. A light breeze brushed Blanka's cheeks in passing – somewhere there must be an air-conditioner.

They turned off, following the curve of another passageway. It suddenly ended. Blanka stopped so abruptly that Nicholas bumped into her. Silently Blanka let the beam of her flashlight roam upward. They were standing in front of a stone passage. Relief sculptures bordered the doorway on both sides – sculptures of wolves hunting.

'That's old,' whispered Blanka. 'It must be even older than Maddalina's convent.'

Quietly they walked through the doorway and entered an underground cathedral. A graceful gothic vault rose above them, designed in a way that made it able to bear a great weight. Awestruck, they looked around.

'So this is where Maddalina and the others fled to,' whispered Blanka. 'They simply disappeared – through a secret passage into the underground convent.'

'Where next?' Jan urged.

Blanka shut her eyes and visualised the plan. 'At the back on the right some other passageways branch off.'

Wide-eyed, they ran through stone passages where ancient sculptures sat in niches. These were not figures of saints but the faces of mortals that looked like chiselled death masks. At a fork in the passage, Blanka looked over at one niche and recoiled in horror.

'Oh my God!' whispered Nicholas. Two skulls were grinning at them.

Blanka turned the flashlight's beam onto the ceiling. A root protruded between two stones. 'The orphans' cemetery is above us,' she said.

'Wrong,' came Jan's dry answer. 'The cemetery is down here.' He pointed to other niches, where several skulls lay, as if in a catacomb.

'If there are no dead bodies up there in the coffins, then what's in them?' whispered Nicholas.

'I couldn't care less,' replied Jan. 'Where's Caitlin?'

The fear in his voice infected Blanka. The passageway got wider again and became an oval room. Stopping all at once, they stumbled and grabbed at each other. Several heavy wooden doors appeared in the flashlight's trembling beam. They were small and almost square, a little over a metre high. The top of the one on the right of the passageway was pointed. There could be anything behind them: a burial chamber, a passage, Hell, or – a prison. The bolt closing the heavy door from the outside was shut. Before Blanka could stop him, Jan ran to the door and hammered on the wood.

'Caitlin?' he called softly. There was a rumbling noise, and then someone moved on the other side of the door.

Every hair on Blanka's body stood up. 'No, Jan!' she cried, dashing to the door. Jan spun around. It was not until the floor came up to meet her that Blanka realised that Jan had pushed her aside roughly and that she was falling. She hardly felt the impact. The bolt slid back with a scraping sound.

'Caitlin!' Jan cried, flinging the door open.

At this moment, which seemed to be everlasting, Blanka learned two things. One, that it took only a fraction of a second to be catapulted out of the world of formulas and hypotheses for ever. The other, that reality could be worse than any nightmare. The creature that crawled out of its room into the light of the flashlight could not be real. Pale limbs groped their way over the stone. Glittering eye slits were surrounded by predatory folds, and the mouth became wider and wider. The beam of light moved over the grotesque face. Terrified by the light, the monster let out a shrill cry and then sprang aside with a repulsively agile movement. Claws scraped over stone like chalk over a slate board, and then all sound ceased, even the panting breath. The creature had discovered Blanka. For a moment, time stood still. For one confusing moment Blanka thought she could see two Nicholases – the one she knew and the one she'd dreamed of in the mask, the wolf mask, a mask that was now baring its teeth triumphantly. Nicholas sprang up at the same instant as the creature, and then the shadows came. With a dull thud Blanka's flashlight fell to the floor and went out. Blanka turned and ran. Her own panting drummed in her ears, drowning out Jan's and Nicholas's voices, which fell farther and farther behind. But the scraping noise behind her was much louder, the raw breath getting closer and closer. Blanka screamed when she brushed against a wall with her shoulder, felt an archway, the wall of a hallway, and a skull that rolled away under her hands and shattered with a dry crash. The creature was faster than she was, much faster. In her mind's eye she could see it pursuing her, bounding like a lion. Far ahead there was a glimmer of light. When Blanka felt the almost loving touch of claws on the back of her knee, she forgot the light and just ran. Then she felt two arms wrapping themselves around her and a bandaged mummy-like hand pressing her lips painfully against her teeth. She squinted into the darkness, but the monster seemed to have disappeared.

'You're frightening him,' a rough voice whispered into her ear. The smell of alcohol was overpowering.

'If I let you go, will you be sensible?' asked Simon Nemec. Blanka pressed against his hand, hoping he would interpret the movement as a nod. He released her. Nearby a match was struck. Concerned, Nemec wrinkled his brow, but he was not looking at Blanka. His glance was drawn to where a whimpering sound was coming from. Blanka reached out for the uneven wall, braced herself against it, and turned around, trembling. The monster sat huddled against the wall, rocking back and forth, as if trying to soothe a pain.

'You kicked him,' Nemec rebuked her.

'It . . . it attacked me,' Blanka replied. She watched in bewilderment as the caretaker bent down and stroked the creature's matted hair comfortingly with his bandaged hand. The monster raised its head and looked at Blanka despondently. It had blue eyes, she saw. Not a predator's eyes. Like a blind person who finally understands what he has been touching, she realised what the monster was. It had been searching for her all along – it had felt for her in its thoughts and had finally found her. And it was a human being. A young man. His skin was very pale, as if he had not seen the sun for many years. His claws were long, horny fingernails. His shoulder bore several barely healed cuts in the pattern of a spider's web. His head hung forward, making him look even more like an animal. What Blanka had thought of as predatory folds were tattoos. Black lines depicting a beast of prey had been drawn on his face, making it look like that of a wolf. The young man looked at Blanka and contorted his face. It pained her to see him trying to smile at her. His molars gleamed. Blanka felt so nauseated that she slid down the wall and covered her face with her hands. It seemed that a long time ago someone had slit open the corners of the man's mouth to make him look more like an animal.

'Who did that to him?' whispered Blanka. Nemec shrugged, took a candle from a niche by the door and lit it with the dying match.

'Maddalina, Hans Haber, Joaquim – all of us.' His voice shook. 'And that means me too.'

'The Wolves, then,' she said. 'And you're one of them.'

'Yes, and sometimes no,' returned Nemec. Apprehensively he

looked round. 'Not at the moment, otherwise you wouldn't be standing here asking me questions.'

'Would I end up like him?' Blanka replied bitterly. 'What did he do?'

Nemec's face softened as he looked at the boy. 'It's his destiny. He knows nothing else, Blanka. He's a wolf-child; he grew up without human contact. Light hurts him, but in the darkness he can even distinguish colours. He hardly feels heat and cold. His senses are sharper than ours – they're so finely tuned that he can even see the colours of our thoughts.'

'That means you locked him up down here when he was just a child!' gasped Blanka. 'You're all crazy!'

Nemec's gaze seemed to smoulder in his sombre face. 'In a way it makes him freer than any of us,' he whispered. 'He doesn't know who or what he is. He's a wolf – with all the capabilities of a man. With all the intuition and powers that most men lost centuries ago. Haven't you felt it, Blanka? His presence is everywhere!'

Blanka looked at the wolf-man. Thinking exhausted her; she felt as if her whole body was trembling. 'Then he's a . . . medium,' she whispered.

Nemec swayed slightly and reached out to the wall to steady himself. 'In a way, yes,' he said, his voice rough. 'He picks up our thoughts subconsciously. In his mind he can go wherever he wants.' He laughed as if he had made a joke.

'Are you drunk?' Blanka's tone was accusing.

Immediately Nemec grew serious again. 'Down here is the only place it's possible to think clearly,' he growled. 'Thoughts vanish into the mist – and the others can't understand them.'

'Can the Wolves?'

Something like pride lit up his face. 'Belverina's gift. We had it once and we'll have it again. For centuries they tried to take it away from us, but the Wolves are learning – they're learning again and transforming themselves.'

The wolf-man let out a soft sound.

Simon Nemec froze. 'He hears them,' he whispered. 'They're going into the assembly room.' Blanka did not pull back when he grasped her by the shoulders. He no longer seemed aware of his injured hand. 'They mustn't find you!' He pushed her roughly and ran off. Without stopping to think she stumbled after him, through dark passageways – it seemed like the same route she had taken on the way here. The round beam of a flashlight confirmed her guess. Nemec almost fell when he saw two figures coming around the bend. Blanka could see Jan's eyes gleaming, wide with fright.

'Don't ask questions,' she hissed. 'Come on!'

The wolf-man was running beside her on all fours; she could feel his breath on her hand. Nemec was heading back to the room from which they had freed the wolf just a few minutes before, running so fast that his jacket billowed out behind him. He pushed the door open. 'What are you waiting for?' whispered Nemec. 'They won't look for you here!'

Blanka hesitated, looking into the caretaker's watery eyes. She could hear footsteps approaching in the distance. She imagined Joaquim and the other Wolves getting nearer.

'Come on!' she commanded Nicholas and Jan. They looked at each other doubtfully, but Blanka took their hands and dragged them along behind her. The wolf-man made a plaintive sound and did not move an inch. Only when he saw Blanka go in did he follow. Nemec slid the bolt across on the outside.

'Are you crazy?' whispered Jan.

'Shut up, otherwise we're finished!' Blanka ordered. It smelled like Mrs Meyer's living room – of animal fur and tanned hides.

Except that the smell was a hundred times stronger. They could hardly hear anything at all through the door: just murmuring and Nemec's grumpy voice in response. Frightened, they waited, huddling close together. After a while Blanka raised her head and looked around. Light came from a tiny lamp in a niche. Animal furs lay on the floor, and some were rolled up against the wall. All around, the walls were covered in scratch marks that looked like outlandish cave paintings. How many hours must the wolf-man have spent searching for a way out of his prison?

The door swung open and Nemec slipped into the room. 'Come on! I'll show you the way.'

'Not without Caitlin!' hissed Jan.

Nemec stared at him in astonishment, then broke into hoarse laughter. 'You came here because of the Irish girl?'

'She's disappeared.'

Nemec made a dismissive gesture. 'She went home. I took her to the airport myself. She was told that Blanka was being expelled too.'

'Why?'

'Copies were found in her room. She was careless enough to say they belonged to you, Blanka. Anyone who breaks into the bookroom and makes copies runs the risk of being expelled.'

'And you had the key to Caitlin's room?'

'Oh no,' Nemec replied anxiously. 'Not me. I don't have any keys to the students' rooms. But in this case no key was needed. You were clever enough to lock your room, Blanka. Caitlin forgot this time.'

'How do you know I lock my room?' Blanka's mouth was hanging open. 'Oh,' she said, it all making sense now, 'It was you, the night the power went out. You tried to get into my room!'

'I only checked to see if your door was locked. It's better to keep the doors locked when the Wolves have decided to do battle.'

'I had the key to the drawer!'

'It's not hard to open a drawer like that, with a piece of wire, for example.'

'You're lying to us!' cried Jan.

The cowering wolf-man growled and straightened up. Nicholas crawled away as fast as he could, to keep as much distance as possible between himself and the wolf.

'He isn't lying, Jan,' said Blanka

'Give me one reason why I should trust him,' returned Jan.

'I won't give you any reasons. I'll just get you out of here, nothing more,' said Nemec.

'Annette Durlain trusted you, didn't she?' Nicholas's knuckles were white, he was gripping the box-cutter so tightly.

Nemec turned slowly in his direction.

'Maybe she was called Klara Schmied, too,' Nicholas added. 'Did you kill her?'

The wolf-man was oblivious, gazing at Nicholas.

'Well?' Nicholas gasped. 'Did you kill her?'

The wolf-man began to bare its teeth in imitation of Nicholas's rage.

Blanka had to look away.

'I don't know who you mean,' said Nemec coolly.

'I mean the woman who was found dead at the foot of the stairs.'

Nemec and Nicholas eyed each other for a long time.

'Meret Johanna Vargas,' murmured Nemec finally. 'We just called her Johanna. No, I didn't kill her. I would never have done that. Never!' He fell silent and made a sound that sounded like a stifled sob.

'What was she looking for?' asked Blanka quietly.

Nemec sighed and wiped his eyes with the back of his hand. He cleared his throat and pointed to the wolf-man, who had stopped baring his teeth.

'Her son,' he said softly. 'She wanted to rescue him. I was keeping watch . . . That evening was the perfect time. The Wolves were distracted, taking the new students around. We just had to wait until the orphans' cemetery was empty. But Johanna . . .'

The box-cutter fell to the floor.

'That's not true,' whispered Nicholas. 'I'm her only child.'

Blanka took a step towards him. Now the incident in her room was making sense – the wolf and Nicholas. Nemec held his head in his hands and slid down the wall until he was sitting on the stone floor.

'So it's true,' he said to Nicholas. 'She told me about you. I just never took it in.'

'She abandoned me for his sake,' said Nicholas. Blanka had expected him to be upset, maybe fall apart completely, but he was quite calm.

'She left you to protect you,' Nemec corrected him. 'It was very hard for her to do that. But she managed to make herself invisible. When she ran away all those years ago, even I thought she was dead.'

'And she simply left the wolf . . . her child . . . behind?' asked Blanka.

Nemec laughed bitterly. 'She was just a child herself. She was seventeen when she got pregnant. By a student.'

'The one who drowned,' whispered Nicholas.

Nemec nodded.

'It was against the Wolves' rules, because he wasn't one of us. Johanna was descended in a direct line from Maddalina and Hans Haber.'

Suddenly Blanka felt stupid. She remembered all the hours she had spent brooding over the chronicles of the witch trial. The answers had been right in front of her nose the whole time! 'So the nuns actually had children themselves,' she realised. 'The witches' sons. And where can you hide children without anyone noticing? In an orphanage.'

'Oh, there were genuine orphans as well,' said Nemec. 'Maddalina wasn't stupid. But it didn't help. The children who weren't condemned and killed at the time of the witches' trial left town and scattered all over the world. But the Wolves searched for them – and they're still searching for them today. All over the world. And often enough, they find them.' He smiled grimly. 'Except for Johanna – Johanna was the best of all. She became invisible. And her second son seems to have inherited this talent from her.'

'What did the Wolves do to her?' asked Nicholas in an expressionless voice. He still could not tear his gaze away from the wolf. 'How did . . . he . . .' He fell silent. The pale-skinned boy stared back.

'For centuries there's been a wolf living within the walls. He has to be here. It's an old place, a mythical place, one that holds the soul of many centuries. As long as the wolf lives, so also do the Wolves, and their memories of the dead. But the wolf had grown old. Its thoughts had begun to fade. Its end was drawing near. Before it could be killed, a new wolf must be chosen: Johanna's child. For a long time she didn't want to accept it. She thought she could simply say "No, thanks" and leave. Then, when her boyfriend drowned, she understood.' Nemec sighed. 'She didn't manage to save her child, but she herself fled. To us she was dead. She hid. She moved around and changed identities so often that she herself often hardly recognised the face in her mirror. But she never forgot her wolf-child. She spent years making all the preparations – she laid trails and created escape routes. And when she contacted me a year ago and told me she was ready to come and get him, I . . .' He swallowed hard.

'. . . helped her.' Blanka finished his sentence. 'You sent her the floor plan. The timing was perfect. She dyed her hair, made herself look older, and went to see the exhibits, masquerading as a tourist. It was the day the new students arrived – good timing again, because that meant the Wolves were busy. She didn't leave the school – she stayed in the building.'

'It was crazy,' whispered Nemec. With difficulty he rose from the floor and wiped his mouth. 'I gave her the key to the museum door – and she went and got her son. But as she was about to flee . . .' He shook his head as if trying to drive out the memory. 'I didn't know that the Wolves had locked the exit to the orphans' cemetery. She turned around and was going to escape through the exhibit room.'

'Where the Wolves found her and killed her,' finished Blanka. 'Did they do this to the wolf-man?' she inquired, pointing to the cuts across his back.

'He ran into the display case. Although he had a fever and the wound wasn't healing, he couldn't let go of Johanna – he looked for her, and he found her – in your thoughts, Blanka.'

'That's why I heard footsteps.'

Nemec nodded. 'Echoes – a lot of people with Belverina's gift hear them. This is an old place. Maybe they're really echoes of the past. That kind of haunting usually occurs with someone who isn't aware of causing such incidents. And the prophetic ability is usually particularly strong in such people.'

'Why didn't you free him yourself?' whispered Nicholas.

'I'm not like Johanna,' replied Nemec with resignation. 'I

never was. I can only be different when I'm drunk. How often can you get drunk? And where could I have taken him? Where could I go myself? I'm a Wolf. They'd have found me, wherever I was.' He hesitated. 'Anyway, I'd only be going from one prison to another. They have me in their power. Forging documents isn't a minor crime, particularly when you're talking about contracts.'

'You were the one who forged the chronicles – and some exams. All on the Wolves' orders.'

'Not all.' He smiled bitterly. 'I forged your exams so you wouldn't be accepted. They only take the best.'

'You stole my notes so you could practise my handwriting. And so the Wolves wouldn't suspect, you bandaged your hand so it wouldn't occur to anyone that you could write forged exams in that condition.'

The wolf-man raised his head and listened. 'Go,' Nemec urged. 'Take him with you – maybe you'll have more luck than Johanna!'

Blanka went over to the wolf-man and stroked his hair. She did not know whether he understood her words, but he would know what she meant. 'Come with me,' she said softly.

The flame of Nemec's candle floated ahead of them in the darkness like a beacon. As quietly as possible they made their way through the passageways. The wolf-man had the least difficulty. He moved so quickly and surely on all fours that it startled Blanka. The passageways narrowed again. They crossed two chambers and came at last to a narrow metal staircase that rose steeply.

'Up there,' Nemec ordered. Without hesitation Blanka grasped the handrail and pulled herself up. Above her head she discovered a hatch bolted shut. When she glanced down, she saw their four faces looking up at her. Nemec gestured impatiently. Blanka nodded and reached for the bolt. As if just thinking about it caused it to happen, it snapped back. Confused, she pulled her hand away. The hatch swung open. Joaquim's face appeared. Thinking quickly, Blanka reached up and grabbed hold of his fur collar. Joaquim swayed a little but did not fall. Something hard hit Blanka's hand, sending jabs of pain shooting up into her shoulder. The faces below her started to spin – and she fell.

Cords cut into her wrists. From time to time Tanya jabbed her between the shoulderblades, driving her on. Blanka had lost all sense of where they were a long time ago. Their path was too long by her reckoning. The bruises on her ribs and legs, where Nicholas and Nemec had caught her as she fell, throbbed. The cloth Joaquim had used to blindfold her was crushing her eyeballs. At every step, pain throbbed at the spot on her neck where Tanya's stick had landed. The room she was being roughly pushed into felt unpleasantly cold. Parquet creaked under her feet. Finally the procession stopped. There were whispers, surprised mutterings, and the shuffling of chairs.

'Who's this?'

Blanka pricked up her ears. It was a woman's voice – a soft voice she knew all too well. 'Mrs Catalon?'

She heard hurried footsteps, then the blindfold was removed.

For a moment everything was blurry. They were still in the underground convent, but in a newer part. About fifty people were gathered in the room. It was brightly lit – a crystal chandelier hung from the ceiling above a large table of polished black stone. Documents lay scattered near a few computer screens. In the background Blanka could see huge bookcases that filled the entire wall. There they were: chronicles, antique books, files. Innumerable files. Mrs Catalon gave Blanka a friendly smile, as if she had just invited her here for coffee.

'Blanka! What a coincidence. We were just talking about you.'

There was renewed muttering.

'So that's her!' said an older man.

'The pair of them broke in,' Joaquim's voice made itself heard.

Blanka looked over her shoulder. Apart from Joaquim and Tanya, only the other two Wolves were behind her. Tobias stepped forward and put Blanka's and Nicholas's mobiles, together with the map showing the floor plan, on the table.

'Who's the boy?' asked Mrs Catalon.

Nicholas jumped when Tanya pulled down his blindfold. Nemec was standing not far from them, right beside the wolf, who was cowering at his feet, whimpering as he hid his eyes from the light. Jan was nowhere to be seen. Taken off, Blanka thought grimly. Oh well, at least he managed to get away.

'Klaus Jehle from the university magazine *Attempto*,' Nicholas introduced himself calmly.

'That's the name of the student who was at Mrs Meyer's yesterday,' a woman called out.

'Well, well, it's Mrs Nyen,' said Nicholas frostily. 'Did you go out there all on your own to kill Mrs Meyer? What did she do? Call you at the town archives and tell you she had Heinrich Feverlin's records?'

A renewed muttering ran around the room. Mrs Nyen went so pale that her wart stood out from her skin like a bluish-black boil. Gradually Blanka recognised some of the other people who were standing in the room. And right at the back at the table sat – Sylvie. Her hand holding the pen still hovered over the paper half filled with writing. Was she keeping minutes? The girl lowered her eyes. Beside the table stood a tall, balding man with round glasses – Dr Almán, Joaquim's father.

'Nemec was going to take them to the northern exit with the wolf,' said Tanya.

A groan ran through the crowd. Joaquim's father stepped out and dragged Nemec forward. The old caretaker fell to his knees. The cut on his forehead that Joaquim had given him with his stick began to bleed again. Rage and panic were reflected in the onlookers' faces. Blanka thought that the crowd was about to rush at Nemec and lynch him.

'What were you thinking?' roared Joaquim's father. The wolf-man ducked down and ran to Nemec.

'Stop!' cried Blanka.

The next moment she sank to the ground, groaning. Joaquim had hit her in the ribs with his stick.

'Shut up, Snow White,' he said.

'Leave her alone!' Nicholas's face was distorted with rage. Tobias and Tanya had to resort to all their fighting tricks to hold him back. It was not until Tobias hit him in the legs that they managed to force him to his knees.

'Put your weapons away,' growled Dr Almán. 'And let go of him.' Three sticks fell to the ground immediately; only Joaquim hesitated. The line of older Wolves eyed him threateningly.

'They broke in,' Joaquim defended himself. 'Into the old section! They were going to take the wolf away. The wolf!'

'Joaquim,' warned Dr Almán softly. Under the strict eye of his father, Joaquim seemed to become smaller. Finally he bent down and carefully laid his stick on the floor.

'Professor Wieser.' Nicholas's voice rang out in the silence. An older man in a grey suit looked up. 'And the gentlemen from pathology,' Nicholas continued. 'So you are involved in this too. No wonder Johanna Vargas's death was declared an accident.'

The name that Nicholas had spoken hung in the air like an echo. From Sylvie's horrified face Blanka could tell what a serious error Nicholas had just made. In five quick paces the professor was beside him, seizing the bonds around his hands and jerking his arms up. 'What else do you know?' asked Wieser. Nicholas groaned. Blanka screamed when she saw a knife gleam in the light.

'That's enough!' The words were not loud, but they were sharp. Wieser's hand froze in mid-air and then dropped. Everyone's eyes went to the door. Blanka blinked. All the Wolves – young and old – looked like children caught with their hand in the cookie jar. Blanka felt as if the ground were moving under her feet.

Marie-Claire Lalonde stepped into the silence, in full command. She was wearing a tailored dress reminiscent of a nun's habit. Her hip-length hair flowed loose over her shoulders, making her look astonishingly similar to the portrait of Belverina.

'Give me the knife,' she ordered. The professor moved away from Nicholas and gave her the weapon, which she took with a nod. Behind her, Dr Hasenberg appeared in the doorway. When he saw Blanka, he cursed. Madame went into the middle of the room, where Nemec and the wolf were sitting. With a graceful gesture she bent down to the caretaker, lifting his chin with one hand. Nemec let her, his bound hands pressed painfully against his back.

'You were going to betray us and let the wolf go, Simon?' she said gently. 'Why?'

Simon's eyelids trembled. 'Because it's not right, Marie-Claire,' he replied hoarsely. 'A man's a man. I didn't understand for a long time – until you showed me what it's like to be locked up in here.'

The headmistress sighed and stood up. 'Oh, Simon!' She did not give the order to untie him, turning instead to Blanka. The Wolves watched in silence as Madame approached her and raised the knife. Strangely, Blanka was not afraid. The headmistress carefully cut through her bonds. Then she stepped in front of Blanka and gently took her face in her hands. Her smile was a little sad. Blanka swallowed. Against her will, she acknowledged how long she had been longing for this contact. At this moment she both hated and loved Madame.

'Why didn't you come to me?' asked the headmistress with gentle reproof. 'I told you to come to me if you were ever worried.'

Blanka turned away.

'But you were in Brussels,' she said. Then she added scornfully, 'And I thought . . .'

Madame Lalonde laughed.

'Yes, a lot of people think that. The alpha wolf is never the one that bites and threatens. The alpha wolf leads, and settles disputes. He only shows his teeth when necessary.' With these words, she swung around and hit Joaquim straight in the face with all her strength. His head snapped back and then he doubled up. 'Give me the fur,' she whispered. Joaquim sniffled but stubbornly shook his head. In one purposeful stride, the head-mistress was beside him, forcing him to the floor. He threw a pleading look at his father, but Dr Almán folded his arms and did not move.

'That's against the rules,' Joaquim gasped.

'José!' warned Madame.

Dr Almán turned pale. The Wolves watched with bated breath. Even so, Blanka thought she saw an almost imperceptible movement. Finally, Dr Hasenberg broke the silence.

'She isn't ready yet,' he said.

'I'm still the one who decides that,' the headmistress corrected him sharply. 'I know her better than any of you. Well?'

The teacher, the doctors and Mrs Nyen all went to stand at Madame's side. Dr Almán and the young Wolves stayed back. Sylvie had not moved from her seat behind the table. Wide-eyed, she stared at Dr Hasenberg, who was still standing between the two battle lines. The psychologist took a deep breath and closed his eyes for a moment.

'All right,' he said finally, moving to Madame Lalonde's side. Dr Almán's eyes flashed with rage. Reluctantly, he went over to his son, taking the wolfskin from his shoulders. Tanya and the other Wolves fell back. Blanka watched with horror as Madame took the wolfskin and held it out to her.

'It's meant to be yours. You found us and proved that you're better than he is. And I expected nothing else.'

Suddenly Blanka realised why Joaquim and the Wolves hated her. Madame had made it clear from the start that Joaquim's days as chief of the young Wolves were numbered. Without being aware of it, from the very first day Blanka had been the intruder who was preferred above all of them and threatened Joaquim's status.

'I won't take the skin,' she said.

Dr Hasenberg laughed. The headmistress threw him an annoyed glance. 'She'll take it,' she answered. 'I can feel it. She's like me when I was younger. And she's in better command of her thoughts than most other people here. When I ordered her to go, she was able to resist me. Me!' She stared at Blanka. 'I called to her while she was sleeping, and she woke up and came to the window.' Pictures began to form before Blanka's eyes. She had to blink. The phantom outside the window! So she hadn't been mistaken when she'd seen the nun's habit. 'You were dreaming,' whispered Madame's soft voice in her ear. 'You saw the past. Only those of us with Belverina's gifts see the echoes of the past. You're one of us, Blanka.'

'No!' shouted Blanka, pulling back. The older Wolves laughed.

'Oh yes,' Madame insisted. 'All of us here are Belverina's children. Centuries ago, Maddalina, Hans Haber and the other two prisoners escaped into the catacombs to their wolf. The children were driven away and scattered to the four corners of the earth. For many years Belverina's heirs lived here, underground, only going out at night to get food from the forest. That's how they survived. For decades now we've been trying to find the descendants of the witches' children. Over the generations they'd ended up all over the place. So we could find them more easily, we founded the Europa International School. And you, Blanka, are something special.' She lowered her voice. 'You're descended from Regina Sängerin and from the wolf-man who lived within these walls in Maddalina's time.'

Blanka felt as if there was not enough oxygen in the room. She was getting dizzy. 'I'm not one of you,' she cried. 'You kill – and you keep human beings like animals!' She gestured towards the wolf-man.

'Let me explain,' said Dr Hasenberg, stepping forward. His manner was so kind and understanding that Blanka would have liked to spit in his face. She looked away in distaste. Nicholas turned his pale face towards her for a moment. She noticed that he was hunched forward and was hanging his head, as if he

wanted to hide his face in the shadow of his hair. Blanka understood. Of course – he too was a descendant of the wolves.

'The order that existed centuries ago was Christian only in
appearance,' explained Dr Hasenberg. 'Belverina is our ancestor.
She was never a Christian saint. She had the gift. Second sight.
The power of suggestion, telepathy and thought control. But
people with special skills are soon betrayed. Her students and
descendants learned from her tragic fate.' He raised his hands.
'And what better place for wolves to hide than in the middle of a
herd of sheep? No one would look for wolves, heathens and
thought-controllers among the Lord's sheep.' The Wolves
murmured approvingly. 'Belverina's heirs could set up their
underground chambers and hide their true character in nuns'
habits and gardeners' smocks, without fear of persecution or
discovery. Their children were born down here, and this is where
they learned to use their skills. They experimented with alchemy
and magic and took, and still take today, the best from all the
sciences. *Porta post portam* – we have managed to push open
other doors behind the last door of the conscious. And the
journey is far from over. Of course, it isn't easy to find all their
descendants. As I told you before, our ancestors also bequeath
their fate to us. Even today there are many orphans among the
descendants.'

'Are all the students descendants of the Belveriners?' asked
Blanka.

'Oh no,' another man spoke. He seemed very familiar to
Blanka. She remembered seeing his picture in the newspaper
once. Of course – he was the mayor. 'Among every thousand
students there are three at the most who have the gift,' he
explained. 'But that still doesn't mean that they can use it or are
really suited to be accepted into our society.' He gave a satisfied

smile, seemingly very proud of being one of the chosen ones. 'Maybe you've noticed the hypothetical questions in our application tests. They're intended to give us an idea of whether the student has this special intuitive talent. Those with the gift are not all necessarily descendants of the Belveriners, and they come from all over the world. It's our task to find them.'

'But even the students without the gift are useful to us,' Madame added. 'We have a network of people who don't know our true mission. People who make a career for themselves and later are in the right place, people who make decisions.'

'Like Caitlin?' asked Blanka. 'Is she supposed to help you to recruit the next generation, when she's a teacher?

'Control the thoughts of others and you will control their deeds,' Madame responded with a smile.

'You manipulate people!'

Madame Lalonde became serious. She bent forward so far that Blanka could see the dark ring around her iris. '"Manipulate" sounds like force,' she whispered. '"Lead gently" is a better way of putting it. Who directs an arrow – you or your thoughts? You draw the bow, point the arrow in the right direction, and think of the target you'd like to hit. The thought counts, Blanka. Let's assume you could infiltrate the thoughts of an archer. He doesn't aim at the bullseye; he aims to the side and loses the tournament. Then you'd have won, without trace, without cheating. Just using thoughts!'

'And then you can make him think of aiming at a person. Is that the perfect murder?' Blanka replied sharply.

'It's possible,' replied Madame, smiling. 'It's far harder to influence a person's thoughts in that direction. We're just beginning to understand this discipline, but we're working on it, believe me.'

More pictures flooded Blanka's mind. She remembered how Nicholas had lied to her. Suddenly it was easy to hate him. Much too easy. Dazed, she wiped her eyes, and then another feeling won the upper hand: anger.

'Don't try that with me!' she hissed at Madame.

The headmistress laughed.

'You see: wolf sense. You have so much talent, Blanka. You should learn to use it.'

'What about him?' The wolf-man was pressing closer to Simon Nemec.

'Our most important member,' said Dr Hasenberg. 'He's everything to us – our medium, our focus, our confidante. Without him, we're nothing. He's our memory, our soul. We are descended from the wolf – call him our totem, if you like.'

'A highly civilised analysis, Professor Hasenberg,' mocked Blanka. 'And yet it comes from the mouth of a barbarian and murderer. You're all murderers!'

'We have to protect ourselves,' replied Dr Hasenberg icily. 'Ourselves and our history – far too often other murderers have taken the lives of our wolves.'

'And for that Johanna had to die?' cried Blanka. 'She was one of you!' Scornfully she let her gaze roam over their faces. No one looked away. Only Sylvie looked down. 'Perhaps Maddalina and the others were martyrs who fought for knowledge,' Blanka continued. 'But that doesn't justify anything you're doing today – anything at all! You're not the martyrs you pretend to be!'

Dr Hasenberg's face was turning red and he was breathing hard. He was about to say something, but Madame Lalonde stopped him with a wave of her hand.

'I don't approve of their killing Johanna,' she explained. 'It was an accident. Joaquim and the others . . .' her tone grew sharper

'. . . discovered her by chance as she was trying to escape with the wolf through the exhibit room.'

'We went down to prepare a little surprise for you in the museum. Joaquim and Tanya wanted to scare you,' said Sylvie quietly, then fell silent again as Madame looked at her.

The headmistress continued. 'A stick hit Johanna in the wrong place. The Wolves don't want to tell us who the mortal blow came from, and we respect their silence. Removing the wolf mark was an act of panic, too. But we don't expel anyone, right, Simon? In our society, mistakes happen – and we're there to protect each other.'

'That's why you didn't come and get me for the test of courage,' said Blanka to the Wolves. 'You had to get Johanna out of the way. Were you going to hide her in Nemec's room until Madame decided what to do?'

'Yes, and we'd have managed it if you hadn't got in our way!' Tanya said resentfully.

'Why didn't you take her to the basement?'

'Because the door was shut,' Sylvie replied for Tanya. 'Johanna locked it behind her. We didn't know that she still had the key on her. We called Dr Wieser and he told us to hide the body in the library – from there there's a passageway directly to the carpark. He was going to pick her up during the night.'

'You have a choice,' said Madame gently, holding the wolfskin out to Blanka again. 'Accept your mission. We're not murderers – we offer people like Jan a chance, and Caitlin too – she comes from a poor family. We pay their scholarships and help children and young people all over the world.' She lowered her voice even more. 'Sadly, as always happens when you're trying to do good, some sacrifices have to be made. Would you condemn someone for panicking and shooting a burglar who's trying to kill his family? Johanna's death was an accident.'

Blanka's gaze fell on Joaquim's unhappy face. His father, for whom he would never be good enough, had moved away from him. Blanka swallowed and looked straight at the headmistress. She was still Madame. Her Madame. There was a huge lump in her throat.

'If I decide to join you, what will happen to him?' she asked, pointing to Nicholas. 'He's not one of you – but he knows everything now. Will you let him go?'

The threatening silence was answer enough. Blanka straightened her shoulders and took a step backward, her heart beating wildly.

'Mrs Meyer's death was no accident,' she said quietly. 'The student didn't drown by accident. And no one deserves the fate of this boy. How barbaric do you have to be, to mutilate someone like that? I'll never be one of you, Madame. To me you're all murderers. And that includes you.'

The scream was stifled, but Blanka still felt it ringing in her ears. The Wolves spun around. Simon Nemec was kneeling beside the wolf-man. His face was contorted with grief. Scraps of bandage and rope hung from his wrist. In his fist, which showed no sign of injury, he held Blanka's box-cutter. As if in slow motion, blood ran down it and dripped onto the floor. Nemec's hoarse voice seemed to bounce off the walls.

'It must come to an end,' he said to Madame. 'And it has come to an end – now.'

The wolf-man lay doubled up on the floor. Blood spread over the parquet.

'Run!' shouted Blanka to Nicholas. At the same moment Nemec raised his weapon again. Sylvie jumped up, and papers fluttered from the table. Nicholas and Blanka both rushed towards Nemec.

The bulbs in the crystal chandelier flickered. The next moment Blanka was standing in darkness as black as pitch. Her hands grasped the wolf-man's upper arm. With all her strength she tried to pull him up, but even just his arm was as heavy as lead. An elbow hit her jaw with full force. The arm slid out of her grasp, and the next moment she was swimming dazedly in a sea of bodies. There was a bang, then a dreadful splintering sound. Sparks flew as a computer monitor crashed onto the floor. Blanka rushed blindly into the darkness and stumbled over a stick lying on the floor. 'Blanka?' The voice was right beside her. The next moment a lighter clicked on. The quivering light of the flame lit up Nicholas's face.

'He's dead!' cried Blanka. 'We have to get out of here!'

Like a nightmare, Dr Almán appeared in front of them. He swung with Joaquim's stick. Then the flame went out again. Blanka felt for the stick at her feet and grabbed it without thinking. Wood cracked. The blow left her hands numb.

'To the door!' she shouted at Nicholas. Hoping she would not hit Nicholas by mistake, she raised the stick and hit out again. Someone groaned. The chandelier flickered on again – two, three times. It seemed to Blanka that she was looking at innumerable disembodied images. One of them was of Dr Almán, slowly getting back onto his feet. Another was of Sylvie grabbing Tanya's arms just as she was about to rush at Blanka.

'Go!' screamed Sylvie. Then the light went out with a final huge bang. Someone grabbed Blanka's arm and dragged her towards the wall.

'Here, Nick!' called a voice. It was Jan! Blanka bumped into a door frame and groped her way outside. Panic-stricken cries and a crash reached into the hallway. There was the smell of burning plastic. Nicholas's lighter gave just enough light for them to duck in time to avoid hitting their heads on the stone roof of the passage where it dipped low. Without any way of orienting themselves, they stumbled through the passageways, got lost, and took side passages that sometimes looked familiar but were more often completely new to them. Again and again they heard cries and pounding footsteps. At one bend Jan recoiled and sniffed.

'Shit!' he whispered. 'Something's burning here too.' Then his face brightened. 'A draught!' He grabbed Nicholas's lighter and held it out in front of him. Blanka could see a fan as high as a man; it completely filled the end of the passage, creating suction as it turned. The lighter's flame flickered and went out. Jan's voice cracked.

'We're in a ventilation shaft!'

'Are we supposed to jump through the fan, one at a time?'

'Don't be stupid. There's always a maintenance passage around a fan.'

Hand in hand they groped along the wall until Jan flicked on the lighter in the shelter of his hand. In front of them was a door with a big bolt. Together they pushed it open. Nicholas coughed. Smoke stung Blanka's eyes. Suction slammed the door behind them with a deafening thud.

After seemingly endless minutes Jan stopped again.

'A shaft and climbing irons,' he cried. 'Up we go!'

Blanka felt rusty metal. Coughing, she hauled herself hand over hand up the shaft. It must have been set at least ten metres down into the ground. With his injured leg Nicholas took forever to make his way up. Blanka's hands were scraped and painful when she finally saw light above her. Jan lifted up a grille, pushed it aside, and helped her, then finally Nicholas, to pull themselves over the smooth marble rim onto a stone floor.

Panting, they fought for breath. Somewhere nearby, birds were twittering.

Dazed, Blanka opened her eyes and saw a chubby angel between cotton-wool clouds smiling down at her beatifically like a drunken man. Disbelievingly she blinked and raised her head. Hidden behind flower decorations and an altar, a railing rose up before them – and through a gothic gateway behind it they could see the early-morning sky over the orphans' cemetery.

'We're in the Belverina chapel,' Jan realised. 'An airshaft that's classified as a historical monument. Very clever.' He took Nicholas's bag, which he had been carrying the whole time, off his shoulder, stood up, and climbed over the railing. 'Come on! Let's go! Let's not get caught again.'

Cursing, Nicholas struggled to his feet. Blanka took his arm and pulled him along. Laboriously they hurried past the tomb-stones to the park. As she walked, Blanka glanced back and shuddered. The cemetery looked like the stage set for a cheesy horror film. Billowing smoke, rising from several graves and the chapel, began to cover the scene like fog. In the distance the siren of a fire engine wailed.

The first thing Blanka saw when the school was in sight was the glass of the library windows blowing out. Flames shot up into the sky, like a harbinger of the sun, which would soon rise behind. Students and teachers were crowding the entrance, pale with fright and freezing in T-shirts, dressing gowns and pyjamas. One of the fire engines pulling in braked so sharply that the gravel of the driveway sprayed up in all directions.

'How did you knock out the chandelier?' murmured Nicholas. Jan looked at him, wide-eyed.

'I didn't do anything to the chandelier,' he said. 'I'd only just found you when the lights went out.' Suddenly he staggered.

Blanka just caught him in time, and helped him sit down on the ground. His skin was cold from shock. 'Maybe the bearing seized,' he mumbled. 'Then the motor overloaded. There was wood everywhere in the museum . . . But that can't be right. I'd built a fuse into it!'

'It wasn't you,' said Blanka loudly. 'The fire could have started for all sorts of reasons. There were candles burning down there – and I saw sparks when a monitor fell.'

'But they may all be trapped!'

'You don't think there was only one entrance, do you?' asked Nicholas bleakly.

BELVERINA'S DESCENDANTS

CARSTEN SEIBOLD HAD NOT HAD TIME for a shower. Unshaven, he sat facing Blanka, looking at the prints of Nicholas's digital photos.

'OK, then. You were doing research for a history essay and discovered that someone had forged the record of the witch trial. That much I understand. But what does that have to do with the fire?'

'No idea,' replied Blanka. 'I've told you everything I know.'

Seibold looked at her suspiciously and frowned. 'Now why don't I quite believe you?' He sighed deeply and took another gulp of coffee. 'You're obliged to answer my questions – you do know that, I hope?' he said rather more severely.

Blanka nodded.

'It must have been a very unusual fire,' continued Carsten Seibold. 'Or there were accelerants involved. We found a tamper-proof lock on the museum door.'

'They said that on the news today, yes,' replied Blanka softly. At the thought of the panic in the assembly room, of the screams and faces, she felt sick again from grief and horror.

Seibold nodded and ran his hands through his hair, agitated. 'OK. You have my card?'

'No. Madame Lalonde didn't give it to me last time.'

He looked at her for so long that she began to feel uncomfortable. Finally he reached into a drawer and took out a card. After a moment's consideration he picked up a pen and scribbled a number on the back.

'My mobile number. You can call me any time, if you think of anything else.'

Blanka nodded and attempted a smile. She found it hard. Sylvie's face swam before her eyes. She could not hold back her tears. Detective Seibold took a box of tissues from the drawer and handed it to her without a word. He waited until she was in control again.

'I have a question for you, Detective Seibold,' she said softly. 'I noticed in the town museum that you donated to the orphans' cemetery. Why?'

She had managed to catch him by surprise. To her astonishment he seemed embarrassed.

'It was my grandmother's wish. After the war she and my grandfather used to meet in the park by the cemetery. It meant a lot to her. And when she died, I donated part of what I inherited towards the restoration.' His smile grew bitter. 'Hmm. If I'd known I was financing the secret passages and airshafts of a cult . . .' He looked up at her quickly. 'Did you know?'

'No.'

He made a dismissive gesture, giving up at last. 'OK, OK. Well then . . .' Slowly he stood up, reaching out to shake her hand. 'I don't imagine we'll see each other again very soon. I expect you're staying in town.'

Nicholas and Jan were already waiting in La Bête. The café was deserted again, the tourists preferring to head out to the ruin of the school and to the orphans' cemetery to compete with the international news stations for a spectacular photo of the salvage operations.

'So?' asked Nicholas without even greeting her first.

Blanka sank into a chair and shook her head. 'I don't think he's one of them.'

The relief left Nicholas's expression soft and a little sad. Shock was still evident in his face. Blanka took hold of his hand under the table.

'Let's wait and see what Seibold does with the information,' said Jan, his voice rough. 'I don't trust anyone in this town, anyway. I'm leaving.'

'You're going home?'

'What would I do there? No, I'm going into hiding. The last thing I need now is having my name appear in some police report.' Nervously he drummed on the table with his fingers. His cheeks were hollow and the deep rings under his eyes made him look older. The carefree, cool Jan had disappeared. 'Caitlin said I should take the next plane to Dublin, but I think it will be better to hitch-hike. And maybe I can do odd jobs somewhere to pay for the ferry.'

'You've spoken to Caitlin?' cried Blanka. 'My mother was quite hysterical because she had called asking for me at home.'

'She's at the end of her tether. But she's not the only one.' He patted the side pocket of his jacket. 'I'm dying to see what she says when she sees her final exam.'

'But it won't be any use to her any more,' murmured Nicholas.

'Caitlin can ace any exam – at any school,' replied Jan.

'Did you tell her everything?' asked Blanka.

'Absolutely not,' said Jan with emphasis. 'That's your business.' He stood up, rapped on the table in farewell, and left. They watched him through the café window as he went across the marketplace, shoulders hunched, towards the main street. Directly in front of the central pillar stood a TV news team, asking passers-by for their comments. An old man was waving his hands dramatically. Blanka had the feeling she was watching the mime-show at a great tragedy.

'Our story,' said Nicholas despondently. He put his mother's bag on the table and took out the records they had rescued from Dr Hasenberg's office.

'Your story.' He pushed a genealogical chart over to Blanka. '"ba" – that's your abbreviation. And here's your ancestral line, back to the wolf-man.' With a bitter undertone he added, 'Belverina's heirs. At least we both know now where we come from.' Blanka studied the symbols and lines. Right at the bottom, Dr Hasenberg had noted down the profession the Wolves had intended for Blanka. 'Neurologist,' she read out. 'And I'll bet they'd have managed it. I'd have spent my life researching brain waves and engrams.'

Carefully she smoothed the paper. There were the names of her biological parents. Both had died on the same day, a year after Blanka's birth. Strangely, the thought of her mother – her mother wearing her restaurant uniform – moved her much more. For the first time in months she could think of the word 'home' without it sounding false and bitter. Nicholas gave her a sideways glance.

'What?'

'Admit it. In the assembly room you believed Marie-Claire for a moment.'

She lowered her gaze. 'Only for a moment. She was really convinced about what she was doing. She believed she was a good person!'

'You miss her, don't you?'

Blanka was silent.

'No more secrets,' warned Nicholas softly. 'We promised each other that.'

She had to clear her throat to speak. 'I liked her.' It was not the whole truth.

Nicholas looked away and surveyed the big town-hall clock. Blanka was still amazed that time was marching on as if the night before had never happened. Through the open door the wind carried the photographer's instructions into the café.

Suddenly Nicholas took Blanka into his arms and rested his forehead on her shoulder. It felt incredibly good to have him so close. 'I'll tell you something else,' he said. 'I don't believe he's dead.'

'Stop!' Blanka pleaded. She turned her head and looked into Nicholas's eyes. 'I touched him – he didn't move. He gave no sign of life.'

Nicholas's voice grew even quieter. 'He was gone. When the light flickered on, he wasn't lying where he'd fallen. Maybe he was just injured and unconscious?'

'Even if he wasn't in the same place – what does that prove? The others dragged him away. Or your view of his body was blocked. After all, we didn't even know where in the room we were!'

She could feel from his arms, still holding her, that he was beginning to relax.

'You're probably right,' he said. 'But I keep thinking about it. There were other exits, weren't there?'

'I can't say, Nicholas. The floor plan only showed the old section of the underground building.'

'But if there were . . . other exits. Do you realise what that would mean for us?'

Blanka looked at her hands and fought against the feeling that the firm ground, which she had only just stepped onto, was beginning to shake again.

For a long time they sat in silence, both listening to the echoes of their own story.

'Three dead bodies have been identified so far.' The TV journalist spoke into the camera. 'Marie-Claire Lalonde, the head-mistress of the Europa International School, José Almán, the chairman of the board of the Maddalina of Trenta Foundation, and Dr Wolfgang Polnoga, the town's mayor. But other teachers at the school and professors from the university are suspected of being members of the supposed cult as well.'

'Hi!' someone called out to the two of them, 'Can I ask you a couple of questions?' Startled, they looked up. A young man stood in front of them holding a microphone 'I'm from *Attempto*, and I'm doing a piece on the Maddalina of Trenta case. What do you think . . .'

'Nothing at all,' said Blanka, pulling Nicholas up from his chair. 'We're not from around here.'

EPILOGUE

Red! It woke up trembling. In Its whole body It felt fear, fear that was crawling over Its limbs leaving a slimy trail, like the cluster of snails that It had once eaten and about which It still dreamed sometimes. With a jerk It raised Its head and sniffed the air. Looking at the colours hurt – a hundred different kinds of green, brown, and wet black in the much-too-bright light at the cave's entrance. And again and again the red of Its thoughts – the glowing, red-hot, roaring thing It had escaped from. The voices and noises still resounded painfully in Its ears – screams and splintering noises, and the snarling of fearful thoughts that had flooded through It. In Its memory they became so loud that It howled in fright. It bared Its teeth and crawled back even deeper into Its refuge. The cave smelled of moss and bark, and its stones felt good – familiar and safe. Its fresh wound, struck by the strong Other's sharp tooth, was hurting. And then there was another image. 'Come!' said the gentle voice. It had lost her, but somewhere, in the distant shadow of Its own thoughts, It felt her gentle presence, quite near. Comforted, It closed Its eyes and waited.

It was not until much later, when the painful colours had turned into comforting grey shadows, that It crawled outside, cowering down in fear. The air around It moved like a living being and It cried out in anguish. But then It sniffed the air and dared to take Its first step. The distance, the quietness, were frightening, and yet something in It began to stir. Nobody called It back, nobody was there to lead It or drive It forward. No strange thoughts disturbed Its peace. Only the shadows and a multitude of unfamiliar smells, seductive and frightening at the same time. Its steps got faster and faster. Soft, feathery undergrowth, like wet fur, flew under Its feet. Its heart beat wildly, and yet It did not feel weariness any more, just a strange, blazing intoxication. The last remnants of fear disappeared, and the pain in Its wounds only pulsed dully, like a dim memory. The distance bore It like a gentle hand across the ground.

And It ran.

It ran.

About the Author

Nina Blazon was born in 1969 and studied German language and literature and Slav languages at university. She worked in an advertising agency for several years. Today she works as a journalist and author. She won the Wolfgang Hohlbein Prize in 2003 for her first fantasy novel.